Turtle Island Dreaming

T0345294

Turtle Island Dreaming

A NOVEL OF SANCTUARY

Thompson Sayer Crockett

iPUBLISH.com
at Time Warner Books

For information address iPublish.com, 135 West 50th St., New York, NY 10020.

Ⓦ A Time Warner Company

ISBN 0-7595-5001-8

First Edition: October 2000

Visit our Web site at www.iPublish.com

Contents

Prologue		I
Chapter 1	Descent	3
Chapter 2	Passing Within	17
Chapter 3	An Intimate Koan	59
Chapter 4	Mirror Dance	97
Chapter 5	A Quality of Light	123
Chapter 6	Dark Circle, Stone Circle	149
Chapter 7	Turtle Dreams	183
Chapter 8	Theatre of the Bardo	219
Epilogue		243
About the Author		245

Contents

Prologue

I'd been thinking of pain and death and loss when the turtles first came to me. I'd been seeking some sanctuary of the spirit—asking for guidance. When I closed my eyes I'd see them—great, graceful sea turtles gliding through the blue waters of my dreams. They came not once, but many times. To understand these visits, I read about sea turtles, photographed them, studied them. But when, in dreams, they still floated up before me, I had to listen to them—to hear the story they would tell. . . .

A woman walks out onto the deck of a ship. It is a cruise ship—the *Blue Pearl*—famous for its level of luxury. It's filled with happy couples, people escaping, people paying for an illusion of the exotic. But it is early morning and still, and she passes no one as she pads softly on bare feet from her stateroom to the lowest of the outer decks—the one that offers no obstructions between the railing and the sea.

She is calm, perhaps more tranquil than she has been in a very long time. Her stateroom is in order. Her small suitcases and camera bag are packed and sitting on the still-made bed. There is a tip for the woman who has cleaned her stateroom each day and arranged for fresh flowers to be delivered. There is a letter for a friend on the dresser, stamped and addressed and ready to be posted. The bottle of complimentary champagne in her stateroom is unopened. She has avoided her prescription sedatives and antidepressants. She has not been crying. The few passengers who might later recall meeting her will not have observed any particular sadness or air of melancholy about her. Mostly, she will not have been noticed at all, as if the light by which we are able to see each other in her had been snuffed out.

She finds a point along the railing more in shadow than the rest. She drags a deck chair into the shadow with her but does not sit. She looks out across the moon-sparkled night sea. It is warm, and the only breeze seems to come from the ship's forward motion. The wind is barely enough to lift her dark curly hair from her shoulders. Except for the humming vibration of the ship's engines, all is quiet. She breathes in the salt scent.

She unties the belt of her silk robe and lets it fall from her shoulders as if casually shrugging off a skin. Naked, she steps up onto the deck chair and swings first one leg then the other over the railing. She finds a ledge, just wide enough for her heels, on the outboard side of the railing and stands up. She steadies herself by holding a vertical brace and takes a deep breath. She is not nervous or frightened. She does not regret. She feels only a primal urge to return to the sea from which her ancestors once crawled.

Her compass spins.

She has strong legs and they carry her surprisingly far from the edge of the ship before she begins to drop. It is a long way down, but she enters feet first, slicing into the water. She is drawn through the curtain of ocean. It is strange and enveloping. The warm darkness wraps around her like a shroud.

Time stops.

CHAPTER 1

Descent

Stopping time—living in the moment—is a sorcerer's trick. But between me and the magician there is an unspoken agreement. I choose to see the fantastic. I assume that sea turtles find their way through thousands of miles of open sea. I invent their navigation from seaweed fields off protected coasts to breeding beaches washed by unrestricted waves. But when I see through this illusion, the turtle whispers, "There is no navigation, no finding. There is only one place, one moment in the life of a sea turtle—here and now."

Marina was quite prepared to die as she hit the water. She had been courting death with increasing abandon over the past several years. She had flirted with death in Bosnia, but no bullet or bomb fragment had so much as grazed her. She had danced with death in Rwanda and gotten only a now-pale scar from the blade of a machete to show for it. It had not frightened her. It had not sobered her. She had gone on to sleep with death in Chechnya, but not even so intimate an acquaintance—lying close to death, in death's embrace—had satisfied her.

There had been countless little moments, obsessive self-assignments, casual brushes with death. She had the photographs to prove it. But each morning she woke up alive.

At first she had lied to herself about this preoccupation. Photojournalists, at least the good ones, she told herself, were expected to put themselves in harm's way. She was just "pushing the envelope," she told herself. It was the images that mattered, and she specialized in suffering. Her passport read like a chronology of conflict: Lebanon, Afghanistan, Iran, Tibet, central Africa, the implosion of the former Soviet Union. She was good at what she did—wars, famine, natural disasters, holocausts. Her photographs had a passion and a humanity that elevated them beyond the merely voyeuristic. At least that was what was typically written on the dust jackets of her books.

She believed that her photographs had once possessed a certain quality, a grace or an honesty that made demands on the heart. But that was before the slide into darkness. Her photographs had been a part of what made her whole, and it was now through her photographs that she saw her illness.

She had not always felt so cut off, so disconnected from what it was that made people want to be alive. She'd had family, friends, causes she had believed in, underlying truths. But it seemed to her that those ties, those things that had once anchored her, had been cut, frayed, or worn away over the years, with nothing to replace them. All she had now were her photographs.

Marina saw those photographs as she expelled the air from her lungs and sank into the warm ocean. Time had been stilled for her in this moment, and she contemplated the irony, smiled at the idea of seeing her life in her own photographs. She had heard people talk about having their lives flash before them in moments of near-death experience. She saw her life now as a slide show. Images that had changed her life or images that reflected her changes appeared to float before her. Only they weren't really her life. Her life was behind the photographs, attached to them marginally, like so many captions and cutlines—black marks on a page.

Lebanon 1978—Refugee Camp

Black-and-white image: A woman in a dust-caked black robe cradles her dead son in the dirt. He is shirtless and slender, perhaps twelve or thirteen years old. There are dark holes in his chest, but not much blood. He lies across his mother's legs, arms splayed out and limp, head back, a Madonna and child. The woman looks up at the camera, but it is not grief that penetrates past lenses and film stocks, papers and printing processes, it is bewilderment. Perhaps later the woman would come to despair or hatred or bitterness. But at this moment, captured in Marina's photograph, the woman simply, silently asks why.

★ ★ ★

It seemed like an eternity since she had made images that held that kind of power. That image was from her first assignment as a photojournalist. She had made other powerful images on that assignment, but this was the photograph that had won her the respect of her colleagues. She had interned at two newspapers and one magazine during her summers, and even gotten some of her photographs published, but to get a foreign assignment like this, just out of college, was rare. Her editor had hoped that because Marina was a woman she might get access to the closed society of Muslim women. She'd gambled that Marina might be able to put a human face to the suffering in Lebanon, and that gamble had paid off.

Marina had been too young, too inexperienced to be afraid. She was open to the pain of others. She had no defenses and no need for them. At that point in her life the act of photographing had been a kind of connecting force for her—one she came to call her heartline. It ran from her heart to the hearts of her subjects. It was her gift, to reveal a moment of humanity in silver halide. She had a way of getting people to open up to her, to relax and forget that they were being photographed. She could make herself, if not invisible, at least insignificant. She could slip between the cracks, observing and photographing as if from another dimension.

Marina spent three years in the Middle East. She learned some of the language, a lot of the culture, and, thanks to her olive complexion and dark hair, could pass for an Arab woman. She made the images that an insider might have made. She showed how the constant fighting of Muslims and Jews, Muslims and Christians, Muslims and Muslims affected the lives of women. She had the ideals of a liberally educated young woman, but she kept her opinions to herself when she was working. Inside, however, she grew frustrated. The conflict made no sense to her. She found no side to claim her moral indignation. No party or group seemed much superior to the other.

In the end she turned her attention to another conflict—one further east—a conflict she thought she could believe in.

Afghanistan 1983—Christophe

Black-and-white image: A young man and a young woman sit side-by-side on an outcropping of rock. They are both dressed roughly, as peasants, or bandits, or pilgrims. A camera sits on top of a leather bag at her feet. A rifle leans against the rock on his side. She wears no shoes, and her head rests on his shoulder. The camera angle is odd and the image is not well framed, but despite these technical faults, the photograph reveals that some secret thing has passed between them. One knows, without understanding how, that these are lovers.

★ ★ ★

This image had won no awards, had never been published, was not even a photograph Marina shared with friends. It was the only photograph she had of Christophe and herself together. It had been made with a timer so that they would both be in the picture. They had slipped away from the guerrilla group they traveled with, to make love, and Marina had desperately wanted a photograph of the two of them together.

Christophe was a French photojournalist. First he was a comrade in the heart of the conflict, then something much more. Their affair was made more intense by the circumstance of constant risk. They made no plans, lived wholly in the moment, and loved always as if there might be no sunrise. For Marina it was her first and only great love. Before Christophe she'd had relationships—some which claimed her body, others which claimed her soul, but never both at the same time. After Christophe she never again allowed herself to give both body and soul.

Christophe died in a helicopter raid, killed by machine-gun fire. Marina had been there; she'd photographed it. His death confirmed her almost-sacred belief in the prohibition against carrying a weapon. Christophe had carried a rifle as well as a camera. Her camera was her shield. It created an inviolate bubble of safe space around her. As long as she trusted it completely, it would make her invisible. If even for a moment she placed her trust in some other form of protection, her bubble, her shield, would crack and fear would slip in.

But her shield had a price. She began to see her camera—her photographing—not so much as a channel to her subjects' hearts but as a barrier around her own. It wore away at her heartline, fraying the subtle connection she had always been able to make with her subjects. It was a little thing at the time. She hardly noticed the change.

She buried Christophe on a mountain in Afghanistan. She had no way of getting his body home. She couldn't even dig into the rocky ground. She piled stones over him, finding it increasingly difficult to breathe as she placed the stones on his chest.

She won a Pulitzer for her work in Afghanistan. She got an agent, produced the first of her books, *Killing in the Sun,* and had her pick of assignments around the world. It was a good time for her. She was well known and well respected. No one, least of all Marina, could yet see the cancerous little shadow that had begun to grow inside her.

She photographed in China, Tibet, and Cambodia. Many images strobed before her in a blur. She could have picked any one and unfolded the story behind it or related it to a moment in her life. She loved the east, but she came halfway west again to photograph both sides of the war between Iran and Iraq. Then came Baghdad and the Gulf War.

Baghdad 1991—Aerial Bombing

Black-and-white image: An old man and an old woman lie in one another's arms. Masonry, plaster, concrete, and steel beams bury their legs. Daylight from a newly cleared section of the bombed apartment building slashes the darkness to illuminate them. Dust hangs in the air like a mist. It is quiet and still. It is hard to tell if the old man and woman are asleep or dead. There are little details that one notices in the photograph after the initial bouncing of the eye between the peaceful repose of the upper bodies and the carnage below. He has pulled her close to him to cradle her. Her hand covers his heart. His lips are still pressed to her forehead.

★ ★ ★

Her bubble—her barrier—had protected her throughout the long night of an aerial bombardment. The building she took shelter in crumbled around her, but still she was unharmed. She clung to her cameras. Her film cassettes were her rosary beads. The walls around her toppled. The floor beneath her gave way and she fell. She was bruised, the wind knocked from her, but she was not more seriously hurt. She spent the night in darkness, trapped as much by the total lack of light as by any material restriction. She heard the moans and cries of the injured echoing eerily through the collapsed ventilation shafts.

When morning came and the first shafts of light penetrated her temporary prison, Marina began to photograph again. She did not leave the building immediately, but went in search of those pained voices she had heard. She refused help for herself—after all she had her magic camera—but led rescuers in the direction of the injured. She photographed what she saw. She found the old man and old woman this way. They had not lived through the night. She photographed them, then turned back to the world of light.

Marina was a well-known and respected photojournalist with an international reputation, but no American newspaper or magazine had wanted to publish these pictures. Marina had spent very little time in America in the preceding nine years. She returned only occasionally to visit her parents in Seattle, her sister in Washington, D.C., and to meet with her agent or publishers, but she still thought of herself as an American. While not overtly patriotic, she was by no means ashamed of her country. She was out of touch with popular sentiment and had no idea that the Gulf War had taken on a life of its own back in the United States as some kind of national healing ritual for Vietnam. Now she began to question her country and it showed in her photographs.

Marina felt that she was simply doing what she had always done—looking for the heart and soul of conflict and capturing it on film. But her family and others questioned her. After all, they had argued, the people of Kuwait had suffered and American soldiers had died in a war we didn't start. Her photographs seemed to imply that America was the aggressor, the heavy-handed power. This criticism incensed Marina and made an expatriot of her.

Cut loose from family and country, she became even more of a gypsy than she had been. Nothing anchored her, and she let the work she did toss her about as an ocean might toss drifting wood.

Haiti 1993—The Tonton Macoute Aftermath

Close-up in color: A brown-black hand extended in a puddle of blood across a plank wood floor. The index finger points like the hand of God in Michelangelo's Sistine Chapel ceiling. But instead of passing the spark of creation, this hand gestures in futility to a long, narrow strip of paper soaked in blood. It is a voting ballot. It is marked crudely in pencil, but it will never be counted.

★ ★ ★

"You should be working in color," they told her. "There are very few publications that print black-and-white photography anymore." Marina knew they were right, these well-meaning friends, her editors, her agent. So she began working in color. It frightened her at first, but she got used to it. She found herself looking at the world differently.

Or was it that she was already looking at the world through different eyes and her shift to color film followed her shift in perspective?

The world that had seemed alive and vibrant in black-and-white seemed dull and lifeless in color. She began to look for graphic evidence to photograph. Sharp vivid colors, contrast, blood and viscera. She had misplaced her ability to see in subtle terms. If she could not whisper and suggest with her photographs, she could still make them scream.

When she wasn't on assignment she was miserable now. She sabotaged every relationship in her life. She sought out shallow and superficial people because they did not challenge her. She lived on the surface of her photographs. She took an assignment to shoot fashion against the backdrop of a burned-out Cambodian village. It paid more than any assignment she had ever done and it cost her twice as much. For the assignment she traveled with a small army of fixers, arrangers, editors, gaunt, beautiful women, and style mavens. She drank heavily, slept little, and smoked opium just to numb herself for the work.

When it was over Marina plunged right back into the world she knew best. She seldom visited America anymore. She lived in temporary apartments, hotel rooms, with friends. She communicated with the publishing world almost exclusively through her agent and friend, Erin. She kicked the opium habit and stopped drinking for a while, but she still found it hard to sleep, and the numbness she had sought in the drugs and alcohol now came unbidden.

Marina began photographing herself, comparing the photographs to younger versions of herself. She was not concerned with aging, the little lines and wrinkles some women look for. She had once been attractive, even striking. Her dark wavy brown hair fell below her shoulders and was usually tied back with some impromptu scrap of cloth. It framed and softened the sharp angularity of her features. Her eyes were almond-shaped and a warm, chestnut brown in color. Her skin had a soft olive glow that was enhanced by the sun. What she looked for in the new photographs she made was the encroaching darkness around her eyes. It was as if her eyes were receding into some dark cavern of her soul. This was when she became fully aware of her slide into the darkness.

★ ★ ★

It was an accident that took her to Rwanda, a chance sexual encounter with a journalist in Sarajevo, made romantic by the fog of fermented and distilled potatoes. She must have lamented the lack of anything dramatic to photograph as they drank in the hotel bar. Or perhaps she cursed her own boredom and emptiness out loud while making love. Whatever the reason, before leaving in the morning he told her that central Africa was where she should be. "Things are just about to come apart there," he told her. "Old tribal feuds. It won't be pretty."

It sounded like just what she needed.

Rwanda 1995—Executioner

Color image: A man stands between two hospital beds. He is jet black and glistening with sweat. He wears mismatched camouflage fatigues with a rifle slung over his back. He is swinging a machete in a wide arc down at the body of a woman who is trying futilely to escape under the bed. He has struck her twice, maybe three times. There is blood on her back, blood on the machete, blood spattering the sheets and the soldier's uniform. Droplets of blood hang in the air as a red blur behind the machete blade. The man's eyes are open wide, his teeth are bared, threateningly white against thick black lips. If he hears the camera shutter recording his gruesome task, he gives no sign of it.

★ ★ ★

Marina had shot nearly a whole roll of film, spinning it off with her motor drive, before he noticed her. Afterward she realized that he had developed some sudden compulsion to leave the little hospital and she merely got in his way. If she had moved aside, perhaps stepping over one of the crying wounded or one of the corpses, he might have passed her right by. For all she knew, her whiteness might have made her invisible to him. But she kept photographing as he came toward her. She backed up and tripped. She fell over an outstretched leg and hit the wooden floor hard. Still she might have escaped injury, but she thrust a leg up at the man defensively and he swung at it with the machete. It bit into her calf muscle and lodged in bone. She was aware of the dull thud of something striking her leg, but the pain did not come until later. She twisted and wrenched her leg hard and the machete slipped from the man's grip. Whether it was the blood on his hands or that he had suddenly lost his enthusiasm for the slaughter, she never knew. He ran past her, leaving her lying on the floor of the primitive hospital among the dead and the dying with a machete blade embedded in her leg.

Marina pulled the machete blade free and poured some dark liquid that smelled like a disinfectant over the wound. She took an antibiotic tablet and a codeine pill (she always carried her own medicines when she traveled), and bandaged the wound in gauze and torn bed sheets. By this time others had come out of hiding to help as they could with the wounded patients. There was little she could do to help and she had not the strength to continue photographing so she limped back to her rented car.

It was a forty-minute drive on the rough back roads between the village hospital and Kigali. She hoped she would make it back to her hotel while the codeine tablet lasted. She thought about HIV infection and other blood-borne tropical diseases as she drove, but she knew there was nothing she could do about that. Now there was only prayer and she did not know to whom to pray.

The capital city of Kigali was in chaos, but the little hotel that catered to western journalists maintained an illusion of safety. She redressed the wound, took more codeine and antibiotics, unloaded her cameras, and labeled her film cassettes—all before falling asleep. She spent a week in her hotel room, drifting in and out of feverish sleep, clutching her film cassettes like charms.

When she was well enough to travel she left Rwanda.

Her pictures were published, somewhere. She didn't even keep track of these things anymore. Her few remaining friends began begging her to slow down and take some time off. She renewed her self-portraiture with a particular interest in the healing of her wounded calf. She had seen a specialist in England and, aside from the scar, was expected to make a full recovery. It hurt her sometimes, but mostly she was fascinated by the numbness she experienced as she ran her fingertips across it.

She began to fantasize about other wounds she might experience. She traveled to Russia, shot a piece about the Russian Mafia, selected and slept with dark men named Yuri or Boris, half hoping they would hurt her, but not knowing how to ask them to.

Chechnya 1996—The Hands

A series of images, all black-and-white, all stark and empty: Most of the images are of solitary trees, bare and leafless, almost black against a gray sky. With a quick glance they might all appear to be trees, but one image is a detail of a hand reaching up from a shallow dirt grave. The hand and the trees are similar in shape. They all seem to be reaching up to something, perhaps pleading. They take up the same space in the composition of the images. They are mournful and yet in some way transcendent.

★ ★ ★

Chechnya was where Marina found the edge she had been circling—found it and crossed over it.

She had been photographing the advance of the Russian army from a little village on the outskirts of Grozny. She was with a mixed group of Russian and western correspondents, some of whom she knew well. It was near dusk, but she was photographing the way she once had. She called it "tapping in." It was that feeling of being connected to something bigger, as though she couldn't make a wrong move or frame a bad image.

They were traveling in a pack, this small cadre of photographers and journalists, shuttling from one area of fighting to another, drawn by the sound of gunfire, down first one alley, then another. They were moving cautiously. They were all veterans of this sort of reportage. They knew the dangers.

There were times, she had learned long ago, when it was good to blend in with a crowd, and times when it was deadly. She knew this rule, had learned it from hard experience, so she knew they were in trouble when she saw the frightened crowd of villagers heading toward them. They were unarmed, as near as she could see, and they were stampeding in the dying light of day. In the narrow alley there was no place to run but back the way they had come, so she ran. Peter Burdett, a stringer for the international wire services, was beside her, but the others were soon lost in the crowd that overwhelmed them. She went down on the cobblestones once and felt sharp pain shoot up from her knee. Peter grabbed her arm and pulled her up, keeping her from being trampled.

There was no fighting the flow of the crowd so they went with it. Marina heard the popping of automatic-weapon fire behind her and the occasional screams of the wounded. She and Peter held onto each other as they ran. Marina's cameras banged against her chest and hips. She felt like she was in a maze. It seemed as if they were running downhill.

Then they stopped.

It was as if the crowd was a wave striking a seawall. The energy of the panicked mass continued to surge forward from the back for a few seconds while the group in front flowed backward. They met in the middle in a crush of people unable to move in any direction.

Then the popping report of automatic weapons sounded louder. It came from the front and the back. A low dull moan grew from the belly of the crowd. It was not a shriek of panic or pain, but an acknowledgment of the inevitable.

A head exploded near her but the body was wedged in too tight to fall. It merely slumped. Other bodies slumped or jerked around her. When enough bodies in a given area had been hit, they sank to the ground under the weight of their mass, leaving others all the more exposed and vulnerable.

She felt a slam in her shoulder, as if someone had punched her, then a burning pain. She felt it again lower in her side and she doubled over. Peter wrapped himself around her, pushing her head into his chest. He held her for a moment. She felt more of the punches, but they did not reach her, and there was no burning pain that followed. Peter began dragging her down to the ground and she let him. She did not know whether he was already dead or mortally wounded when he slumped over her, but there was little she could do for him anyway. He covered her like a heavy blanket, still and unmoving. Then there was more weight on top of her as more bodies piled up. Her leg was twisted underneath her and uncomfortable, but the way Peter had fallen created a kind of shelter over her, so, though she lost consciousness, she was not crushed.

She woke up in an impromptu Red Cross hospital. Peter was dead. He had probably died quickly, she was told. The other journalists were also dead. She learned later that Russian soldiers had continued to fire into the crowd long after no one was moving. Then they had blown up a building on one side of the alley and bulldozed a thin layer of dirt over the rubble to bury the evidence. Fortunately, they had been in a hurry and had not done the job properly. The Chechen fighters pushed the Russians back the following morning, but still it had been almost twenty-four hours before all the bodies had been exhumed from the mass grave. She was one of five survivors. She had been shot in the shoulder and the side and taken an additional bullet in the thigh, but her prognosis looked good. Even her cameras survived, though this was most likely because they were strapped to her body.

Later she would find the solitary hand image on a roll of film still in one of her cameras. She could not have taken it herself. She was unconscious when they pulled her from the pile of bodies, and she could not imagine anyone stopping to take a picture with the camera while it was still tangled around her. Her best guess was that it had fired accidentally as they pulled her free of the dirt and rubble.

She could not bring herself to publish any of her pictures from Chechnya, but she did allow "The Hands" to be made into a poster. It sold well considering its gruesome subject matter, but she asked that the proceeds from the sales go to Peter Burdett's wife and daughter.

★ ★ ★

There were no pictures after Chechnya, but there was no relief, either. She went on pilgrimages to holy places, read ancient sacred texts, sought answers, tried turning inward, but all she felt was empty. There was nothing romantic or exciting about death now, but there was nothing exhilarating or important about being alive, either.

When Erin, her only remaining real friend, recommended this cruise, Marina had gone along with it out of apathy and exhaustion—not knowing anymore what to do. "You could shoot some landscapes or people," Erin had prompted enthusiastically. "It'll be fun."

Marina had not yet decided to end her own life, but the thought was with her. She could just disappear in the night, slip back into the great dark womb. There would be no mess, no chance of complications, no body for family or friends to identify. It seemed clean.

And now she had done it. The letter she had left in her stateroom was for Erin. Within that letter was another letter, this one to her parents. It was not a kind thing to do to Erin, giving her this responsibility, but Marina was afraid the letter might be lost if it wasn't entrusted to her agent. In the letter she had tried to explain why this really was the best thing to do. She wasn't happy with the suffering she would cause her family, but she could no longer go on as she had been. She'd once taken pride in her own hidden resources, her inner strength. Now she was tapped out.

On the cruise she had searched as much of her soul as she could find. She had asked, pleaded, begged for an answer. She wanted a sign from a god she didn't really believe in—but there was nothing and no one, and she was alone.

She opened her mouth and let the water in.

There was no time to taste the salt, for she was coughing and gagging reflexively. Her lungs hurt first, then quickly her face, and the inside of her head burned. She kicked and clawed at the water for a moment, then relaxed. She was floating now. How odd, she thought. It had only hurt for an instant.

She opened her eyes and was surprised that she could see—not far, but a little way around her. There was a light above her, but beyond a few feet she could see nothing. It was like being in a fog or heavy mist. Fish seemed to materialize in front of her, swim past, and fade away. Fish with stripes, wide fish.

What were they called? she wondered. Angel fish? Would she see angels soon? she thought. She seemed sleepy, dizzy. So this is what it feels like, she told herself. But she couldn't remember what "this" referred to.

She thought about sharks and things that might eat her. She wondered if she could still feel a bite or tear. Would she even know if she was being devoured? She was not afraid, but she was curious.

Something circled her. She caught glimpses of it at the edge of the misty range of her vision. It was big and graceful. She thought it was round, then it seemed like a woman, then it was round and almost glowing yellow green in the water again. It rolled and did pirouettes. It had a halo. It's an angel, she thought. It's my angel.

Her angel drifted close to her, studying Marina. It had the face of a woman. It probably had the body of a woman as well, but Marina could not see beyond the gentle face.

"Why?" Marina heard the question without hearing it. It seemed to go straight inside her head. She wanted to give this angel an answer. She had a hundred answers and a photograph to go with each one of them, but her brain would not make her mouth work. She tried thinking the answers she wanted to give, but this was too much work, required too much concentration. It was all she could do to keep her eyes open.

"Dreams?" The word came to Marina, but she was not sure if she had heard it or if she thought it.

Yes, she thought, take me into dreams. Let me dream one long dream and never wake up.

The woman before her, her angel, she supposed—though something inside her balked at the idea and did not believe in angels— turned in the water. As she turned, her back became rounded. There was a pattern, like a map of interlocking islands, painted on her skin.

It was beautiful. Marina had never seen a painting more beautiful. It was alive. It undulated and moved. It was like the shell of a large sea turtle, but it was also more. It was green and blue with hints of accents of red and golden yellow.

The painted islands became the continents of a watery planet, and she saw them drift together and apart, accelerated as if through some kind of time-lapse photography. Mountain ranges pushed up, lowlands filled with water. She drifted close to it.

Once while visiting her sister in Washington, D.C., she had seen a film at one of the Smithsonian's theaters. It had been shot from one of the space shuttles and showed the planet Earth as a beautiful blue, cloud-stroked orb. It seemed so incredible, this vantage point. She recognized places she had been, but they appeared so different from just a matter of miles up in space. None of the scars showed. She had paid to see the film three times in a row. When her sister finally dragged her from the darkened theater she felt oddly at peace.

She felt this way now as she hovered over the painted planet—the turtle shell islands. She was in low orbit. It was sweet and serene from this distance. There could be cultures and civilizations being born, fighting their wars, dying off, and evolving on those island continents, but from here it was an elegant ballet. She reached out to it, not with intention, but by letting her arms drift to embrace it. Her hands found a hard, smooth edge. She could still move her fingers so she held onto it. She wanted to lie over this planet, wrap her skin around it, become a mother goddess for this beautiful little planet.

She felt herself being pulled through the water—faintly aware of momentum. She clung to the edges of the turtle's shell and laid her cheek down among the island continents. Her eyes closed and she surrendered to angels, and turtles, and islands, and currents, and dreams.

CHAPTER 2

Passing Within

There are competing theories to explain how sea turtles navigate over great distances. It has been posited that they use celestial navigation to find their way—that each time a turtle surfaces for air at night it studies the stars—that there are, perhaps, certain turtle constellations that mean "steady on for food," "this is the path," or "this is the place from which you came and to which you must return."

I once dreamed that I saw pictures in the stars, but in the moment of my waking the pictures fell apart like a puzzle. Now when I look to the night sky, I'm only aware that there is something I've forgotten.

★ ★ ★

When you die, you move down a long tunnel, drawn by an intense and beautiful light.

This was the thought with which Marina awoke. Surely this was the light. It was a golden light, intense and burning. There was an irregular but dull rhythmic throbbing that sounded both close by and distant at the same time. Marina's eyes were closed and still the light was blinding and warm. Should I open my eyes? she wondered. Can I open them? What would it mean to look into the light? Would I cross some line that I could not step back over? Wasn't there some test about looking or not looking in the land of the dead?

Marina opened her eyes, blinked, closed them, then tried opening them once more. There were colors at the edges of her field of vision.

Blue. She could see blue around the edges of the light. A pale blue that ran to brighter, almost turquoise, shades. Sky blue, she thought, almost immediately aware that she was, in fact, looking at sky.

The bright light was the sun. It was directly overhead in a vivid blue sky. She was staring right into it and could not seem to look away. She closed her eyes. If sight was a sense that one still needed after death she did not want to jeopardize it. She had not spent much time imagining what death would be like, but she was sure that she did not like the idea of being both dead and blind.

She concentrated on looking away. It took a great deal of effort, much more than it had taken to open her eyelids, but with time she found she could move her eyes and bring other things into her field of vision. To the right, there was more blue sky and the wisp of a cloud high up and bannerlike. Further to the right, and this took even more effort, the sky met a horizon—part water, part land. Sand. She was on a beach. The distant pulsing rush she had heard were waves, though they still sounded oddly distant, as if her ears were plugged, or, more likely, filled with water.

When she looked down all she could see was the familiar out-of-focus abstraction that was her nose. When she rolled her eyes back she saw more sky and a line of something darker, perhaps the tops of trees.

She looked left and realized that her head must be inclined slightly in this direction because she could see the sand and the ocean and one of her arms stretched out away from her. The arm was an angry shade of red and blistered, but it did not hurt. She realized for the first time that she could not feel it at all. She tried moving it. She tried wriggling fingers, clenching a fist, but nothing moved. She tried to feel other parts of her body but they were equally lost to her. She could see that she was lying on sand, but she could not feel the sand. She felt some warmth from the sun on her face, but felt none in other parts of her body. She could control no muscles. She felt no pressure against her skin, neither the ever-present resistance to gravity nor the places where her body must be coming in contact with other matter. Even her somatic sense, the understanding of where her body was in space, was confused. She had no idea how her body was arranged on the sand.

She closed her eyes again.

She would not have imagined death to be like this. She had hoped it would be a liberation, that her spirit would fly free of her body and she would move on to some beautiful peaceful place. But this seemed more a punishment than a liberation.

Was this what death was really like? Would her spirit remain trapped in her body while it decomposed? Would she spend long nights on this beach while crabs tore the skin away from her body and birds pecked out her organs? Perhaps this was hell. Once her body had been dried, devoured, and bleached clean by sun and salt, would her spirit then be free? Or was this all there was? She was not a Catholic, but she knew that Catholics believed that suicide was a mortal sin. Were they right? Was she condemned to this for taking her own life?

★ ★ ★

Marina slept for a while, or at least a period of time passed that she recalled neither thinking nor dreaming.

Something firm but gentle pressed against her right cheek and a hard edge touched her lower lip. Something cool ran into her mouth, a few drops of sweet fresh water. There was a pause and then a few more drops trickled in, not a lot, but enough to make her cough because her tongue and throat were not working in unison. She closed her lips and concentrated on learning to swallow again. After a moment she parted her lips again and more of the cool water poured into her mouth. She swallowed better this time. She repeated this ritual several more times and, like a child nursing, found that water was always available when she opened her lips.

She felt a shadow pass over her face and carefully opened her eyes. The sky had been replaced by a face. It was a woman—an old woman with thin, tangled black hair streaked with gray. She had the features Marina associated with South Pacific Islanders—a mélange of ethnicities—delicate European nose and mouth, honey-toned Asian skin, and deep-set, dark, jade green eyes, perhaps the blood gift of some Jewish merchant or Spanish sailor. She would have been beautiful as a young woman. She was, in fact still beautiful. She looked at once familiar and foreign. Marina felt as if she had seen this woman before, but she could not remember a place or a time.

Marina tried to speak, tried to say "thank you," but all that came out was an unintelligible, hoarse whisper. The old woman cocked her head to the side like an animal that knows it's being addressed without understanding the message. She studied Marina. The old woman had thin lips, and it did not take much of a smile to expose shining white teeth. She said nothing but held up the shell with which she had been pouring water into Marina's mouth, offering more. Marina tried to shake her head no, then tried to say the word no, and finally settled for closing her lips.

The old woman seemed to understand. She leaned back and Marina could see that she was sitting cross-legged in the sand. She was bare-chested and her breasts hung low and pendulous. She was a small woman, tight and compact, but she looked strong. She wore a short, ragged skirt of dark green grasses or seaweed that looked more deco-rative than protective. Her hair, Marina noticed, was more than just tangled. There were things in it—feathers, twigs, leaves, a piece of shell. She wore a necklace of beads around her neck—polished white coral, and black pearls threaded on a cord of twisted fiber.

Marina watched as the woman surveyed her from head to foot. Slowly, the old woman scanned with her eyes. Sometimes she squinted and pursed her lips, other times she made faces, poking her cheek out with her tongue, closing her lips and blowing both cheeks out while bulging her eyes. Marina wanted to laugh, but the old woman seemed to be concentrating intently on what she was doing. She put her hands over Marina's face, not touching her but several inches away, and bounced her hands as if against some invisible barrier. She made some noises in a high singing voice, but Marina could not tell if they were words, prayers, or simple vocalizations.

Then, as if satisfied, the old woman stood up abruptly and walked away. Marina tried to call out, tried to say "Don't go!" and "Please stay!" but her own voice was unrecognizable to her and barely more than a whisper. Left alone again, Marina tried moving her head, tried moving some part of her body, but felt nothing. What is this place? she wondered. What is happening to me?

But this time Marina was not alone for long. Soon the old woman was back. She set two carved wooden bowls down in the sand and sat next to Marina again. She cradled Marina's head with her right hand and slipped her left hand under Marina's shoulders. When she lifted Marina into her lap it was almost effortless. She held Marina's head gently at an angle so that she could see her surroundings. The sea was in front of her, as was the setting sun low on the horizon. She was, as she had thought, on a beach. Her feet were in the water and the waves surged as high as her thighs, but she could not feel this. She noticed that she was naked, but this bothered her less than the color and con-dition of her skin.

Every inch of skin that she could see was an angry red. In some places the skin had bubbled and broken to create open sores. Her legs were splayed and twisted unnaturally. She could have seen the machete scar on the back of her calf if the rest of the skin around it had not been so burned from the sun. She wondered if one or both of her legs were broken. In some places—her right knee, her right hip, her left ankle—she noticed swelling. On her abdomen she noticed a dark bruise, purple-black beneath the burned skin.

She felt panic rise up within her. Her breath quickened. She saw her burned breasts rise and fall on her chest, but she seemed, at the same time, disconnected from the source of her breath. She was, she realized, disconnected from her whole body. She felt none of the pain she would expect from such injury. In fact, she felt nothing. Her pain, her panic came from a different place.

Again she thought, Is this death? Am I watching my body die? Now she was truly living in her head. If she was living at all.

Something cool dripped onto her forehead and ran into her eyes. The old woman dipped her fingers into one of the bowls and let more of the liquid drip onto Marina's forehead. The liquid was soothing and smelled faintly of flowers. Marina realized that her face must be as burned as her body, but she felt no pain, only the cool liquid that the old woman first dripped then painted on with light strokes of her fingers.

Marina closed her eyes. The old woman hummed to herself and rocked gently from side to side. This is what angels must be like, Marina thought.

Sleep or stillness came over her again, as though it required great effort even to maintain awareness in this place. When she opened her eyes it was twilight. The sun had dropped into the ocean and the sky had hissed red, orange, and then pink, before shifting to evening blues. There was still enough light to see and the first thing Marina saw was the turtle's shell.

It was close to her, upright and almost heart-shaped in the sand. The pattern of interlocking plates was a deep green and blue with details in red and yellow. There were five on either side and five down the center. The outer edge formed a border of smaller plates. Where had she seen this pattern? She balanced on the edge of recognition. She tried thinking backward. She had seen this shell in a dream, her dying dream. She recalled it now. Her angel had been there, but her angel had been a sea turtle. It didn't make much sense to her, but she recalled clinging to the turtle's shell.

Slowly, the shell she was watching began to move, but it did not move the way she expected shells to move. This shell undulated, bent, twisted to reveal arms instead of long reptilian flippers. A human head rose up as if from within the shell itself, but as it continued to turn Marina realized this was no shell but a picture of a shell. It was painted, no, it was tattooed on the back of the old woman who had given her water and cooled the burn on her face.

It covered all of the old woman's back, from her neck to the base of her spine where the seaweed skirt hung. It spread out to wrap halfway around her sides. It covered so much of her that when she sat, head hunched down and arms pulled in, all that showed was the beautiful shell design.

The old woman turned to look back at Marina as she stood up. Marina was surprised to see that she did not look as old as she had seemed earlier. Her face was less lined, her skin tighter, her breasts sat higher on her chest, and her waistline was more narrow. She still wore the same necklace and her hair, while a bit more lustrous, was still tangled with the detritus of the sea.

She also seemed to step more lightly as she walked up the beach out of Marina's line of sight.

For a long time Marina was alone. She did not sleep or close her eyes. She watched the sky go from cerulean to navy. She watched stars come alight in the night sky, forming patterns she did not recognize. She looked for clusters of bright stars and made patterns of them as she had when she was a girl, before she knew that there were such things as constellations. She named them silently to herself. There is a ship, and a bear, and an arrow.

"A sea forest, an egg, and the north stone," a voice added. It seemed to come from above and behind Marina, though she could not tell for sure. It seemed so much a continuation of her own thought that she wondered for a moment if she had heard it at all. She could see each of the shapes she had heard spoken. There was a sea forest, and an egg shape made from seven stars low on the horizon. She could even see a single bright star in an irregular cluster of stars, like a diamond glinting from a rock. Somehow she knew this was the north stone, though she did not know what this meant.

"The north stone is the way there and the way back," the voice answered. It was a woman's voice, almost familiar. In tone and pitch it sounded like the singing of the old woman, but it also seemed lighter, more youthful. The words were accented strangely and assembled with the precision of someone not used to speaking English.

Marina tried to look behind her, but she still could not move her head. She rolled her eyes back, but stars were all she saw. "Hello," Marina said. Her voice came out a little clearer than it had earlier in the day. "Who is there?" There was no answer. "Hello," Marina tried again. She used more breath this time and spoke a little louder. "Is someone there?"

"Why are you here?" the woman's voice asked softly.

"I don't know where I am," Marina answered, though this was not an answer to the question.

"Why are you not knowing where you are?" The construction was awkward but Marina understood the question. What she did not know was how to answer.

"I don't know where I am because I'm dead." It came out more sharply, more impatiently than she had intended, so she softened it by adding, "I have died, haven't I?" If she wasn't dead, but merely paralyzed below the neck, well ... she didn't even want to contemplate it further. It was quiet for a long moment, then the woman spoke again.

"What is *dead*?" she asked, emphasizing the word dead in her question.

"Dead is not living."

"You were not living before?" The way the woman made a question of her response confused Marina. She was not sure if it was a comment on her life or a misunderstanding of her explanation.

"No, I was living before, now I am not living. That is being dead."

"I know death, but not dead."

"Then I am in death," Marina answered. This made the woman laugh and made Marina feel like she had miscommunicated. "This is death, isn't it?" she added. Again there was a moment of silence.

"Death is out there," the woman said. A shell or stone plopped in the water down by Marina's feet. "Death is a . . . ," she seemed to search for the correct word, then found it, "current." She was pleased with her choice of words. "It carries you here."

"Then I am dead?" Marina asked. She disliked having to belabor this point but this was not what she had expected death to be.

"You are not . . . living." She said this slowly and carefully and

Marina wasn't sure if it was because the woman was not certain herself or if she was just being careful of Marina's feelings.

"So this is what death is like," Marina whispered, more to herself than to the woman.

"This is what death likes," the woman pronounced, as if it answered Marina's question. Again Marina suspected that this was not simply a miscommunication. Either the woman was deliberately not answering her question or she honestly did not know how to answer it. Something about the woman's voice made her doubt dishonesty, so she tried a different approach.

"Then who are you?" Marina asked. By way of answer, a head moved into her field of vision. She knew at once, even in the darkness, that it was the turtle woman she had seen before, but now she seemed even younger, almost girlish. She wore the same necklace, had the same wildly festooned hair, but she had the glow and aura of youth about her. Marina knew that this young woman, the older woman she had seen at sunset, and the old woman who had given her water and cooled her forehead, were one in the same. And now she began to recall seeing this woman before. She had seen her in water, in a dream of water. She had been the angel that had come to Marina. "Are you an angel?" Marina asked hesitantly.

"An-gel." She drew the word out, playing with it, almost tasting it. The young woman moved to sit beside Marina. She laughed and said the word again, "Angel." Even in the dark Marina could see the young woman's eyes glisten as she tried the word on. "Angel. Turtle," she added as if comparing the two. "Angel." She held out her left hand as if holding something in it. "Turtle." She held out her right hand and appeared to be gauging the weight of an invisible object.

Marina watched in silence. She was struck by the quality of play in the young woman, as if everything was fresh and new to her. Vaguely, through a great mist of time, she recalled possessing that quality herself. When she looked up, the young woman was studying her with that same head cocked to the side, that same almost animal curiosity that she had shown earlier in the day when she had seemed so ancient.

"What will happen to me now?" Marina asked. Once again the woman did not answer right away. She looked up at the night sky as if looking for an answer or, at the very least, searching for the right word. She put a hand on Marina's chest, covering her heart.

"Healing?" The way she accented the end of her words made everything she said sound like a question, or, perhaps this was meant to be a question.

"Healing?" Marina repeated, intending for it to be a question. "If I am dead, why must I heal?"

"Dead?" the woman asked. She looked confused.

"In death," Marina added impatiently. "If this is death, if I am in death, why must I heal?" Again, the woman looked confused. Her forehead wrinkled and she brought her hands up to her face.

"Death . . . is a current," she was speaking slowly and deliberately as though Marina were a child.

"I know, you said that," Marina interrupted. "Death is the current that brought me here. I understand that. This is where you go, this is what happens to you when you die. I know I am dead. I know I am in death. What I want to know is what happens now?" The woman nodded her head, smiled, then began again.

"Death is a current, there." She gestured out to sea. "Life is a current," she looked around, then gestured in the opposite direction, "there." Marina closed her eyes in frustration. "Current brings you here in death. If you heal, you may find your way, there." Again she gestured in the direction she had assigned to the life current.

"Do you mean that I can live again?" Marina asked. There was a tone of bitterness she heard in her voice that she had not intended.

"Maybe." The woman smiled, but did not seem certain.

"Do you mean that I will be reborn, reincarnated?" Marina asked.

"Re-in-car-na-ted," she rolled the word slowly out of her mouth and laughed. "Reincarnated." She seemed pleased with the word, but Marina had no idea whether they shared an understanding of its meaning.

"I don't want to live again," Marina explained. "I was no good at it."

"Good at it," the woman repeated, nodding her head.

"Do you understand? I wanted to die. I ended my own life. It was my choice. I was not good at being alive. I wanted death." Marina repeated herself, saying the same thing several different ways in an effort to make the angel or woman, or whatever she was, understand. "Now I just want to move on, to see what comes next. Do you understand?"

"Move on." She nodded her head. "Yes, heal to move on."

Well, Marina thought, I can understand that. If I have to heal to move on to the next level or place then that is what I will do. "How do I heal?" she asked. "Can you help me?"

"Maybe?" Again Marina could not tell if it was meant to sound like a question. Then she added, "I don't know."

"Isn't that what you're here for?"

"Maybe?" the woman answered and again it sounded like a question. She was smiling, though, and did not seem to have been bothered by the question.

"Then will you help me?" Marina asked softly.

"Maybe?" she answered brightly, but then for a moment she looked troubled.

"What is it?" Marina asked. "Have I said something wrong? Don't you want to help me?"

"It is . . . hard," the woman answered haltingly. "I don't know the . . . ," she faltered again, as if searching for a word, "the way you speak, your . . . your . . ."

"Language?" Marina completed the sentence.

"Lang-uage." This was another of the words that seemed to please the woman. She said it softly several times, as if laying claim to it. "Yes, language."

"No," Marina interrupted, "you speak my language very well." The woman laughed at this, and her laughter made Marina's eyes tear.

"Not this lang-uage," she said through her laughter. She drew the word language out as she had done with the words angel and reincarnation and touched Marina's lips with her fingertips. "This language," she said as she touched Marina's chest over her heart.

There was a moment of silence between them, then the woman stood up. "Wait," Marina said. "What should I do?" The woman seemed to ponder this question for a moment, then she dropped to her knees in the sand beside Marina.

"Decide," she said, and this time it did not sound like a question. She held each of her hands palm up as though there might be something in them. "Angel?" As she said this she lifted her left hand and cocked her head to the left gesturing out to the ocean. "Turtle?" She posited this word as though it and not devil or demon were the common antonyms for the word angel. At the same time she lifted her right hand and cocked her head to the right, gesturing in the direction she had identified with the life current. "Angel? Turtle?" She repeated the choices and the gestures that went with them, then she laughed, stood quickly and was gone.

"Wait," Marina called out again, but this time there was no answer.

Decide, she thought, decide what? What did it mean to decide? But even as she turned the question over in her mind she knew what it meant. She didn't understand all of it, but somehow she was being asked to decide whether she would do what it would take to move on with this experience. While she was not certain that this place was death, it was clearly not life. Perhaps this was a way station, a step in the process of transition from life to death. Well, she thought, let me get on with it. I'm ready.

★ ★ ★

The sun woke her in the morning. She felt it on her face. As far as she could tell nothing had changed. She had not moved. She still felt nothing below her neck. She still heard the waves rolling ashore along the beach on either side of her. She smelled the salt air, and she was thirsty.

Almost as soon as she was aware of her thirst, the old woman, the old turtle woman was there beside her with water in a scalloped shell. Marina drank, in sips, most of the water from the shell. She looked up at the old woman. The eyes, the mouth, the shape of her face were identical to the young woman she had spoken to, more alike than even a mother and daughter could be.

"I am ready," she said quietly. "I have decided." The old woman cocked her head in that peculiar way that Marina recognized from the day before, but showed no sign of understanding her. "I am ready," Marina tried to explain. "You know, angel . . . turtle," Marina repeated what the young woman had said, but the old woman still looked puzzled. "You remember," Marina pleaded. "Last night, you said that I needed to decide. Didn't you? Wasn't that you?" Again the old woman just looked confused, as if she wanted to understand Marina but couldn't.

She stood up and turned her back to Marina. The turtle tattoo was still there. It was beautiful, fascinating in its detail, intricate and precise. But Marina was confused. Why couldn't the old woman understand her when the younger version of what Marina was certain was the same woman, could? Had she dreamed the conversation in the dark? Could she trust any of her senses?

The old woman walked up the beach, out of Marina's range of vision and for a few moments Marina was alone again. Then the woman was bending over her, lifting and folding Marina's arms across her chest. Next she felt her head and shoulders being lifted. The old woman lifted her by the shoulders and began dragging her backward. Marina saw again the burned and sun-scarred condition of her own skin. She saw the tracks in the sand made by her limp legs.

As she was pulled backward her view of the beach expanded. A wide white band of sand extended as far as she could see in either direction. The waves rolled ashore powerfully, but seemed to break further out, their force blunted by some sandbar or reef. A barrier of palms and other trees began just beyond the dune line and quickly became a dark tangle of undergrowth.

When the old woman stopped dragging her and laid her down, she was next to a shallow trench in the shade of a particularly full palm tree. The trench was about six feet long and two feet wide scooped out of the sand to about eighteen inches deep. Beside the trench was a pile of wet seaweed. The thick, broad fronds appeared to be coated in a slick, almost slimy, translucent film. As Marina watched, the woman layered the seaweed in an overlapping pattern to cover the bottom and sides of the trench. She did this carefully and it took time to complete. Marina found herself mesmerized by the simple repetitive activity.

She had almost drifted off to sleep when she felt herself being lifted off the ground. When she opened her eyes, the old woman, who was easily a foot shorter than Marina, had lifted her up as if she were a baby. She was limp in the woman's arms and felt herself being lowered into the trench. Once down, the old woman pulled and tugged Marina into place. She straightened Marina's arms and legs, pulled back her hair, and pushed sand beneath the seaweed layer to form a support for her head and neck.

"What is this?" Marina asked. "What are you doing?" The old woman smiled at her but said nothing. Instead she began layering the remaining seaweed strips over Marina. She molded them carefully around Marina's feet, calves, and thighs. She covered her belly and breasts, wrapped her arms and shoulders, and ended by wrapping her throat carefully. Marina felt none of this, but watched it with an eerie detachment, as though this was someone else's body that must be causing someone else, somewhere, excruciating pain. While the old woman wrapped, she sang. Her voice was pretty and melodic, but Marina could not make out any words.

When she finished her wrapping, she stood up and walked into the forest. Within a few feet she was outside of Marina's view and Marina felt, once again, alone. She wondered if this seaweed wrap was to help her heal. The old woman had laid several strips across Marina's forehead and cheeks, and it did feel cool on her face.

After only a few minutes, the old woman returned carrying an armful of flowers. They were tiny coral red and pink orchids. She had never seen such small orchids in such intense colors. The old woman knelt beside Marina and let the flowers fall into the trench. There were not enough blossoms to cover Marina's body, but the woman arranged and distributed them evenly. The scent of them was honey-sweet but also sharp, with a hint of citrus and cloves. The odor filled Marina and she closed her eyes just to concentrate on it.

When she opened her eyes again, her feet were gone—covered in sand—and her legs were fast disappearing.

"What are you doing?" Marina cried. "No! Stop! Please stop." The woman was methodically but rapidly pushing sand down into the trench to cover her. Marina suddenly thought of flowers at funerals. She thought of Chechyna. She thought of wanting to die, but she was already dead so how could she die again?

"Wait," she called out. "I did choose. I want to heal and move on. You said I had to decide. I have. I have decided." The old woman ignored her. She sang to herself and pushed sand into the trench to cover Marina's torso. "I don't want this, please don't." She was crying now as the old woman pushed sand in around her neck and head. Despite the futility of it Marina found herself taking deep breaths, as though this would give her some protection from being buried alive. As the sand came close around her face she closed her eyes, waiting for the dark, waiting for the smothering weight of sand.

But it never came. When she opened her eyes again, the old woman was smoothing the sand over her. She had pushed and packed the sand around Marina's head, right up to her face, but no further. She brushed the sand off of Marina's face and patted her head. Then she drew handfuls of gray and black powder from another pouch and sprinkled it over Marina. The powder was lighter than sand and some of it blew into Marina's face. Ash. She could taste burnt ash. What bizarre burial ritual was this? she wondered. The ash marked the mound that covered Marina. The old woman inspected her work, nodded her head in approval, and left.

Several times during the day the old woman returned with a basket of tightly woven grasses. She poured fresh water from the basket over Marina's buried body. Though she could not feel it, she knew the cool water must be trickling down between the folds of her seaweed wrapping, keeping her skin moist and cool. She also helped Marina drink water from the scalloped shell. Never a lot, but always enough to keep her mouth and throat cool and moist.

She did not speak again to the old woman. She had not decided if this old woman was her savior or her tormentor. With all this careful watering, she wondered if something was supposed to grow from her grave. Or was her skin supposed to just decay beneath the earth and slip from her bones? Would she be free, then? Free to move on to some other place, some other level?

With the night, a woman came out of the sea. It was clearly the younger version of the strange turtle woman, for even in silhouette against the moonlight, her youthful figure stood out. She stood up with the waves making foam about her ankles and stretched her arms up to the night sky. She dropped her head back, and Marina could not tell if she was stretching or worshipping the moon or simply studying the sky. Turtle Woman, Marina thought. She had no other name to use for the young woman. I will call you Turtle Woman.

"Why are you here?" It was the Turtle Woman. She had slipped silently up the beach while Marina was studying the stars. Why am I here? Marina thought. Wasn't that the same question she had asked the night before? I'm here because I'm dead! She wanted to shout this. She thought it. But she remembered how difficult it was to explain dead to the woman, and, besides, she wanted to talk to someone. She decided to try a different approach.

"I'm here to heal," she said. She didn't really understand what she was saying. She did not know how she could both be dead and need to heal at the same time. It seemed pointless, but it was the language the Turtle Woman had used, and Marina thought it might be what she wanted to hear.

"Dying . . . healing." The woman stood over her, her legs on either side of the shallow grave Marina was buried in. She held up both of her hands as she had the night before, miming a kind of scale. "Dying?" She bounced one hand as though judging the weight of something resting in her palm. "Healing?" She bounced the other hand. "You are still choosing, yes?"

"No," Marina said. But it was true that she had made no conscious decision to heal. She had not really chosen anything. She could not choose something she did not believe in. "Well, yes," Marina admitted softly. "It's just that I don't understand this, any of this. I just wanted to die."

"Then get up. There is the current." She gestured at the ocean. "Go to it. Continue dying. Or . . ." she paused, put her hands on her hips, ". . . come again to the living."

"I told you I was no good at living." Her voice was angry now, with traces of desperation. "I just want to die." The Turtle Woman gestured with both hands toward the ocean, but said nothing. "I can't move, damn it. If I could, I would. I died once. I can do it again." Marina was actually not sure she believed this, but frustration was building within her. "Why can't I move? If I'm dead why am I crippled?"

"Are you crippled?" the Turtle Woman asked.

"Would I be lying here, buried like this, if I had a choice?"

"But you chose not to be with the living."

"This is not how it's supposed to be," Marina snapped. She strained her body, willing it to move with all the muscles in her face. She felt her eyes bulge with the pressure she was creating, but nothing moved. It was like trying to lift an object securely bolted to the ground. She fought the sand, the dead weight of her body, gravity itself, until she had nothing left to fight with. "I can't . . . ," Marina fumbled. "Please. Take me to the current. Let me move on." Her voice was weak, defeated. She never liked asking people for things. It made her feel diminished.

"I cannot," the Turtle Woman said. She sat lightly in the sand beside Marina. The moonlight reflecting off the water and the white sand created just enough of a glow for Marina to see the Turtle Woman's face. It was a beautiful face, dark but radiant. She had a young girl's mouth, full and quick to smile. There were no lines in her face yet, but her eyes seemed still to belong to the older woman. They were a mother's eyes. "I can help you to walk, but the path you must choose. . . ." She did not finish the sentence. She did not need to. Marina knew the Turtle Woman was telling her the truth. It did not please her to know she still had choices to make. Choices were what death was to have resolved.

"Who are you?" Marina asked gently. Then, without waiting for an answer, she added, "I mean, are you an angel or a spirit? What are you?" The Turtle Woman seemed to be considering her question. She looked as though she would speak several times, then didn't. She looked out at the ocean. Marina had the impression that she was searching for words.

"I am like you," the Turtle Woman began hesitantly. "Now I am woman. There . . ." she gestured up to the night sky, "I am mother." She pointed out to the ocean. "Then I am . . . tur-tle." She said turtle slowly, breaking it up into two distinct syllables, as if she found it both amusing and fascinating to associate herself with this word. "Here," she touched Marina's forehead, "I am angel." She looked at Marina closely, as if to see whether she understood. "Many things. One thing." She seemed pleased with her own explanation.

"You come from my head," Marina asked, "don't you?"

The Turtle Woman wrinkled her forehead, thought for a moment, then answered. "Yes," she announced, pleased with herself. She touched her fingertips to the point between her breasts where her heart beat. "I come from your head." As she said this she touched Marina's forehead again. Then she put her hand on the sand that covered Marina's chest. "You come from your head."

"I mean," Marina struggled to explain, "that this is all a fantasy, a dream. Isn't it? Even though it seems like a long time, it's probably only taking seconds, right? Somewhere my body is drowning right now. I'm unconscious and this is my last dream. Right?"

The Turtle Woman seemed to contemplate Marina's perception for a long time. In the silence, Marina thought about what she had just expressed. Like the moment when one becomes aware of being in a dream, Marina half expected to have her surroundings begin to fade, to be snapped back to her drowning body. But nothing changed. Her surroundings, if anything, seemed more real. Minutes seemed to go by as neither of the two women spoke. Then the Turtle Woman patted the sand firmly.

"This is a real place," she said in a quiet but serious voice. "This is also a dreaming place. Maybe you are dreaming me. Maybe I am dreaming you. Maybe Turtle Island is dreaming us both. Turtle Island is a mother. Maybe we are daughters in her dream." Marina's head began to swim.

Can I stand this? Marina asked herself. Can something be both a dream and real?

"What is a photographer?" the Turtle Woman asked. She said the word again, playing with it as, Marina noticed, she did with all the words that seemed new to her.

"A photographer makes pictures," Marina answered, though she knew as she said it that it was not a satisfactory answer.

"Draws pictures?"

"Not really drawing."

"But pictures?" She leaned and turned slightly touching her own back where the turtle-shell tattoo covered it. The colors were brighter than Marina had remembered from when she had seen it before.

"Yes, pictures," Marina said, "but not with ink, not drawing."

"How, then?"

"With light," Marina answered, though she did not really know how to explain this simply. "I catch reflections of light to make pictures."

"Hmmm." The Turtle Woman nodded her head. Somehow she seemed to find a connection, some way in which this could make sense to her. "How?" she asked. She leaned in close to Marina, expectant and curious. Marina was not sure where to begin.

"Film," she started to explain. "Something sensitive to light."

"Like skin," the Turtle Woman interrupted. Marina thought about this for a moment.

"Yes," she admitted, "like skin." Skin was a surface that reacted to light. It changed color, darkened, with exposure to light. "Like skin, but more complicated."

"Complicated?" the Turtle Woman asked. It was another curious word for her. Actually, Marina thought, it is not more complicated. What could be more complex, more magical, than the natural chemical reactions of the body in response to its environment? Still, she was looking for some way to explain the almost magical clumping of microscopic particles of silver halide on film.

"Light," Marina began, "focused by a lens." She stopped to see if the Turtle Woman understood this word. "A glass," Marina tried. "A crystal," she added, and at this the Turtle Woman nodded. "Light, focused by a crystal, makes patterns on a sensitive surface that reflects what we see."

"What we see?" the Turtle Woman asked with emphasis on the word "we."

"What everyone sees," Marina tried to explain, though she knew as she said it that it was, at best, an imprecise answer and, at worst, a falsehood.

"How much light?" Marina had expected to have to further explain how she could possibly record what everyone sees, but the Turtle Woman seemed contented with her explanation and ready with a different question.

"Only just the right amount of light will work," Marina began. "Too much light will make a negative go dark. When I try to make my image from that kind of negative it will appear all white with no detail, no patterns. Not enough light and the negative will appear clear. Then the print will be too dark to see the detail or the pattern." Marina realized this explanation was probably too complex, but the Turtle Woman seemed to be thinking about it.

"Then you need some light, and some dark," she announced, clearly pleased with herself. This was technically not a correct observation, but at a deeper, more essential level, it made perfect sense.

"Yes," Marina decided to agree, "some light and some dark."

"This is good," the Turtle Woman responded.

"Why good?"

"This is your language," the Turtle Woman said. She emphasized the last word and Marina remembered that they had used the word in their conversation of the previous night.

"What do you mean?" Marina asked.

"You think . . . ," she hesitated, "you speak to your body in this language."

"What language?"

"Light," she said as she stood up. "Light and darkness. This is why you are here. This is what you have to heal."

"I don't understand," Marina said.

"Too much darkness," the Turtle Woman said. She laughed a little and smiled, clearly pleased with her discovery. "You have too much darkness. You cannot see the patterns. You cannot see your own image clearly anymore." Marina was silent. "You rest now. Tomorrow, maybe you will sit up." As she said this she backed away from Marina with light dancing steps.

Marina watched the Turtle Woman run to the water. She ran out into the surf until she could run no further. Marina expected to see her dive headfirst into the water, but, instead, she bent at the waist and lowered herself into the water, so that the last thing Marina saw was the turtle-shell tattoo floating just above the waterline. Then she was gone.

Marina became aware of the odor of flowers again, as if the blossoms that had been buried with her were percolating their sweet scent to the surface. Too much darkness, she said to herself as she closed her eyes. Too much darkness.

★ ★ ★

Thirst woke her. It was day again and the sun was already high in the sky. Broken sunlight filtered down through the palm fronds and for a while Marina watched the pattern made by the light progress across the sand that covered her.

Shadows and light, she thought. What it takes to make a pattern.

It was not by movement and it was not all of a sudden that she became aware of the old turtle woman next to her, for the Turtle Mother, as it now seemed more appropriate to call her, sat so still that she might have been a rock or the brown stump of a cut tree. Marina became aware of her slowly. One moment Marina was alone, the next she was almost certainly alone, then she was in the presence of someone, then the Turtle Mother was with her. All this occurred without word, sign, or movement.

The Turtle Mother sat cross-legged in the sand, back bowed slightly, hands palm up on her knees. If she breathed, it was with excruciating slowness, for Marina could not see her chest move at all. Her eyes were open, fixed on some point on the horizon. Her face was serene and relaxed, and much closer to the young Turtle Woman she knew from the nights.

"Please, I'm thirsty," Marina whispered. "May I have some water?" The Turtle Mother unfurled her right arm slowly and lifted a shell from the sand at her side. She brought it to her own lips and drank. Then she set it back in the sand beside her.

Marina did not know what to make of this. She had not known the Turtle Mother to be mean spirited. She had only experienced her kindness. She had been frightened by being buried in the sand, but it seemed clear to her now that the woman had meant her no harm. Perhaps, she thought, she did not understand me.

"May I please have some water?" Marina said a little louder. Again the Turtle Mother lifted the shell and drank herself. Marina could see a rivulet of water run down the Turtle Mother's chin and trickle between her breasts. She found herself opening and closing her mouth as the Turtle Mother drank. She made little moaning sounds like an infant dependent on a breast or bottle. She was so thirsty.

The Turtle Mother refilled the shell with water and placed it in the sand over Marina's heart. Marina wanted to cry. What is the purpose of this? she wondered. Is it not enough that I am trapped here? Must I suffer as well?

Almost as if in answer to her unspoken question, the Turtle Mother slowly stood up. She stretched lazily, and even this seemed an affront to Marina. She walked down the beach to the water's edge, then out into the gentle surf. She seemed to walk a long way without disappearing and for a moment, Marina had the impression that the Turtle Mother was walking on the water. Then she bent and lowered herself down as she had the night before disappearing slowly into the calm surf.

The water was inches from Marina's mouth. She could almost smell it. This was agony. She was so thirsty and the water so close. Her mouth was dry, her throat burned, her skin itched. Water was the antidote, cool, sweet water, water inside her, water to soothe her skin. It was just within her grasp. If only she could move.

Wait, she thought. I can feel my skin!

She had not been able to feel anything against her skin before. She could not even feel dull pressure. Now she could feel a stinging at her thighs. Her skin tingled. She wanted to scratch it, but she was far from irritated by it. It was a confirmation of something. There was some life left in her. Life, she thought, or whatever this is. At least there was some feeling below her head. It was a little thing. She still could not move. She tried. She focused her attention on her legs and willed them to move. She was not buried deeply, and it was only sand. She could break free with even just a little movement, but nothing moved. Still she could feel the skin on her thighs.

She concentrated on experiencing the burning she felt. She wondered if she could feel anything else, and, for the first time since she had awakened in this strange world, she was aware of her heart beating. She felt it thumping inside her.

It no longer seemed odd to her that she might be both dead and experience a beating heart at the same time. Death was clearly dreamlike.

Still, it was her heart she felt, and her heart was a muscle. Maybe there were other muscles she could feel again. She thought she could feel muscles in her neck. She strained and flexed them, and sure enough her head moved just a little.

She picked a muscle in her neck that she seemed to be able to contract and relax at will. She imagined this muscle plugging into another muscle that ran beneath her skin to her shoulder. She flexed both muscles. Then she imagined that muscle in her shoulder connecting to another muscle in her upper arm. In this manner she slowly built a lifeline of muscle that extended from her jawline to the tip of her right index finger. It was not enough to move an arm, reposition an elbow, or shift a shoulder, but when she put her mind behind it and concentrated, she was convinced that she felt her finger move.

With uncharacteristic patience she brought movement back to her right hand. First she could flex a finger, then two, then she could squeeze a ball of damp sand in her hand. She could open and close her hand and wrap her thumb around to make a fist. She compacted the sand around her hand to create a space, a hand cave that she inhabited with her whole awareness. She felt the roughness of the sand against the back of her hand, and, while it did not hurt, the skin on her hand was sensitive. It was as if she had grown new nerve endings for this skin. She remembered how badly burned her skin had been and wondered if with feeling she would also get pain.

She could move her hand—open and close it and compress the sand into it. Could she dig herself free? She judged the distance she would have to dig. There were eight, maybe twelve inches of sand, some of it moist, but the top half was surely loose and dry.

She scratched the ceiling of her hand cave. Sand fell around her hand, but not enough to bury it. Slowly she clawed her way up, aware all the time of the great dead weight of her arm. Marina watched the sand that covered her. She saw the first shifting over the place she expected to see her hand. She saw a small crater form, then a finger, then another. Then there was a hand, her hand, and her arm emerging.

Somehow this image seemed familiar: the single hand clawing its way free of the earth.

Her arm was more than just dead weight now. It had found strength. It was moving sand aside and she could see from her shoulder to her hand.

Her skin was greenish black and wrinkled like dried leather. She had a moment of panic, then realized it was the seaweed that the Turtle Mother had wrapped her in. She rested for a moment with the victory of her liberated arm, then she picked up the shell of water and brought it to her lips. Her hand shook and her arm was unsteady. She spilled some of the water down her chin, but she also tasted it. It was warm, but sweet, and she held it in her mouth for a moment before swallowing it. She drained the shell then set about to dig out her other arm.

She could not really dig into the sand that covered her chest but she pushed it toward her legs the way a dog would dig a hole with two forepaws. It took time because she tired easily, but it was also exhilarating to be doing something after such a period of inactivity and helplessness. She became aware that it was getting darker, as if night and the progress of days had returned with the life in her limbs.

She carved a depression of sand over her chest and created a small hill over her pelvis. She pushed and scratched her way down to her left hand and met it clawing its way up. To feel both hands touching, to feel with both hands, was like a meeting between two lost friends. Marina laughed out loud.

She worked her head free of the sand and lifted herself onto her elbows. Most of the sand fell away from her chest and she saw sand-caked patches of seaweed molded about her chest. With great and deliberate effort she began to pull herself backward, up and out of the shallow depression she had been buried in. She grunted and strained and pulled her limp legs out of the sand. She still felt nothing below her waist. She could not make her knees bend or wiggle her toes, but she could feel new power in her spine and neck as she twisted and rolled to free herself.

Darkness came quickly, and it was a deeper darkness than she had known before. No moon and no stars penetrated the clouds, but there was still enough light for her to see that she had dragged her whole body free of the sand. Content for the moment, she closed her eyes.

★ ★ ★

"Too much darkness."

At first Marina was not certain whether she had thought this or heard it. She opened her eyes in the darkness. She could hear the waves washing ashore maybe fifty yards from her but she could not see them. "Too much darkness." She heard the voice again and recognized it. It was the Turtle Woman, the young one who came at night. She was somewhere behind where Marina lay. "It took a lot of light to bring you out of the earth. Now . . . ," she paused, "there is too much darkness."

"You said there was too much darkness in me. Is that why it is so dark now?" Marina asked.

The Turtle Woman did not answer right away and when she did speak it was in that hesitant manner she used when trying to find the right way to say a thing.

"Not a fault, I think. It is a balance. You called on a lot of light for your balance. Now, maybe, you must give some light back."

"How do I do that?" The part of Marina that struggled to understand things did not understand this and even before the Turtle Woman could answer she added, "I mean surely this light must be infinite. How could any one person use it up?"

"The light is always there, but not always for you. You must find the balance."

"You mean, I must find more light?"

"More light now, later, enough light." The Turtle Woman reached out and stroked Marina's hair. "It is like this film you think of." She exaggerated and stretched out the word film. "Too much darkness and this film is sick. But too much light and this film is also not whole. It is not living its purpose."

"Are you talking about me?" Marina asked. "Am I the film? I know you said that there was too much darkness in my life, but what good will it do to find light now. I have no life now. I have no purpose to live." There was a long period of silence.

"Maybe," the Turtle Woman finally continued, "you will choose to come again to the living. Maybe you will come this time with balance, with enough light and enough dark to make a whole person."

"My heart has no strength for living again."

"And yet your heart has the strength for coming out of the sea to this place. Your heart has the strength for coming out of the earth. I think this must be a strong heart."

This was all too confusing. She couldn't stand the thought of being powerless, trapped in the sand, the loss of control, but at the same time she believed that death was the right choice for her. It had not been some quick emotional response to a crisis. Her decision to die had come slowly, over time, in the full light of reason. She had been as ready as anyone could be, she thought, to give up her life. Now she seemed to be in some in-between place where death and life were both options.

"Yes, this is an in-between place." The Turtle Woman had plucked the words right from her innermost thoughts. "This is a dreaming place. Maybe you will not decide life or death so quickly here. Maybe you will heal some wounds and then decide which way you will go." Marina had nothing to say to this. She had no arguments to counter it.

"Can you sit up?" the Turtle Woman asked.

She used her arms to push herself into a sitting position and tried to lean forward, but with her legs directly out in front of her she just fell over on the side. She tried again, using her stomach and back muscles to hold herself upright, but she could not seem to find a position of balance. Again she fell over. This time the Turtle Woman came to help her. She lifted Marina up into a sitting position from behind and dragged her onto a little pile of sand. Then she pulled Marina's limp legs into a crossed posture and steadied her. She wobbled and almost fell several times but Marina found that she could sit up if she held onto her ankles and braced herself with her arms. The Turtle Woman settled in behind her and sat cross-legged with her back against Marina's, supporting her.

"Can you see any light?" Marina did not understand what the Turtle Woman meant.

"Light?"

"Up there." The Turtle Woman gestured into the sky.

"You mean stars? No," Marina answered, "it's pitch black."

"Look softer. Make the light come to you."

"What light? I don't understand."

"Up there, when the clouds break."

Marina looked for a long while but saw no break in the rich darkness. "I'm sorry, but I just don't see anything," Marina said in frustration.

"Then just practice sitting. Find your balance point so that you can sit without falling over." This Marina could do. She had come to know her body more intimately in the last few hours or days or whatever measure of time had elapsed. She could travel within her body and find points and connections. Now she found her balance point, like a pendulum suspended within her body, something pointed her to the center that would keep her perfectly aligned. Slowly, tentatively at first, she removed her hands from her ankles. She tilted, a little uncertainly, then regained her balance point. Next she leaned forward, creating a slight space between her back and the Turtle Woman's. She was sitting up on her own. She reveled in the accomplishment of it.

A flicker of light caught her eye, then disappeared. She looked up at the sky. It was as dark as it had been. "Did you see that?" Marina whispered.

"Yes," the Turtle Woman whispered back. "It is a good start. Remember to look softly. Maybe you will call some more light to you."

Marina relaxed into her sitting. She found she could do this now that she had found a balance point. In fact, she found it was easier to remain balanced if she didn't think about her balance. She looked up at the sky and half-closed her eyes. She made her focus soft, the way she did when she was photographing and wanted a sense of the balance of light and dark areas in a composition.

The darkness, which had seemed so solid before, now seemed to be streaming past. She realized that she was looking at clouds moving very fast across the night sky. Once she was aware of this she began to see wispy places where the clouds were not quite as thick. She sent herself out to those places, those gauzy thin patches of cloud, and willed them open. She did not will them with strong intent. She did not try to tear them or rend open spaces with her imagination, but sent herself as a soft breath to disperse the clouds where the clouds themselves were of a mind to be dispersed.

When she saw her first flash of starlight through the cloud cover, even though it was brief, it made her giggle. The Turtle Woman behind her giggled as well. Marina was stunned by the realization that, however fleetingly, she was happy.

It took a long while to open her next clear patch of clouds, and, strange as it seemed to her, she did believe she was opening up these places to allow light through. It made no sense to her, but if she could quiet her skepticism, acknowledge her disbelief and let it pass over her, in just those moments she could influence the thickness of the clouds.

Soon the night sky was alive with light. Moonlight broke through clouds to strobe the water. Stars scattered across irregular fields of clear night sky looking like reflections of stars in pools and puddles on the ground. Then there was more light than darkness, more open night sky than clouds. She felt both calm and exhilarated. She felt connected to the light, as though she truly had called it and the light had come to her.

Morning came and it was gray blue, then blue, then purple, then pink, then blue again. There were no clouds in the sky and the colors were crisp and clearly defined.

The Turtle Woman had left her at some point in the night, but Marina found several shell bowls of water in the sand around her when light came. She drank two of the bowls but reserved the third. She could see all around her now, and, though she could probably drag herself across the beach, she could not see where the Turtle Mother found fresh water. She drew her legs back into the cross-legged position, adjusted her balance, and contented herself with sitting.

The sun was almost straight overhead and filtering tinted green light down through the palms when the Turtle Mother returned. Marina first saw her as a tiny speck at a great distance walking along the beach. As she got closer, Marina noticed that she was carrying the woven water bag and another woven pouch slung across her shoulders. She still wore the loose grass skirt and the necklace of coral and pearls. Her bare breasts swayed back and forth as she walked, and her hair was still a wild tangle decorated with the remnants of sea life.

She came to Marina first and refilled the now-empty shell bowls with water. She still said nothing, but she smiled at Marina and stroked her head as Marina drank greedily from the shells. She dropped the shoulder pouch she was carrying and walked to the edge of the excavation where she had buried Marina. She circled it once, inspecting it, then dropped to her hands and knees and began digging another small hole in the center of the trench. She did not dig for long, and it was not a big hole, but Marina began to think she might be buried again. She wondered if she was strong enough to stop the woman this time. But the Turtle Mother did not try to drag her to the hole. Instead, she gestured for Marina to lie down. She also gestured to indicate that she wanted Marina to lie on her stomach, but it was not a gesture Marina understood and, eventually, the Turtle Mother simply flipped her onto her stomach like a beached fish.

The Turtle Mother sat next to Marina. She placed a small woven mat under Marina's face to keep it out of the sand and dipped more water from the woven basket. Marina felt the water running through her hair. The Turtle Mother picked things from Marina's hair and combed it with strong fingers. Marina saw some of the things the Turtle Mother tossed aside as she groomed her hair and it made her laugh. She had thought the Turtle Mother and the younger Turtle Woman's hair a strange tangle. Now she realized hers was probably no different. She saw a crab's claw, strands of seaweed, bits of driftwood, and a bone form a pile in the sand next to her.

Next she felt the water run down her neck and over her shoulders. It was neither cool nor warm, but it felt soothing. After a few moments the Turtle Mother began picking at her back and tossing limp bits of seaweed into the hole she had dug. This process continued down her back. Water would soak the dried seaweed, then the Turtle Mother would remove it. Sometimes it came loose in big swatches like bandages. Other times she had to pick at it like peeling skin. The Turtle Mother continued removing the seaweed from her buttocks and legs, though she felt very little of this, then bathed her once again in water dipped from the bag.

The Turtle Mother stood up. She gestured for Marina to stay as she was and carried the now nearly empty water bag into the thick tangle of trees. Marina propped herself up on her elbows to watch where the woman went, but she disappeared within a few yards of the jungle.

Soon, however, she was back with a full pouch of water. She gestured for Marina to roll onto her back and, this time Marina understood. She flipped herself over with some success, though her legs lagged behind and needed the Turtle Mother to uncross and adjust them. Beginning with her face, the Turtle Mother bathed and removed the seaweed patches. Then she repeated the slow soaking and peeling process down Marina's torso and arms. It was odd and a little uncomfortable to have the woman bathing her breasts because she could feel every touch with a kind of raw intensity. She expected pain from her burns, but all she experienced was a disturbing sensitivity to touch. She felt little or nothing as the Turtle Woman cleaned the seaweed from her lower body and she was grateful for the reprieve from the intimacy of the process.

When she was done, the Turtle Mother poured water over her again, carefully bathing her. Marina felt a light breeze on her skin as the water evaporated. She lifted herself onto her elbows and looked down at her body. She had felt no pain during the process of removing the seaweed, but she remembered the burned and blistered condition of her skin. She was not certain what to expect, but what she saw surprised her.

Her skin had healed.

There were no blisters, no raw red burns, no open sores. Her skin had recovered its rich olive tone. There was no variation in her coloring, no sign she had ever worn a bathing suit in the sun. This was like a baby's skin, she thought. Indeed, it did seem less wrinkled, less traumatized than she recalled her skin being. She checked for scars. Yes there was a pale scar on her abdomen from the surgery after her bullet wound, but she could not find the scar from the shoulder wound. She had had a scar on her upper arm from a bad scrape she had gotten as a child, but now she could not find it, either. Nor could she find her childhood vaccination scar. She sat up and inspected her calf. The machete scar was only a faint pink track where it had been an angry puckered gash.

What is happening to me? she wondered. She collapsed back onto her elbows. "What is happening to me?" she asked the Turtle Mother. "How is this possible?" But she knew the woman would not or could not answer her. She lay back in the sand and her hand came up to touch her own face. Both the skin of her face and the skin on her fingertips tingled at the point of contact. She wondered what her face must look like. Was it still her face? she wondered.

Marina lightly touched the skin at her throat. Her hand trailed between the delicate skin of her breasts. She felt the bone of hidden ribs and then softness as her hand crossed her belly. She passed the point where the only sensation she registered was coming from her fingers, and it felt odd, almost as if she was touching someone else's body. Her fingers wandered through the dark curls between her legs and then to her thighs. She felt muscle beneath the clean new skin.

Marina remembered, with a start, that she was not alone. She brought her hand back to her face and opened her eyes. The Turtle Mother was not looking at her, but was rummaging in the grass shoulder pouch she had dropped in the sand. She drew from it some simple tools, a sponge, and several clamlike shells tied shut with fibers. Marina watched as the Turtle Mother sat at her feet. She lifted first one then the other of Marina's legs. She seemed to be weighing them. She turned them to one side then the other. Finally she seemed to select Marina's left leg. She bent it and pulled it across her lap at an angle that caused Marina to roll onto her right side. In this new position, Marina could not see what the woman was doing to her with the tools and shells. She felt a kind of rhythmic tapping but little else.

Whatever the Turtle Mother did took a long time, and Marina drifted off to sleep. When she woke the sun was setting again. The Turtle Mother was gone and there was a bandage around her ankle of what looked like more seaweed strips tied in place by grassy fibers.

She also felt pain.

It was not serious pain, but it was startling because it came from her ankle and traveled up her left leg. It was feeling. She was feeling something in her legs. She sat up and drew her legs to her. She massaged her calves and thighs and she could feel the pressure of her hands. It was still a numb and distant sensation, but it was more than she had felt before.

She also became aware of the sand she was sitting in. Feeling seemed to be extending below her waist now. She could feel the sand against her buttocks.

She leaned back on her elbows and tried to extend her left leg. At first there was no movement. She grunted and strained but could not get the leg to budge. Then she tried her right leg. Nothing moved.

She went back to her left leg and pushed. This time something did move. The leg straightened a bit, pushing sand ahead of it. "Yes!" she said aloud. She pushed again and again there was a little movement. She tried her right leg and it too moved a little. She alternated legs, straining first the left then the right, like riding a bicycle.

She worked her legs until the sun was completely below the horizon, and by the time the young Turtle Woman came to her she could move them with some degree of certainty and control.

"So, I think soon you will be ready to leave." The Turtle Woman squatted in the sand next to Marina.

"Leave?"

"Yes. You remember. You wanted to continue with your dying. Soon your legs will carry you back to the sea, or . . ." She paused.

"Or what?" Marina asked.

"Just another choice."

Marina was aware that the Turtle Woman's speech, her choice of words and syntax, was more confident and assured. She wondered if the Turtle Woman was learning from their conversations or if she was simply imagining her differently now.

"Look," Marina explained, "isn't dying kind of the end of choices? Shouldn't you just tell me what to do next, where I should go?"

The Turtle Woman smiled and shrugged her shoulders. "There are always choices. Even choosing not to choose. Sometimes you find stillness, a moment in which you may not need to choose anything, but always choices return. They are like the waves. Sometimes they are calm and hide beneath the water, but they will always come back."

"So what are my choices?"

"The sea." She gestured toward the water. "The beach, this way or that. The jungle."

"And what is it I am choosing between?"

"Paths. All to different places, different ends. Some paths continue your dying, some paths continue your living."

"How will I know which path?" Marina asked. She didn't really expect an answer from this enigmatic creature, but she did not know what else to say.

The Turtle Woman seemed to really consider the question for a long moment before answering. "Can you live in the water?"

"What?" Marina asked.

"Can you live in the sea?"

"No."

"Then you know where that path leads. The other paths . . . I don't know. But before you can make these choices you must learn to stand again. Can you stand?"

"I don't know. I haven't tried yet."

"Then try." The Turtle Woman stood up herself and moved around behind Marina. She put her hands underneath Marina's arms as Marina brought her knees to her chest and positioned her feet beneath her. With surprisingly little effort considering the difference in their sizes, the Turtle Woman lifted Marina into a standing position. Her legs buckled almost immediately and she would have fallen if the woman behind her had not supported her. She had taken standing for granted and realized that she needed to concentrate in order to stand. This time she fixed her attention on her legs and braced them. When the Turtle Woman released her she wobbled slightly but managed to stay upright.

"Okay," Marina said, "I think I can stand on my own." But almost as soon as the Turtle Woman moved away from her she teetered and fell. It was not a hard fall and the sand cushioned her, but it was frustrating.

"You must learn to stand again," the Turtle Woman said softly. "You are once more like a baby." She caressed the skin on Marina's arm as if to reinforce her point.

She picked Marina up into a standing position but this time she put one hand over Marina's pelvis and the other against her lower back. Gently she shifted Marina's center of gravity. "Bend your knees a little," she instructed.

Marina found her knees were locked and she had to use muscle to keep them from buckling as she bent them. Again the Turtle Woman pushed Marina's pelvis, shifting her center of gravity, and this time it seemed to relieve some of the muscle tension she felt in her thighs.

Next, keeping one hand against Marina's lower back, she pushed lightly on her chest until she was standing up straight. Marina felt as though all of her vertebrae were stacked carefully and precisely on top of each other.

"Now lift your chin. Look at the sea."

Marina realized she had been looking at her feet, focusing her conscious mind on the act of standing, as if not being able to see what her still-unfamiliar legs were doing beneath her would cause her to fall. She looked up. She looked at the sea. Then she looked higher into the night sky. She looked for the stars she had seen the first night. Then she began to tip backward. The Turtle Woman steadied her.

"Look only straight out to the horizon," the Turtle Woman reminded her.

After a while she could stand on her own and the Turtle Woman came around to face her. Almost instinctively she tried to step forward, lost her balance, and fell. The Turtle Woman laughed, but it was without malice, and Marina laughed, too.

"First stand, then walk," the Turtle Woman said as she lifted Marina back into a standing position.

"Just stand?"

"Stand and breathe," the Turtle Woman answered. "Here, like this." She held her arms out in front of her as though she were holding a large inflatable beach ball. She bent her knees, shifted her hips, and straightened her spine as she had shown Marina to do, though it seemed much more natural for her, as though this was the way she always stood. "Breathe in and fill your arms with air." When she inhaled her arms expanded ever so slightly. When she exhaled they sank back. Marina copied what she saw. Soon she was not thinking about standing but about breathing.

Together the two women breathed. They only spoke when Marina would lose her concentration or her will and fall. Then she would make fun of herself, or curse under her breath. Once she cried. It was hard work, this standing. Her thighs ached, her arms and shoulders ached. Sometimes she wanted to give up. Then she would slip in between some space of breath and time would seem to move on and leave her. She felt, at those moments, as though she could stand forever. She was rooted in the earth like a tree, not like one of the shallow-rooted palms behind her but oaklike and old.

Her eyes were closed and the Turtle Woman could have slipped away as she usually did when dawn approached, but this time she touched Marina lightly on the shoulder.

"I must leave now," she whispered. "You should rest. Soon you will learn to walk."

"Where is it you go?"

"Go?" She seemed confused by the question. "I am always here."

"But only at night. Where do you go during the day?"

"Ahh," she seemed to understand this better. "The day is for sleeping. I sleep. Sometimes I dream I am a little girl, sometimes an old mother. But always when I open my eyes, I am here. You must sleep now, too."

Marina was sleepy. She let the Turtle Woman lower her back to the sand and she lay on her side. Almost as soon as her head found the little grass mat the Turtle Mother had left behind, she fell deeply asleep.

★ ★ ★

Marina awoke in sunlight with pressure from her bladder. It was a familiar sensation, but she could not remember experiencing it since she had been here, wherever here was.

She rolled over onto her stomach and brought herself up onto her hands and knees. She carefully stood up. Her muscles seemed strong enough. They were sore from the exertion of the previous night's standing, but they supported her as she stood again. She tried a step forward. Her right leg did all that she asked of it, but her torso betrayed her. She teetered like a baby, waving her arms for balance, on the edge of falling. She drew her right leg back and this shifted her balance forward—too far forward. She pitched over onto the sand, landing on hands and knees. She would have tried standing again but the pressure that had woken her was growing unbearable.

She tried crawling.

She could crawl reasonably well. She made her way to the edge of the jungle where sand sprouted palms. She relieved herself, squatting with her back to one of the palm trees and found the experience oddly pleasurable. When she was finished she scooped sand over the little wet spot she had left and crawled toward the water. She wanted to wash. It was partially an instinct, a remembered habit, but part of it was also an exercise in control. She wanted to do for herself.

It was late afternoon and about a hundred yards to the sea. The crawling was slow but steady. It seemed to take longer than it should have, and it tired her more. She marked the change in the texture of sand, from loose and hot to cool and flat. The first lapping of waves that reached her was warmer than she had imagined it would be. She crawled out into the water a bit and then lay on her back, letting the gentle surging of the waves lift her for a moment before settling her back into the sand. She let the water wash her, wash over her, wash through her.

Later, as the water retreated, leaving her lying on the moist packed sand, she watched the sun track across the sky and descend toward the horizon. Changing light always inspired a kind of frenzy in her. She used to see it as a commodity in short supply. As a photographer she knew the best light, the most magical light, was at dawn and at dusk. It was also the least predictable light. It was fickle and fleeting and no amount of coaxing or pleading would alter its behavior. It was hard for her to simply enjoy a sunset.

She was not surprised to find the Turtle Mother sitting beside her. She was by now used to the silent coming of her guardian angel. The Turtle Mother sat cross-legged in the sand, her eyes closed, swaying gently to some internal music or prayer. Marina studied her again. It was the same face she saw when she looked at the woman who came after dark, only marked by time. They could have been mother and daughter. What had the young woman said to her? That sometimes she dreamed of being an old woman. Was this silent old woman the dream of a young woman? She had spoken to the young Turtle Woman, and though she was enigmatic and often frustrating, Marina thought of her as being more real. And yet hadn't the old woman, the Turtle Mother, cared for her physical body? Hadn't she healed her burns, quenched her thirst, helped bring feeling back into her limbs? Why did she assume the Turtle Mother was the dream? Perhaps the younger incarnation was the dream of this woman.

As the sun reached the water, somewhere far off in the distance, Marina sat up and touched the old Turtle Mother's hand. The old woman opened her eyes slowly. The green of them glowed in the orange light.

"Thank you." Marina wasn't sure why she felt compelled to say this now. She had a sense that with the sun setting, some chapter was closing. She might not have the chance to say this again.

The Turtle Mother cocked her head to the side as she always did when Marina spoke to her.

"Thank you," Marina said again and squeezed the woman's hand.

This time she smiled at Marina and nodded her head.

Marina could not tell if the Turtle Mother understood her or not, but something passed between them.

The Turtle Mother reached across Marina to knead and pinch her right shoulder and arm. Then she repeated this with the left arm and shoulder. She poked and squeezed Marina in several places, all the time nodding her head. Marina felt as though she were getting a physical exam from a doctor. The Turtle Mother worked her way down Marina's right thigh, calf, and ankle. She twisted Marina's foot in her hand and seemed satisfied. Then she repeated her examination on Marina's left leg.

When she came to the ankle she stopped. She lifted Marina's ankle into her lap. Marina had almost forgotten about the bandage around her left ankle, but now the Turtle Mother unwrapped it. She carefully removed the outer leaf, then drew back the seaweed strips. She inspected the place for a long moment. She poked it gingerly and looked to see if Marina reacted, but Marina felt no pain, only the pressure of the woman's finger.

Satisfied, the Turtle Mother patted the ankle and set the leg back down. Marina could see a tiny dark spot on her ankle, almost like a bad bruise, but before she could examine it more closely, the Turtle Mother had stood up. She walked around Marina then squatted beside her again. She took Marina's face between her hands and looked into her eyes. Marina had the feeling that the woman was looking for something.

After what seemed like a long moment the Turtle Mother released her face and stood up again. She turned and walked out into the ocean. The water was shallow for some distance and what had once seemed to Marina like walking on water now seemed perfectly understandable. The old woman walked until she seemed quite tiny and the water was only up to her waist. Here she stopped, turned a complete circle, as if getting her bearings, and lowered herself into the water. The turtle tattoo on her back was visible for a few seconds, then it, too, disappeared.

Marina watched the water's surface for several minutes, but nothing else broke or disturbed it. She looked down at the bruise on her ankle. She drew it close to her to see it better in the fading light. It was on the outside of her left ankle, just in the hollow behind her anklebone, but it wasn't a bruise. It was a tattoo. A tiny sea turtle etched with black ink lay poised to swim up her calf. Delicate swirls of red and yellow ink marked the interlocking plates that formed its shell on a field of blue and green. Marina was astounded. The work was intricate and precise and beautiful. It also seemed alive, the way the Turtle Mother and the younger Turtle Woman's backs were marked. Their tattoos were not just decoration, they seemed a part of them. Marina touched her own tattoo. It too seemed a part of her.

"So are you ready to walk now?"

The voice didn't really startle her. The sun was now set and she had been expecting the young woman.

"Yes," Marina said, looking up at her beautiful companion. "Do you think I am ready? I mean, I tried earlier, but it didn't seem to work."

The Turtle Woman extended her hands. "First stand." Marina took the woman's hands and let herself be pulled into a standing position. She bent her knees as she had been taught and found her center of gravity. She carefully aligned her vertebrae and balanced her head atop. She shifted her weight back and forth between each of her legs until she found the point at which an equal amount of weight was carried by both of them.

"Good!" the Turtle Woman laughed. Then she dropped to her knees beside Marina and put her hands on Marina's hips. "Now shift all of your weight to one leg." Marina tried to lean to the right, but the young woman held her hips in place. She said nothing but pushed Marina's hips to a position roughly centered over her right foot. This was different than leaning. It was steadier, less precarious.

"Now step out with your left leg, but don't put weight on it." Marina tried this. "Now shift your weight over your left foot like this." She gently but firmly directed Marina's hips to slide out over her left foot. "Feel the point where half of you stands here," she touched Marina's right leg, "and half of you stands here." She touched the left. Marina paused when she reached the halfway point, where weight was equally distributed between both of her legs, then she continued until all of her weight was carried by her left leg.

They repeated this process, slowly at first, with Marina's hips under the careful guidance of the young woman, then facing each other. The Turtle Woman held her hands for steadiness and took every step Marina took, only backward. They might have been sisters, or witches, or lovers dancing on a moonlit beach, but Marina's mind was absorbed by the subtle flow of her own weight shifting back and forth between her legs, and she could not fathom where the younger woman's thoughts took her.

Eventually Marina walked on her own. She learned to walk with the slow graceful shifting of weight, then she leaned into her walk and trusted her stride and momentum to balance her. She ran, skipped, spun, fell, rose up, and ran some more. She was giddy with her new power of movement.

Breathless, Marina sprawled in the sand and panted. The Turtle Woman came and sat beside her.

"So now what?" Marina asked after she had recovered her breath.

"Now, you are not a baby, a little one, anymore."

"But what does that mean? Where do I go?"

"When little turtles dig out of the sand they choose to go toward the sea. This is life for them and the urge to go there is very strong. It is not easy to take this path. Most . . . well, most will be caught up in the great current and return to be born again and again. Sometimes though, a little one will choose not to go to the sea. They will choose death. Maybe they are lost or frightened or sad, but still they choose death." She paused for a moment and looked at Marina with eyes so green she could even see their color in the moonlight. "What would you do if you found such a turtle on your beach?"

"I'd take it to the water's edge," Marina answered without thinking.

"Yes, you would, but if that turtle was determined to die, then what?"

"I don't know, what else could I do?" Marina was beginning to understand the direction of the story. "The turtle has a right to choose. I would just want to make sure that it was choosing and not simply lost."

"And this is all I can do. In the morning, when you can find your way by the sun, you will not be lost, but you will have to choose."

"But I did choose. I chose to die. It was hard enough to choose to do once. Are you saying I must choose to do it again?"

"The choosing may be hard, but the going will not be so hard. You are halfway there now. It will be harder to go back."

"That's fine because I don't want to go back. I just want to get on with it." Marina pushed sand around with her hands and looked out to sea.

The Turtle Woman said nothing.

"It's not that I don't appreciate what you've done for me. It's just that living was too hard for me. I had no . . . place." Marina could not recall ever having said this, ever having put it into words, but it felt true.

"Did you ever have a place?" the Turtle Woman asked.

Marina thought about this. Her family's home had once been her place, then her apartment during college had been her place. In a larger sense the United States had been her place, but now it wasn't. She made light of the fact that she lived like a gypsy, but even that was an unfair stereotype. She had photographed Hungarian Gypsies. It wasn't that they had no home; they took their homes with them. They made where they were their place. No, she couldn't claim to be a gypsy.

"Do you remember when you lost your sense of place?"

Marina thought back. There was a time when she did not feel out of place, when she felt that she belonged. When she was younger, out on her first assignments, she felt grounded and connected. She knew there was always a home she could return to. It gave her strength.

She could not say what had happened to that sense of place. It had not gone all at once. She could not think of any moment or crisis that had precipitated its disappearance. It had left her gradually. As she returned home less and less frequently after longer and longer absences, her sense of home abandoned her through inattention, as if home was an act of will manifested only by the power of her imagination.

"No," Marina paused, "I don't remember when I lost it. After Baghdad I suppose, or perhaps before that."

"What else happened, then?"

"I don't understand."

"I mean what else changed?"

"Well, I sold my apartment, broke off a relationship, stopped speaking to my family, but other than that . . ." She laughed, waited for the Turtle Woman to laugh, then sighed. "See what I mean. I'm clearly a failure at being alive."

"But how did the light change for you?"

"I don't know what you mean."

"The light," she fumbled for the right word, "these light drawings you do. Photography. When did they change?"

"After Baghdad? I don't know—I guess color was a big change for me."

"Color?"

"Yes, before Baghdad I photographed almost exclusively in black-and-white and after, I started working in color."

The Turtle Woman seemed to deliberate over this for a moment.

"And is color better or not better?"

"It's complicated," Marina replied, though the answer in her heart was not complicated. She had hated working in color. It had robbed her of her sense of the beauty of light. In black-and-white her images could be both powerful and moving as well as beautiful. In color her images could only be dramatic. She had to go to extremes to find the viscera that could replace the lost light.

Thinking about this reminded her of something the Turtle Woman had told her. "Light and darkness," she said it out loud. "You said that I was here because of light and darkness. You said that is what I have to heal. Does this have something to do with my photography?"

"Perhaps." Marina waited for the Turtle Woman to speak again, but she seemed to be having a difficult time finding words. "The photography is not what is wrong, but it is a mirror for you."

"I still don't think I understand."

"Are you a good photographer?"

Marina had no false modesty about her skills as a photographer. She was good at what she did. She was technically and stylistically a perfectionist.

"Yes," Marina answered. "I'm very good."

But as she said this she hesitated. She had gotten better at certain aspects of her job as a photographer—her timing, her instincts for action, her ability to deliver good images under pressure. But she also felt that in some ways she was not as good as she once thought she would be. Her vision, her ability to see beauty in her subjects, had left her. Like her sense of place, she could not say when she had lost her ability to see beauty, but one day it was just gone. It had been like waking up to discover that a lover had left her in the night.

"What makes a good photographer?" The Turtle Woman interrupted Marina's thoughts.

"A lot of things. A sense of composition, technical skill, reflexes." Marina rambled on for a few moments, almost stalling for time until the real answer, the true answer, bubbled up from her heart. "A good photographer sees everything in terms of shadows and light."

The Turtle Woman let Marina think about what she had said for a moment.

"Then a good photographer has balance?"

"Yes, I suppose so." The Turtle Woman was silent, but she did not need to speak. Marina understood. "I have lost my balance. That's what you're saying, isn't it?"

"Is it?"

"Of course. All I can see are the shadows. I can't find the light anymore."

"But isn't the light everywhere the shadows are not?"

"That's the problem. I just can't find those places anymore. I am so good at finding the shadows, but the shadows don't make me happy. Maybe I don't even believe in the light anymore. Maybe that's why I died."

"Then maybe that is why you are here. Maybe you have a little time to try to find the light you lost."

"I wouldn't know where to look."

"But will you look or will you continue dying?"

Marina thought about this. She didn't understand what was expected of her. Was she being offered a second chance? Did she even want a second chance?

"Are you saying that if I find this light, if I regain some kind of balance that I won't really be dead?"

"I think there must be several things for you to learn here, but you do not have much time to learn them. Follow the turtle's mark." She touched Marina's tattooed ankle. "You must find the things you need while the turtle's mark shines bright on you. As it fades, so the call of death will grow strong in your head again."

The early morning sky was brightening.

"So am I dead or not dead?" Marina didn't really expect an answer to this question. She had asked it before and gotten nowhere, but it was out of her mouth before she could stop herself.

The Turtle Woman just laughed at her and stood up. "Dead. Not dead." She held her hands facing up as she had before and pretended to be weighing two things in her palms. "Come with me, or go your own way."

The Turtle Woman began backing down the beach away from Marina and toward the water. Marina stood up, uncertain for a moment with her new sense of her body and its movement. She took a few tentative steps toward the Turtle Woman, then a few more. She felt water wash over her toes and soft sand beneath her feet. She took a few more steps out into the water. Waves lapped gently at her calves. She was choosing water. She was choosing to continue dying. A few more steps and the water was up to her knees. She looked into the Turtle Woman's eyes. They were deep and beautiful. She felt a stirring, a kind of attraction. She wanted to be seduced.

Marina glanced back over her shoulder and was startled to see that she had walked more than a few steps out into the water. The beach was a long way off. She remembered how the sandbar seemed to stretch out so far into the water. She looked back at the Turtle Woman. It was almost imperceptible, but in the growing light she seemed not as young as she had before. Still Marina felt an attraction. She felt like she was truly walking the fine edge of two moments. She glanced back at the beach again.

"Go back." Marina turned to the Turtle Woman again. She had heard her speak, but her lips were not moving. "Death is easy. It will be hard enough to resist my nightsong if you linger on this island too long, but for now you have the strength. Go, see what you will see." The words went right inside Marina's head. It was the same voice, the same singing cadence and odd pronunciation, but it was not carried on the air.

The Turtle Woman reached behind her neck and untied the necklace of black pearls and white coral. Then she lowered herself below the surface of the water. Marina realized that they had somehow moved further out into the ocean. The water was almost up to her waist. She felt the Turtle Woman tie the string of beads around her right ankle, then she stood up. The water matted her jet black hair and beaded on her skin.

"For balance," she said, this time speaking the words, or at least mouthing them as she sent them into Marina's mind. She took Marina's face between her hands and kissed her softly on the lips. It was a strange experience, both gentle and friendly yet erotic at the same time.

The Turtle Woman turned her back to Marina and walked a few more steps before bending at the waist and lowering herself into the water. For a few moments all Marina could see was the turtle shell tattoo, mesmerizing in its detail, floating in the clear blue water.

The growing light told Marina that somewhere on the other side of the island the sun must have cleared the horizon. She looked back at the island and for the first time she could see that a lush, green mountain, most likely an ancient volcano, dominated its center. She wondered what was on the other side. In that moment of wondering she found herself in water only up to her knees, as though she had walked halfway back to the beach without being aware of it.

She looked for the Turtle Woman's painted back floating in the water. She thought she could see it, floating in the distance, then it was gone. She stood there a moment longer, thinking about balance and light, living and dying, the salty kiss she still felt on her lips.

She had made a choice without wanting to, without intending to. She turned back and studied the place. Then, for the second time, she came out of the water and onto the beach. She still did not know where she was or what she was, or even if she was. The Turtle Woman had told Marina that she had come from death and Marina knew she had come from the sea. The sun set on this side of the island, so perhaps this side of the island was death. Maybe the other side of the island, around or over the mountain, was life.

She could not say that she had chosen life, but she had chosen to find what was on the other side of the island.

CHAPTER 3

An Intimate Koan

Some researchers believe that turtles navigate by the same senses that have grown dull in people who live cut off from nature. They need no extrasensory organs to explain the turtle's amazing feats of navigation. It is all smell, and taste, and sensitivity to subtle shifts in water temperature. The turtles of my dreams taste their way across salty South Pacific seas. They smell Fiji and Bali and Maui like delicacies cast off from the banquet table that is ancient Australia, Asia, or the Americas. They find their way through the infinite by attending to the intimate.

Marina walked all morning and into the afternoon. She moved through a world of only four colors: the dark verdant green of the jungle to her right, the azure blue overhead, the turquoise wash of waves to her left, and the winding path of ivory before her. The necklace of black pearl and white coral the Turtle Woman had tied twice around her ankle clicked softly, creating a rhythm from her steps. The anklet was all she wore, but her nakedness was dreamlike and somehow natural, without the embarrassment that sometimes accompanied even her dreams of being naked.

Several things occupied her mind and intrigued her as she walked. She noticed that if she set her sights on some distant feature along the beach and walked toward it, she would never reach it. Sometimes the beach curved out and she could not see around it to what lay ahead. Other times it curved inward and she could see a great distance away. But whatever she saw in the distance was never the same when she passed the place where it should have been. If she took her eyes off a landmark, looked down at the sand or out at the water, the landmark would shimmer and disappear. She tried to discipline herself to keep her eyes focused on one feature, walking toward it steadily without removing her eyes from it. But if she did this, if she maintained that level of intense concentration on a landmark, she found that she would never move any closer to it. It felt as if the island was creating itself solely to satisfy her experience of walking.

And then there was the walking itself. She felt the warm sand molding to her feet. Her toes dug into the damp sand when she drifted into the tidal range. Her narrow graceful feet imprinted the sand as she walked, but her own track disappeared behind her. She discovered this quite by accident. She passed a pink spiral shell and almost stepped on it but did not pick it up. After a moment she decided to go back for it. She followed her own footprints back and saw the distinctive pattern her feet had made in the sand become rough indentations evenly spaced by her stride, then shallow depressions, then smooth sand—all within twenty paces. No waves washed up far enough to have eroded the footprints. Time might have eroded the marks if she had been taking a step every hour or two, but she was walking far too briskly for that. She checked this several times, but it was always the same, and when she followed her footprints back to the furthest point out, the point at which she had turned around, her footprints had faded just as surely, just as quickly.

It seemed as if her entire existence on this island took place within a narrow window of time.

Most intriguing was her turtle tattoo.

It was moving.

She could not see it move, but it had begun in the hollow of her left ankle and now it was on the back of her calf. It was still small and brightly colored. Marina checked the tattoo carefully, though she had to twist her leg awkwardly to see it. It had not faded. If anything, it seemed brighter, more alive. It did not seem possible that the tattoo could have moved, so she questioned her memory of it being on her ankle to begin with.

In this landscape of death or dream or some mélange of both, Marina was afraid of what she might conjure up. And so, when she saw the women sitting on the beach ahead of her, she approached with great caution.

There were three women sitting, facing each other and forming a triangle. They all wore black robes with hoods. One of them rhythmically slapped a skin drum stretched over a round wooden frame. The other two shook rattles made of bone and tiny copper bells. They rocked back and forth in ecstatic trance to the beat they kept with their drum and rattles.

"Excuse me," Marina said softly, "I'm sorry to interrupt you but . . ."

The women continued singing, as if they did not or could not hear her.

"Excuse me," Marina tried again, louder this time. She waited, but no one acknowledged her. She stood up and moved toward one of the women. No one looked up as she passed between the women. She still could not see their faces. Their heads were down, hidden in the cowls of their robes, totally entranced by their own singing. Marina knelt beside one of the rattling women and reached a hand out to touch her.

"Don't do that!" Marina was startled. It was a man's voice and it seemed to come from outside the triad of women. At first she was confused and she looked carefully at the women.

"Don't touch them." The voice was softer now, less emphatic, gentle. "It hurts them if we touch them."

Marina stood up. A man squatted on the bent trunk of a twisted palm tree that grew almost horizontally out of the jungle growth. She could not say how long he had been there.

"I'm sorry if I scared you. But it's best if you don't touch them."

"Who are they?" Marina asked as she stood up and walked tentatively toward the man.

"I don't know really. My wraiths, I suppose, my punishment. I just know they are here for me."

"Do you talk to them?"

"They can't hear us. They're barely here now. In a few days they will be stronger." Marina looked back at the women, and indeed they seemed to shimmer and become transparent in places. She could see the ocean and the sand through them.

The man still made no move to approach Marina so she walked closer to him. He seemed young, perhaps in his twenties. He was lean and muscled and tanned from the sun. His hair was dark. He wore a short, brightly colored wrap around his waist and a smooth circular stone on a leather cord around his neck, but little else.

For a moment Marina tried to shrink her body down to something inconsequential. She was aware, suddenly, of her own nakedness. A moment before she had not been and now she was, like Eve taking a bite from the forbidden fruit. At the same time it seemed like there was little she could do about it, and her desire to talk to someone overcame her discomfort.

Throwing her shoulders back and standing proudly, she said, "Who are you?"

"My name's Rafael." He still made no attempt to move from his perch. He did not seem threatening. He seemed calm and still inside and once again Marina felt uncomfortable.

"Are you an angel?"

He laughed and it was a rich laugh with only a trace of irony. "No. Are you an angel?"

And now it was Marina's turn to laugh. "My name's Marina." She wanted to say her last name. She remembered the idea of last names, but she couldn't remember hers. "I'm . . . ," she paused, began to form the *d* for "dead" with her lips, but what came out was different, "dreaming."

"Or dead," Rafael said it matter-of-factly, and Marina realized without having to ask that whatever she was in this place, on this island, he was more like her than the Turtle Woman or the Turtle Mother had been. "I know," he added, "it was confusing for me at first, too. You just get used to thinking that this is your dream and then you find out someone else is dreaming it as well."

"Then you're dead, too?"

"If I'm not, I should be." He said this casually, but Marina caught an undertone of self-recrimination in his voice. "I think I died—was dying—but something happened along the way." He gestured around him. "This place."

"Did you . . . take your own life?"

"We all take our own lives," he said, half under his breath, clearly not comfortable with the topic, then continued, "in one way or another."

Before she could ask anything else he jumped from the tree and landed lightly in the sand. He was not short, but Marina was tall and they stood almost eye to eye. There was something unnerving about his physical presence. She felt the prickling of attraction and wished she had something to cover herself with.

"Come on." He gestured toward a path that led between the palms into the jungle. "You're probably hungry." She hadn't been hungry, but as he said it, she realized that she was very hungry. "And you're probably tired." She'd not been tired but now she was. Her legs ached from walking and she wanted nothing more than to sit and rest.

Rafael started up the path, but Marina hesitated, and he turned back to her.

"What about them?" Marina gestured toward the women, but when she turned to look for them they were gone.

"Soon enough for them, I think. We have a few days." He did not explain this but took hold of her hand and gently led her up the path.

★ ★ ★

The place to which Rafael took her was not far inland, but Marina was surprised at how quickly the jungle sloped upward. They soon picked up a stream and followed it to a clearing. The shelter where Rafael lived and worked was a wooden structure of four posts thatched over with palm leaves. There was a raised wooden floor covered with woven leaf mats and a simple patterned carpet. Three sides were open to the jungle and the fourth side faced a freshwater stream that splashed over stones.

There was a blackened fire pit ringed with stones in the sand between the hut and the stream, and a loosely woven hammock was strung between two trees. The hut had clusters of fruit and coconuts hanging from the rafters. There was an old wooden chest that looked like it might have contained a pirate's treasure and several other smaller boxes and bundles that looked like they, too, might have washed ashore. A slab of stone with a smooth bowl-like depression filled with water sat by the carpet and an assortment of little colored bottles were clustered around it.

But what dominated the space under the thatched roof was the loom. A weaver's loom stood against one of the open-sided walls. It took up most of the wall. In front of it was a cushion on the floor, several skeins of brightly colored yarn, and some wooden pieces that Marina thought were called shuttles.

The weaving on the loom was easily four feet wide and almost as tall, though still in progress at the base.

It was breathtaking. In the same way that the Turtle Woman's tattoo had seemed alive, more than a mere drawing, this weaving seemed to have a life of its own. Marina had the sense that the weaving told a story, though she could not decode it. It seemed to be bright and full of possibility at the top, then it darkened and the colors grew somber in the middle. Next there was a band of deep blue, then the colors began to return. This was where the weaving stopped, almost as if the weaver had forgotten how to weave with the colors he had once used and was struggling to remember.

"You wove this?" Marina asked, still in awe.

"Yes." Rafael answered simply but seemed unwilling to talk about it more.

"Is that what you did before? Weave?"

"No! No, I was never much good at making things, only at tearing them down. Would you like something to eat?" He seemed uncomfortable talking about the weaving and was clearly trying to change the subject, so Marina did not press it.

"Yes, thank you."

"Here," he said as he handed Marina a bundle he had pulled from one of the boxes. "You might be more comfortable in this." It was a short jacket that belted in the front. It was soft, like silk, but had more body to it, and she recognized that it was the same fabric that Rafael wore around his hips. She also recognized the weaving style from the loom.

She slipped it on. It felt good, but it also made her more aware of her skin at the places where the fabric touched her. She sat cross-legged on the floor, tugging the jacket down between her legs to cover herself. She could not explain it, but she felt more sexual wearing the jacket than when she had been wearing nothing. Somehow, by acknowledging her nakedness he had broken a spell between them. In an instant, the fact that she was a woman and he was a man had gone from being inconsequential to being charged and significant.

Rafael set about gathering fruit from his rafters. He sliced and seeded fruits that Marina almost recognized and laid them on a large, shallow wooden bowl in front of where she sat. The fruits were salmon and pale green, deep purple and creamy yellow in color. They glistened with their own sweet juice where they had been cut. They were sensual foods and Marina was famished. She could smell them and the smell alone was intoxicating.

"Be careful. You haven't eaten in a while and food here is . . . well . . . potent." Marina laughed at this description as she lifted a handful of what appeared to be melon to her mouth. She wondered if every exchange between them was going to take on this air of eroticism.

"I think I can handle it." She took a bite of the melon and it seemed to both melt and expand in her mouth. It was sweet like honey, but it was also tart and there was another flavor that she could not identify. It washed over her and made her dizzy. She wanted another bite and she took it. It was incredible. She had never tasted anything like this before. She took another bite, then another, barely chewing the soft fleshy fruit before swallowing.

"Slow down." Rafael reached a hand out to her and she backed away like a threatened animal guarding her food. She took another deep bite of the fruit. The juices ran down her chin and dripped onto her chest. She bit into it again and again.

Rafael started to move the bowl away from her, but she quickly grabbed a handful of soft, wet fruit. He took hold of her wrist, gently but firmly. "Please," he said, "be careful."

Marina jerked her hand away, amazed at the instincts that seemed to possess her. She slid back and tried to stand up. She felt dizzy and intoxicated. She dropped the rind of the fruit.

Everything spun, then went black.

When she woke she was lying on the carpet, her head supported by one of the cloth bundles she had seen. She saw Rafael by the fire ring building a small fire.

"What happened?" she croaked. When he saw that she was awake he came over and sat down beside her.

"The fruit," he began, "it's the first food you've taken here. It's like you're tasting for the first time. It happened to me, too."

"Is it safe to eat?" She realized this was a stupid question even before it was completely out of her mouth. What am I afraid of, she thought, being dead and being poisoned?

"You'll get used to it. What's important is to take it slowly for now. You'll find that all your senses are heightened. I don't know why or how, but I think it is part of the path."

"You know about the path?" Rafael nodded his head but didn't speak. "I mean, are you on the path? Are there others? Where is this place? How long have you been here?" The questions poured out of her.

Rafael smiled. He seemed gentle and compassionate, and he stroked her head softly. "I don't have very many answers. I don't know where this place is, but I understand it is somewhere . . . in-between. I have met others. Not many, but a few. They moved on. I'm . . . not ready to move on yet. There is something I need to learn—something I must complete." He gestured to the weaving on the loom. "Perhaps soon." She detected a note of sadness in his voice as if perhaps he did not relish completing his task.

Marina started to ask another question, but he stopped her. "First eat, then ask questions."

"Can I eat? Will it happen again?"

"The trick is to eat slowly. Experience each bite—each flavor—fully. Pay attention to what you're eating."

He held a small piece of the salmon colored fruit up to her lips, and she opened them. She let him slide the moist fruit into her mouth. Again the flavor of it seemed more intense then it should. This fruit tasted like figs but with a sweet center that reminded her of ripe pineapple. She held it in her mouth and let it dissolve. It was exquisite.

She let herself be fed this way, slowly, one piece at a time while he named the fruits. The names he gave them were Spanish, and she did not ask for translations. She liked the strange ringing sound of the names and imagined that she was memorizing the taste of each name. They played a game where she closed her eyes and identified the fruits he gave her by taste alone. He was right about her senses. If she took it slowly she was not overwhelmed by the flavors. It was decadent and sensual to be fed like this. They were like children, and they were like lovers. She could not recall a moment in her life more erotic than this and yet the closest they came to touching was when his fingers would brush her lip.

★ ★ ★

She woke in the morning, still lying on the little carpet. Rafael was at the loom. The shuttle flew from hand to hand, silently gliding down the channel of alternating yarns. With each toss he leaned to one side then to the other and she watched the muscles in his back flex beneath his skin.

She watched him do this for a long time, but eventually he seemed to be aware of her watching him. "So, how did you sleep?" he called, without turning around.

Marina took this opportunity to stretch and yawn. Her legs were stiff and a little sore, from walking the day before, but otherwise she felt good. "I slept fine, thank you."

Rafael turned to her and smiled. "There's some tea in the clay pot by the fire and a little broth in the bowl next to it. Just remember—"

"I know," she interrupted, "take it slow."

"Listen, I have to work for a while." He stopped and looked around at the jungle. He was fleetingly uneasy about something, as though he was being watched. Marina looked around, too. "I just have to get a certain amount done." Marina had the sense that he was trying to explain something to her without having to be explicit about it.

"It's okay. I'll make myself scarce." She wanted to ask questions. There was so much she wanted to know, but he had been kind to her and now he seemed distracted. "Can we talk later?"

"Sure. I'll come find you after I've finished my work. If you follow the path by the stream it'll take you down to a little cove."

"What's in the other direction?"

"Don't know. I've never looked."

Marina found this hard to believe and it aroused her curiosity. She would have to look, she thought to herself, but not now.

Rafael had turned back to his weaving, ending their conversation.

Marina got up and tried some of the tea and a little of the broth. The tea tasted of flowers, and the broth was mildly salty with a pungent flavor of fish. It didn't take much to satisfy her, so she rinsed the bowl out in the stream and turned it over on a stone to dry.

Marina picked her way down the stream path. She could hear birds high up in the canopy of the jungle and rustling noises in the undergrowth around her, but nothing seemed threatening. The path was alternately sand and stone with occasional roots that required her to climb. She reveled in the exercise, enjoying all the textures beneath her bare feet. She could not remember when she last immersed herself so fully in the experience of being barefoot.

It was like the fruit, she realized. Her sense of touch was as heightened as her sense of taste. When did she stop feeling, tasting, smelling the world around her? she wondered. She was not even aware that anything had changed before she had died. She had been dull, depressed, without joy. Nothing beyond the extraordinary moments of violence and fear she had photographed had been powerful enough to tear through the heavy veil with which she shrouded her senses. But she had not been aware of this, could not have been aware of this except by contrast. This place was that contrast. Everything felt new, almost unbearably sensual. It was ironic, she thought, that on this island of the dead she felt more alive than she had in many years.

She came to the cove Rafael had described. She heard the rush of water splashing from a height into a pool almost at the same time she rounded a thicket of palms and other twisted trees. It was a serene open space lit by a shaft of unfiltered golden light. The azure sky to which she had grown accustomed was painted over the cove like a cathedral fresco.

Marina circled the cove, picking her way over stones and wading through the stream below where it overflowed the main pool. On the other side she found a little strip of sand that allowed her to wade into the pool gradually. The water was warm, almost the temperature of a bath. She slipped out of the jacket and laid it over one of the stone slabs.

She eased into the water. A few strokes took her to the center of the pool. It was deep enough there that she had to tread water to stay afloat, but she luxuriated in even this slow-motion exercise. She swam back and forth across the pool several times, sometimes dipping her head beneath the water, sometimes floating or doing the backstroke.

When at last she tired of the swimming she picked her way over the rocks to where the waterfall splashed into the pool. She found a smooth stone just below the surface that she could sit on and lean her head back into the stream of water. This water was cooler than the sun-warmed pond and drummed against her head, massaging her scalp. It relaxed her deeply and made her tired.

She angled herself to allow different parts of her body to feel the massaging effect of the waterfall. She let it throb against her neck and pound her back. She moved her legs under the water to feel it surge against her sore thighs and calves. She was interested, but not surprised, to notice that the turtle tattoo had migrated to the top of her left thigh, just over her knee.

After a while she pulled herself up onto one of the warm stone slabs that jutted up from the pond like the shells of turtles. She lay back, her feet dangling in the water. She felt the sun linger over her bare skin. She closed her eyes.

When she opened them again she could not say how much time had passed. The sun was still visible through the opening in the canopy of trees, but it had drifted close to one of the edges. She lay still for a while, studying the sky, but gradually began to sense that she was not alone. She did not look right away. She forced herself to be open to her perceptions. She heard no sound that was out of place for the jungle. She saw no movement on the periphery of her vision. Everything was still, and yet she felt a presence around her.

She lifted herself onto her elbows. Ahead of her, on the other side of the pond, stood one of the women in black she had seen on the beach. She still wore the cowl of the robe pulled over her head, shrouding her face. She did not move. She stood looking in Marina's direction, but Marina could not say whether or not the woman saw her.

Off to her right another of the women stood at the edge of the pond. She too was hidden by the folds of her dark robe, but she seemed to be looking in the same direction as the first woman.

Marina sat up and turned to look behind her. She knew before seeing her that the third woman was standing behind her on the strip of sand near where Marina had left her jacket. This third woman had the cowl of her robe pulled back so that her face was exposed. She was young, perhaps seventeen or eighteen, with pale skin and short, dark hair. Her features were delicate and her expression sad. Her dark eyebrows seemed to weigh on her. She was looking down at the water, as though she could see through it.

Marina too looked down at the water. She watched as the woman knelt in the sand and dipped her hand into the water. Marina caught her breath as she saw the woman's hand disappear beneath the water without breaking the surface. Her hand seemed to pass through the water as if it was an illusion. There were no ripples on the water from her hand, no disturbance of the surface, and still she seemed to bring ghostly water up when she withdrew her hand. Hazy droplets fell away from her cupped hand but never struck the pond. The woman touched moist fingertips to her own forehead in a gesture that seemed almost Catholic.

Marina was intrigued by these women, but also discomfited by their presence. She slipped off her stone slab and swam slowly toward the shallow edge of the pond where she could walk out of the water. She stopped long enough to pull her jacket on and belt it around her waist. She carefully and quietly waded ashore onto the sand strip where the young woman still knelt. She remembered what Rafael had said about not touching the women, but she had no desire to touch them now. Even though she was fairly certain the women could not see her, she tried to slip past the young woman quickly.

Suddenly, the young woman swung an arm toward her, as if swatting at something barely perceived but annoying. It happened too quickly for Marina to avoid. All she could do was watch as the woman's hand and arm swept through her leg. Marina's intuition told her that this was what would happen when the insubstantial encountered the substantial, but she was unprepared for the feeling of cold that shot up her leg.

She was also unprepared for the wailing cry of the young woman. She cradled her arm as if she had been burned and cried out in misery. The other women cried out as well, like dogs joining in a howling ritual.

Marina stumbled backward a few feet into the brush. She panicked for a moment. All she wanted was to get away, but she felt hemmed in by the thick jungle growth and the boulders. She scrambled up several stones toward the top of the waterfall. It was not an easy climb, but it allowed her to avoid the low side of the pond and the other two women.

The cold in her leg subsided but her heart pounded and she was short of breath as she climbed. When she pulled herself over the edge of the top boulder, she still had the stream between her and the trail back to Rafael. She splashed into it without caution.

The wailing of the women had grown louder and higher in pitch. Marina glanced down at them. They now seemed to be looking up in her direction, though not specifically at her.

They can sense that I'm here, Marina realized, but they can't see me. I'm as much of a ghost to them as they're ghosts to me. Rafael had tried to tell her something like that. Her foot slipped on a slick stone beneath the surface of the stream and she fell. Her leg hurt, but she stood back up instantly. She took another step and slipped again. This time she went down in the stream on her hands and knees.

"Easy, Marina. Slow down." Rafael appeared before her as if from nowhere. He caught her in his arms and held her for a moment. She struggled against him briefly, then let him hold her.

"Who are they?" she asked breathlessly.

"It's okay, they won't harm you. They've come for me, not you."

"But why? What do they want? What are they?" Marina heard the hysteria in her voice and worked to suppress it. She usually didn't panic in stressful situations.

"I told you before, I don't really know what they are. I once knew who they were. I only know that they are here because of me. I brought them with me when I came here, and I won't be able to move on until I appease them. I'm sorry you have to see them at all. Sometimes I don't see them for weeks, but I'm getting close to finishing my weaving, and that always brings them closer."

"I don't understand. What did you do to deserve this? And what does your weaving have to do with this?"

"I'll explain as best I can, but not here, not now. Let's go back to the hut." Marina allowed herself to be led from the stream. She even allowed Rafael to hold her hand as they walked back up the trail. She found this strong, young man enigmatic but reassuring. There seemed little that was threatening about him and she could not imagine what he had done to warrant the unholy attention of the women in black.

Back at the hut, Rafael set about preparing a meal for them. He cut up more fruit and roasted some plantains in the coals of the fire. She offered to help, but he would not let her. So she found a comfortable spot and watched him work.

He was deliberate, absorbed in the task of preparing the food. He cut each piece of fruit open with reverence and arranged the slices on a wooden platter like an artist. She realized that he did everything with this attention. When he was weaving, he was totally weaving. When he prepared food or when he had fed her the night before, he had been totally in the moment. The only time Marina had lived in the moment was when she had been behind the lens of a camera, and even then, toward the end, she had been unable to maintain that level of attention for long.

When at last he brought the tray of sliced fruits and vegetables to her, she made no move to feed herself. She meant this as something of a joke, but he matter-of-factly lifted a piece of fruit to her mouth. She bit down on its juicy sweetness. It was delicious, nearly as powerful as it had been the night before, but the sensation did not overwhelm her this time. She allowed herself to taste it, to press it against the roof of her mouth and feel the juices run down her throat.

He lifted another piece to her lips but instead of biting it, she picked up a piece and offered it to him. He took it and chewed it slowly, indulging in it. Then she took the piece he offered.

In this way they fed each other in a silence punctuated only by wet chewing noises and sighs of pleasure and surprise. After they had finished, Rafael took the wooden platter down to the stream and rinsed it off. Marina's own fingers were covered in sticky sweet nectar, so she got up to rinse them off as well. Both her legs ached as she stood up but her right leg, the one she had fallen on in the stream, hurt sharply. Rafael noticed her limping to the stream.

"You should let me work on that," he said as he splashed water on his face.

"So you're a doctor as well as a weaver?"

"I just may be able to help, that's all."

"How?"

"Massage. I have some oils that might help."

"Oils?"

"When I first came here . . . ," he seemed to think a moment, as if trying to recall how long ago that had been, "a woman lived here. She taught me how to weave. She also showed me how to use these oils. She said they contain highly distilled essences of plants and other things."

"Where did she go?"

"I don't know. Up the trail I think." He gestured up the trail in the direction he had told her that he had never looked. "She was ready to move on. I couldn't. I haven't seen her since."

"What do you mean about being ready to move on? You've said that several times and I don't understand. Can't you leave whenever you want?"

"Not really, though I don't understand why not. I just know I'm not ready."

"And where will you go when you are ready?" What Marina didn't say, what she really wanted to know, was whether Rafael would choose living or dying. She wanted to know if he had to make the same choice the Turtle Woman had offered her.

Rafael didn't answer her right away. Instead he opened the trunk near his loom and took out a little wooden box. He set this on the floor near where Marina sat on the little carpet and knelt down beside her. He pushed her gently and she lay back. He put a pillow beneath her head then moved around to sit at her feet.

"How is it that you don't know that living is better than dying?"

"You're very young," she snapped. "You haven't seen what I've seen." He was silent for a moment and she regretted her tone. "I'm sorry. I chose death because I lost faith in the living . . . lost faith in myself actually." Rafael smiled at her. He was not judging or evaluating her. His question had not been intended as a reproach.

He opened the little box, drew a cobalt blue bottle out and uncorked it. Instantly there was a new scent in the air. It was vaguely sweet, like vanilla, but also spicy. He lifted her right foot and shifted himself so that her ankle rested on his thigh. "May I?" he asked, touching the dangling string of coral and pearls.

"Yes," Marina whispered. She knew that he was asking if he could remove the ankle bracelet, but she felt as if she was saying yes to much more.

Rafael drizzled a little of the scented oil from the blue bottle into his hand. He set the bottle down and rubbed his hands together spreading the oil from palm to palm in a circular motion. Gently, with light but firm strokes, he began to massage her foot.

"I know that if I am given the choice again, I will choose living."

He said this quietly, looking at the weaving. Marina too looked at the weaving. It was beautiful and marvelously asymmetrical. At the top it was a tangle of colored threads almost without visible pattern. The chaos of the weaving seemed to increase during the first third of its length. Then an abrupt band of blue slashed across the woven space. This blue reminded Marina of the sea and the sky together. It seemed to absorb the chaotic pattern and color that had come before.

"It's the story of who I am." Rafael had noticed how Marina was studying the weaving. "When I can fully tell the story, perhaps I can move on."

"But it looks like it's almost finished." The weaving had nearly filled the capacity of the loom. All of the strands and colors that had seemed so tangled above grew out of the blue band in delicate and ordered patterns. The only tension in the pattern that remained was created by three irregular islands of black that descended from the band of solid blue. They seemed to be descending toward the open space of the yet-to-be-woven.

"Are those the women in black?" This was just an intuition on Marina's part, but Rafael nodded.

"I'm not sure if they are to be part of the weaving, but they are part of my story and I can't seem to keep them away."

"But who are they? Why do they haunt you?"

"I have much to atone for."

"You're so young. You're a wonderful artist. Look at what you've made. What could you have to atone for?"

"I was not always so good at weaving things together. When I was a boy, all I could do was tear things down. This is the way of boys without fathers. My mother was a good woman, but I never knew my father." Rafael paused, shifting his position to massage further up Marina's calf. "I don't mean that as an excuse. I am what I chose to be, but it is true that without a father or a strong man in a boy's life, he cannot learn how to build things, how to care for others, how to be responsible.

"Anyway, I was a wild boy, little king of the Barrio. All I was good at was destroying things. I tagged and spray-painted, set fire to things, broke windows, tore down everything good someone tried to build in our neighborhood. When I got bored with destroying things, I moved onto people. I was out of control. I found reasons to fight, first with my hands, then with chains and clubs, then knives. Eventually, I got a gun and I was like a little god. Everyone was afraid of me."

Marina found Rafael's story hard to believe. His hands and fingers were smoothly kneading the muscles of her calf, working around her sore knee and gliding up onto her thigh. He was beautiful and serene in the flickering light of the candles. His long black hair hung about his shoulders framing his face, and though his eyes seemed sad and distant as he spoke, they were also gentle.

"It's true," he said. "You can see it in the weaving. Look." He gestured up at where the tangle of colored threads seemed chaotic and patternless. She could see no pictures or words in the weaving, but it was a story nonetheless, and she knew it was a true story.

"I hurt people any way I could. Boys who disrespected me, I hurt with my own hands. Sometimes I cut them, or beat them. Girls I hurt in other ways, in the heart maybe, or by giving them babies. The only ones I would not hurt were my mama and my little sister, though I know now how much my behavior must have hurt them both. Then I just thought that I was being strong for them. I didn't know what being strong meant."

Marina found it hard to connect this gentle, young man with the person he described. He was strong. She did not doubt that he could hurt people if he chose to. And he was handsome. It was easy to imagine girls being attracted to his dark, sad eyes. But his touch was so tender as he massaged her thigh. His fingers drifted underneath the edge of her jacket making her keenly aware of her nakedness, her vulnerability, but there was nothing overtly sexual in the movement of his hands. Sensual, she thought. It felt so good to be touched like this. But even that was imprecise. What she really meant was that it felt so much to be touched like this. She could not remember when being touched had been so intense for her. She was almost disappointed when Rafael stopped and shifted himself again to begin massaging her left foot.

"I'm not sure I believe that you are the same young man you describe. Surely you must have had some good qualities."

"If I did, I don't know what they were. Perhaps it was my love for my mother and sister, though even that was twisted."

Marina closed her eyes as he continued with his story. The spice and vanilla scent of the oil filled her nose. Her right leg was deeply relaxed and did not ache at all.

"When I got older I joined a gang. Then I was the gang. It was my gang—Blood Walkers, we called ourselves. We ran the Barrio. You name it, we did it.

"I had a woman, a girl really, she was only sixteen. She was beautiful. Her name was Carita and I loved her as much as I could love anybody. Not so much as my mama or Theresa, my sister, but a lot for me. She was a kind of beautiful treasure, a trophy. I couldn't see women as being more than possessions, you know, property. Still, I thought I was on top of the world. I was invincible. I was eighteen, maybe nineteen, and I had managed to avoid being arrested for anything, or even being seriously injured in any way. I told people that I had the luck of the spirits. Some people believed me. I would see them make the sign of the cross when I passed. I was such a fool."

"Wait!" Marina interrupted. "Where was this? I mean where did you grow up?"

Rafael paused. "I . . . can't recall a name for it." He seemed genuinely perplexed.

"Was it in the United States?"

"Yeah, I think . . . It's weird, the names of cities come to my mind, but Los Angeles, or San Antonio, or Miami . . . they're just names. I can't say that I came from one and not another."

"It's okay. It's not important. Go on with your story."

"Well, I thought I really was untouchable. I did drive-bys. I shot people. I killed people. Terrible things."

Again Marina was struck by how incongruous these words were, coming from this man. She had only known him a short period of time, but she had always had good instincts about people. It was one of the things that had kept her alive in dangerous situations over the years—the ability to know whom to trust.

"I was way out there, totally reckless. I made enemies, measured myself by my enemies, and these enemies eventually came for me. They caught me at my mother's house. I wasn't staying there regularly. It was too dangerous. But Carita stayed there. She was pregnant by then and her father had kicked her out, so she was staying with my mother and sister. I visited her there."

"And is that where you . . ." Marina did not know how to finish the sentence but Rafael just laughed softly and finished it for her.

"Died? No, that would have been a blessing." His voice betrayed a hint of bitterness. "But then again, maybe yes, maybe I did die, then.

"Here I was, this macho man hiding behind women, behind my mama and my sister and Carita. And I got away. I was so proud of myself. I slipped away, cheated death. I was the master of my world."

Rafael paused for a long time. Marina looked up at him, studied his face in the flickering candlelight. His eyes were closed and his hands were still firm and gentle as he massaged her leg.

"It wasn't until later that night that I heard. They had killed mama and Theresa and Carita. I had killed them really—began killing them the moment I was born. I guess I died then, though it took a few more hours for me to find death. I told myself I wanted revenge, but I just wanted the pain to go away. I went out alone. I think I had a gun, but in the end I never even took it out of my pocket. I walked the streets in the early hours of the morning. I cursed God and shouted taunts. I imagined enemies in every dark place, but just found my own shadow. I crossed borders. It took them a long time to kill me. I think they thought I was some kind of holy fool. We confused religion and super-stition a lot in the Barrio. We were children. We made up our own myths, our own rites of passage.

"In the end, though, they could not let me live. They killed me. I don't remember how really, only that I was glad of it, relieved some-how. Then I woke up here."

"And when was that?" Marina asked. "How long have you been here?"

"I don't know really. I've lost track of time." He gestured at the weaving. "At least that long, though I couldn't really tell you how long I've been working on it."

He was silent after that. He had finished massaging Marina's legs and though she wished he would offer to continue, she said nothing, letting him sit with his memories.

After a while she touched his hand. "I believe you must have changed from the person who did those things," she said solemnly.

"Changed? Yes, I suppose that is the best we can hope for, that we change over time. But we can never escape from what we've done."

"How do you bear the past?" Marina asked. "I mean, I have terrible memories. I feel weighed down with guilt. It's why I chose to die. I still can't imagine going back, being alive again. I would just be returning to that pain."

"Well, I suppose I just take every moment as a kind of gift. I try to see it for what it is."

"You mean you don't think about the past?"

"No. I think about the past. I think about what I've done, but I do it fully. When I think about the past I give it all my attention. I try to avoid lingering half in the past and half in the present or future. I think you should be in one place, in one time, as completely as you can."

Marina considered this. "And where are you right now?"

Rafael smiled at her, understanding the subtle tug back into the present. He cupped his hands together and brought them prayerlike up to his face. He opened them slightly, closed his eyes, and inhaled deeply.

"Vanilla, cinnamon, cloves," he intoned the words like a mantra, like an incantation, "coconut, the oils from your skin, the oils from mine, heat, passion, a little regret, uncertainty, a bit of lust."

He read the scents and the moment accurately and it made Marina blush. She did not expect the desire that had been building in her to go unnoticed, but she also did not expect to be rendered so transparent.

She sat up slowly until her face was inches from his. She wanted him to kiss her, but instead found her mouth drawn to his. She kissed him and he kissed her back. It was a soft kiss, passionate, but tentative. When she pressed a second kiss, he backed away.

"Not yet," he whispered.

"Why not?" Marina asked. She was breathless and agitated.

"You're not ready."

"No, I am," she pleaded, but he touched her thigh and drew her attention to her leg. They both looked at the little turtle tattoo. It had moved to the top side of her thigh, halfway between her knee and her hip.

"Soon, perhaps, but not now. You are not strong enough yet. You are still learning to walk. Besides, I have work to finish in the morning."

Marina slumped back onto her elbows. She knew he desired her as much as she desired him, but he seemed determined. "How do you know that's what the turtle means?"

"It's what I learned when I first came here. Now try to sleep." Rafael stood up in one easy, fluid movement. He moved like a cat, extinguishing the candles he'd lit earlier. He left one next to Marina and placed his palm against her cheek. She closed her eyes and inhaled. She tried to smell the scents he'd described. The vanilla and cinnamon came easy. She could even find the coconut. The other smells, hers and his, she could only find by imagining them.

When she opened her eyes again, he was gone. She could see him outside of the hut, swaying in the hammock, bathed in moonlight. She contemplated going to him, rising up, slipping from her jacket, and offering herself. She wanted to make love to him, to have him make love to her. She was still attracted to him despite everything he had told her about his past. She was not usually enamored of dark and dangerous men, so her attraction was not simply a habit. She still couldn't join in her imagination the angry and violent young man he had described with the Rafael she sensed now. It was a strange feeling, this desire.

She had once had relationships, long periods of time spent with only one man. Sex was good—passionate and later comfortable. She enjoyed the physicality of these relationships, but her life, her career, were hard on others. Long separations took a toll on her relationships, and her focus on her work drained much of the energy she might have had to commit to a man.

Eventually love affairs replaced relationships in her life. Short intense bursts of passion shared with colleagues thrown together in difficult circumstances made up the life of her heart. She was usually aware that she was only escaping into someone else in these affairs. But she knew that the men she slept with were escaping into her as well.

When love affairs became simply lovers, she had all but lost interest in sex anyway. It wasn't that she didn't want and sometimes crave it, but it was never satisfying. It was an itch that no amount of scratching seemed to relieve. She only felt distant and empty afterward, a bit player in her own erotic drama.

So she had given up that part of herself, lived celibate, and convinced herself that she was happy—or at least as happy as she was capable of being. And now, here she was in some kind of afterlife, craving the feeling of a man. Well, why not, she thought, if I can be hungry here, if I can hurt, if I can taste and smell and feel, then why can't I make love?

Marina contented herself with remembering the feeling of Rafael's hands on her legs. Both her legs felt deliciously relaxed. She realized she was tired. She blew out the candle, and, while she did not fall asleep immediately, neither did she stay awake long.

★ ★ ★

She woke early in the morning, but Rafael was already at work on the loom. Marina ate some fruit and sipped a cup of tea in silence. She rinsed off in the stream and studied the turtle tattoo. It had moved a little, higher and to the inside. It now seemed alive to her, as if it was following some instinctual course across the landscape of her body. She thought about walking back down to the pond, but did not want to run into the women again so she sat as quietly as she could. It did not last long.

"Will you finish today?" Marina finally asked when she could keep quiet no longer.

"Maybe, I'm not sure. Soon, though. I must finish soon." Rafael did not turn to look at her but continued weaving as he spoke.

"Why?"

"I must have the story woven. It's . . . it's my full confession, and I must tell it all before they come."

"Before who comes?" As she asked the question, she already knew the answer. "The women? Your wraiths?"

"Yes. They are the guardians. I cannot move on until I have satisfied them."

Marina thought about this. "Do I have guardians?"

"I don't know." He was answering in short, clipped sentences. Marina recognized the pattern. Whenever she was working, absorbed in a task, and others asked her questions, she tended to answer the same way. She knew she was distracting him, but she couldn't help from continuing.

"What was it like when you first woke up here?"

Rafael's shoulders slumped in recognition that he was not going to be left to work in silence and that he could not do two things simultaneously. Resigned, he turned to face her. All at once Marina felt guilty about pulling him away from his weaving. She knew she was being selfish, but she wanted to indulge herself. The look on Rafael's face, however, was not one of disappointment. Somehow in the turning toward her he had resolved to answer her questions with the same presence and energy he had put into his weaving.

"I was angry. I was very weak, almost an invalid, but still I tried to hurt myself. It felt, at first, too much like being alive. I wanted to be punished, I wanted pain, and here I felt almost nothing. Later I gained some strength, began to get feeling back. Then it occurred to me that I was alone and that terrified me worse than the prospect of any physical pain.

"I had always been afraid of being left alone. My father had left us when I was an infant. Sometimes my mother would leave us alone when she went to work and couldn't find anyone to stay with me and my half-sister. So I became good at making myself the center of things. I was never alone. I had my gang or my women, or my family . . . always someone. Then I was here and alone.

"I survived. There was fresh water and fruit, and I learned to catch fish. I lived on the beach then. I explored a little, but there seemed to be some limit to how far I could go. I could walk along the beach all day and when I turned around it was always only a short walk back to where I had started. I wasn't ready to move on, though I didn't understand any of that then."

"So no one came to you, you didn't see . . . ," Marina struggled with what to say—what to call the creature who had helped her get her strength back and learn to walk again, "a Turtle Woman?"

Rafael shook his head. "No . . . no one, but Mai-Ling saw her. She had the same tattoo as you, though I'm not sure what that means."

"Who was Mai-Ling?"

"The woman who was here before me. The woman who taught me . . . ," Rafael paused, smoothed the cloth wrap he wore and picked at its edge, "how to weave." Marina sensed there was more to this story, but she was also aware of Rafael's discomfort.

"So . . . this was her loom?" Marina probed gently.

"No. She found it here, found all of this just as I did. She wasn't even a weaver. She carved beautiful wooden bowls." Marina had noticed the wooden bowls they ate and drank from. They were smooth and polished with dark oils. They seemed to fit her hands perfectly. She glanced at one of the bowls that held a candle.

"Yes," Rafael added, "the bowls are hers. She left them behind."

"But you said she taught you to weave. How could she do that if she wasn't a weaver?"

"I'm not sure either of us ever understood that. She seemed to be able to teach me to weave, to find patterns, to bind strands into a whole fabric, even though she herself did not weave. She said it was what she had to teach me, and I'm sure it was something I had to learn."

"Then was she like the Turtle Woman I met? Was she a teacher or a spirit?"

"No . . . she was as real as you or me." He laughed as he said this and Marina laughed, too. "She could recall her own death and her coming to the island. She spoke of an old woman with a turtle tattoo on her back. She even had a turtle tattoo, though hers looked different and moved more slowly."

Marina touched the tattoo on her own thigh. "You said she had something to teach you. How do you know that?"

"You always meet people who have things to teach you, if you're open to it. That's just the way the world really works. At least that's how we came to understand it."

"You and Mai-Ling?"

"Yes."

"Then what did you have to teach her?"

This question seemed to trouble Rafael. He took a long time to answer and Marina was about to ask another question, to change the subject, when he finally spoke.

"At first I couldn't imagine that there was anything I could teach her. She seemed so calm, so centered, so at peace with herself—everything I wasn't." Marina found it odd that if she had to describe what fascinated her most about Rafael, it would be these same qualities. She considered telling him this, but he continued. "But what she didn't understand was how beautiful she was." Marina was silent. She waited for Rafael to go on.

"Mai-Ling was an artist. I had never known anyone like that before. She was maybe thirty when she smoked enough opium to make it pretty painless to slit her wrists." Marina remembered the painless fog of her own opium days. She winced at the image that came to her and caught herself on the edge of an opinion about a woman she didn't know. Who was she to pass judgment on someone else's decision to end their life?

"She said that she'd wrestled with depression most of her life and in the end it grew to be too much for her. When she was younger a man she'd been in love with burned her face with a hot iron. She had a terrible scar, up here." Rafael made a gesture about two inches long up near his right eye. "But it didn't matter, you know, she was still really beautiful. She kind of glowed from the inside, but she never saw that when she looked in a mirror. She taught me how to make something, how to find a center like she had, and I showed her how attractive she was. I suppose it was a fair trade."

Suddenly Marina felt guilty. For all her questions and her probing, she had shared little of herself. All she'd done was take since she'd arrived—as if Rafael, and in fact everything she encountered on the island, was there for her benefit.

Slowly, carefully, she offered her story, and he accepted it as though it were a gift. She talked about waking up on the island and the turtle women, then realized she had to go further back. She went back to the dream she had had as she drowned, which took her back to the cruise and beyond. She told him of her career, of her loss of feeling, her emptiness. He asked questions and sometimes she digressed. He prepared food for them, they ate, the day slipped away and still she told her story. In the end, when she could think of nothing more to say, she stopped.

She was aroused by the conversation, by sharing so much, excited by a man who would listen so patiently, so completely. For Marina, this was as much foreplay as any kiss or caress could be.

"So what do you have to teach me?" she asked coyly.

"What do you need to learn?"

"The Turtle Woman said that I needed balance. She said that I needed light to balance my darkness. Do you have any light?" She smiled as she said this, aware that she was leaning close to him, conscious of the flirtation.

"I don't know what I have to give you. I didn't know what I had to offer Mai-Ling at the time."

"Perhaps you are supposed to teach me to weave." She wrapped her hand over his hand, twining her fingers in between his fingers. She said this half in jest, but he answered it as though she meant it seriously.

"I don't think so. You're already an artist. You have that ability to find beauty in the world, to see the patterns. You may not honor or value your gift, but you know you have it. No . . . I have nothing to teach you there."

Again they were both silent. An idea came to Marina. "Then teach me to be centered like you. You are so into everything you do. I used to have that experience when I photographed, but I can't even remember what it feels like anymore."

Rafael laughed and his smile was warm. Marina still held his hand. "Yes . . . maybe. It isn't anything I ever thought about teaching, but Mai-Ling taught me."

"How did she teach you?" Rafael appeared to be thinking about this, but when he didn't answer, Marina continued. "Were you lovers?" Marina instantly regretted the question, regretted her own erotic impatience.

"Yes, we were lovers, but we weren't until we were."

"What?"

"She taught me to experience the moment as fully as I could, not to live in the past and not to live in anticipation of the future, no matter how attractive that future seemed."

"But I like the anticipation, the sexual tension. It heightens the experience."

"Only if there is an experience to heighten. If the anticipation is unrealized it turns to regret, embarrassment, longing."

"So . . ." Marina touched Rafael's long black hair. She was only half capable of understanding anything he was saying. She had moved beyond words and was growing impatient. "Will there be an experience?"

What am I doing? she thought. And then, I don't care. I want this. I need this.

"Only if you learn to feel one thing at a time."

"And how will I learn that?"

He didn't answer immediately. He seemed to think about this for a while, then answered suddenly. "Take your jacket off and lie on your stomach."

As much as she had flirted, as much as she had wanted this, Marina was suddenly reticent. He had seen her naked on the beach the first day, but not since then. What if she wasn't as attractive or as young as Mai-Ling? She was grateful when Rafael got up to light candles. She quickly slipped from the jacket and lay face down on the little carpet while his back was to her.

Rafael sat next to her with his box of oils and selected several. She watched him mix small amounts from several bottles in his hands. She

could smell something that reminded her of India—jasmine and perhaps sandalwood with a hint of something heavier, muskier. She closed
her eyes.

"Now . . . don't think about the past or the future. Don't anticipate.
Just feel what you feel."

He placed his palms against the small of her back and she felt an
electrical tingling. He didn't move his hands, however, and the tingling
soon subsided. It seemed as though he could tell when she had relaxed,
because he began slow circling motions expanding out from the small
of her back. He did not press hard but let the oil lubricate her skin. His
hands stroked higher and lower at the same time—shoulder blades and
buttocks, shoulders and the back of her thighs, her neck and her calves.
She didn't believe his reach could extend much further.

Then he was at her feet, working oil-slick fingers between her toes,
around her ankles, up her calves. As he massaged her thighs, she subtly
shifted her legs apart just a little, hoping he would touch her there. But,
while he came close and she felt his fingers brush the curls of hair
between her legs, he did not touch her the way she'd hoped, and she
brought her attention back to the places he was touching.

He rubbed more of the scented oil into her buttocks and hips, her
back and shoulders, her arms and hands. He massaged her neck and
scalp, pressing places that made her almost melt. When he whispered
for her to roll onto her back, she almost couldn't. She hadn't the
strength. But he helped gently turn her, and she lay exposed and weak
in the candlelight.

Her eyes were closed, so it was a surprise when she felt him back at
her feet. Again he worked his way up her legs, but this time he moved
them. Lifting them up into the air, bending them carefully, pulling and
deeply stretching the muscles. She could not have been more exposed,
more open. She felt like a doll—like a child. She felt his hands again
near the place she wanted to be caressed and tried not to want it.

He pooled more of the scented oils in the hollow of her belly and
spread this across her abdomen. He made light wrapping strokes around
her ribcage, between her breasts, up to her collarbone. Then he cupped
her breasts in his palms and held them. Despite her relaxed state, Marina
felt her heart race. She felt her nipples stiffening against his palms and
was embarrassed, but he did not take his hands away. He kept them over
her until her heart began to calm and her breathing evened out. Then
he began with slow soft strokes to work the oil into her breasts.

Next he moved on to massage her throat and then her face. He made tiny circles with his fingertips across her forehead and temples, down her cheeks and along her jawline.

It took a while for Marina to realize that he was no longer touching her. She slowly opened her eyes. He was sitting next to her, watching her.

"Thank you," she whispered. She didn't know what else to say. Seldom had anything felt that good, that relaxing. She tried to lift a hand up to his face. She wanted to pull his mouth down to hers, but she was too relaxed and her hand fell over his thigh.

"I want you," she murmured.

He smiled and bent to kiss her. "Remember, one thing at a time." The kiss was sweet and his lips were moist, but Marina could barely focus on the experience. She knew she wanted him, but she also knew she could not have him, not like this anyway.

"Stay with me . . . please." She patted the carpet next to her. "Sleep next to me." It was all she could do to ask. She hadn't the strength to stay awake for the answer.

★ ★ ★

Sometime in the early morning, at the first edge of light, Marina woke from a dream. In the dream she had been making love to a beautiful Asian girl with a scar over her right eye. They were kissing and rubbing languidly against each other in the shallow water of a pond. It was night. There were bright stars in the sky and candles floated in hand-carved wooden bowls. She woke aroused, and with the peculiar sensation that she had actually intruded on Rafael's dream.

He was there next to her in the pale blue-black light. He lay on his back, breathing heavily, deeply. Marina was on her side with one leg wrapped over his, her hand on his chest, his cool, smooth, stone circle talisman tangled around her fingers. She slowly ran her hand up to his throat, feeling the smooth muscled flesh as she went. She touched him very lightly, looking more for the pattern of him than the substance. She caressed his cheek and teased his lower lip with her fingertip. He swallowed, but did not stir.

Marina let her hand glide back down his chest, circling his nipples without touching them. She wondered if they were as sensitive as hers. Some men's were and she always found it fascinating. That sensitivity to touch or tongue or the brush of soft hair was like a key to a secret place—best used judiciously.

Her hand drifted down. His belly was relaxed, but she felt muscle and definition at his sides. She took a deep breath and placed her hand at the juncture of his legs. He was hard. She could feel him even through the woven cloth kilt he wore.

She looked up to see if she had woken him, but he seemed still lost in sleep. She wondered what he was dreaming of, who he was dreaming of.

Emboldened, Marina propped herself up on her elbow and studied him. She rubbed her thigh, still lubricated by the massage oils, up Rafael's leg. She used her foot to caress his calf, but still he did not wake. She reached across his waist, searching for the little bone button that fastened the kilt. Her fingers found it, and she gently pushed the smooth polished bone through the eyelet. She paused again, but Rafael showed no signs of moving.

Gently she uncovered him. He was large, but not unnaturally large. His penis bounced and twitched in its erection, now free of the fabric it had pressed against. She wrapped her hand around him. Marina did not have small hands, but he filled her palm. He was warm and smooth, uncircumcised. She felt the blood pulse through him as he swelled and hardened even more in her hand.

Rafael moaned under his breath.

"Beautiful man," Marina whispered. It felt like an invocation.

A kind of rapture came over her. She dipped her mouth to his nipple and drew it into her mouth. It grew hard against her tongue and his body shuddered. She let her hair wash over him as she seeded long, slow, moist kisses across his chest. She rolled against him, rubbing herself along his thigh and pressing her breasts into his belly. She felt a moistness between her legs and knew she was already opening to him. She slid down further on his body, felt his warm, hard organ cradled between her breasts, kissed his stomach and felt him tensing, coming slowly out of his dream.

Before he could fully wake she slid even lower and took him in her mouth. He moaned aloud again, but did not open his eyes. For a moment Marina wondered if he was imagining another woman, but the wave that carried her was powerful and she knew that she didn't care who he saw behind his closed eyes. If he wanted Mai-Ling, she would be Mai-Ling for him.

She took as much of him as she could into her mouth in long slow strokes. She pumped with her hand as well. She felt his hips begin to thrust instinctively, even though she was providing the motion. She tasted a pearl of salt from him, felt him begin to come, then stop.

His hands were in her hair, clasping her head gently but powerfully pulling her mouth from him. He curled up to meet her and drew her mouth to his in one smooth motion. His tongue slipped between her lips and plunged into her mouth.

He seemed to know by instinct when she needed to breathe. He would move away from her mouth and kiss her face, her neck, her shoulders. He was sitting up now and she knelt in front of him. His eyes were open. She could see that in the pale light. He knew her.

She held his penis in both hands as she straddled him. She guided him toward her. She was slick and open and the head of him slipped into her easily. She lowered herself down slowly, prolonging the strange sensation of enveloping him. She felt stretched, filled, impaled. She looked down between them but could see only shadow as the last of him was swallowed inside of her.

Immediately, she wanted to ride him, to slide up and down his length, but he held her firmly down, his hands circling her hips.

"Wait," he said, "just feel it. Don't move."

She tried to do as he asked. She let him hold her still. He stopped kissing her. He stared into her eyes. When she was still by herself he removed his hands from her hips and ran them slowly over her back and arms, belly and breasts, buttocks and legs. He kept this touch very light, sometimes almost not touching her at all. It made her tingle all over. She felt an odd kind of energy building between them. It was like an orgasm, but not something she could control, and it frustrated her. It made her impatient.

With a laugh she began moving again. "I'm sorry. I can't hold still." She lifted herself up with strong thigh muscles and let herself fall back onto him. Again and again she pumped and he let her. He seemed to be studying her, playfully, passionately. He touched her nipples briefly, then the base of her neck, her buttocks, behind her knees and then the soles of her feet. These were all sensitive places for her and he seemed to know them from experience. His hands moved deftly and firmly, as if he were sculpting her body out of soft clay, modeling her muscles, smoothing her skin, giving her form.

She was panting now, sweating and moaning as she felt the beginning of the little wave in her. It started far out to sea within her, and she willed it ashore, feeling it build and surge as it moved. It felt good, so good. It overwhelmed her, pushed her deeper and deeper, further and further down into some secret place within herself where the faces of other lovers flashed before her. Smells and images and tastes came to her from someplace in the past. It was like she was cycling back through other experiences, like she was lost and looking for a sign, some star to navigate by. One moment she was present, alive with anticipation. Then . . .

She was outside of herself looking on. She saw two people coupling wildly. They sat facing each other like Tantric statues—Shakti riding Shiva in an orgy of worldmaking. Their bodies glowed from sweat and some inner furnace in the growing light. It was beautiful but empty. Here she was, outside of her own passion, the ultimate cliché for a photographer, a voyeur of her own experience.

It was not, of course, the first time it had happened, but she hoped this time might be different. Sex had become confusing and frustrating. Something about the sensation, the sheer sensual weight of the experience, had somehow become too much for her. She had taken to abandoning her body in the face of it.

When it had first happened, this flight from her own body, she'd tried to reenter her own experience, to force her way back, but she knew she could not make it happen. She knew no way back in. Usually the partners of her brief encounters would be none the wiser for her absence. But if she let them stay around too long, even the most insensitive of them would come to resent her retreat from ecstasy.

She would come back to her body slowly after these experiences. Once the thrusting and sliding and moist rhythms had ceased she would be drawn back to pretend satisfaction and closure.

She had had bad lovers, clumsy and awkward men, self-centered grunters, but this problem was hers, not theirs. Even Rafael's careful attentions were not enough to keep her in her skin. She had hoped this great erotic failure of will had been left behind when she died, but . . .

"Is it better from outside, or just safer?"

Marina was startled by the voice. It was Rafael speaking, but at just this moment the Rafael she saw had one of her own breasts in his mouth. "You won't find that center from out here, you know."

A shimmering, semitransparent version of Rafael hovered in the air, cross-legged, on the other side of the embracing couple. Startled, Marina thought herself backward and she drifted back a few feet. She had never realized that she floated when she left her body.

"I'm sorry. I . . . thought I could do this. I want to be with you, I really do, but this happens to me. I can't control it."

"But you can control it."

"I can't. I've tried."

"How?"

"I've tried concentrating, forcing myself to stay in my body with all my willpower."

"And does that work?"

"No." Marina felt drained, as though she might suddenly cry. She wondered if she could cry outside of her body.

"So if fighting it doesn't work . . . ." He paused as if she would understand how to complete his thought.

"I don't understand." Marina felt thick and slow.

"What you are fighting, perhaps you need to surrender to."

"I still don't understand. I wasn't fighting anything just now. The sensation just got to be too much for me, and . . ." Something hovered at the edge of her awareness. Something important.

"What were you thinking about . . . just before."

"Falling. I was falling down into some dark place."

"And what did you see?"

"Old lovers, old wounds, I don't know."

"So what scared you most—the falling or the past?"

"I don't know, the past I suppose."

"Could you surrender to the falling and stay in the present?"

"I don't know how."

The shimmering Rafael floated over to her. "When that little current begins within you, where does it begin? Here?" He passed his ghostly hand into her belly and down as if he could touch her most private places from the inside. Oddly, she felt the touch and moaned, but the sound came from the Marina locked in Rafael's embrace on the floor below her. "Or here?" His hand passed up through her, inside her head to some center of passion. Again she moaned with pleasure despite herself, and again the sound came from her physical body below.

"Here?" He touched her once more between the legs. "Or here?" He tickled some place within her head that set her trembling.

Both places excited her. Both places seemed to be the center and the source of her pleasure. It was like a puzzle. She knew her own body, knew the places that needed to be stroked and fondled to set the wave in motion, but she knew this was partially illusion as well. She had read that it was theoretically possible to induce an orgasm in a person by direct electrical stimulation of the brain.

Both places were the source and neither was.

The wave that washed over her, that dragged her down, threatening to pull her into some dark secret place, came from somewhere else. But this place was not a third place, not a different site, rather it was an amalgam, a paradox, a place made out of being neither one location nor the other. If she didn't fight the contradiction she could almost hold this new location within her, but she couldn't hold it tightly. It had to flow.

Yes, that was it—flow. It was like knowing where to point her camera's lens, seconds before the action occurred. It was what photographers called the decisive moment. She'd spent her life in pursuit of the paradox of decisive moments. That thing which cannot be manufactured, cannot be contrived, without robbing it of life.

Marina was panting with excitement. But which Marina? This was a trick of being in two places at once, she thought. No, not two places, many places. She knew this trick. It was the secret of her best photography, her highest art, when she was not a voyeur, not separate from the action around her, but intimately connected to it, flowing with it.

Her nipple ached. She saw/felt Rafael nurse greedily from her. The photographer's gift, her gift, was not and never had been the ability to see. It was the ability to be there—to be where the life was, to tap the source of desire, to prick and watch blood flow. Not attached, but connected.

The ghostly Rafael's face hovered close to hers. His eyes were dark black pools. She saw her spirit-self reflected in those pools. She saw her physical-self through those eyes. Two wave patterns spread out from her head and from her thighs, like pebbles dropped in either end of a pond. She heard herself make noises that she could not control, could not stop.

She was one wave, then the other, reckless for the collapse, holding both crests, crying, salt sweat in her mouth, biting down on her own lip, tasting blood, delicious sensations, polished stone circle on leather cord banging between them, crashing, back to her body as Rafael exploded inside of her, hot and wet, and then she was exploding, trembling, clinging to him, legs and arms entwined, not Shakti now, but Kali, erotic goddess of death and fiery creation, squeezing every last surge from him, then, and then, and then . . . suddenly weak, spent, melting in a pool of sweat and semen, her moisture and his, blood, and tears, and traces of scented oil, jasmine . . . sandalwood . . . musk. . . .

Sleep. Little death.

★ ★ ★

Again she woke first. The sun had risen, started to climb. She untangled herself from him gently and rose on still-unsteady legs. She walked a little way into the jungle to relieve the pressure in her bladder. Then she bathed herself in the stream.

She was still sore from his being inside her and her skin was sensitive in places from rough caresses, but she felt happy, full, almost buoyant.

She brought fruit and cool water to him. She bathed him with a cloth dipped in the water and he reveled in it. He stretched like a cat, allowed himself to be fed juicy bits of fruit, and eventually sat up. He kissed her gently on the lips and they both rediscovered the little cut from her bite. She wanted to thank him, to say something, but there seemed to be no need for words between them.

After they ate, he left to wash himself and rinse the wooden bowls. He wetted his hair and squeezed the excess water from it. It hung long and glistening in the sunlight. Then he came back to her. He still had not refastened his kilt. She saw him look at the weaving, saw an uncharacteristic shadow flicker over his face.

She stood then, intending to give him time to weave. He had been more than generous with her. But he caught her thigh in a strong grip and pulled her toward him. She stood in front of him and let her fingers comb through his damp hair. He ran a hand slowly up her right thigh. She knew by instinct that he was tracing the path of the turtle. He twisted her thigh gently and she opened herself to him. His finger glided inside her thigh and then stopped. He laughed.

Curious, she bent to look for herself. The turtle was half hidden in the dark curls between thigh and abdomen. Rafael kissed her there and she held his head with both hands. He kissed her again and again, and then he was licking her, parting her flowery folds with his tongue, making lazy circles, then frantically lapping, then pausing.

She stood as long as she could. She draped a leg over his shoulder for a time, then shifted it back, needing both legs to stand. When the tremors came she slumped down, pressing herself hard against his mouth. When she could stand no longer, she let herself be guided down until she knelt over him, riding his mouth with liquid convulsions. Soon, however, even that was too much, and she fell to her side. But still he would not leave her. She let herself be rolled onto her back, allowed him to devour her like some carnivore.

When she came this time, she did not fight against it, but surrendered to it, risked the plunge, held onto the impossible duality of the experience, and remained in her body.

They lay together after that, stroking and exploring one another more slowly. He inspected the traces of her wounds and showed her his. He seemed at times like a surveyor mapping her every mound and estuary.

They made love again. They did it slowly and she let him hold her still this time, experiencing the intimate connection. They spoke playfully while they coupled. She made him come in her mouth and between her breasts. He made her come by touching herself while he watched. She lost count of the times she felt the rush of orgasm, but she felt it fully and completely every time.

★ ★ ★

They slept again, but something woke her. It was late in the day. But was it the same day? Could they have done so much in just one day? She felt like she was waking from a dream.

Something hurt. Her head hurt. An odd high-pitched sound rang in her ears. Rafael sat up, too. He looked stunned, dazed. He stood up, held his hands over his ears.

"No, it's too soon." He looked about frantically. "I have time. I still have time."

Marina held his arms. "What is it Rafael? What's wrong?"

"The weaving. It isn't done yet and already they're here."

"Who's here?" Marina yelled. She had to yell to be heard over the noise. The ringing had turned to wailing and she already knew the answer to her question.

All at once Rafael regained his composure. He had momentarily lost his center, but then he found it again. He picked up his kilt from the floor and buttoned it around his hips. He picked up the jacket he had given Marina and helped her on with it.

"What's going on?" she asked.

He took her by the shoulders and said calmly but firmly, "You must go now."

"What do you mean go? Go where? Why?"

"They will be here soon and you cannot be here."

"I'm not leaving you like this, Rafael. It's my fault that you didn't finish on time. I'll tell them it's my fault."

"Please, Marina, it's me. I don't want you to see me when they come."

"I don't understand." Rafael took the stone circle from around his neck and placed it around hers.

"I could love you, but I'm not free to love now. Maybe soon. I almost finished this time. Perhaps next time I will complete it, but now I have to begin again, and you can't be here for that."

"But it's my fault. If I hadn't come, if you hadn't helped me, you would have finished. It's not fair."

The wailing was growing louder, even more uncomfortable. Marina and Rafael were shouting at each other just to be heard.

"I was supposed to help you. You were supposed to help me. But we are moving at different speeds. I have a heavy penance. I have nowhere else to go. You have to learn certain things. This place, all of this is a great gift. Do you understand that?"

"I don't know. I don't know." Rafael kissed her, hard and passionate, then pulled away softly. He hugged her to him and spoke directly into her ear so as not to have to shout.

"Take the forest trail up the mountain. It's the way Mai-Ling went, and I know in my heart she must be safe. Go now and don't look back, please."

Marina had tears in her eyes. She wasn't sure she could do it, but she could sense how urgently he needed for her to try. She turned away but he caught her wrist.

"Wait." He pulled her back. He scooped something off the floor and knelt in front of her. It was her pearl and coral anklet. He tied it around her ankle. He let his hand slide up the inside of her leg, caressed her thigh briefly, then turned away to his loom.

Marina stood a moment, then turned and ran from the hut. She couldn't see the wraiths, but it sounded as if they were all around her. The sun was dropping below the tree line and the trail was taking on shadows. She climbed a gentle sloping trail upward for what seemed like twenty minutes.

The sound of the wraiths faded, and the farther away from it she got, the less she liked having fled the hut. What would they do to him? she wondered. What was the power they had over him? When she finally decided to turn back, the trail was even darker and harder to follow. She crept down it, unfamiliar with it even though she had just climbed it. She listened for the wraiths but heard nothing. When she was almost certain that she would never find the hut in the darkness, that she had somehow wandered off on a side trail, she recognized the stream where she had bathed only that morning.

The hut stood off to the side, but it was empty, no loom, no chests or bundles, no carpets, no hammock. No, that wasn't true, either. She could see something. There was a mist blowing past the hut and every now and then through patches of it she could see the hut as she recalled it. She crept closer. Candles burned in the hut. Rafael was there, seated in front of his loom, but instead of weaving, he was pulling threads from the beautiful cloth, unraveling it, unmaking it as she watched.

He was weeping. She couldn't hear him, but she saw his eyes glistening by the candle glow. The mist shifted and she saw the women in black. They sat around Rafael on the floor, patient and silent. Their hoods were thrown back and their robes were spread open to reveal skin and dark terrible wounds. Rafael's family, Marina realized.

There was an older woman with a dark gash across her belly, a younger woman, the one Marina had accidentally touched by the pond, and a little girl. The young woman must be Carita, Marina guessed. There was a great bloom of black blood high on her chest, and her belly was rounded. Rafael had said she had been pregnant with his child. The little girl had her back to Marina, and while she could see no wounds, she knew they must be there.

Rafael did not look at them. They were his own private ghosts, and they haunted him in mute testimony as he sadly pulled apart his great weaving.

She wanted to go to him, but he had not wanted her to see this.

Another patch of mist blew through and her vision was again obscured. The mist was unusual. She had not recalled seeing mist or fog since she woke on the island. As she pondered this she realized that it was not mist obscuring her vision of Rafael and the women and the hut, it was their transparency. They all shimmered like ghosts before her. She and Rafael had both looked like this briefly when they had left their bodies.

They were slipping away from her now, like shadows. She watched them as long as she could, feeling sad, feeling empty again.

At last she turned and started back up the trail. It was dark now and the trail was hard to follow. She walked as long as she could, but when she began to trip and stub her toes, she found a mossy spot just off the trail at the foot of a tree with low overhanging branches. It provided a sense of shelter even though she was not cold, was not worried about rain, and was not afraid of wild animals.

She lay awake for a while, sitting up, clutching her legs to her chest. Rafael, as she had just seen him, was more ghost than solid form, and yet her body still ached from him. He was painfully real to her. Then she remembered the little stone circle talisman Rafael had given her. It was still fastened about her neck. She squeezed her fingers around it, grateful for something to hold on to.

CHAPTER 4

Mirror Dance

It has been proposed that rather than gross or subtle clues to position and direction, it is movement itself, some kinesthetic sense, that provides the secret map of sea turtles. Perhaps they know themselves so well, live so much in the present, that they feel their way across oceans, knowing the physical "rightness" of muscle strain versus current drift. What flotsam and jetsam, what waterlogged and wasted cargo would I need to jettison to see my way so clearly?

Morning noises woke Marina. They were the noises she had come to expect as the jungle changed shifts with the light. The night hunters made their way to burrows, lairs, hollows, and nests, while the colorful things that needed open blossoms and bright light to spot dangers, took their place. It was a morning symphony of exotic squawks, calls, whistles, and roars. She heard each one not as a dull drone or annoying background, but as part of a great whole.

There were smells here, too, that intrigued her. She had never had a keen sense of smell, but now she was aware of a rich, moist, loamy smell—the smell of peat, of wood and leaves composting. Woven into this blanket were other subtle smells: almost-sweet floral aromas, something odd and surprising, like vanilla bean or caramel, a hint of salt in the breeze.

She thought of Rafael's essential oils.

Rafael.

Marina had slept sitting up, her back in the round of a great exposed root. She was sore and stiff. Her legs ached, but she could not say if it was from climbing the jungle trail or from making love with Rafael. Worse, she felt an ache, an emptiness that began between her legs and seemed to spread upward. At least I know it was real, she thought, as she ran her hands over her thighs and belly. That at least was something to take away.

But she had more than that, and she knew it. She was changed somehow. She felt as though she had crossed a bridge into another country. The process that had begun when she dug herself free of the sand down on the beach had somehow been completed with Rafael.

When she had learned to walk and regained her balance, she had resurrected some somatic sense of her own body moving through space. This had been a revelation in itself, but her other senses had seemed annoyingly sensitive, out of her control. They had threatened to overwhelm her. What she had wanted to do was suppress them—to push them down and hide them somewhere inside herself.

Rafael had showed her another way. He had dared her to give her senses free rein. Rather than controlling her capacity for the sensual, he encouraged her to attend to it. The expansion she'd experienced expressed itself in the language of eroticism, but her experience with Rafael had been about more than just sex, more even than just passion. She had had both in her life before, but this was something different. She could truly say that she was living fully in her body. She could not recall when she had ever felt so aware of her senses. Perhaps as a child . . .

Images of her youth flickered before her. A gangly girl of twelve or thirteen, suddenly awkward when running, off balance with swelling breasts, embarrassed by boys. Full of the smells of a late summer evening: cut grass, barbecued chicken and roasted potatoes, citronella candles, sweat, her own perfume—half baby powder, half desire. The tastes of lemonade and bubble gum mingle in her mouth. She can still taste a trace of blood from a cut lip—an accident—a prize got wrestling with the boys. Grass itches her skin. She is aware of her bee sting, the little pink bandage over the cut on her foot, all her glorious wounds. She hears the cries and laughter of children, full into their make-believe. She hears the murmur of adult conversation, the clink of ice in glasses, Joni Mitchell on the stereo from inside the house. Then there are the birds, the crickets sawing in the high grass of the fields, and the toads calling down by the pond.

That girl on the edge of becoming a woman had been alive like this.

She was still alive inside Marina. Rafael had found her.

Part of Marina wanted to go back. She wanted Rafael in a physical way. She had tasted something that had only just whetted her appetite. But there was another reason for going back. She owed Rafael something. She had taken what he had to teach her and given nothing in return. She had been the cause of his not completing his weaving in time.

She wondered what it meant to have to begin again. How long would it take him? How many times had he started over? Would he have another chance? Would he want her back? Could she even find him again?

Marina stood up, pulling herself to her feet by a low-hanging branch. She ran her fingers through her hair and rubbed the sleep from her eyes. She opened her bright little jacket to straighten it and noticed the turtle tattoo. It had moved from its dark nest between her thighs. She remembered Rafael's kissing her there and it made her shiver. The little turtle had now moved to her belly, inches from her naval. She studied it, poking and stretching the skin beneath it. It was the closest she had been to it yet.

The detail in the turtle's shell was fascinating. It was hard to imagine that the old woman she had called Turtle Mother had done this. It seemed the work of an artist.

The interlocking pattern of shells inked onto her skin formed a map like the tattoo on the Turtle Mother and her younger incarnation's back, but it also formed a tiny labyrinth. She wondered what propelled it. How did it travel across the ocean of her body? She never saw it move. Did it move only while she slept? How did it know where to go, and where was it going? The colors of the ink still seemed vibrant, but were a shade less bright than they had seemed when the turtle had navigated the channel that was her thigh. Now, in the open ocean of her belly, was it fading?

What did that mean?

Both the Turtle Woman and Rafael had said something about time. She had only a limited amount of time to do or learn something. She had only the time while the mark of the turtle was visible.

The tree she had slept beneath was only a little off the trail, but in the few steps it took to find the path again she knew that she would not go back. She wanted to. She felt she had an obligation to. But she had also a higher calling. Rafael had wanted her to continue on her path. With all his guilt and sorrow, he still could not believe that Marina would not choose life over death. Though she herself was still not certain about what she wanted.

Marina decided she could best honor Rafael by pursuing the course that seemed to revere life. After all, she thought, I can always go back. I might only have a limited amount of time to go forward.

Marina belted and straightened her jacket. She looked down the trail in the direction from which she had come, turned in the opposite direction and started to walk. The coral and pearl anklet clicked softly and seemed to reinforce a strong, confident stride. It made her aware of the swing of her hips and a way of walking that was distinctly feminine. Sometimes she stopped to listen to the sounds of the jungle. She would walk carefully then, shifting her weight over first one foot then the other. She found that she could walk almost noiselessly this way.

Her only other possessions were the colorful woven jacket that draped about her shoulders and the little polished stone ring that hung from the leather cord around her neck. Sometimes her hand would drift absentmindedly up to the stone and fondle it. She rubbed it, polishing it with her fingers, and occasionally a finger would slip through the hole in the stone. This caused parts of her body to tingle in an odd echo of erotic vibration, as if the stone resonated with the energy she and Rafael had unleashed with their passion. It was not an unpleasant sensation, but it was distracting, and she had to force herself not to indulge in it, at least not while walking.

Late in the afternoon, after what felt like hours of gradually climbing into the jungle and the interior of the island, Marina became aware of her thirst.

She wondered where she might find water. The trail had followed a stream in the morning, but she had left that hours ago and could hear no trickling sounds off in the distance. Surely there must be streams and springs even in the high interior of the island, she thought. The trick was in finding them. She considered going back, but decided against it.

"I will go on faith." She said this out loud to the jungle. "I need water, I will find water. If I am supposed to be here now, then water will be provided."

She laughed at herself, but not out loud. To whom was she speaking? she wondered. She did not believe in a god, but, at the same time, this island seemed alive with spirits. Perhaps one of them was listening.

Her request, more a statement than a prayer, really, was answered in a way that made her remember her father telling her to be careful what she wished for.

It began to rain.

She heard it before she felt it. The rain seemed to need to quench the thirst of the canopy of trees first. Then, only when the canopy had drunk its fill and topped off its reservoirs, did the excess pour down on the forest floor in torrents. In some places the rain fell evenly. In other places it gushed as if channeled through the downspouts of some high cathedral.

Marina took her jacket off and rolled it up tightly. She broke off a large leaf, rolled her jacket bundle up in it, and tied it with a supple bit of vine. She drank her fill from leaf bowls, letting the cool water spill across her chest. Then she picked up her bundle and continued hiking in the rain.

The trail soon turned to mud beneath her bare feet and she felt it squish between her toes. She had walked naked on the beach the first day she had left the Turtle Woman, but that had been different. It had felt dreamlike. Now it felt exhilarating. She enjoyed the feeling of rain splashing on her shoulders, running through her hair. It called up memories of a younger Marina.

She was perhaps seven, maybe eight years old. She had spent the summer with cousins on a farm in Georgia. They grew peaches in an orchard, raised some cattle, grew corn and soybeans, and, most important, had enough wooded property that Marina could get truly lost. She found the workings of the farm interesting and she liked her aunt Beth, her mother's sister, but of her cousins, Alice was several years younger than she and Dawn, several years older. This, according to her mother and Aunt Beth, was no problem, but in reality there was too much of a gulf between them for anything more than polite play while the grown-ups were watching. When not required to put on a display, Dawn retreated to the barn to fuss over her two horses, and Alice preferred to be indoors with her dolls and their dramas. This left Marina free to explore.

It had been a drought year, hot and sticky. Marina had been following a dried up stream bed carved through cracked red clay when it started to rain. She was too far away from home to avoid being soaked by the rain on her trip back so she decided to stay out in it. She continued to follow the creek bed, fascinated by the way the red of the clay deepened to blood, then wine, as it was saturated by the rain.

She was, as always, barefoot, and her feet were red from the clay. Her cut-off jeans and T-shirt were already soaked through so that when she found the little hollow filled with red mud and clay, it didn't seem unreasonable to explore it.

She took the precaution of slipping out of her clothes first, hiding them under a low bush, before wading into the warm mud. She sat down into it then lay back. She debated for a moment whether she should get it into her hair, but it was raining hard and she was sure it would rinse out. She looked down at where her body should have been but there was only thick red mud. She let her head sink into it. The only part of her that was out of the water now was her face. She closed her eyes and let the rain fall on her.

When she opened her eyes again it was because of some movement. She could barely hear anything. Her ears were below the mud line, and the steady drone of the rain masked the more subtle sounds of the forest, but she felt subtle vibrations that made her eyes open. Not five feet away from her a stag was drinking from a little pool of clearer water.

It was not unusual to see deer on her aunt and uncle's property, but always at a distance. Marina had never been this close to a deer, especially one so large.

It moved closer to her as if she were not there. Marina blinked her eyes slowly, like a cat. She felt connected to the stag in a way that was both strange and wonderful. Marina, mud, earth, deer, rain, clouds—she could not say where one began and the other ended. There was something in this moment that changed her or, more precisely, shifted her direction.

Eventually the stag moved away, disappearing into the rain. Marina climbed from her hiding place. She stood in the rain and rubbed the mud and clay, as much into her body as off of it. It was hard to rinse the red clay from her hair. For a week after, she would tint the shower water red when she stood under it in the evenings. She pulled on her soaked underpants, shorts, and T-shirt and made her way home in a kind of daze.

Marina tried to tell her aunt about the stag. She listened politely, but Marina knew that the experience, the moment, was one she could not communicate with words.

She spent the rest of the summer in the woods with her camera, sitting still for hours at a time to photograph a deer, a raccoon, squirrels, birds. She used up all of her summer allowance, the money her mother had given her for ice cream, sodas, and treats, on film for her camera. She never saw the stag again, but by the end of the summer when she returned to Washington she had a portfolio of little black-and-white snapshots. Some were blurry, out of focus, under- or overexposed. Some showed animals barely visible against the forest background into which they were designed to blend. But some of Marina's photographs even made her father take notice. One in particular, a deer that had come close enough that Marina could have reached out and rubbed its snout, was good enough to be enlarged and her father sent it off for this honor.

Later, of course, Marina's interest in blending in and being the invisible observer expanded to the photographing of people, but it had begun as a child, in the forest, in the rain, in a liminal moment when she could have been one thing or the other and she chose the other.

It began in a place not unlike where Marina now found herself.

When she came to a crossroads where the trail divided, she stopped. She had not yet had to make a decision about which path to choose. There had been other paths that led off the main trail before this, but it had been clear which was the main path and which a diversion. This fork offered no simple choice. The branch to the right was steeper and water flooded down it, almost as though it were a stream. The branch to the left was not as steep, but appeared to curve and wind off into the distance. Both appeared to have been well used, the right branch perhaps a bit more traveled, but the channel of water sluicing down it made it look like a slippery and uncertain path.

Marina took the trail to the left. It wound up more gradually, as if here the giant steps had eroded and rounded out. The rain stopped, and as it did she could hear the sound of running water echoing through the trees. It sounded like only a small stream tripping and falling over rocks, puddles, and pools on its course downhill. The trail led her to the stream and Marina stepped over it easily. From there, however, the trail seemed to follow the stream to its source in lazy S-curves that climbed, crossed, and recrossed it.

The source of the stream was a steady trickle of water that flowed from a worn crack in a wall of carefully arranged stones. She might have missed it altogether, as the wall was set back from the trail several yards within a grove of trees. She found it more by sound than sight.

The wall was taller than Marina and seemed to define a kind of terrace. The terrace itself was well hidden by thick old trees that grew up closer to each other than seemed natural for the jungle. She could find no easy way around the wall, so Marina tossed her jacket bundle up onto the slab and scrambled up the face to find the source of the water.

It was getting late in the day. The sun had come back after the rain, but Marina could tell by the glimpses of it she got through the canopy that it was setting. She should find a sheltered spot to spend the night, she thought, and if this was a source of drinking water that was off the trail and protected, it just might serve her needs.

The pool itself was deep, dark, and still. Some leaves floated on the surface, but the only motion was at one edge of the pool where the water overflowed the stone border and spilled out over the rock face Marina had climbed.

It was unnaturally round, and it took several moments for Marina to understand why. It was man-made. Old cut stones, now almost completely obscured by moss, ringed the pool in a perfect circle. Ferns and other plants had sprouted up from the cracks and depressions in the stones, but it still retained its shape. Around the pool and back for several yards the ground was clear and free of all but the smallest plants. It was covered in a spongy carpet of more green moss and tiny white flowers. Beyond that was the ring of trees that grew thick and tightly packed, their roots and branches so entangled, that they looked as if they had been planted to create just such a wall. The pool backed up to a rock face with a shadowy opening.

This seemed a good place to stop for the night, so Marina dropped her jacket bundle and knelt by the pool. She dipped her hand into the dark water and was surprised at how cool it was. She brought some to her mouth in a cupped hand. It was sweet and clean. It must come from an underground spring, she thought.

She lay down on her stomach to drink more deeply from the pool. The moss was like fine velvet against her skin, cool and soft. She put her face close to the surface and lifted cupped palms full of water to her mouth. When she had drunk her fill she rested her head on folded arms and watched the water quickly return to its mirrorlike stillness.

That's when she noticed her own reflection in the water. She seemed younger than she remembered. The little lines were still there at the corners of her eyes and the perimeter of her smile, but the dark circles that had grown to be a fixture underneath her eyes were gone.

That alone seemed to take several years off her age, but there was more.

She had been photographing herself for the past several years, something she had never done before. She would turn the camera back on herself in the middle of moments of stress. She would photograph her body or just her face in cracked mirrors in little hotel rooms. She made close-up photographs of her scars. She had an entire collection of work locked in a safe deposit box in a bank that no one knew she kept an account at. She had been obsessed.

Always in these photographs, there was something oppressing her, some shadow that seemed to shroud her. In the darkroom she tried adjusting exposure times and contrast filters, she even experimented with infrared film, but she could not bring a sense of translucence to her own skin. She could find it in the images she made of others—that subtle glow of life—but not in her self-portraits. It was as though her skin was too thick, almost a disguise. In the end this had made it easy enough to choose to die, when she could find no evidence of life within herself.

Now her skin seemed to fit her better. Even in her reflection in the dark pool she could see a radiance, a glow.

Her reflection smiled.

Marina had not smiled, but was unaware that she hadn't.

Her reflection blinked, slowly, like a cat, like Marina had as a little girl when she had seen the stag.

Marina had not blinked. She brought her hand up to her face, touched the corner of her mouth.

Her hand in reflection did not move.

Marina reached out to touch the reflection on the surface of the pond, was reassured to see a hand reach up to meet her. But when fingers met, the reflection did not give way. There was no melting away, no penetration of surfaces, only light resistance, pressure for pressure.

Marina gasped.

"She is only your reflection. She cannot hurt you."

Marina sat up sharply, looking around. The grove of trees and the stones surrounding the pool created odd echoes. It was hard to tell where the voice was coming from.

"Don't be frightened, child. I am right here."

Marina found the source of the voice. A woman was sitting cross-legged on a stone near the opening in the rock face. She had rich dark brown skin and long gray hair that hung about her shoulders in dread-locks, with some thick rolls curled crownlike around her head. Marina could not guess at the woman's age. Her body was covered in a long robe dyed in patterns of moss green and cerulean blue, revealing only her pink-soled feet and tiny folded hands.

Though she thought it silly and a little late, Marina unrolled her bundle and pulled on her jacket. "I'm sorry. I didn't know anyone was here."

"It's quite all right. I don't get too many visitors. Most of them pass this place by. Only those who have lost something of themselves come here."

"What do you mean, lost something of themselves?" She seemed to have abandoned the need for introductions and polite preliminaries. She was at once ready to enter almost any discourse, especially with someone who might know more than she.

"If you had not lost some part of yourself, you would not be here."

"That isn't really an answer, you know." But as the words were leaving her lips she realized that she had probably misinterpreted the woman's answer. She continued to clarify. "Unless you mean that it is why I am here . . . ," she gestured up to the sky and around her, "not just here." She finished, patting the moss-covered stones.

"You came to Turtle Island to find that part of you that understands what a gift life is. Yes?"

"I came here by mistake actually."

The woman smiled at her serenely, knowingly. It annoyed Marina. If this woman had something to say she should just say it, she thought.

"What?" Marina asked. "What did I say that was so funny?"

"Do you really still believe in mistakes and accidents?"

"What I mean is that I meant to die, and I ended up here."

"And do you still want to die?"

Marina did not answer this immediately. It was an important ques-tion, and, even though an answer leapt to her lips almost instantly, she felt like she should be careful before she spoke aloud.

"No. I don't think I want to die now . . . but surely it must be too late for me."

"Never too late for finding." The old woman's eyes sparkled. "If you find what you've lost you won't die." She paused. "Now living, well, only if you are strong enough, but at least you need not die."

"I don't understand."

"Come, my name is Atana. Stay the night with me. I have food and you must be hungry. The moon will be out tonight, the lovers will swim." The old woman gestured at the pool. "A good time to find what is lost. I will tell you what I know."

The sky was darkening and Marina had no place to go and no reason not to stay, so she agreed. The old woman led Marina into what had appeared to be a shallow cave from the outside, but was actually quite spacious on the inside.

"My sister and I keep the mirror pool."

"Your sister?" Marina asked, looking around.

"We take turns. I am the waxing sister. I watch the mirror from dark of the moon to full. My sister watches the waning."

"And what is your sister called?"

"Atana." Marina looked perplexed and the old woman laughed. "We are never here at the same time so it causes little confusion. It is the way it was with my mother and her sister and her mother and sister for as long as anyone knows."

Atana lit a few candles in the cave and Marina realized that while some of the cave had clearly formed naturally, other parts had been etched into the stone. There were raised stone benches carved into the sides of straight, smooth walls. Carefully cut and fitted stones that looked ancient and worn by time formed tables and shelves. Niches had been cut into the stone to hold candles. Images of the moon were carved or painted on almost every surface. There were the makings of a little cooking fire set into a corner in a stone fireplace, but it was not lit and Atana did not choose to light it.

She bade Marina sit on one of the woven mats in front of a low stone table and brought her food. There were more fruits, some like those she had eaten with Rafael and some she didn't recognize, and little salty bean-curd cakes. She washed this down with the sweet water of the spring.

Marina ate slowly despite her hunger, tasting every new food fully before swallowing it. Atana ate very little, and seemed to be studying Marina. They ate in silence, then Atana cleared away the food and returned with a stoppered gourd and two small wooden bowls. She poured a silvery-black liquor from the gourd into each of the bowls and handed one to Marina.

Marina wanted to ask what it was, but Atana was already sipping hers slowly and it seemed impolite to question. Marina brought the bowl to her lips and sipped. It was heavy and sweet and cooler in her mouth than it had been against her lips. It tasted like the juice of silvered pears. Marina knew this wasn't possible, but the poetic description that popped into her mind seemed more appropriate than any rational combination of flavors she could think of.

She finished it faster than she'd intended, but Atana just said "Good," as she took the bowl from Marina.

"Come," Atana said as she stood and took Marina's hand. Marina let herself be pulled to her feet by the little woman and led outside. Marina felt a little dizzy, intoxicated by the silvered pear liquor, but she followed and sat next to the old woman on the mossy stones beside the pool.

"The moon will come tonight," Atana said pointing up. The trees formed a circular opening overhead like a skylight through which she could see a dark night sky sprinkled with stars. "How do you call the moon in your place?"

"I don't understand."

"Do you say the moon is a woman or a man?"

Marina had heard folktales in which the moon represented male deities, but in most of the stories she could recall the moon was feminine. "A woman, I guess."

"Ahh . . . well, the thing to remember is that when water is a woman, the moon will be a man. He will enter her here." Atana gestured at the pool. "She will be drawn to him and push away from him, strong, like the tides. It is a good time to look for lost things."

"You said that before. . . ." It was hard to frame complete thoughts, but Marina's mind was filled with images. ". . . That I had to find some part of me that was lost. I don't know what you mean."

"You have many women living here." Atana put her hand on Marina's heart, slipping just her fingertips inside the jacket to touch skin. "Girls, young women, mothers, lovers, grandmothers. You can give these pieces of yourself away. This is a great gift. You can also lose them."

"What do you mean lose them?"

"They can be driven away by fear, misplaced by inattention. They can seek places that better nourish them. There are many ways to lose these things."

"Have I lost . . . ?" It was a silly question and she stopped herself from finishing it. Of course she had lost something. She hadn't always woken up sad and heavy. She had once been able to find beauty and meaning in things.

"The question is not have I lost, but what have I lost," Atana said softly. "Can you name the pieces you have lost?"

Marina's head was spinning. She looked up at the night sky. Could she name the lost ones? There was the little girl in the woods of Georgia, the Marina who felt in her heart the connection between her life and everything around her. That little girl had been gone for some time. The Marina of the past few years had felt nothing but disconnection and disorientation in her life.

And what about the artist—the artist in Marina who had always been able to see beauty and pattern and, above all, the light? She had left Marina sometime after her assignment in Baghdad. Sure she could still make incredible photographs, but the light had gone out of them. Marina made them from instinct and habit, not from passion.

Then there was Marina, the lover. She'd lost her virginity at twenty. She knew this was late. It seemed that all her friends had matured much sooner. She hadn't been afraid of sex or intimidated or embarrassed by it. She just hadn't been ready for it. She made up for her late start with passionate and uninhibited affairs. She'd loved Christophe body and soul, but something inside her had died along with him. Afterward, she could still enjoy sex, enjoy the erotic attention of men, but it was never the same. She could never abandon herself to the passion. She'd gotten some of that back with Rafael, but what good would that do her now?

"I'm curious." Marina asked, "Can I get these pieces back?"

"You have already found some of the most important pieces."

"When? I mean how do you know?"

"Well, you have the turtle's mark on you. What did you discover on the beach?"

Marina wondered how the woman could know about her tattoo, but glancing down at her own chest she saw the head of the little sea turtle just visible between her breasts in the *V* formed by the jacket. It had been on her belly this morning and now it seemed to be heading for her throat.

"Balance!" The word came quickly to Marina. "Something about balance. Physical balance, but something more than that. She talked about a kind of emotional or maybe spiritual balance. That I needed to pay attention to the light as well as the shadow."

"And did this make sense to you? Do you know the part of you that once kept you balanced?"

An image came to Marina of her mother. Her mother had been sensual and emotional, even unpredictable, but she had always been optimistic. She could find beauty and wonder in the most commonplace of objects or experiences. Her father, on the other hand, had been a brooder, a deep thinker, introverted and intense. He was an academic, a historian who wrote about genocides and holocausts, great rents in the fabric of humanity. But despite this, he had found his own balance in life. His daughters and especially his wife were his lifeline, his way up and out of the darkness into which he often wrote himself.

Marina had a little of each of them in her, both the brooder and the optimist. She realized for the first time that this meant she must have spent a good part of her life with that one aspect of her personality functioning as the lifeline for the other part. Now she had no lifeline, no way back. Her mother's spirit within her had gone. She had stopped nurturing it with observations of beauty and wonder. This was her balance.

"My mother," was all she said.

"Call her back, then."

"How?"

"Look for them in the mirror." Atana made a circular pass with her hand over the pool. It was still and jet black now, but a light glowed at one edge. Marina looked up through the circular opening formed by the tall trees. The moon was just edging into the dark circle of sky. It was almost full and reflected off the surface of the pool.

"Call them back. Call them all back."

Marina slid closer to the edge of the pool and knelt facing it. She leaned forward and looked down into the water. She couldn't even see her own reflection very clearly, just a darker shadow that seemed to blot out little sparkles of stars.

She turned back to Atana. "I don't see anything. What do I do now?"

"Keep looking, child. Ask them to return."

"What am I looking for?"

"Reflections. Look for your reflections." She wanted to question Atana's use of the plural, but understood that she was just avoiding what she knew she must do.

Marina felt awkward about speaking out loud, so she tried focusing her thoughts and willing the pieces of her soul back. She thought about the little girl on the farm in Georgia—the naked, clay-covered, wild animal. She thought about her mother. She pictured herself as an artist like her mother had been. Her mother had worked in a studio, her paintings were abstractions based on landscapes. She had not required people, and yet she had been very sociable. Her relationships with friends mattered almost as much as her art. Marina's art required people and yet in the past several years she had come to see them simply as props.

The water shimmered in the area of her cast shadow. She thought she saw a woman's face. It was her mother's face, then her face, then her mother's again.

Marina tried to picture the lover in her. She instantly saw herself with Rafael. Yes, she thought, this is how I want to see the lover in me—passionate, absorbed, present.

The water shimmered again and she saw herself clearly. An image filled the shadowy area. It was her image, but not a reflection. She saw herself lying on her back, naked, glistening with a fine sheen of sweat, her pupils swollen, her body flushed with orgasmic exhaustion—ecstatic fatigue. She looked powerful and strong and deeply feminine. She thought of the great sculptural representations of the erotic goddesses of India. It was as if this image of her own body was a manifestation of that energy. Her hand traced a line in the perspiration from her lips to her throat, down between her breasts, over her belly to touch the turtle tattoo between her thighs.

Then the image held a hand out, palm level with the surface of the water, as if she was touching a glass or mirror from the other side. Marina hesitated, then extended a hand out over the surface of the water. The image floated closer to her so that she didn't have to bend out far to touch the watery hand. She put her palm over the image of her palm and pressed lightly into the water.

Her hand met resistance. Instead of sinking into the water her hand touched another hand, palm to palm. It supported her weight. She leaned on it tentatively. The image lifted another hand and Marina placed her palm down over that one. She leaned forward. Her image supported her. She felt strange, giddy. She knew this was not possible, but . . .

Her knees were at the very edge of the moss-covered stones lining the pool, and as her image drifted back into the center of the pool it pulled Marina with it. She was off balance and sprawled into the water, but she never splashed or broke the surface. She seemed suspended against her image at every point where her body made contact. It felt like floating, like weightlessness without the pressure of water around her.

"Call them back, Marina." She heard Atana's voice as if from a long way off. "Make a place for them."

Marina laughed. She felt absurd, even surreal. She looked down at an image of herself as if pressed against soft glass. Her image seemed to be aware of her, patient, waiting to be seduced.

"Come back," Marina whispered. She felt self-conscious, but spoke anyway. "Please, I need you."

Almost at once Marina felt herself slipping through the glass—spinning around and into the water. Her point of view shifted radically and she became the erotic image of herself. She was looking up and saw herself, floating face down in the mirror pool in her colorful jacket.

At first it felt awkward to be inhabiting her own erotic body. Then, gradually it became more familiar. This was not a foreign place, after all, only a long unused, unvisited, unrecognized place within her. How do I bring this back? she wondered. How do I make room for it?

But even as she thought this, she was aware of some essential part of herself filling this powerful feminine body—slipping into the unoccupied spaces. This image she was exploring was not her. It was not a complete person. It was more of an archetype—the divinely erotic feminine—a potential and a possibility that she'd once had access to. She'd lost or severed her bond to this goddess. Now she wanted it back. She drew this image around her, expanding into it until she could not say what was her and what was archetype.

She flipped again and was looking down once more. This time she saw her mother beneath her. Her mother alone. Her mother alone in her studio. Her mother and herself as a child. Her mother was teaching her to dance. She was young again in her mother's studio. The radio was playing something classical and her mother was teaching her to waltz. She did not need to know how to waltz. In fact, she already seriously doubted if she would ever have occasion to waltz, but her mother's laughter and enthusiasm was infectious. They danced out of the barn that her mother used as a studio and across the lawn, finally collapsing in the grass almost beyond earshot of the radio.

"You will be very pretty and talented and people will say great things about you. They will also be jealous of you and say hurtful things." Her mother toyed with Marina's hair. "Just remember that the voices inside you are the only ones that can hurt you and the only ones that can keep you truly happy."

Marina vaguely remembered this event from her childhood. Her mother was often taking her aside to tell her what seemed to be important things. And every time, Marina promised herself that this time she would remember the advice. But the little bits of shared wisdom didn't seem to have a place in her childhood and were too quickly forgotten.

There was something she wanted to say to her mother or something she wanted her mother to say to her. She slipped again beneath the water, into the body of her mother. It was a strange feeling. This too was not her body. In an odd way, however, it was comforting. She had, after all, once spent nine months in the body of this woman. If she listened carefully she could hear her mother's feelings and contradictions.

Marina's mother, Maria, was acutely aware of the amount of energy she possessed. She saw herself as an artist and a mother, but she knew that both of these challenges tapped the same source of energy within her. She constantly struggled to find the balance between her art and being a loving and nurturing mother. These were not constraints placed on her by society. Maria cared little for social conventions. This was a struggle formed from her own self-awareness, her own drives, her own passions.

Marina recognized this contradiction in herself. She had unconsciously made a choice where her mother had found a compromise. Her mother was a talented artist with a regional following. She still painted, she still sold pieces, but she had not pushed herself into the kind of prominence that Marina had achieved.

Marina had an international reputation as a photographer. She was known by her work around the world. But she had no children, not even a steady relationship. It was not that she believed that these things were necessary for happiness or fulfillment, but they did represent the choice she had made.

Now, looking up at herself from her mother's body, Marina saw a confident and vibrant woman, a daughter and a person well loved. This was how her mother still saw her. She regretted the letter her mother must have received by this time, the note that calmly and rationally explained why Marina had decided to give up the gift of life her mother had given her. She thought about the pain it must have caused. She had known it would be a sad thing for her family, but had not realized what that truly meant until now.

Marina didn't have time to cry. She flipped once again into her own body. Her mother was gone and in her place was the little child she had recalled earlier. Actually, all she saw was her face, as she'd once been, buried in the warm red clay as the rain pelted down on the hot summer afternoon. She almost laughed. Was that what she had looked like? The little girl seemed so intense, so focused on her experience. How old had she been then?

It did not surprise her when she slipped into her child body. She wanted it, wanted to remember the warm mud, the rain on her face, the intimacy with the forest, the sense of connection. She looked at herself through her own young eyes. She was delighted by how easy it was for the young Marina to see herself as a woman. She'd always had a kind of self-confidence about her abilities that was unusual enough in a child but somehow extraordinary in a young girl. It often made adults ill at ease with her, but it also meant that she had a clear view of her future. To a young Marina, the woman she saw floating in the water above her was a mixture of mother and father and something else, something powerful, but unpredictable. How can I bring this part of me back? she wondered. Perhaps by seeing as she saw.

Marina abandoned herself to the sounds of the heavy rain blanketing the Georgia forest. It was a dull sound that had rhythm and almost a song to it. She saw the stag drink water from the little pools that formed close to her. She saw a salamander slither from some hiding place. She saw birds overhead in the trees—crows, blue jays, a solitary owl. She saw a turtle crawl slowly around the edge of her mud wallow. It stopped to look at her in a way none of the other creatures had. The rain and forest song grew more insistent. The turtle. There was something about the turtle that reminded her of something. There was something she was supposed to remember.

It grew suddenly darker and Marina felt as if she was sinking. The image of herself as an adult receded as she descended. The song became a voice, a familiar voice, but one she could not quite identify. She tried to will herself back into her body. She imagined herself as an adult again, but it did not help. She sank still deeper into the pool.

"Marina." A voice called to her. It was not Atana's voice, but it was familiar. "Are you ready to come back to me?"

Marina could see no one. She was also not sure how to answer. Not sure if this was her imagination or some real voice.

"Marina." Again the voice called. It was a woman's voice, strangely seductive. "Have you chosen?"

Chosen, Marina thought, chosen what? A hazy shape began to materialize out of the darkness. Marina realized she was holding her breath. She had not been aware of breathing or not breathing when she had shifted perspective between herself and the lost pieces of her self, but now she felt pressure in her lungs.

"Yes, just take a breath and come to me." The ghostlike image in the water coalesced into a body. The body took on soft feminine curves. She began to recognize it. The Turtle Woman, the young incarnation she had first met, floated in the water before her. Her dark hair floated like a tangle of seaweed around her head. When she floated back her hair engulfed her face. When she moved closer to Marina her face emerged from her hair like a hesitant sea creature. "Come with me now. It will only get hard for you if you continue."

There seemed to be something overwhelming and attractive about surrendering to the Turtle Woman. She knew that surrender was what she was being asked to do. She had wanted that surrender before. She recalled dropping into the night dark sea from the cruise ship. The Turtle Woman had been there, too. She had surrendered to her then, but now some part of her hesitated.

Must I? she wondered.

"You must surrender to one thing or another. You have only a short time to walk this edge."

"Is my time up, then?" She was not aware that she was speaking, but her thoughts seemed as good as conversation.

"Very nearly."

"And if I choose your way, it means death, right?"

"My embrace just carries you further down death's path. You knew this before. It is what you said you wanted. Don't you remember?"

"Yes, I know, but you said I could choose a different path. I don't understand how I can, but I don't want to die or go on with my dying right now. If I can live, I might do it better this time."

"That path will get harder before it gets easier, Marina. Come with me now and I will show you worlds you cannot imagine." The Turtle Woman floated closer to her.

Marina looked at her own body. She was not a little girl anymore.

She had her body back. She had the body that had jumped overboard, determined to die.

The Turtle Woman pressed against her, wrapping her arms around Marina. She closed her eyes. She expected soft flesh but what she felt was hard and firm. When she opened her eyes the Turtle Woman was gone and Rafael held her once again. He pressed his mouth to hers, probing her lips with his tongue. She wanted to let him inside her, opening herself in every possible way, but something inside her resisted.

He pressed harder, squeezing her tighter and tighter. A battle raged within her. Her lungs ached.

She parted her lips lightly against the phantom Rafael's press and tasted water. She inhaled in spite of herself and choked. Water filled her nose and mouth and burned her. She was drowning. She recalled the sensation. When she had drowned before it had hurt, but she had also been resigned to it. The experience had been passive and oddly dream-like. Now she struggled against it.

Rafael—or was it the Turtle Woman?—held her firmly the way a mother might hold a struggling child or the way a lover might hold a partner who was saying no but meant something altogether different. She was no longer certain who it was, but she was in no mood to be cradled and supported into oblivion. She pushed and kicked against the figure that held her. She broke its grasp and pushed it from her.

The hazy figure once again coalesced into the form of the Turtle Woman. "Go, then." The Turtle Woman gestured up, but up seemed as dark as down, and Marina did not know whether to trust this direction. Her ability to think clearly was failing. She felt desperate but also tired, as if she might drift off to sleep.

She kicked up. She seemed to rise fast. She looked up, trying to see light. The pool could not be this deep, she thought. The water seemed to shimmer around her and grow a little brighter, as if she were swimming in a shaft of light. Moonlight. She realized she was swimming in the shaft of moonlight that had penetrated the pool. It seemed to be drawing her up, pulling her toward the source. She felt embraced in a different way. The light overhead grew brighter and brighter until there was nothing but light, then nothing.

When she woke she was once again on the smooth, cool stones beside the pool. Her jacket and hair were not wet, not even damp.

Atana sat where Marina remembered she had been, solid and unmoving, like an onyx statue, her eyes half-closed.

The moon had gone, passing beyond the circle of trees, and the night sky seemed to be coloring with the first light of morning.

"So, what will you do?" Atana asked.

Marina sat up slowly. "I want to go on. I don't know what that means completely, but I think it's what I need to do."

"You have found what you lost, then?"

Marina thought about this. Yes, she felt somehow as though she was more complete, more whole. There was a little girl in her that could still be awed and amazed by beauty—connected to every living thing. There was a mother, nurturing and caring, a balancing force. There was a lover, present and attentive, inside of her—someone who could live in the moment—a woman who could fully accept her erotic power.

"Yes," Marina answered. "I have found some things I thought I'd lost forever. And there's more. I think . . . no, I know I'm ready to live again. I think I could do it better now."

Atana said nothing, and after a moment Marina continued. "That is what this is all about, right? That I might have a second chance?"

"And what do you think would happen if you returned to the life you had been leading?"

Again Marina thought a moment before trying to answer. "I'm not sure what you mean. I suppose I would try to live a better life."

"And had you been living a bad life?"

"No," Marina explained, "My life has not been bad. It's been very rich, actually, but I've been living it badly. I lost touch with things, lost parts of myself, like you said. But now I feel as though I have them back."

"And can you keep them?"

"Keep them?"

"Can you keep these souls you have recovered?"

"All I can do is try."

"And how will you try?"

"I'm sorry, I don't understand what you want me to say. Isn't it enough that I've recovered my lost souls and that I'm aware of them within me?"

"There is something you still need to learn, child. It's the real reason you are with us here. This is Turtle Island, the island of sanctuary. You are here not just because you were in need of sanctuary. Sanctuary was ever-present around you. No, you came to us because you couldn't find sanctuary in your life. You couldn't define it or create it, so you had no respite, no relief. Your souls scattered because you offered them no safe place. If you do not learn how to make sanctuary in your life, you will not long keep them."

"I've been to sanctuaries. I've been to retreats. I've been on pilgrimages, but none of that seemed to help me much." Marina's head was spinning. Here was a person who seemed able and willing to answer her questions. She had so many questions.

"Sanctuary is different things to different people. First you must come to sense the sanctuary in places. This is sanctuary." Atana spread her arms and gestured to the pool and the circular grove of trees. "But it is only a reflection of this sanctuary." Atana touched her own chest lightly.

She was silent a moment, then, as if dissatisfied with her own explanation, she continued. "No, that is not entirely true. When a place of some subtle energy comes to reflect sanctuary for many people over time, it becomes a sanctuary of great protective and healing power. The mirror pool has reflected souls for many of the lost and wandering. It is a powerful place in its own right.

"Not everyone who crosses Turtle Island comes to the mirror pool. You needed to see yourself more clearly so you found it. Do you know what you have learned since coming to Turtle Island?"

Marina thought about the question for a long while. She looked at the anklet the Turtle Woman had tied upon her. The word "balance" came to her mind. "The Turtle Woman spoke to me of balance. When I was first here, I couldn't move. I couldn't feel anything. I suppose it was like my life before. I couldn't really feel anything when I was alive, either." Another correlation crossed Marina's mind and it excited her. "I couldn't move myself out of my depression, either. I couldn't move and I couldn't feel when I was alive and that's what I experienced after I died. Why did I think it would be different?" Marina asked the question without actually expecting an answer, and Atana offered none.

"She said I needed to find balance, to find light to equal my darkness. Basic rules of exposure." Marina said this last sentence more to herself than to Atana—speaking in the language of photographers.

"And what else?"

"Rafael," Marina said softly. "I was to learn something from Rafael, wasn't I?"

"There is purpose in every experience—both here and in your world. Your task is to understand that purpose."

"Was Rafael real, then?"

"As real as you or me."

"But was he like me? You said I was one of the lost and wandering. Was he lost and wandering too?"

"He exists apart from your needs. He is on his own path. You will meet others like him if you go on."

"What will become of him?"

"I don't know. That is up to him."

"Did I cause him pain? Did I interrupt his search?"

"I think you know the answer to that."

Marina searched inside herself. An answer came to her but she wasn't sure she trusted it. "I was as much a part of his journey as he was a part of mine, right?" Atana nodded. "But he helped me understand something incredible about my own senses, about living in my body, living in the moment. What could I have taught him?"

"What did he do for you?"

Marina smiled and her left hand went absentmindedly to the stone talisman about her neck. She considered telling this woman about the sensations she'd experienced, but something more important, more relevant popped into her mind. "He sacrificed his own progress to help me move on."

Again Atana nodded, clearly pleased in Marina's answer. "And don't you think it was valuable for Rafael to know that he could act this self-lessly? You brought him this opportunity."

"Will I see him again?" She wasn't sure why she asked this, but she'd said it before she could stop herself.

"Here," Atana gestured around her, "who knows. But in some life it will be hard to avoid him."

"What do you mean?"

"You ask so many questions. I cannot answer them all now. You must make your own way forward or go back now."

"I want to go forward. Whatever I have to learn, I want to learn."

"Then go now and see if you can learn the art of sanctuary." Atana stood up in a slow, graceful motion like a flower unfolding and offered Marina her hand.

Marina took it and allowed herself to be pulled to her feet. She stood a head taller than the old woman, but somehow felt small in the woman's presence.

Atana led Marina around the stone pool. At the far side of the stone face with the cave entrance in it, a path led between the trees. Marina had not noticed it before and it seemed almost as if it had opened up at Atana's request.

At the foot of the path, just where stone met packed earth and twisted roots, a bundle lay waiting. Atana picked it up and handed it to Marina. She inspected it and found some sort of waterskin in a pouch with a long strap. There was also some bread and dried fruit wrapped in large leaves.

Marina thanked her and slung the pouch over her shoulder. She looked up the path between the trees. Daylight was filtering slowly through the dense canopy. She looked back at Atana.

The old woman took a few steps to the pool and knelt beside it. She dipped her hand and arm into the water holding the sleeve of her robe out of the way with her other hand. She did not reach down far before grasping something and removing her hand from the water. Marina could not imagine that the bottom of the pool might be that shallow. She was sure it must extend far below the level of the ground.

Water dripped from her fist as she extended her hand to Marina and opened it. A smooth flat pebble shined like black glass in her palm. Marina picked it up and marveled at it.

"It is a little piece of the mirror pool. Take it with you to remember the souls you carry within."

Marina looked at her own reflection in the black stone. She could see herself in surprising detail. The first thing she noticed was the turtle tattoo. It was now crossing her face. It marked her high on a prominent cheekbone and made her look almost feral. It was a tribal mark, wild and significant, but it was also much fainter than she had recalled. She turned to Atana and started to ask.

"Yes, child, you have little time left. When the turtle's mark fades you will be without compass. You will be as lost as you ever were. Go now, and I will dream for you."

Marina took the old woman's hand and bent to kiss it. She pressed her lips against the back of the woman's still-damp fingers and tasted the strange silvery flavor of the water. She turned then and started up the path.

She had not gone far before she was out of the grove of tall ancient trees. When she looked back she could see no clear path back into the grove, only a path forward.

She realized the stone was warm in her hand and she stopped to look at it.

She saw her own reflection, but then that grew cloudy. Out of a mist that seemed to fog the stone from the inside, a moving figure materialized. It was the Turtle Woman, young and beautiful, her wild hair floating about her. She blinked languidly and smiled. Marina was both attracted and repulsed. This was the same woman or spirit who had helped her, who had encouraged Marina to make this journey. Now she seemed to be calling Marina back.

Marina shoved the stone into the shoulder pouch she carried and walked on hurriedly. The path ahead was clearly marked. It led up through an open forest. Each time she looked back, what had seemed like a well-defined trail ahead of her appeared in retrospect a random selection of turns.

She wondered how she could know if she was truly going in the right direction. Was she moving backward or forward? The Turtle Woman had said something about Marina's finding her nightsong irresistible. Was she moving toward life or back to the death she had so willingly sought?

She was, for the first time, frightened. She was frightened of the attraction she felt for returning to death's embrace. She was frightened that what she had learned, what she had recovered, would not be enough to see her through.

She was no longer dispassionate about the journey she was making. Until that moment she'd taken what she'd found with little desire to choose one course over another. Now life called her and she wanted to answer.

CHAPTER 5

A Quality of Light

While some argue that it's the stars that steer sea turtles on their great migra-tions, others pledge allegiance to the sun. Would the warmth on my back be enough to guide me? Breaking the surface every thirty minutes for sunlight and air, could I find my way? We know our way by time as much as by compass now. There are great stone turtles half buried in jungles where time is reckoned differently. These turtles carry sundials carved into their backs, though the sun no longer penetrates the green canopy to cast the telling shadows.

Marina walked on.

She climbed steadily during the morning, crested a ridge around noon, and walked on fairly level terrain into the afternoon. She stopped to rest several times, drinking water from her pouch and eating the dried fruit.

Late in the day she began to notice a change in the trees around her. They seemed to open up. The trees themselves were taller and the trunks wider. There were fewer trees and more sunlight filtered down to the forest floor. It didn't look like island ecology. It reminded her more of the redwood forests of northern California or the old growth stands of timber she had hiked in as a girl.

The trees were majestic and the plants on the forest floor seemed almost arranged, like a Japanese Zen garden. Ferns and delicate lacy plants with tiny white blossoms dotted the ground. Purple and blue flowering shrubs colonized little ponds of sunlight. Stones thrust up from the ground, almost artful in their randomness.

There was something odd about the trees as well. Some of the smaller, younger trees seemed to have twin trunks that grew together. Even some of the taller trees seemed to have once had two distinct trunks. Though fused together now, she could still see where they had been joined. She also began to notice that some of the younger trees had trunks that bulged voluptuously in places, as though the bark had grown over human forms. With a little imagination she could see the whole forest as alive with dancing giants. Perhaps they had been frozen into the shape of trees by the spell of an evil sorcerer, or perhaps it was her own presence that caused them to disguise themselves.

But as strange as the shape of the trees might have been, Marina was even more fascinated by the light. To an untrained eye, the sunlight cascading down through the trees would have been spectacular, but to Marina it was almost unbelievable. It was golden and green, sepia and olive-tinted. Some shafts seemed almost red-orange, as if they had shone through a shard of stained glass lodged somewhere high up in the trees. She knew she was seeing not just the color of the light but the colors the light illuminated. All of that and something more.

She wished she had a camera with her, and this thought surprised her. She had not felt the desire to photograph so strongly in years. Of late, she had come to spend most of her professional time getting to a place. Her cameras went with her, and, when she arrived at the confluence of some moment and some event, she photographed it. She never thought about whether she wanted to photograph it or needed to photograph it. She seldom thought about photography at all. It was a job for her, perhaps an obsession, but no longer a passion.

I could be passionate about this, she said to herself as she studied the light.

She wandered, forgetting about a path, looking up, looking around.

She had once loved life, loved beautiful things. As an adolescent, she had tried to make beautiful pictures with her camera. She studied Ansel Adams, Edward Weston, Andre Kertész, Imogen Cunningham. She looked at the way they used light in their images. It was a palpable thing, this light. She could feel it, harness it, work with it in her own photographs.

Her early work was so beautiful that some editors refused to run it. It looked staged, set-up, they told her. No one could get that lucky, so consistently. But fellow photographers came to Marina's defense. She wasn't lucky, they told their editors. She was more patient, more sensitive, more skilled at taking advantage of the play of light. Journalists and photographers who traveled with her were amazed at her uncanny gift for knowing how the light would fall on a subject and when the trajectory of subject and light would intersect.

It was a delicate gift. While she honored it, it served her well. But once she squandered it with angry work, work meant to prove a point, it abandoned her. After Baghdad she gradually lost her ability to sense the movement, the weight, the very presence of the light. When it showed up in her images, it truly was luck.

Now, here, in this place, she could feel the light again. It was like a force, like a warm presence. She stood in a little puddle of light and stretched her arms up the shaft. She felt like Danaë, locked in her father's high tower, visited by her lover, Zeus, in the form of a shower of gold.

"You can really feel it, can't you?" a man's voice asked.

"Yes." She answered the question before registering that it had come from another person and not just her own thoughts. When it occurred to her that someone else had actually spoken, she snapped her arms down to her side and looked around. At first she saw nothing.

"Here," the voice spoke again and this time Marina followed it to its owner. A man sat cross-legged beneath the low-hanging branches of a huge tree. "I'm sorry. I didn't mean to startle you."

Somehow, once Marina realized that the man must have been sitting there before she arrived, and that she was the one who had wandered into his space, she relaxed. She wasn't certain what the protocol for territory was on Turtle Island, but she had yet to meet anyone who had intended her harm. Still, she was cautious.

The man seemed to sense this and made no move to approach Marina. "I'm Téves," he said. This helped Marina little, but it seemed meant as a friendly gesture.

"My name's Marina." She didn't say Marina Hardt, but she was suddenly aware that she had remembered her last name. She wasn't sure when it happened. When she first woke on Turtle Island she could not remember her last name, now she could. It had just come back to her.

"Welcome to Adytum Wood." He still made no effort to rise but spread his arms to gesture to the grove around him and made a little bow. Marina moved closer, self-consciously adjusting her jacket as she went. The little belted jacket was still all she wore and, while it covered her upper body, breaking just below the tops of her thighs, she tended to get careless about how she wore it and sometimes it revealed more than she was conscious of. This hadn't mattered when she was with Rafael, or Atana for that matter, but now it did seem to make a difference to her. It was as if she was regaining some sense of propriety as she traveled across the island.

"You're not sure why you're here are you?" he asked.

Marina observed Téves carefully. He looked to be in his early sixties. He seemed a rather round and bearlike man. He had wild gray hair and a short gray beard. He was dressed in a rough brown shirt that had long sleeves and only one button up near the collar. It fit him loosely, more like a tunic than a shirt. He wore dark green trousers that were baggy and loose as well. He was barefoot, but she noticed leather sandals set neatly beside him.

"Excuse me?"

"I'm sorry," he added, "all of this can be confusing. Do you know why you're here?"

Marina was not sure what question Téves was asking.

"Do you mean why I'm here?" She opened her arms to embrace the space around her. "Or why I'm *here*?" She put special emphasis on the word here and pointed to her feet. She was repeating the same semantic conundrum she had stumbled upon when answering Atana's questions.

Téves laughed, and it was a big laugh, hearty and reassuring. "Come, share some food with me. I'll give you a place to sleep and you'll give an old man some conversation. Maybe we'll find out why you have come to Adytum Wood."

She had been walking all day and she was tired. She hadn't thought about what she would do when night came. Somehow, she'd always been provided for. She just assumed she'd find food and shelter as she needed it, and here it was being provided for her again.

"Thank you," she said as she watched Téves stand up and slip his feet into his sandals. A gnarled wood staff leaned against the tree trunk behind him and he took it up. He did not appear to need the staff. He seemed healthy and vigorous. There was life in his step and he strode purposefully. Marina had to walk quickly just to keep up.

They didn't walk far. Téves often turned around and walked backward so that he could look at her and point out plants along the way. At first this made Marina nervous. She was sure he would trip over exposed roots, rocks, or downed branches, but he'd been looking at it. Sometimes he'd stop and lay his hand upon a tree. Then he would lean close to the trunk and whisper something. Sometimes he would appear to have heard an answer, and sometimes Marina thought he was actually conversing with the tree. Other times he would reach out and caress a tree trunk in passing.

It was perhaps because she was looking down at some flower or shrub that Téves had drawn her attention to that Marina did not notice the three great trees until she was right upon them.

"Well, here's home," Téves said gesturing to the trees.

The trees were huge, like redwoods she had seen. They were so big that she had to step back just to take them in. When she looked up into the tree closest to her, she almost lost her balance trying to find its top. Something coiled around the trunk like the pattern on a barber's pole for as far up as she could see. She had to follow the pattern back down the trunk to realize that it was a ramshackle circular staircase made of wood and heavy vines, tied in place with rope.

"Don't worry," Téves said, touching her shoulder gently, guiding her toward the stairs without pushing her. "If it'll hold me, it'll hold you."

Before she knew it, Marina was climbing. She wasn't normally afraid of heights—she had dangled from many precarious perches to get just the right angle for a photograph—but this climb made her dizzy. The steps seemed sturdy enough, but the whole staircase slipped and shimmied against the trunk every time they moved. She tried not to look down, but looking up was equally disturbing. They seemed to be climbing toward a shadowy platform that was suspended on several thick branches between the three trees, but for most of the climb she concentrated on where she would place her foot next.

When they reached the platform Marina was breathing heavily and perspiring from the climb, but Téves seemed undisturbed. He led her onto the platform and to her relief she found it much sturdier than the stairs had been. The platform was a triangle of rough-cut logs tied together like an oddly shaped raft. There was a heavy railing that ran around all three sides and a triangular hut sat back against two of the edges.

The hut had a simple door and small windows shuttered with twig panels. The roof was thatched. Two low stick chairs with sloping backs sat on the widest side of the platform in front of the door. A black iron brazier sat on a tripod of iron legs to the side of the door next to a pile of fatwood, twigs, and small cut logs.

"Come," Téves gestured as he opened the door to the hut.

It was bigger inside than Marina would have guessed. There was a wooden bunk with a rough mattress and wool blanket. There were several wood hutches and cabinets, a counter space that seemed to be reserved for preparing food, and a workbench. On one wall hung an assortment of handmade saws, axes, and other tools she didn't recognize. Aside from the tools, there were few personal possessions in evidence. In the center of the room were a rough triangular table and two chairs.

"Sit and rest. I'll make us something to eat."

Marina set her shoulder bag down against the wall and sat in one of the chairs. "Did you build all of this yourself?"

Téves stood preparing food with his back to her. He took a long time to answer and Marina was about to ask the question again.

"It was here when I came, but I suppose I've rebuilt it twice since I've been here. It seems like such a short time, but then I'm most used to the time of trees. Even a full life is a breath to some of these trees."

He turned and set two wooden plates and two wooden cups down on the table. The plates had fresh fruit, bread, and a salad of mixed greens. He poured a pale golden wine from a clay carafe and sat down opposite her. He bent his head for a moment, murmuring a quiet prayer.

She had not grown up with prayer before meals but always had the odd suspicion that she should pray. It made her vaguely uncomfortable when other people did it. She often found herself bowing her head as well, though she had no clear notion to what or to whom she was praying.

They ate in silence, and though Marina had questions for Téves she appreciated the chance to taste the food. It was a simple meal. The bread was crusty and textured with nuts and seeds. The greens had a slight bitter taste offset by a fruit vinaigrette. The fruit itself included sliced apples, pears, figs, and a small red fruit she couldn't identify. The wine was sweet and tasted of honey and the nectar of summer clover. While the sensation of eating and tasting was not as intense as it had been with Rafael, she was glad to see that she could still really experience the tasting of things.

After they finished, Téves cleared their plates, brushing the few scraps into a clay pot. He poured them each another cup of the sweet wine and led Marina to the low chairs on the wide edge of the deck. The sun was fading fast, and with it, the day's warmth. Téves placed the blackened brazier between the chairs down by their feet and started a small fire.

"Now I've fed you, lit a fire for you, and given you a roof for the night. You owe me a story," Téves said as he settled into his chair. He slipped his sandals off and extended his feet toward the fire.

"A story?"

"Your story. Tell me how you came to my woods. I'm always interested in the stories of travelers."

Marina hardly knew where to begin. How far back should I go? she wondered. Does he know that I'm dead? How would I explain that? Am I still dead? All of these things ran through her mind, but she found herself beginning the tale anyway. "I came here on the back of a sea turtle. . . ."

Téves listened intently as she told her story. Sometimes he interrupted her to ask her a name or to have her retell a part of the story, but he never questioned her version of what happened or how. Even the parts of her story that seemed, now, as she retold it, most improbable, he accepted as absolute fact.

She told the story in great detail and, when she finally completed it, ending with her meeting Téves, she found that the sky was black and the only light came from the brazier. She had a blanket over her legs, though she couldn't recall either of them fetching it, and yet another full cup of the honey wine.

She was sleepy and perhaps a little intoxicated. She could not remember how many cups of wine she had drunk.

"So how about you? Where do you come from? What's your story?" Marina was not slurring her words, but it seemed an effort to get them out.

"Me, I've always been here. At least it seems like that. I took my vows here when I was a boy."

"What do you mean, your vows?"

"My Greening vows. Do you not know of the Greening?"

"Are you a priest, then? Is it a religious order?"

"Ahh, I see you come from one of the times when the Brothers and Sisters of the Greening kept their order a secret."

"Perhaps there is no Greening where I come from." As she said this, she wished she had put it more gently. She had no idea of whether he would be offended or not, or even whether he could handle the idea that his religious order was not universal. He seemed unshaken, however.

"No, the Greening is everywhere. In some places the order is secret. In some times the order exists as a heartfelt belief with no organization, no code, no Landbond, but it is always there."

"What is the Greening, then? Who do you worship?"

"Worship?" Téves seemed perplexed by this question. "We worship nothing . . . and everything . . . all of this." He gestured to the trees around him. "We keep the Landbond. We tend the sacred trees, the rivers, the mountains, the seas."

"I don't understand. How do you tend them?"

Téves began again as he might have spoken to a child. "When I was very young, my family saw the gift in me—that I could feel the living places. Now I believe this is not so much a gift. Most children are born with this sense. We can only lose it. Well, it was strong with me so my parents let me study the Greening."

"I'm sorry," Marina interrupted. "What's the Greening?"

"The Greening is a path, a way of seeing the interconnectedness of all things. It teaches that the air, the water, the stones, the soil, and especially the plants and animals are part of us. They are vessels for universal spirit. Resting places for when we are between lives.

"So I studied the Greening and decided to take my vows. As a young man I traveled to many places before coming to Adytum Wood. The caretaker before me was old then and ready to pass on. This was my special place. It called to me, so I made my Landbond here."

"And what is a Landbond?"

"The Landbond is a vow and a relationship. I am the guardian of this place, but I do not own it. I may take nothing more than sustenance from it. I may marry, and I may have children, but my children have no claim to this place. I have my duties, my sacred tasks. I help others pass on and I speak for the land. That is the Landbond."

"Does someone own this land, then? I mean, what if someone wanted to cut these trees down and sell them?"

"That is what the Landbond is for. It is a relationship. At present Adytum Wood is owned by no one, but it has been owned by people in the past. It may come to be owned in the future. The Landbond says that a person may own land and take a livelihood from it, but any alterations to the land must be negotiated between the caretaker, a Brother or Sister of the Greening, and the owner. In this way the land has a voice."

"That's more like a story, a fairy tale, than anything I know of the real world. It's too beautiful. But, I wish it were so where I come from." Marina was gazing up at the stars that peeked through the canopy of trees. Her eyelids were getting heavy and she knew she would sleep soon.

"But it is so where you come from." Téves's voice sounded far off. "You may not have the Landbond, but the Greening is alive. There are those who can feel the pulse points of the earth, the sacred energy. They are the living seed of the Greening."

Marina closed her eyes. Half in dream already, she imagined people as radiant seeds, seeds in her hands, glowing seeds tossed from the treehouse platform, falling away like fireflies in the night, landing softly, sprouting fast, rising up, strong vines shooting past her, wrapping around her, carrying her off the platform, lifting her up past the canopy, into the night sky, surrounded by more radiant seeds and stars.

★ ★ ★

She woke in the morning to light coming through one of the windows. She was on the mattress in the bunk inside the hut. The blanket was pulled over her and she was warm, but she couldn't remember getting herself to the bunk and was suddenly embarrassed at the idea that she had needed to be helped. She also wondered where Téves had slept. He was not in the hut and she could hear no movement outside.

Slowly, she stretched and slid her legs over the side of the bunk. She stood up and folded the blanket neatly over the mattress. There was water in a pitcher on the table and a clean wooden cup. She drank some of the water and wandered out onto the platform.

It was frightening and exhilarating to be so high up. The three trees to which the platform was attached were each so large that half a dozen people with arms outstretched still couldn't encircle the smallest of them. Though the platform on which she was standing was already high up, these three trees seemed to continue up so far that she could not tell where they ended.

She walked over and put her hand against one of the trees. She felt a pull, a kind of tingling in her palm and she drew back. She pressed her hand against the rough bark. Again and again she felt the odd sensation of something pressing back. She crossed the deck to the second of the trees that supported the front side of the platform. She pressed both hands lightly against the trunk.

At first she felt nothing. This is silly, she thought to herself, and started to pull her hands away. She felt the tremor coming from a long way off. It seemed to begin at the root of the great tree and ripple up the trunk. Leaves and branches vibrated. Birds flew up in alarm and squirrel-like creatures flung themselves to other nearby trees.

She could not have removed her hands now if she had wanted to. The whole platform began to shift back and forth. It was inconceivable that something so huge could actually sway, but that was what the three trees were doing. It was frightening but also exhilarating to be riding such a powerful force. She held on.

After a few moments the tremor seemed to recede. It rolled lazily back down the tree and into the ground. As Marina disengaged her hands from the tree, she shuddered, expressing a deep involuntary tremor of her own.

Shaken, but not afraid, Marina started down the twisting spiral staircase to the ground. She didn't so much want to get away from the trees as she wanted to tell Téves what had happened, or ask him about what she had experienced. From the platform she had not been able to see him below, but as she got closer to the ground she could make him out. He was methodically stacking cut circles of wood into little pyramid piles.

"Did you feel that?" Marina called down as she got within range. She was flying down the steps now. Whether it was the difference between going up and coming down, she wasn't sure, but she seemed to have lost her uneasiness over the way the steps bounced and swayed against the tree. "The trees, I mean. Did you feel the trees shake?"

"Having a conversation with old Jeremiah, were you?" Téves seemed to have completed his stacking task and was taking a long draft of water when she finally reached him.

"No, it was the tree. I put my hands on the tree," she gestured to the large second tree, "and it started to shake. I thought the whole platform would come down."

"I doubt that Jeremiah would have let that happen. Anyway, you should consider yourself lucky. Jeremiah doesn't speak to just anyone. . . ."

"Who's Jeremiah?" Marina interrupted. "Do you mean the tree?"

"Of course, Jeremiah is one of the old ones. He was caretaker here long, long ago."

"The tree?"

"The tree holds his spirit now. That's what you felt. You did feel something when you touched the trees, didn't you?"

Marina didn't know what to make of this. She wondered if the old man was crazy. "Well, yes. When I touched the first tree—"

"Sybil," Téves interrupted to supply the name.

"When I touched the first tree," she began again; she was not yet prepared to use the name Téves had supplied, "I felt a kind of tingling or vibration in my hand. But when I touched the other tree it seemed to come alive."

"They are alive. They're all alive. Most people forget how to listen though. They forget how to talk to trees and stones. "

"I'm not sure I spoke to anything. I just put my hands on the tree."

"Ahh, but you listened, you see. You had an open heart when you touched the tree, so you could hear it. There is nothing more flattering than having someone who truly listens to you."

"But I don't know what I heard. I don't know what was said to me."

"From Sybil, I would say you got a simple greeting, an acknowledgment of life energy. Sybil is a bit shy and takes time to open up. Jeremiah on the other hand is much more verbose. He's like a living library. There's little that he can't comment upon."

Marina had to laugh. "I'm sorry. This is just too much for me. I've seen a lot since I've been here, but I'm not sure I can believe in talking trees."

Téves was not angry or perturbed. He only smiled and said, "Come, walk with me. Perhaps I can explain better." He shouldered a long saw and tucked his hand ax through his belt. He also pulled a knapsack over one shoulder. He began walking and Marina followed.

They walked through the morning forest for about an hour. Marina saw more of the strange trees with twin trunks. She also saw more of the beautiful sunlight filtering down through the trees. They were not following any path she could see, but Téves seemed to know his way.

Every so often he would stop and have her put her hands on different trees. Sometimes they were young trees with smooth bark, sometimes they were older, with rough scaly bark. Sometimes he'd have her touch one of the great old trees like the giants in which he'd made his home. He told her to keep her heart open as it had been when she touched the trees before.

She wasn't sure how to do this, but she did try to empty her mind. She practiced breathing the way the Turtle Woman had taught her—deep and slow from her belly. And she did feel something.

The more trees she touched, the more convinced she became that the something she experienced was real. The young trees seemed to hum and buzz. The sensation she drew was that of oscillation, like a wave pattern. The older trees were sometimes silent or vibrated with a steady low-pitched rumble that reminded her, for some reason, of snoring.

The giants were always unique. Some were quiet, some were loud, but all expressed themselves with distinct patterns of energy. Téves asked her what she felt at each tree, but refused to confirm or explain any of Marina's experiences.

Sometimes he would stop and ask her to simply describe what she saw. Though he didn't ask her to do this, Marina understood, that in some way, she was really to describe what she felt. She always began with the light. The light was the first thing she experienced each time he asked her to describe something. She also began to notice different things about the light.

As a photographer, it had been her business and her passion to understand light. She knew how to capture and record light as well as anyone she knew, but now it seemed to her that light was so much more. It seemed to be telling her things—suggesting more than just superficial patterns painted on the landscape. She could see the light now, not as simply casting patterns in shadow and light, but as illuminating underlying patterns, fundamental distributions of energy. It was as if the light was not just giving her clues to what might be, but was mapping the structure of the only thing that was truly essential.

Again Téves said little as she tried to put these new discoveries into words. He just smiled or nodded his head, answering each of her questions with another request for her to touch some tree or describe some space. She began to wonder as she walked behind him if she could capture this new understanding of light on film. She felt this was more than just an imagined perception, but she wondered if she could render or manifest it. She also realized that she was thinking about things she might do if she were still alive or could be alive again somehow.

She caught herself wanting it.

Téves had moved ahead of her in her reverie and when she caught up with him he was kneeling before a fallen tree. The tree was old and decayed. None of its branches bore green leaves. It looked as if it had toppled over in a storm some weeks past. Téves had both hands on the tree and seemed to be whispering to it. Marina stood back. Some instinct for ritual kept her from questioning Téves.

He turned and gestured to her to join him. She knelt next to him and placed her hands on the fallen tree. At first she felt nothing. Then the faintest hint of what she had come to expect from touching the trees with her heart open like this washed over her. It was soft and faint, like the echo of a song just before it fades away.

"This is Carolis," Téves said quietly. "She's been here since the time before I was caretaker. She was a singer of bright songs, a mother to four daughters, and the great love of two men."

"Do you mean that this tree stands for her?" Marina was struggling to make sense of what Téves was saying. She knew from her own touch that somehow everything he said was true, but her logical mind could not grasp it. "Is it a symbol? I mean, was it planted in her honor?"

"No. This is Carolis. She came through these woods once just as you have. She was lost, hungry, looking for a place to rest. She chose to stay."

Marina stood up and backed away from the tree. She stepped backward a few more paces, then turned and walked a little ways into the woods. She looked around at the strange trees and for the first time saw them for what they were—bodies frozen and modeled of wood. It was true that they had reminded her of human forms when she first saw them, but she'd thought then that it was only her imagination playing with her. It had been a game to see them as people, like seeing dragons in clouds. Now she saw them as actual bodies grown to wood.

They were rooted in the ground with arms outstretched in a tangle of what must have once been fingers. On some she saw curving breasts and flaring hips, on others she saw broad strong legs and barrel chests. Legs sometimes grew together, fusing into one trunk. New branches sprouted higher up on the older trees, and on some she could almost see faces hidden by the heavy cowl of enfolding bark. Some seemed to watch her. She was certain that if she turned at just the right moment, she might see an eye blink or a mouth form a soundless word.

It was at once beautiful and terrifying. She knew there was incredible peace here. These spirits were not trapped or bound by the trees around them. They were living urns, vessels for the spirits that had come here to rest. She also knew this was not the place or time for her spirit. *Does Téves have the power to lock me to the ground, to make a tree of my lost and wandering spirit?*

"You needn't fear me. All are free to choose here. Come or go as you wish." Téves had slipped up behind her but kept a respectful distance so as not to frighten her. "Every spirit in Adytum Wood has chosen to rest here. It is not a prison."

"I'm sorry. It's beautiful, really. It's just not for me."

"Of course not, you are Marina—of the sea. When your spirit is ready to rest it will find water."

Many things flashed through Marina's mind at once. Her name did mean "of the sea." She'd chosen for her spirit to rest in the sea. She hadn't thought about it consciously at the time, but suicide by drowning, especially in the vast deep ocean, was the only way of taking her life that felt even remotely right to her. She also thought about her spirit coming to rest, and she knew she had crossed some threshold. Her spirit was not ready to rest. She had things she still needed to do, wanted to do. If she could go back to the world of the living, she wanted to.

"I'm sorry." She said it again for no other reason than that she couldn't think of what else to say. She had not meant to insult Téves or his beliefs. He seemed a caring and gentle soul. "I—"

"Come," he interrupted, "help me find the heartwood." He held out his hand and she took it. He led her back to the fallen tree and placed her hands on the trunk. "Move your hands along the trunk and tell me where her heart is."

Without really knowing what she was feeling for, Marina opened her heart and listened. In some places the faint song she had heard was stronger. She went back and forth several times until she had isolated a single section where the tingle and vibration was strongest. "Here," she said.

Téves nodded and smiled at her. He picked up his long saw and cut into the tree. It took time, but his saw was sharp and eventually he cut through the trunk. It creaked and fell apart just a little, and Téves began sawing again, cutting a four-inch thick slab of wood from the tree. This he rolled out and laid on the ground.

"See," he gestured to the slab and Marina approached. She could see a dark blue shadow in the center of the tree. "This is all that's left of her. Her spirit's shrunk back, condensed, ready for new life." he turned the slab slightly and all at once the blue shadow became a recognizable form. It looked like the silhouette of a woman's body wrapped in a long blue gown.

"What will you do with it?"

"Set it free." Téves slipped the heavy slab into his knapsack and shouldered it. "It is part of my duty here, part of my vows."

They walked back in silence. Marina was surprised to see that the sun was beginning to set. The day had not seemed long. Téves had once again moved out ahead of her. Even with his heavy pack and tools, he moved with grace and speed through the forest.

Marina found herself preoccupied with thoughts of living again. Up to now living again had seemed an abstract possibility. Now she began to make it concrete. There were things she wanted to share with people. There was work she wanted to do. She owed her family more than she'd once thought. She had reasons to be alive.

Alive.

The woods around her were alive.

She had stopped walking without realizing it. She was standing in a little open space between some of the biggest and oldest trees she had seen all day. Light fell around her, almost palpable. If the rainbow light of spinning crystals could become almost solid, she thought, like snowflakes that might melt before hitting the ground, that would come close to what this light is like.

She was intensely aware of the energy around her. She was not touching anything, but it came up through the soles of her bare feet. It misted and danced about her with the light. She could smell it and taste it. It sang to her like silvery wind chimes and breathy flutes. She crumpled to the ground and wept.

It was some time before she realized that Téves was cradling her. He held her like a little baby and rocked her in his arms. She felt drained from her crying, weak and tired. Too tired to even apologize.

"It's all right," he said softly. "You are so open now that the energy can overwhelm you. This is a sacred place even within a sacred place."

"Is that what I feel here? Energy?"

"It's one of the pulse points. There is energy all around us, but in some places that energy is concentrated through time, or will, or intention. These places can recharge us if we know how to find them."

"I don't feel recharged. I feel drained."

"When you step into the flow, it cleanses you. It pulls away the undergrowth that's sapping your strength. The first time that happens it can be disorienting. Stay here awhile longer, then come to me. Jeremiah and Sybil are not far away. Listen for them and you'll find your way."

With that Téves gently untangled himself and stood up. Marina straightened her jacket and drew her legs up in a cross-legged posture. She watched Téves walk off until he disappeared. Then she stilled her breathing as the Turtle Woman had taught her and waited. There was something about this experience that called to her. She was learning something important, something she had to learn. Atana had said something about sanctuary. She had to learn about sanctuary. She had thought sanctuary meant some church or temple, some religious or spiritual monument. But wasn't this simple grove a kind of sanctuary?

She thought about what she knew of sanctuary. Monasteries had once provided sanctuary against the concerns of daily life. Churches offered sanctuary against the abuse of temporal power. The Sanctuary Movement among certain progressive churches in North America had provided safe haven for refugees of political violence and instability. But sanctuary seemed to have a deeper, even more relevant meaning. It was more than just a place of physical safety. It was a place to rest, to heal, to renew and recharge.

We are not meant to live in sanctuary, she thought, but we don't seem to be designed to live without it. We need places that revitalize us. If we can't find energetically rich and active places with our own senses, we must trust to tradition. Perhaps this is why so many people make pilgrimages to holy sites. Her mind was racing now. It seems like the more chaos and upheaval is in our lives, the more frequent our need for sanctuary. This need can't be met by the traditional sanctuaries. They are too few and too far between. We need new senses. We need to find the little . . . what was it Téves had called them? Pulse points? Places like this. Places where . . .

Marina felt a new kind of energy rising up within her. She felt it between her thighs, deep within her belly, passing through her solar plexus, into her heart like an arrow of light, up through her throat, tingling at her forehead and erupting from the crown of her head. It lifted her up and she was standing. Then she was spinning, dancing, and spinning again like a Sufi dervish, caressing trees as she passed them, taking and giving energy with each step. The child in her laughed out loud and sang a song she did not know that she remembered.

All at once she was at the foot of the great tree Téves had called Sybil, the staircase tree. She was out of breath, but she turned and bowed formally to the trees around her. "Thank you. Thank you." She bowed again, blowing kisses like a diva to her adoring audience. Then she turned and climbed the stairs, still laughing, still happy.

Night seemed to fall as she climbed, though it could not have taken her that long to ascend the rickety steps. When she reached the platform, Téves had a little fire in the brazier and a meal laid out for them both.

They ate again in silence—bread, a thick vegetable soup redolent with herbs, and deep red berries wrapped in a pastry shell. She was glad for the silence, the chance to taste the wonderful flavors in the food, but it was hard not to say the things that crossed her mind.

"It's like I've had blinders over my eyes," Marina said after helping to clear their simple dinner dishes. She felt giddy with enthusiasm, like a child discovering some new fact about the way the world works.

Téves poured some of the honey wine for each of them and they went to sit in the chairs that overlooked the night forest.

"I don't understand how I could have not seen all of this energy around me. Will I always be able to see it," she hesitated, "even if I go back to my own world?"

"I don't know your world, but I have to believe that the life force, the energy, is there. I see it in you, and you are a product of your world."

"What if I can't find it back there? Knowing it's there but being unable to feel it would drive me crazy."

"Not everyone senses the energy patterns in the same way. Some people hear them stronger than they feel them. Other people feel them but can't see them. There are Brothers and Sisters of the Greening who can sense the energy in plants, but not in water, or in stone, not in the air. You seem to see it in the light."

"Yes, the light. There is something wonderful about the way I am seeing the light now. It's like what some people call an aura, but it's so much richer than I imagined."

"Then that will be your way back in. If you ever lose your ability— your awareness of the patterns—look for the light."

"But I've always paid attention to the light. It's what I know better than almost anything."

"I cannot see the energy fields in the light the way you seem to, but I've known people who could. When I feel the energy, it's as if I have to feel for what is there and what's not at the same time."

"The shadow and the light." Marina said it softly, almost to herself.

"Yes, perhaps that is the way of it for you. If you soften your eyes, your focus, it may come easier." Marina tried this—blurring her vision slightly and looking slightly away from the object of her attention. It did seem to make it easier to see the glow of light around things.

"But what does the aura mean? I mean, what's it telling me?"

"You will have to find that out for yourself. There is no easy interpretation for the patterns. So much of it is connected to your way of seeing them."

"Then what does the Greening have to do with sensing this energy in things?"

Téves did not answer immediately. He poured them each some more of the honey wine. Marina felt warm and safe, tired, but not yet sleepy. The fire and Téves's voice cast a kind of spell over her. "There is a story I learned as a boy about the first Greening. It is only one people's version of the Greening, but I think it a good one. Perhaps you would like to hear it."

"Yes. Tell it. Please." Marina could hardly imagine anything she wanted more than to sip the sweet wine, to sit by the fire, and to hear a story told.

"This is the story of Oriolis, who some call the Green King. It was first told by the Bandu people of the Upper Vrali about a child lost from a caravan. This child was called Oriolis. His mother, Sara, was the first daughter of a great trading family who traveled the desert caravan routes. It is said that his father was the mad poet, Leotis. As a boy, Oriolis was troubled by dreams of his father's madness and dark dreams of the desert. Some say he shared a touch of his father's madness. But his mother cared for him, and when he woke in the night crying from his desert dreams, she would sing him to sleep with songs of cool oases.

"The caravans of the great trading families crossed the Assouh Desert with cargoes of oil and spices, aromatic woods, fine cloth, and precious stones. The great lumbering Gimba beasts carried sacks and casks and the belongings of the families. By day the children walked alongside, but when crossing the fiercest tracks of the Assouh by night, they rode in hammocks strapped to the sides of the furry creatures.

"It was on one such night that Oriolis slipped from his hammock to the soft sand and was left behind in the desert. For many days he wandered in the desert, surviving on such skills as all desert-going children learn: conserving energy during daylight hours, finding water in the root of the tak-tak plant, and navigating by the stars at night. Though his family searched for him, he had wandered far from the caravan route, and eventually they lost hope of finding him. They said prayers for his spirit and returned to the Upper Vrali.

"Oriolis traveled until his strength and skill failed him. One evening after having sought shelter in the shade of a boulder all day, Oriolis decided he could travel no more. He was at the limit of his strength and the story of Oriolis might have ended there were it not for the Blue Bakoo.

"The Blue Bakoo were elusive creatures who lived around the remote oases of the Assouh. Their intelligence was legendary, as was their gentle nature and good humor. The Blue Bakoo were actually white, but a shade of silver-blue ran through their fur, which made them look distinctly blue by the light of the moon. Sadly, the Bakoo are no more, but they once lived where no man could ever long survive.

"They found Oriolis near death, but they took him in and nursed him back to health. For many years Oriolis lived among the Bakoo. He learned of their culture and their reverence for the land. He learned how they cared for the plants around the oases and how they never took more from the land than the land could give.

"Oriolis was happy. He had young Bakoo with whom to play and old Bakoo from whom to learn. He grew strong and confident on the fruit of the Assouh fig trees. But as a young man, his dark dreams of the desert returned. In his dreams the desert grew larger and larger, washing over fertile farmlands like a great wave. The dreams kept him awake at night and seemed to draw the strength from him.

"In the end it was his adopted mother, Nannu Passa, who told him what he must do. 'You must go into the hottest part of the hottest desert where the Grandfather Spirit of the hot, dry wind dwells. You must ask this spirit about your dreams.' Nannu Passa told Oriolis that he must go to the Abo Flat of the Assouh.

"Oriolis walked by night to the rim of the Abo Flat and prayed to the Great Mother Spirit for protection. At dawn he started to walk down into the Abo Flat, God's Kiln, the hottest place known to the Bandu. By noon the sun and the Grandfather Spirit had sapped his strength, and, for a second time in his life, he lay down to die in the desert.

"It was then that he had a strange and powerful dream.

"The hard-packed earth beneath his back grew soft and dragged him down. His legs and torso, arms and neck were swallowed up. Finally the sand closed over his head and all was darkness. In the last moment of his last breath, his hand found something to cling to. His fingers closed around a thick vine that struggled upward through the sand. Oriolis held onto the vine with both hands, and it carried him free of the desert sand. He held it tightly as it lifted him off the ground. He noticed for the first time the green leaves of the vine and felt them cool on the back of his hands and against his brow. Higher and higher the vine lifted him until he could see all of the desert, and the mountains, and the lush green forests beyond. It was beautiful and rich and vibrant with living energy. The higher he went, the more the desert looked to be a dry island of brown in a sea of green, but the island was growing, and the sea of green was drying up. Still he marveled at the view.

"At its height, when the vine could carry him no higher, it began to shake him from his reverie. Oriolis clung to the vine as it swayed from side to side, but with each dip it grew more strained. Finally it snapped. Oriolis fell an agonized and twisting fall to land hard—broken in the darkness of the black desert night.

"For many days Oriolis lay as a dead man, ruined on the desert floor. In his hand was a broken branch of the great vine that had given him his vision. He had no strength left but to cry. He cried for the world he had seen from his great height. He knew that the desert he had seen was not a true desert, but a desert in the hearts of the people. They could no longer see the life in things. They used the land badly, for selfish ends. They lacked imagination and could not conceive of the land as a fragile and living thing. It had always been theirs for the taking and so it would surely remain.

"He cried for his world, and his tears, the last of his water, dropped onto the desert sand and called forth the Greening. First one tiny shoot, then another, pushed against his back. They lifted Oriolis up as they grew around him. They gave him water and sustenance and he saw their patterns. In awe and joy he watched the plants grow in the desert, and all at once he knew the meaning of his dreams. He knew his destiny.

"Now, how much of this was dream and how much truly happened, no one can say. Perhaps there is little difference, but after many days—far longer than any man had survived—Oriolis walked off the Abo Flat and out of the Assouh desert. He had with him the branch of the Greening Vine that grew to become his staff. He learned all there was to know about plants and trees. He came to know their names, their needs, their natures, and even their innermost thoughts. He traveled far and taught others to see the living energy around them.

"As the years passed, Oriolis became first a teacher, then a preacher, then a prophet of what he called the Greening. Wherever people were gathered together, Oriolis would speak of planting, nurturing, cultivating, and listening to the living song of the world. He would sing wonderful songs of the mythic forests of his dreams and frighten children with tales of hot and lifeless deserts.

"To some Oriolis was a fool. Those who remembered the strange little boy he had once been said he was surely touched by the madness of his poet father. To others he was a dangerous man, deranged by his years of wandering in the desert. When he first proposed the Landbond, some talked openly of imprisonment or worse. Most people paid little attention to Oriolis, and he might have died in obscurity if not for his dreams. His wild dreams of the Greening came to the shaman artists of the Bandu and other people as well. Soon paintings of the Greening were seen and songs of the Greening were heard. Slowly the Greening came to have a place in the world.

"No one is quite certain what became of Oriolis. Like most figures of legend, his ending is obscure. Some believe that when his time was over, he walked into the desert as his father had before him, never to be seen again. Others believe that he found his primal forest and grew into a great tree that still stands there to this day. Still others believe that he can be seen on moonlit nights in green places, secretly tending to young plants and trees. Oriolis had no children, but every Bandu village can point to a great ancient tree that, it is said, was planted by Oriolis himself."

Marina thought the story beautiful but also sad, and it made her think again about forgetting what she had learned. "I'm afraid I will forget all this," she confessed. "I'm afraid that if I should somehow make my way back to my life I'll forget what I've heard and be no better off than I was before. What if I lose these new senses? What if I can't find sanctuary?"

"Even in your world, I'm afraid you will not simply find sanctuary. You may find a place of power, a pulse point, but you must build sanctuary." Téves's knapsack lay at his feet. He pulled it to him and drew a small leather pouch from one of its pockets.

"I don't understand. Do you mean that I have to build some kind of structure for it to be a sanctuary?"

"Some people build temples, some build simple houses in the trees. But you, I think, are a traveler. Your sanctuary must travel with you."

"I still don't get it," Marina said. She was getting sleepy now and frustrated by her own questions.

"Here," Téves said, extending the leather pouch to her. "Some within the Greening use this tool to feel the force of the life energy." Marina opened the pouch carefully and withdrew a simple but beautiful polished crystal pendulum. It was about the size of an acorn and hung from a fine silver chain. "Perhaps it will help you find your way."

"It's beautiful," Marina whispered. She was tired and could feel tears coming to her eyes for this gift. She had not the strength to stop them. Fortunately, Téves seemed distracted.

She watched as he took out the disk of wood he had cut earlier that day. The heartwood, he had called it. He touched the blue silhouette lightly with his fingertips and laid it onto the brazier with careful reverence. Neither of them spoke as they watched it burn. Marina's eyes grew heavy in the dance of the flame and she'd almost surrendered to sleep when the fire began to sputter and pop. It whistled and crackled and finally released some pent-up force in a fireball that hissed skyward in a shower of sparks.

"What was that?" Marina asked.

"Carolis's spirit. She is free to be reborn now. Watch."

Marina watched as a beautiful plume of blue-white smoke wafted up into the canopy. At first it was nothing, then it took on the shape she had seen in the cut log—a woman in a long gown, and then it was smoke again.

"I think you should find your bed," Téves said softly.

"What about you? Where will you sleep?" Marina asked as she stood up.

"I often sleep out here on the deck. I'll be fine."

Marina was too tired to argue. She soon found the little bunk, pulled the blanket around her shoulders and fell into a deep sleep.

★ ★ ★

Marina woke in darkness, her travel alarm sounding insistently. She could see by the luminescent dial that it was 3:00 A.M. She felt the gentle rocking of the ship. She had slept on top of her made bed so there was little to straighten as she slipped off it and into her silk robe.

"Marina." She heard the voice from far away. A high, musical voice, familiar and yet strange at the same time. She looked out the cabin window. It was quiet and still as she had hoped it would be.

"Marina." The voice called to her again.

She took a last look around her stateroom. It was neat and everything was in order. She had repacked all her belongings into her travel bags so there would be nothing for anyone to have to go through. She had thought this all out carefully.

She slipped from her stateroom, leaving the door unlocked behind her. She was barefoot and so moved quietly as she went down the steps to access the lowest of the outside decks. She saw no one.

"Marina." It was louder now, more musical.

She found the spot she had reconnoitered earlier. She pulled the deck chair to the railing and climbed over the edge.

"Marina. Come back to me, Marina. You remember the way." The voice that called her was delicious and intoxicating.

"Marina." Impossible to resist and yet she did. She hesitated for a moment, teetering on the edge of the railing. Something wasn't right. There was something she wasn't remembering.

"Marina. Come now. Your time is nearly up. Come back to me."

Still she hesitated. What was that thing she was forgetting. She would jump, she was ready, but there was something she must recall first. Some little thing.

"Marina. I will show you such wonders. We will fly, yes, you can fly. Fly to me now."

The song was irresistible. A nightsong. She remembered something about a nightsong. But was she to swim toward it or fly from it?

She swayed, tipped, could fight the song no more, felt herself fall forward as she had once before. No, she had not fallen before. She had jumped out. It was passion, not gravity that had carried her

Something caught her, held her in midair. "Marina!" A different voice, alarmed but commanding. "Marina." Softer now. "Adytum Wood is not the place for you to stop."

Téves was holding her, his arm around her waist. She opened her eyes. He had pulled her back from the other side of the railing. "It's a dream, Marina. But it isn't yours. Not yet, anyway. I think you still have time."

Time, Marina thought. What do I know about time? She looked around her. It was still dark but the first hint of dawn was lighting the sky. The turtle tattoo. She suddenly remembered it.

"My tattoo," she said, turning to face Téves. "It was here last time I saw it." She touched her cheekbone. "Can you still see it?" Téves turned her face to catch some of the light from the embers that still glowed in the brazier. He pushed her hair back off her forehead and tilted her head forward.

"I can just see it, here." He touched her hairline with his thumb. "But it's very faint."

"Atana said I must get to the other side of the mountain before the tattoo fades completely. How long will that take me? Can I make it before the sun goes down again? I'm not sure I can make it through another night."

"I'm sorry, but I just don't know. I can take you to the edge of Adytum Wood. There is a trail that leads up from there, but I've never taken it myself."

"Then, I'm sorry, but I must go now."

"Right," he said firmly and set about filling her water pouch and packing some food for her. Marina slipped her pendulum in its sack into her little bag next to the stone Atana had given her.

Quickly and quietly they both descended the stairs that wrapped around Sybil's great girth. Téves again led the way through the dark forest and Marina followed closely. She was amazed that despite her agitated state, she could still see and feel the auras of the trees around her. As the light came up, however, the forest began to change in character. She could still see some of the patterns of energy, but there seemed to be less spirit, less life at the edges of Adytum Wood.

Finally Téves came to a halt. He gestured to a path that clearly led up. "This is as far as I may go. Follow this path and I think it will take you where you need to go. I only hope I have not caused you to linger too long in my woods."

"If I've lingered, it was to learn what I had to learn. Don't feel any guilt on my behalf. You've given me a great gift." She felt like crying again, but bit her lip instead.

"Well, if you choose it, you will always be welcome here."

Marina kissed him quickly and impulsively on the cheek, then turned away. She had no time for crying now, no time to waste. She did not know how she could be so certain, but she knew that she had to be over the mountain before the sun set again. It was the only way back to the life she knew. It was a slim chance. She did not know by what mechanism or philosophy she could return to life, but it was a chance she wanted.

It was an odd feeling after so long, to want something again.

CHAPTER 6

Dark Circle, Stone Circle

Those who study such things have discovered that biogenic magnetite crystals—submicroscopic bits of lodestone—form naturally in the snouts of sea turtles. Could it be that they carry some deep sensitivity to the ley lines, the magnetic ebb and flow, the dragon lines of Feng Shui? In a ruined temple in Central America a Great Mother Turtle Goddess has a body carved of one kind of stone and a head carved from magnetic ore. How could they know? It is almost as if she might one day use this compass to find her way back into the molten sea from which she was born. Or, barring that, she might somehow pull her heart's desire across thousands of miles of open sea to share her temple of stone. What would I give to remember my heart's compass?

Now the path grew steep and the climbing was hard. For the first time since leaving Rafael's hut, Marina questioned whether she had the strength to climb up and over this mountain. She kept hoping to find an intersecting path that perhaps wound around the mountain, offering a more gentle trail to the other side, but, in her heart, she knew she must climb this mountain or turn back. There was no soft path for her now.

That the intensity of her desire coincided with the difficulty of the climb seemed appropriate. If she had wanted it less or the grade had grown steep sooner, her will might have failed her, but she now was determined.

As she walked into the morning, she still saw faint auras of shimmering energy around the trees. Occasionally she would walk through patches of fog, thick mist that obscured the detail of things, but through which she could still see the trees and plants. When she no longer noticed the auras, it wasn't so much that she stopped seeing them, but rather that she had to work so hard to lift and place each foot along the rock-strewn trail that she couldn't look anywhere but down.

She had been barefoot since waking on Turtle Island, but now, for the first time, it hurt her feet to walk. If distracted for even a few seconds by the raucous call or bright plumage of some bird, she would place a foot wrong, twisting, scraping, stubbing, banging. She fell once, skinning her knee and bringing a blush of crimson blood to the surface.

Her clumsiness and inattention made her mad, and then it made her cry.

She stopped to pour water over her wound and rest, breathing in deep, chest-wrenching gulps. She looked at the skin on her legs. Aside from her fresh wound, her legs were still smooth and supple. She still had the skin she had been reborn to when the Turtle Mother had wrapped her, buried her, and forced her to dig her way free—almost a baby's skin. The scar from the machete wound was still a thin, pale, pink line on her calf. She had to feel for it before locating it. I must be more careful with this skin, she thought.

There was no mark on her ankle where the Turtle Mother had tattooed her. She wondered where the tattoo was by now. Was it crawling through some dense forest of her own dark hair? Was it even still visible? She brought her hand up to her scalp. She found a leaf tangled in her hair.

How many days had it been since she'd bathed or washed her hair? Three? Four? She hadn't felt dirty before. Now the bright woven jacket Rafael had given her seemed worn. It was damp with her own sweat and hung open unevenly. The shoulder bag that Atana had given her pulled at the right side of the jacket, opening it and exposing more of her breasts than she would have chosen to reveal if anyone else had been present.

She set off again—moving before her knee could begin to ache. It was past noon and hot, though the sun was still filtered by the canopy of trees. She had little concentration to spare on reverie and thoughts of her own past, but the exertion of the climb seemed to draw sense memory from her own muscles.

Despite herself she slipped back to other times and places where she had climbed hard like this.

In her pilgrimage period, after Chechnya, she had climbed all the sacred mountains she could find. She was never sure what she expected to find at the top, but she climbed them all the same. She explored the ruins of Machu Picchu. She clambered up the steep step pyramid of Chichén Itz· in Mexico. She climbed mounds in Ireland and Wales, scrambled up Ayers Rock in central Australia, and climbed with the tourists and pilgrims to the top of Mt. Fuji in Japan. She trekked in Nepal and visited Lhasa in Tibet.

She had made these climbs to get her strength back after being bedridden from her wounds in Grozny. At least this is what she told others. In truth, she was searching for something—something she thought she would find high up in places of power. She sought out holy men and religious leaders, but could never be still long enough to hear the answers behind the words. She supposed now that all she had really been doing was confirming the opinion she had adopted— that there truly was nothing more than pain and suffering in life.

Emptiness is what she had gone in search of and emptiness was what she found. When she failed to call out across the mountain and into the canyon, no echo returned to her.

Gradually she lost enthusiasm for the pilgrim's road. She stopped looking.

But there was another climb, deeper in her muscles, that she recalled now. Not lush and green like this, but hot and hard across sun-blasted stones. She'd been climbing with Christophe through the mountain passes on the northern border between Pakistan and Afghanistan. They had not been alone. They were tagging along with smugglers bringing American arms supplied by the CIA to the Mujahedin guerrillas.

She had few illusions about the side she was photographing. Their fundamentalism would in time make them terrorists, and they would not know they'd crossed any line. But for now, they were fighting the good fight, resisting the full weight of the Soviet war machine with weapons that could be carried on the backs of camels and donkeys.

It had been an excruciating ordeal, that climb, made worse by the men's clothing she wore. Her hair had been oiled, tied back, and piled under a wool hat. Sweat, gritty with dust and sand, had dripped constantly into her eyes. Her breasts had been bound tight to her chest with long strips of what had once been a turban. She'd worn a rough wool shirt, heavy brown vest, baggy trousers, and old leather sandals. She'd balanced her cameras and film on either side of her in tired leather pouches.

She'd fooled no one in the party she traveled with. No matter how many days she had been away from water, soap, shampoo, or perfume, the men could still smell the woman in her. She also hadn't looked, for all her efforts, nearly mannish enough to pass close inspection. But, at a distance she could pass for a man. And this was all she needed, to avoid drawing attention to the party she traveled with.

Christophe had been dressed as roughly as she, though he carried it better than she did. He'd had the luxury of removing his hat, or opening his shirt to take advantage of a light breeze. He'd been bronzed by the sun to a shade darker, but more reddish, than her own complexion. His hair had been black and he'd had a rough stubble of beard on his angular face. He and Marina had been the same age, nearly the same height, and strangely similar in some of their features. If Christophe, who had an ear for dialects and spoke several languages fluently, had said that Marina was his sister, he would have been believed.

Still, despite her discomfort, she recalled walking along behind him, distracted by erotic fantasies. They had been lovers for six months, in and out of Afghanistan. When they traveled across borders like this as man and man, they had the added thrill of finding ways to make love secretly as they camped at night. Sometimes they would lay close, as all the men did for warmth, and share a single blanket. Feigning sleep, Christophe would explore her body beneath her clothes and bandages, making her nipples ache and her thighs quiver, and causing her to mimic the shifting of a restless sleeper to disguise her orgasms.

Other times they would wander away from camp after dark and find some sheltered ledge upon which to lay down together. She would let him open her shirt, then, and unwrap her breasts in the moonlight, the stone still warm beneath her, the air cool around them. Their unwashed bodies did not distract them, rather the raw scent of sweat and attraction added to their excitement. Sometimes Marina would insist that they both remove all their clothes and make love naked and exposed. Other times it was only important that he take her clothes from her. If Christophe kept rough shirt and trousers on as he slipped against her, it made her feel more open, more vulnerable. She sometimes imagined herself being taken half against her will.

She still could not cry out when making love. When the surging rhythm crested within her she would pull Christophe down over her mouth to silence her screams—so much of her passion held inside.

These were the things she'd thought about as she walked along behind Christophe. It had taken her mind off the heat, the boredom, the discomfort.

She'd loved Christophe. There had been things they disagreed about, sometimes violently, but she had not loved him less for their arguments. The thing she'd hated most was the rifle he carried over his shoulder.

Christophe had been a good photographer. He had been lucky and brave and smart when it came to getting good photographs, but that had not been enough for him. Marina believed that life with the hard mountain rebels had challenged Christophe's notion of what it was to be a man, to believe in things, and to fight for them. He'd still carried a Nikon, but he'd also carried a captured Kalyshnikov rifle. He had practiced with it and knew how to use it, and that scared Marina.

She had tried to explain to Christophe her belief in the shield a camera wrapped around a photographer, but it had been no use. He would not convert to her religion. There had been times when they had separated. She wondered if he had used his rifle during those times. She was afraid he had. The men had seemed to treat him differently. They had a name of respect for him.

It wasn't that she believed him wrong for wanting to do more than just record events. She had felt the same pull herself—the desire to be more "in" life than "beside" it had come over her numerous times. But she felt, perhaps, less distanced from the world by her profession than Christophe had. When the photographing was good, when she was in the channel of the moment, she felt no distance at all from her subjects, her world. Afterward perhaps there was guilt, or remorse, or some soul-numbing wall that went up, but in the moment she truly felt linked to everything and everyone around her.

She had been thinking these thoughts as she'd trudged up the steep mountain track, lost in the rhythm of her stride and her breath and the banging of camera bags against her hips. Some part of her must have heard the familiar rumble of helicopter rotors, because she'd found a camera in her right hand even as she'd run into Christophe, who had stopped suddenly in front of her.

They had all stopped. Strung out along the narrow trail, some had looked up, some simply listened with cocked heads. The donkeys had been skittish, stepping backward and forward, constricted by the wall of stone to their right and the drop to their left. Bringing up the rear, Marina had taken several steps backward. If they had to run, she hadn't wanted to be trampled by stampeding pack animals. She looked for some place that might serve as cover.

Christophe was looking for cover, too. She thought it was for the both of them.

"Down there," he yelled over the growing roar.

They could not yet see them, but the helicopters had been close. He'd taken Marina by the arm and led her to the edge of the mountain path. Just below the trail an overhanging boulder had offered some shelter from above. It was a steep drop but a short one. She'd thought they were making it together, but when she hit the loose sand and gravel, sliding hard into the boulder, she had been alone.

"Christophe!" she'd yelled. "No!"

He had pulled the rifle from his shoulder and was aiming it along the ridge above them at the point they knew the helicopters would appear.

"No, damnit!" Marina was screaming, but Christophe could not hear her.

What had happened next took seconds, but in her memory, replayed countless times over the years, it had become an agonizing slow-motion ballet. She'd brought her camera up to her eye, focused, and zoomed in on Christophe in one smooth, practiced twist of her wrist. Perhaps some part of her wanted to extend her shield around him. She'd brought him up sharp in her viewfinder, caught the first of the dark spinning blades emerging over the ridge in front of him. She'd pressed the shutter button and let the motordrive spin the film forward.

Little clouds of smoke had popped from the Kalyshnikov. Christophe's shoulder had jerked back repeatedly. Marina remembered a blue bruise on Christophe's shoulder. He'd made some excuse for it, and she'd accepted it.

She'd seen him, one eye to the viewfinder, one eye open, tracking.

She'd seen when the little jerks of the rifle's recoil had become a big slam against his chest. He'd spun once or twice, still clutching the rifle. Marina had seen no blood. Perhaps he's simply lost his balance, she'd thought.

He'd come to a stop, still standing. He'd bent at the waist, leaning on the rifle, its smoking muzzle in the dirt. He'd clutched at his chest, then pulled his hand away. It had been moist and red. He'd studied it, turning his hand over and back.

Then he'd turned his head and looked at Marina. He'd reached out his hand to her, as if she could somehow come to him, somehow help him. He'd taken a few staggering steps toward her, but she had not moved. He'd looked at her quizzically. He had not looked sad or in pain, merely surprised. Then he'd smiled at her. And she had realized why he was smiling. She had been looking at him through the viewfinder of her camera. No, it had been more than that. She had not been calling his name, not crying, not running to drag him to cover. She had been photographing him.

The next moment his knees had buckled and he'd dropped down and forward. He had not moved again.

She could never remember how long the little firefight took. It had been so quiet in the mountains, then so loud, then, as quickly, so quiet again. She'd heard a whirring in her ear long after the helicopters had gone and the gunfire had ceased. She'd realized she still had her finger on the shutter release of the Nikon and that the motor drive had still been whining even though she had shot her whole roll.

There had been survivors, but not many. There had not been enough of them to even bring the bodies of their comrades down off the mountain. She had buried Christophe as best she could beneath a pile of stones. She'd buried him with his rifle and said a few words for him. She'd built a cairn to mark the place he lay. Marina had taken the St. Christopher's medallion he'd always worn to give to Christophe's mother. For his sister, she had taken his journal and the little Leica rangefinder he still carried. For herself she'd taken nothing. While he had been alive he had given her everything she needed or wanted from him.

She still had the roll of film she shot that day. It had been in her camera bag in her cabin on the ship. She had never developed it.

She had begun to hate herself then, to hate in some little way how she hid behind the lens of her camera. Some little shadow was born in her on that mountain—some infection of the spirit. She could replay the event in her mind and examine it rationally. She knew that she had brought her camera up to her eye by instinct. It was what every good photojournalist did. It was what Christophe should have done. If he'd remembered to be a photographer and not a soldier, he would not have died. She could get angry at him for this. She also knew that the firefight had lasted only seconds. There was nothing she could have done for Christophe short of dying with him. But, in the end, none of these facts mattered. She dwelt on Christophe's last image of her—coldly documenting his death—and she could find no forgiveness for herself.

It was not that she had lost the man she loved, it was that she had failed him, failed herself in some way. She had thought to hold back death with the talismanic power of stainless steel and ground glass. But had instead silently invited death to walk with her.

★ ★ ★

When the trail Marina was climbing grew so steep as to be an exercise in scrambling over boulders, it suddenly changed from a straight course up to a series of switchbacks. She also moved out of the cover of trees for the first time. The sun was setting behind her and that was a good sign. She knew that she was still moving in the right direction.

She could see down into a valley, over a lower set of hills and ridges and then down to the beach. Beyond the beach, a ring of coral reefs seemed to spread out half a mile into the sea, forming a pale halo around the island. It was where she had come from. She knew that instinctively, but there were no features she recognized from her vantage point. She thought perhaps she could see the cove and the little waterfall and pool near Rafael's hut, but she wasn't sure.

She could not see much of the eastern side of the island, but she could see what was directly ahead. The trail wound back and forth up the west face of the slope before disappearing over the crest. The way looked easier than the climbing she had been doing, but it also looked as if it would take time. Without the switchbacks it would have been much too steep and dangerous for her to climb. Avoiding the switchbacks was out of the question, as was any hope of circumnavigating the peak. The only way was up and over. She glanced down at the sun on the horizon. It seemed to be falling fast into the sea.

She turned back to the trail and hurried on.

She wasn't certain where her urgency came from. Perhaps her

dream of jumping again from the *Blue Pearl* lingered with her. Perhaps it was that voice that had called her. She wasn't afraid of death. She had faced death, fully willing to go down that path, but she had learned things she had not known. She had a chance that she knew she would not get twice. She did not intend to waste it.

The long looping trail took even longer than she had feared. It was dark when she passed between two huge and eroded boulders to cross the western crest of the mountain. But even then she still hadn't fully crossed over.

She saw now that the mountain was a volcano. Ancient and perhaps extinct, but still a volcano. There was a deep caldera—a bowl sunk down on the hardened lava dome. Its base was filled with water—a still, black pool—sister to the mirror pool Atana had shown her. The path to the other side led down and up the far wall. It looked steep and it was hard to judge the true distance, but there was no other way. The moon was not yet up and she could just barely find her way by the light of the stars.

She wondered if she couldn't wait out the night and cross this place in the morning. She had, after all, made it to the top. The mountain had come to symbolize a turning point in her journey back to the living world. Perhaps it was only a symbol. Was crossing over truly necessary?

She knew that it was.

With a dark foreboding she descended into the heart of the shadowy volcano. She picked her way down the trail. The black pool was larger than it had appeared. As she went down into the bowl of the volcano, the terrain changed dramatically. Glittering black sand and rock surrounded her. She could see nothing green, but dead, twisted branches seemed to claw up from the ground around her.

She had gone down several hundred yards, almost falling twice, before she heard the voices.

"Marina." She recognized the voice. It was the voice from her dream the night before, a voice so like the Turtle Woman, but also different. This was the voice that had tried to lure her back. For a moment she wondered if she was asleep. But no, she hurt too much to be asleep. She didn't answer the voice.

"Marina. You've learned so much, you're so close." Marina felt as if she was hearing the voice in stereo. It seemed to be coming from all around her.

"Come back to me."

"Go back to them."

Marina heard both of these statements at the same time. They sounded similar, as if they had come from the same person, but now Marina could sense something different. It was not that the voice was coming from all around her. Two different voices were calling her. They both sounded like the Turtle Woman she had known and they both sounded different.

"Go!"

"Stay!"

Marina ignored both voices. She was coming down to the pool now. The path seemed level. It appeared to run close to the pool in a half circle before ascending the eastern ridge on the other side. The bank into the pool was black and steep. It looked slippery and it sparkled with the shimmering black sand around its edge.

"What are you most afraid of, Marina?" It was eerie to hear her name called by the disembodied voice.

"You must face what you fear most before crossing this place." This was the second voice. Still Marina tried to ignore them both. She kept her eyes on the trail at her feet and tried not to look at either the pond or the high circular wall around her.

"Marina."

"Marina."

Both voices called softly, seductively. She risked a look at the black pool. Something moved. Twin ripples spread out from different places in the pond as if two pebbles had landed at the same moment. She stopped and watched. As the wave patterns crossed, the interference pattern seemed to run back to the source of the ripples. At first she thought she saw little islands, then she saw shells, turtle shells.

Two women stood up slowly at the same time. It was the Turtle Woman who had helped Marina and what appeared to be a perfect mirror image of her, only Marina could not tell who was the original and who the reflection.

She was afraid of them both, but felt malice from neither of them. One seemed to want her to continue, the other wanted her to come back, but there was no self-interest in their pleas. It seemed to Marina as if this was simply what they were made to say.

"What do you fear most?" Was this the one who wanted her to go forward or turn back? Marina wasn't sure.

"There is a way for you not to face that thing, Marina," the second woman said softly. They both began to move toward her, wading through the thigh-deep black water gracefully.

"You cannot avoid this. It is one of the reasons you came here."

"I can help you. Come with me and never feel pain or fear again." This was the one who wanted her to turn back. Marina sensed this instinctively. She was the one Marina feared most. But no sooner had she identified the Turtle Woman's dark twin than they crossed in front of each other and crossed again. Marina lost track.

"What is it you are not remembering?"

"What is it you do not want to remember?"

It was hopeless. She could not keep them separate in her mind. She wanted to turn, to run, but her legs seemed frozen.

"I don't know what you want from me," Marina cried, addressing them for the first time.

"Come with me."

"Why are you doing this to me? I thought you wanted to help me."

"We do." They both spoke in unison, and it was chilling.

"Think of what you cannot remember." Only one of them spoke now, but which one?

"How can I think of what I can't remember?" Marina asked.

"Yes, how?" One of the women was closer to her and reached out a hand. Marina could not have reached it from where she stood, but it made her want to step off the path and slide down the bank into the pool.

"Remember, Marina."

"How can I think of what I can't remember?" The woman with her hand outstretched had repeated Marina's words in Marina's own voice to her sister.

"Remember what?" Marina asked of the second Turtle Woman who stood back a bit in the water.

"The time you can't remember."

"But she can't remember." The women closest to Marina answered her sister with a laugh. "She can come with me now and never need memories again."

"Think, Marina. There is a dark place in you, a cold spill of black ink. It sucks all the light into it."

"Come, come with me. Don't think."

Marina's body was listening to the woman who beckoned. Her

heart was listening to the woman asking her to do the impossible. She stepped forward, at the same time casting her mind back.

Remember, she thought. My childhood? That seemed too far back. What dark place do I have? What more recent place? Most of the traumas of her recent past she recalled all too well. She had seen her own life as if through a lens. She knew the very grain of these experiences as if she had labored over them in the darkroom, pulling forth every shadow and detail.

She thought of herself in a darkroom. . . . No, it was a dark room. . . . No, not even that. She saw herself in a dark place. What couldn't she remember? All those bodies falling on her, pressed against her. There was a time—twenty-four hours. No, longer. She couldn't recall. No, that wasn't true. There were moments she could recall between the slam of the first gunshots and the narcotic return to life in the Red Cross hospital.

She began to slide down a slippery bank, but she was not sure into what. . . .

A crush of bodies.

Cries and moans and the surreal popping of automatic weapons sounded around her. Oh God, she thought. Not again. Something hurt. It came in waves. She grew dizzy. Was she asleep?

"Stay alive, damnit!" It was Peter Burdett's voice. It was tight and pinched and whispered in her ear emphatically. She could move a little. Her legs were trapped, and something pressed her down. It was Peter. He had formed a kind of shell around her. He was wedged on elbows and knees over her, but it protected her from the press of bodies so that she could move a little.

Unconscious again, then awake. Machinery noises vibrated over her. They're coming to save us, she thought—but they weren't. They were pushing dirt and the bricks of a fallen wall over the pit she was in. It grew quickly dark. Dirt fell in her face and she coughed. There was more pressure on her legs. She could hear other voices sobbing. She envied those that had died instantly.

"No you don't." It was Peter's voice, soft but strained in her ear. Had he read her mind or had she spoken her thoughts aloud? "Stay alive. Stay alive." She wasn't sure if he was talking to her or to himself. "Stay alive and get out. Tell Cath I love her. And tell Angie . . ." He didn't finish the sentence.

Cath was Peter's wife. He had shown Marina pictures. Angie was his daughter. She looked to be about five or six in the photos. Marina knew she should say something, but couldn't. There were no comforting words she could muster up. She wanted just to close her eyes and die like the others around her.

But they didn't die, not all at once. She swam in and out of consciousness. She knew who was breathing, wheezing, coughing around her, and when they stopped. She wondered if there was some way to make herself die more quickly. Just get it over with, she thought. But she could not move enough to aid her own death, so she lay in the dark, buried alive, waiting until she could hear no one else move or whimper or breathe.

So this is what I wanted? she asked herself. This is the place I've been searching for. I thought I was cheating death, but all along I was chasing it. Was it like this for Christophe? Did it take this long? Did he have time to hate me? Did he put this seed in me, this little wound, this dark desire?

No, she thought, I infected myself with this disease. Christophe gave me only love—more love than I could give myself. So I have this little wound, and I've worried at its edges, picked at the scab of it until it is such a big rend that it could swallow me up. How did I do this? I would not let myself be alive, but I could not die simply. Am I such a coward that I've been courting my own executioners? Well, now I've found what I was seeking. Is it still what I want?

In her dark tomb, Marina saw the ghost of her mother hovering over her. Wait, she thought, my mother's not dead. Do the living look like ghosts to the dead? Am I already dead? The ghost hovered for a moment, too far away to reach Marina. "What do you want?" she thought she heard it say. Then it disappeared.

"Stay alive," Peter whispered again. But Peter was already dead. She knew this. She had seen his spirit leave his body. She had seen other spirits float up, but not her own.

I will not be left alone down here. She was light-headed. Some part of her knew that she must have lost a lot of blood. Is that how I will die? she wondered. Or will I suffocate? Will I spend my last few moments in an agony of choking, gasping for breath, or will I drift away from loss of blood?

She tried to move again. There was something hard and familiar in her hand. A camera, she was still clutching one of her cameras. Even in death, she thought, and it made her laugh. Laughing hurt, and pain woke her up.

She worked her arm free and rolled onto her back. The little shelter that Peter's crumpled body had formed now offered her more room in which to maneuver. She pulled and kicked, trying to free her legs, and the pain in her side almost made her black out again. She rested.

"What the hell am I doing?" she asked herself. She said it out loud, just to hear a voice, to see if she could still make a sound, to see if she was still alive.

She kicked again and drew a leg up in a tucked position. That hurt worse, but she had one leg free. It took time, but she managed to work the other leg free as well. She pushed through the little tunnel that Peter had created for her and felt for some open space on the other side. She inched forward, pulling herself along on legs, bent necks, long hair, clothing. Her camera was in her right hand and she used it to bang away at obstacles—bricks, stone, dirt, bone. If she couldn't go around it, she hammered at it until something broke.

She imagined that she was swimming in a sea of the dead. Sometimes it felt like hands grabbed at her legs, her arms, her clothes, and pulled her down. She did not know if they were living hands or if she was tangling with the crooked rigor mortis of dead hands. Still, she fought her way up.

There was little more that she seemed to remember. The dirt was packed tighter and fell into her mouth more and more as she climbed. She passed out or slept many times, but always woke to dig a few more feet. She must not, she realized, have gone far on her dark journey, but it took everything she had.

Finally she ran out of strength. It was as if there was no more air for her to breathe and she began to gulp in panic at empty space. She could feel bodies beneath her, holding on, clinging to her, but only dirt and stone above. She scraped at the dirt with her camera and pounded up at it. It was solid and hard and she made no progress through it. Her struggle weakened. She had nothing left.

She pushed the camera up against the dirt one more time. It felt massive and heavy like a lead brick, but this time something broke. Her hand didn't stop. It went up and up, and she felt cool air rush down the length of her arm.

Air and something else. Was that light? she wondered. And what was that noise? She felt the slap of a shutter in her hand then heard a whirring sound like a camera's autowinder rewinding a film cassette, then nothing.

I should wake up in a Red Cross hospital now, she told herself. But she was not waking up. She was sliding back down into the sea of the dead. She felt the pool of their blood cool about her ankles. It wasn't supposed to be like this, she thought. They dug me out. I survived.

"Part of you survived." She knew the voice but it didn't belong in this dream.

"Part of you got left behind." The same voice, but different. She was still sliding down, but her left hand found something to hold onto. She clutched at a small branch that poked up from the ground. It stopped her slide.

"What is the opposite of shadow?" She recognized the Turtle Woman's voice. It was just the kind of question she would ask.

Where am I now? she thought. About to be buried alive or about to drown?

"I don't know." She cried.

"Only your shadow crawled out of that grave, Marina."

"You must go back for her."

Marina couldn't tell who was speaking anymore. It may have been one. It may have been two.

"Look down, Marina."

Marina looked down and saw herself looking up. Her hand was extended, reaching up. Was she floating in the pool or buried in dark earth? Marina couldn't be certain. Her own face, distorted by the black water and her own tangle of dark hair looked passive. She did not look as if she cared whether Marina pulled her from the water or not.

Is that what I've become? she wondered. Is this some trick, some ruse to get me to turn back from life forever? It was all she could do to hold herself out of the water.

"What should I do?" Marina cried into the night. Her own voice echoed back from the caldera walls. But there was no answer.

She looked down again. Her twin was drifting away. In a second she would be beyond reach. Without thinking, Marina lunged with her left hand. She felt the branch in her right hand crack, but it did not give way. She caught her twin's wrist and dragged her up out of the water. Slowly and carefully her twin climbed over her. She worked her way to the level edge of the path and dragged herself up and over.

With her twin's last push, Marina felt the branch in her right hand snap, and suddenly there was nothing to stop her from sliding into the pool. She reached wildly up and out with her left hand and something caught her. Now it was her twin that was pulling her up the slippery bank onto the level path.

She rested a moment on her back, panting into the night sky. Then she felt the trembling. Her twin was pulling Marina to her feet, but the ground beneath them was dissolving. The level path was collapsing into the pool. Her twin pulled her forward for a few yards then Marina was running on her own.

It was like running on dunes. The earth gave way like black sand beneath them as they circled the pool. They both fell, got up, and fell again. Sometimes her twin pulled her up. Other times she saved her twin. Even when they reached the far side of the caldera the ground continued to shift. Sometimes they were scrambling up on hands and knees. Boulders and big stones that seemed to offer solid purchase for a moment fell away after they had passed them, their foundations melting away. They ran and climbed at a sluggish nightmare pace. The black pool bubbled and steamed below them. Voices still called them, but these voices were angry. These were not the voices of the Turtle Woman or her reflection. Marina ignored them.

And then they were over the edge and sliding down the eastern face, trying to control their descent, trying to stand, falling, rolling, banging into each other—sometimes occupying the same space at the same moment in time—until, at last, they came to a stop. But there was no they. There was only Marina.

Which of me has survived this time? she wondered, as she slid to a stop. She looked down at her right hand. She still clutched the broken branch in it. The branch was short, like a bouquet of dried, dead flowers, and made up of many twisted branches. It looked like the winter trees she had photographed before Chechnya, and, in turn, like the single dead hand reaching up from its grave that she had photographed accidentally when she herself crawled to freedom.

I took that photograph, she thought. She was pleased to remember this. How strange, she continued, that I should be pleased to remember a thing like that.

Like so many things that had happened to her since coming to Turtle Island, Marina did not know how she could know this, but she was certain that both she and her twin had indeed made it out of the dark pool and over the edge of the volcano. Her twin, her light reflection, whatever it was that was the opposite of a shadow, was inside her now.

Something made her look up behind her.

A dark, handlike shadow seemed to be feeling its way over the edge she had tumbled down. It looked like black fog and blotted out the stars behind it. Marina didn't like the look of it. She quickly stood up and looked around her. It seemed as though the trail picked up just below her and continued down the eastern face in the same lazy switchback pattern with which it had climbed the western face.

She picked her way carefully down to the trail. It was awkward holding the branch, but somehow she couldn't bring herself to discard it. She thought of the story Téves had told of Oriolis. He had fallen from the sky with a branch in his hand. Perhaps this was her Greening Vine.

At first the going was easy. The trail was not steep, and once the moon rose, there was plenty of light by which to see. But the black fog continued to ooze down the side of the volcano. Because of the switchbacks Marina was forced to follow, it soon caught up with her and threatened to engulf the path she was on. She wanted to yell at it, to tell it to go back. She had made it over the volcano and she was not going back, but the closer it came, the more it frightened her.

She rested for a moment to think about what to do. She took out the little pendulum Téves had given her and let it spin from her hand. It made her think about the auras and patterns she had been able to see in Adytum Wood and after. All at once she could see the auras and patterns in the trees below her, but when she looked back at the inky mist she saw nothing—no life, no energy, no pattern. She put the pendulum back in her pouch and ran down the trail.

It was a hard thing to do in the open, under the full light of the moon. It was even harder when she crossed the tree line. She tripped and fell, kicked roots and stones hard with her bare feet, limped along. But always the fog was just behind her. It seemed she could not outrun it. It was all she could do to stay a few paces ahead of it. It allowed her no rest. No breaks for water or to nurse a cut or bruise. She began to wonder if she would make it. She had known somehow that she was supposed to be over the mountain before dark and she hadn't done it. Did that mean that all her struggle was in vain?

She would not accept that. The fog herded her forward like the cold, foul breath of a stranger spitting and wheezing on her back.

When she thought she saw a stretch of trail that was relatively flat and straight and unmarked by rocks and roots, she sprinted. She intended merely to gain a few precious yards in her race with the phantom fog, but she was soon running too fast to easily control her motion. Her ankle struck something and she looked down. Suddenly she was not on the trail anymore. She was not even on solid ground. She was rolling, twisting, tumbling down. Her head struck something solid and then the black fog washed over her.

★ ★ ★

She dreamed of being lifted up, pulled from the ground, gently but firmly. Someone carried her, placing her body in the bed of a truck that bounced down a rough, pocked road. They were cutting away her clothes. There were gauze pads and bandages, antiseptic smells, needles in her arms. These things she could feel as if from a great distance away, but she could not see. Her eyes seemed to be weighted from above. She had no strength to pry them open.

Marina woke slowly to something familiar. Her head throbbed, her ankle ached, but there was a familiar smell, a comforting motion on her skin. She resisted the temptation to open her eyes and tried to identify the scents first. She smelled vanilla, cinnamon, cloves, an oil base, perhaps coconut oil. What did it remind her of? Something intimate, lust, Rafael. Yes, she thought, Rafael. She was dreaming of Rafael. She felt the gentle lazy circles around her breasts, the long strokes along her sides that pulled and stretched muscle all the way into her thighs. It felt so good, so real.

Too real, she thought. She was not dreaming. She was back there, back with Rafael. Perhaps she had never left. Maybe she had dreamed all of her experiences since Rafael. Or maybe she had them all to live over again, like some twisted time loop. Was she doomed to live the same experiences over and over again? Worse, she thought, what if I'm trapped here? She remembered the phantom black fog. Was this the price she had to pay for failing to cross the mountain before sunset?

She opened her eyes.

He knelt beside her legs, bent low and stretched out so that all she saw was his long black hair. Then he drew his hands back down along her sides, returning to a kneeling posture as he did.

It was not Rafael.

It was not even a man.

A woman knelt beside her. She was beautiful and almond-eyed with skin the color of golden honey. Half her face was hidden by long black hair, but still Marina recognized her from someplace. Something made

her suddenly awkward. An erotic dream she could not be held respon-
sible for intruded into her thoughts. She had dreamed of this woman.
She had dreamed she was making love to this woman. Wasn't this Mai-
Ling, Rafael's Mai-Ling?

She felt a blush spread across her chest and up to her face. She wondered if this woman noticed it.

"Mai-Ling?" Marina asked. The woman seemed surprised that
Marina knew her name. But she also seemed used to surprises. She
accepted the fact gracefully and smiled.

"Yes, my name is Mai-Ling. Have we met before?"

"No," Marina fumbled, feeling even more awkward. "I stayed for a
while with Rafael. He told me about you."

"Ahh . . . Rafael," she said almost to herself, as if remembering
something intensely pleasant.

"He said you were an artist and that it was you who taught him to
weave."

"We taught each other some things, I'm sure." She laughed. "I'm
sure you taught each other some things, too."

Marina began to blush again, unsure of what to do with her hands,
what to cover. Mai-Ling pulled a wide piece of sunflower yellow silk
over Marina's body. Marina was grateful for the drape.

"I'm sorry for intruding, but when I found you . . . Well, you were
pretty dirty and disheveled. I couldn't tell what were injuries and what
was just soil. I couldn't seem to wake you, so I put you on a blanket
and dragged you here. I'm afraid I bathed you and combed out your
hair in the little pool. I didn't know what else to do. Touch is the only
healing tool I have, so . . ."

"No. Thank you. Really. I don't know what I have to be embarrassed about. I've worn little more than that jacket since I came here.
I'm sure you did what you thought was right."

"I washed the jacket," Mai-Ling offered, "but it's pretty torn up. It
looks like you had a bad fall."

"I don't remember much of it. Have I broken anything?"

"I don't think so. Your ankle was swollen, you had some bruised ribs
and a cut on the back of your head, but nothing else I can find."

Marina blushed again to think that she had been so carefully
inspected while unconscious, but she supposed she would have done
the same thing.

"How long?" Marina did not need to finish her sentence.

"I found you yesterday morning. That's a day and a half. You were in one of my stone circles."

"Your what?"

"Stone circles. They're my little altars. I've laid them out in different places around here."

Marina pinned the silk across her chest with her arms and leaned up on her elbows. Her head pounded and for a moment she saw flashing lights, but it passed quickly. She looked around.

She was in a structure that looked much the way Rafael's hut had looked, except that there were woven reed blinds that unrolled to the floor, creating translucent walls on some sides. Some of these blinds were rolled up, and she saw a stream-fed pool outside that trapped water temporarily before it plunged over a far edge. She could hear the splashing of a waterfall. Beyond the pool the landscape dropped away sharply and she could see the tops of the trees that flowed gracefully down to the sea.

"I fell," Marina said, remembering. "I had come over the mountain, the volcano, after dark. I had made it, but something chased me. I got as far as the tree line, then I must have tripped and hit my head."

"You got farther than just the tree line," Mai-Ling corrected her gently. "It's a long way from here to there."

Marina was confused. Was she remembering correctly? She had dreamed of being picked up and carried, but that was after Chechnya, wasn't it? Thinking about it made her head hurt more.

There were woven mats with pillows on the rough plank floor. There were also a number of low tables at the height for sitting and working on the floor. One of the tables had pieces of wood and simple hand tools for cutting, carving, and sanding. Another of the tables had candles, flowers, fruit, and colored stones in little wooden bowls. She recognized the wooden bowls. Rafael had said that Mai-Ling carved the beautiful vessels. There were cabinets and boxes as well. It seemed that Mai-Ling had possessions.

Marina saw her own possessions. Her shoulder pouch was beside her. Neatly arranged in little wooden bowls were her ankle bracelet of coral and black pearl and her circular stone from Rafael. Beside them was the little branch she had carried out of the volcano. She assumed her other things, the stone from the mirror pool and Téves's pendulum, were in the pouch. They were few and simple treasures, but they were all she had. Each object contained the essence of so much experience.

She sat up and drew her legs into a cross-legged position. She winced at the pain in her tender ankle and the silk cover slipped. She covered herself again, trying not to appear self-conscious.

Mai-Ling stood up in a single rocking motion—forward, to tuck her toes, back to shift her weight, and then straight up. She was wearing a pale pink shirt of silk, with short sleeves and tiny cowry-shell buttons. Her midriff was bare and smooth in the gap between shirt and skirt. Low about her hips she had wrapped and tied a piece of turquoise and jade green silk. She was a small woman and the wrapped skirt hung straight from her hips. She wore no jewelry that Marina could see.

She went to one of the cabinets and opened it. She pulled something out and brought it to Marina. It was another silk piece. This one was block-printed in a subtle pattern of orange and black over red silk. Marina slipped it on over her head. Thin little straps held it up, leaving her shoulders bare. It felt good against her skin and her breasts glided against the fabric. She was grateful that it was not too small. She was larger than Mai-Ling and couldn't imagine her wearing this.

"Where do you get these clothes?" she asked, hoping she wasn't being rude.

"I sometimes see people from the lower island. I trade my bowls for what I need." Mai-Ling gestured in the direction of the pool and the view beyond.

"There are other people, then?"

"Yes, not far, maybe half a day's walk. Can you stand up? I'll show you how to tie this on." She lifted the long, yellow silk square in her hand.

Marina found that she could stand up. Her ankle did hurt, but it was more bruised than sprained. Putting weight on it didn't make it hurt any more. She let Mai-Ling take the silk from her and once again she was self-conscious about standing there only half-covered.

But Mai-Ling quickly wrapped the square of yellow silk low around Marina's hips several times, tying and tucking it intricately. She undid it and redid it several times so Marina could study the technique. Finally she let Marina try it. The tying went well but the tucking was not as graceful. Still, in the end, she'd managed it and felt proud of herself.

Standing, Marina noticed her reflection in an old scratched mirror that leaned against one of the support posts for the hut. She turned and looked at herself. She was not used to seeing herself in such bright colors. For years her wardrobe had been utilitarian khaki, warm subtle earthtones, black or gray. Now I look like an Indian princess. . . . Or a temple prostitute, she thought, though she caught herself smiling to think this. There is, after all, a goddess within me. Shakti would approve. The red, orange, and saffron yellow were sensual, hot colors against her skin. She had a fuller figure than Mai-Ling and the skirt emphasized the curve of her hips.

There were other changes, though. She'd seen herself reflected in still pools as she traveled over the island, and she had grown used to the almost-new skin she'd had after emerging from the sand and seaweed wrap on the beach. Now her skin was the skin she recognized, the skin she had grown into over the years. She walked close to the mirror. She could see the little lines again, and some of the scars had returned, but there was also something different. Something illuminated her from the inside now. Yes, the little lines around her eyes had returned, but she had never much minded them anyway. Now, however, her eyes seemed to sparkle. She looked hard at herself and liked what she saw.

"I've always hated mirrors," Mai-Ling volunteered, as if she thought Marina was about to make some self-deprecating remark. Rafael had said something about Mai-Ling, something about how she saw herself. Marina looked at Mai-Ling in the mirror and caught a subtle brushing of the hand as Mai-Ling instinctively touched the scar by her eye. She has touched that scar a thousand times a day, Marina thought. She's keeping it alive. She wasn't sure where this observation came from. It seemed to spring up suddenly in her.

"Well, how do I look?" she asked, changing the subject. She twirled once to feel how the fabric moved. Despite the little aches and pains of her fall, she felt like a young girl again, trying on clothes with a best friend.

"Beautiful," Mai-Ling said softly, but the way she said it made Marina feel sad.

They ate a meal together and afterward they sat on stones by the little pool and talked as the sun began to descend behind the volcano. Marina was amazed that she had come so far down the trail before falling. It seemed much farther than she remembered. She also looked out and down to what Mai-Ling called the lower island.

The same ring of white coral that she had seen from her vantage point high on the western face of the volcano continued around to the eastern side of the island. There appeared to be a little channel of deep blue that cut irregularly through the coral near the farthest eastern point of the island, but otherwise the island was well defended. She could see some flickering lights far below, but if there were buildings down there she couldn't see them.

"What's down there?" Marina asked. She'd hiked up her skirt to let her feet dangle in the cool water of the pool. It felt soothing to soak her ankle.

"I don't know. I've not been down there." There was nothing simple about this answer, but Marina proceeded cautiously.

"Don't you want to go on?" Marina assumed that if Mai-Ling was, as Rafael had said, like her, she would understand what this question meant.

"I'm not . . . I don't think I'm ready yet. You'll understand when you get closer."

"Closer?"

"Closer to the world of the living."

There, Marina thought, Mai-Ling had broached the subject. They had been circling the topic carefully. Now there was an opening.

"I thought once I crossed the summit I would be back in the world of the living."

"I thought that, too, but I think we are still in the shadows here. We are close, but we have not crossed some final threshold. We are not ghosts exactly, more like fairies." Mai-Ling paused a moment, then continued. "People from the lower island do occasionally wander up here. If I want them to see me, I can be real and solid, but if I sit very still in one of my circles, they can pass right by and not see me." Again she seemed to think for a moment, then added. "Except children. I can't seem to hide from children." They were both silent for a while, then Marina spoke.

"Was it hard for you," she gestured at the volcano, now silhouetted by the sun, "the crossing?"

Mai-Ling shuddered and looked away. Again Marina saw her fingers unconsciously trace the scar beneath her hair. Marina noticed that Mai-Ling kept her straight black hair pulled back behind her left ear, revealing the beautiful shape of her face, but on the right it fell so far forward as to almost hide her right eye. Done purposefully, it would have been a mysterious and seductive style, but it seemed only sad in this situation. What little she could see of the scar was not that dramatic or disfiguring. Marina suspected that, like an iceberg, the true scar ran much deeper than it appeared.

Marina changed the subject.

"Rafael said that you had a turtle tattoo when he met you."

"Yes." Mai-Ling brightened. "The Turtle Mother gave it to me. It's gone now though. Did you have one?"

"Yes." Marina touched her scalp. "It was headed this way last time I saw it. But it was pretty faded by that point."

"I didn't see it when I washed your hair."

They were both quiet for a moment, vaguely uncomfortable.

Then they compared stories. They did this carefully, discussing the events of their journeys without touching on the content or the significance of those events. Mai-Ling did not say how she came to Turtle Island, but Rafael had said that she had slit her wrists and Marina did not push her for more details than she was willing to volunteer. She had not been paralyzed as Marina had, but she spent several days wandering blind along the beach. An old woman had helped her regain her sight, an old woman with a turtle tattoo on her back. Mai-Ling had named her Turtle Mother. She did not recall a younger version of the woman.

"With my sight back," Mai-Ling continued, "I wandered until I found an abandoned hut. There was a loom and different tools in the hut, so, to pass the time, I began to carve little wooden bowls. In life I'd been a sculptor, but after death I had no desire to carve anything in the image of anything else. I carved little bowls more as a meditative practice, trying to find the bowl inside the burls and chunks of wood I found in the forest around me. I carved more bowls than I could use, so I set some afloat on the stream and imagined them being carried out to sea. Perhaps, I thought one would find its way back to the land of the living."

She'd burned the remaining bowls in little ceremonial fires. It was one of these fires that had brought Rafael to her. They'd become lovers. She admitted that. She helped him figure out how to work the loom, and though she had no interest in weaving, he seemed to take to it well. He'd been angry then and sometimes he would rage against death, but gradually he grew to understand his fate. She'd taught him to mix and prepare essential oils and to heal with his hands through massage. She'd brought these gifts with her into death.

She enjoyed Rafael's company, but he was haunted by the sins of his life and found it hard to relax his vigilance. In time, she came to understand that she was to move on, even though she knew Rafael was not yet ready.

She took only her tools when she left and from that point, her experiences and Marina's diverged dramatically. Mai-Ling described wandering aimlessly for days, unsure of her path, quite lost and despondent. She spoke of a long, dark cavern and a torture of mirrors. She dreamed and redreamed her life, never able to change a thing or wake from the dream. She did not tell Marina the nature of any of the events she alluded to reliving, but it distressed her even now to recall it.

Marina asked her if, at the time, she'd understood that she might work her way back to the living as she crossed the island. Yes, she answered, she understood that was an option, but it had not been what motivated her to continue.

Had she been aware of learning anything important on her journey? Marina asked. Marina herself had been keenly aware of what she was learning, was in fact, hungry to learn. Yes, Mai-Ling answered, she'd been aware of coming to new understandings, but she admitted also that she was still struggling to integrate what she'd learned.

"I would not do this again," Mai-Ling held up her wrists for Marina to see. There were two neat scars running lengthwise up the insides of her wrists, following the veins. This had not been a cry for help or an accident, Marina observed silently. Mai-Ling had wanted to die and knew how to do it. "But I don't seem to know how to go back yet."

Marina appreciated Mai-Ling's honesty. She herself, even in her recently kindled passion to return to the world of the living, had not really thought about what it meant.

"So here I sit and wait, building my circles by day, watching the lights of the living at night. I'm waiting for a sign, I guess." She traced the scar again without thinking.

★ ★ ★

Later, in the dark, Mai-Ling came to sleep beside Marina. At first Marina did not understand what was happening. Mai-Ling carefully arranged what looked like a set of her wooden bowls in a ritual circle around Marina. Then she slipped silently beneath the light, cotton sheet and pressed her smooth body against Marina's.

Marina had never had a woman as a lover. She didn't want to hurt Mai-Ling's feelings. Mai-Ling might have saved her from losing her chance at life. She was grateful, but uncomfortable. What would be done to her? Marina wondered. What would she be expected to do?

But Mai-Ling merely nuzzled close to Marina, cupping her breast lightly, as if holding onto something secure, and fell asleep. After a time, Marina relaxed, timing her breathing to Mai-Ling's. She seems so fragile, Marina thought, for someone who's made it this far. Marina did not think of herself as fragile, but then she'd never seen herself that way. Mai-Ling was like an unfired clay teacup. The beauty of the form, the potential, was there, but a strong or clumsy hand could still break her. She could not yet hold tea, or realize her purpose.

★ ★ ★

In the morning, Mai-Ling was not beside her and the bowls were gone as well.

Marina washed and pulled on her bright silk top. She was pleased with her ability to tie on the yellow skirt herself. She found a brush and brushed her hair. There were almost no tangles, which she found unusual, until she remembered that Mai-Ling had washed and combed out her hair while cleaning the cut on her scalp. She felt the place where she'd struck her head and decided that it must have been a small cut, for it was nearly healed over.

Mai-Ling returned with fresh fruit, and they ate breakfast together, neither one mentioning the previous night.

"Would you like to see my circles?" Mai-Ling asked after they'd finished eating. "I mean, do you think you can go for a walk?"

"Actually, I think it would be good for me to walk. But what are these circles? You've mentioned them several times. Did you say you built them?"

"It would be easier to show you," she said, pulling Marina to her feet.

As they walked through the forest, Marina practiced seeing the auras of the trees. It was not easy at first. It did not come as naturally as it had with Téves in Adytum Wood, but gradually it came back to her. She tried to talk to Mai-Ling about it, but Mai-Ling did not seem to understand that there was something that could be seen. She seemed, however, to feel the energy in some way, because wherever Marina detected the magical patterns in the filtering sunlight, she found that Mai-Ling had built a stone circle there. Her gift, it seemed, drew her to the places as if by magnetic attraction.

The first circle they came to, Mai-Ling called Dragon's Heart. It was composed of smooth river stones painted with tiny mythical creatures. Marina got on her hands and knees to inspect the stones. The detail was incredible. Most of the stones had images of dragons painted in red and orange and yellow and gold. But some had other creatures Marina could not identify. Between each of the large stones were little hollows dug in the ground. In each hollow was one of Mai-Ling's little bowls. The bowls were charred and filled with ash, but still held their shape.

"Go ahead, step inside," Mai-Ling said.

Marina did, and she felt the change immediately. It was almost as powerful as the old trees that had spoken to her in Adytum Wood. Energy coursed and crackled through her. For the first time Marina wondered if Mai-Ling was as fragile as she had supposed.

The second circle Mai-Ling brought Marina to was one she called Bone Music. It was constructed of twelve small wooden tripods, each supporting three polished black stones. The stones sat up off the ground in their tripods, each stone smaller than the one beneath it. Upon close inspection, Marina noticed that between each stone was a pressed green leaf. The wooden tripods were lashed together with braided grass cord, and they'd been stripped of their bark so that they looked as white as bleached bone.

She tried this circle as well. The energy was cooler and greener here. The story Téves had told her of Oriolis flooded back over her as vivid and alive as when she'd first heard it. Mai-Ling was clearly pleased that Marina could sense the flavors of energy so distinctly.

She pulled Marina along anxiously to the third circle.

"This is Molten Dreams," she announced.

Each of the stones that formed this circle was chipped and crudely, but effectively, carved into a human form. There were female forms and male forms, though they did not alternate evenly. Marina asked if she could pick one up. They were light, she noticed, almost porous. "It's lava flow," Mai-Ling offered. "It's old, but I know where to find it."

"They're beautiful," Marina said as she set the stone back in place. Mai-Ling adjusted it compulsively with her toe.

Marina didn't need to ask or wait to be invited. She stepped inside the circle. This energy was more refined. Autumnal, Marina thought, though she did not know why. It was an energy for slowing down, for going to sleep. It was hard to step outside of this current. She could easily let herself be swept up in it.

The fourth of Mai-Ling's circles was called Earth Work, and it was deceptively simple. It also broke the pattern in that it was not truly a circle. It was a hexagram defined by five sets of five river stones. Each set of stones was wrapped or decorated differently.

Mai-Ling pulled Marina inside the hexagram and made her sit. It was a small form and Mai-Ling knelt behind Marina, directing her hands to each of the five sides. The side they began with had stones wrapped almost completely in the petals of different colored flowers. These petals had dried and shrunk, molding to the stone like a rainbow skin. The second line was made up of smaller stones interpenetrating carefully carved wooden stakes that had been sharpened at both ends. They looked sinister and weaponlike. The third side had stones bundled in reed jackets and tied with red grasses. They looked like little samurai warriors dressed for war in bamboo armor. The fourth side was composed of standing stones, gray obelisks that looked like Stonehenge, simple and unadorned. The last side was made up of five rounded, heart-shaped stones. Each stone had been carefully split in half then bound back together with dried vines.

The energy within the hexagram was erratic but personal. It seemed to be telling Marina things about Mai-Ling. Each side was a code, Marina was convinced, but she didn't have the key. She could not quite get inside it.

For the final stone circle, Mai-Ling led Marina back to the stream that ran past the hut and over the waterfall.

This circle, Spilling Water, she called it, was built of large stones. Some undoubtedly had been found in place, Marina couldn't imagine Mai-Ling moving them, but others had been rolled, pushed, or cajoled into place in such a pattern as to form a circle of steps ranging from about three feet high to ground level. On each stone step was one of Mai-Ling's bowls, each with a tiny hole drilled into its side. Again Mai-Ling pulled her into the circle and made her sit.

"Close your eyes," she said. "Just listen."

Marina saw her dip a ladle into a tiny pool of water and pour this into the highest of her little wood bowls before she closed her eyes. The water trickled from bowl to bowl creating a strange but beautiful musical scale. The sound and the energy spiraled around her. It took her down and brought her back up again. She still imagined she heard the water long after Mai-Ling had stopped refilling the first bowl. Mai-Ling did not rush her from this last experience, but let her sit until she was ready to get up.

"They're so beautiful," Marina said as they walked back to the hut. "Why do you build them, though? Where do you come from?"

Mai-Ling's stone circles did something to the energy patterns that Marina had learned only recently to sense. They channeled and smoothed out the wild energy. They amplified it and made it more intense.

"I don't know. I do them because I can, I suppose. I do them to celebrate and honor the energy." Marina felt that Mai-Ling was only telling her half the truth. There was another reason, a deeper more significant reason. "They're my altars." This, Marina felt, was closer to the truth but still not entirely the truth. "Anyway, you should tell me why I build them." Marina didn't understand this challenge, but she couldn't forget it, either.

★ ★ ★

That night Mai-Ling came to her again. She had fallen asleep this time and did not see Mai-Ling arrange the little bowls in a circle around where she slept. She came awake slowly to the warm press of Mai-Ling's body and the light stroke of her hand.

She seemed again to have no agenda beyond comforting and intimate touch. Marina wondered if this was a slow acclimation, a slide into seduction. She invented boundaries in her drowsy mind. She imagined borders on her body, which, if crossed, would require some sort of defense, but she had not much strength to resist this soft invader. In the morning she could not recall if any of her borders had, in fact, been crossed.

Time passed thickly and slowly with Mai-Ling. They spent their days as sisters, fellow artists, explorers. Marina taught Mai-Ling to see like a photographer, even though they had no camera with which to practice. Mai-Ling taught Marina the sacred arts of wrapping and arranging.

If they were lovers by night, Marina could never recall it in the morning. She had delicious dreams with Mai-Ling beside her—moist, floating, water dreams, but nothing hard, specific, anatomical.

Marina began to experiment with her own altar. She tried careful arrangements of the sacred artifacts of her journey. She had told Mai-Ling, that for her, an altar would need to be portable. She needed to define her own sacred space, her own sanctuary wherever she found herself. Mai-Ling carved a little wooden box for her to carry her stone from the mirror pool, her pendulum, and the circular stone Rafael had given her. The leather cord had broken in her fall so she didn't wear it now, but it was no less important. She still wore the coral and pearl anklet, but took it off at night and kept it on her altar. When Marina began to play with the little branch as a way of supporting both the anklet and the pendulum, Mai-Ling carved a hole in the box to support it as a stand.

Mai-Ling also surprised her one day with a rich brown bowl, striated with blond tones and inlaid with mother of pearl. It too joined her altar.

She found that the elements of her altar were a kind of secret language that only she understood. The anklet threaded around the top of the little branch reminded her of balance and cautioned her against her propensity for the dark side of things. The stone circle made her think of a little lenseless magnifying glass. Live in the moment and pay attention to the details, it told her. If she twisted the shiny black pebble from the mirror pool just right she could see different reflections of herself that reminded her of her own mother, her childhood, and other women inside her that needed to be honored and cared for. The pendulum suspended from the branch encouraged her in slow spiral dances to keep an open heart and search for the patterns. The branch itself was a sign of her strength and her will. She would never again slide helplessly into death and despair. She would not seek death out, but neither was she afraid of it. Mai-Ling's cup she felt was important, but she did not yet understand the language it spoke.

To her collection of sacred symbols, Marina added flowers, found stones, seed pods, feathers, candles. Mai-Ling gave her two little bottles of essential oils, one the vanilla, cinnamon, and cloves mixture, the other a light, floral smell with an overtone of moss and ferns. This second scent she began to wear regularly, touching it to her ankles, wrists, and the hollow of her neck. She did this almost unconsciously, and when she thought about it, she wondered who she was doing it for. Was this for Mai-Ling? she wondered. Was she playing a part in her own seduction? She'd always associated perfumes and scents with something put on for others, but this oil she wore for herself. She liked the subtle scent around her.

Gradually she began to develop little rituals for her altar. She would take the placement of no single object for granted. Each day she would spend some time with her altar. She would not let dust settle long on any of her sacred treasures. She cleaned them each day with a soft cloth. She replaced the flowers as they wilted. She picked up each object and held it for a few moments, feeling its particular energy and spirit. As she replaced each object, she tried it in a new position or orientation until she felt it was right. Her altar was dynamic, not static. Some of her found things spent only a short time on her altar before being carefully and thoughtfully returned to the forest.

These rituals reinforced positive patterns of energy, building up her focus and will. The rituals and then the altar itself calmed her and protected her. It offered her a secret garden into which she could always escape for a moment's respite.

"How do you think a cathedral like Chartres can resonate with such power?" Mai-Ling asked her one day. "It's nothing more than an altar on a grand scale. Some Druid or perhaps some early European shaman felt the energy that resonated from a certain site. That shaman marked the site with stones. Later a priestess of some lost goddess religion would replace the stones with a sacrificial slab. Druids would plant a grove of trees around it, and Romans would dedicate it to the Goddess Diana. Later, Christians would usurp the site and build their churches and cathedrals over it.

"Over time, all the devotional energy absorbed by that site gives it an immense and transformative power. It comes to have a life of its own. I believe this is how our altars work. They focus our energy through ritual and repetition."

That night Marina dreamed of sacred groves and standing stones. She saw Mai-Ling as a priestess, a shaman, a wise woman celebrated and honored by her tribe. She saw Mai-Ling burned at the stake for witchcraft. The dreams ran on into other dreams, some inviting, others disturbing, but the blast of a ship's steam horn woke her in the dark night. She was alone. Mai-Ling had not come to her. She listened for Mai-Ling's breathing across the room. It was arrhythmic, not the steady breath of sleep.

Marina got up and went to her. Her wooden bowls were spread around her in a sacred circle. Marina crossed over them and knelt by Mai-Ling. She lay on her side with her back to Marina. She was crying. Marina could see the tears glinting even in the darkness. She stroked Mai-Ling's soft hair and whispered, "What is it?"

Mai-Ling rolled onto her back in the dim light. She was naked and had no sheet over her. "You will leave tomorrow, and you still haven't told me why I build the circles."

"You told me you build them to honor the energy. You taught me what altars and sacred spaces are for." Marina was confused.

"But why do I build them? Why am I stuck here? Why can I go no further than this?" Mai-Ling's hand went of its own volition to the scar on her face.

Marina had seen her do this hundreds of times, but this time she caught Mai-Ling's hand and stopped her. With her own hand, Marina caressed the raised white burn scar. Mai-Ling winced, but not from pain. Marina bent and kissed the scarred place, but she did not immediately pull her lips away. She let her lips feel the irregular surface. She let her tongue gently taste the old wound.

Images startled her like electrical current. A man Mai-Ling had loved had done this to her. Rafael had told Marina that much. Mai-Ling had never spoken of it. Now Marina saw the man. It was no accident, no drunken rage. It was sober and deliberate and evil. She'd loved him completely with a full and open heart, and he'd surprised her just as completely with his cruelty. When he'd tired of what she gave willingly, he took still more from her. He'd raped her and marked her with a knife heated to a red glow in a candle's flame. He might just as well have torn out her heart and sewn up her chest, for there was no trust left in her.

She could love. She had learned that after death. Turtle Island had helped Mai-Ling find her heart again, but she was stuck here and could not go forward.

Marina pressed her lips to the burn scar once again.

"You build the circles from fear. That's why you can't move on." Marina whispered this in Mai-Ling's ear, soft like a lover's secret. She was not sure where her answer came from, but she knew it was true as she heard herself say it. "You are keeping this alive." She kissed Mai-Ling's scar as she said "this." "You are so much more than this wound." Marina ran her hand lightly along Mai-Ling's cheek, over her throat, across her small breasts, smooth stomach, past the silken juncture of her thighs, as far as she could reach. She could not recall if she had ever touched Mai-Ling like this before. It did not feel familiar.

"Let go of this pain." One last time she kissed the scar, then she kissed Mai-Ling's lips. They were soft and tasted of salt tears. It reminded her of a dream that now seemed long past. If Mai-Ling had asked her at that moment, she would have made love to her. She would have done it with abandon and with a full heart. She would have wrapped herself around her, found ways to be inside her. She would have held nothing back.

And if Mai-Ling had asked her at that moment she would have promised never to leave her.

But Mai-Ling asked for neither of these things.

"Hold me," she whispered. "Sleep beside me one more time."

And so Marina curled up beside Mai-Ling and slept. She did not hear Mai-Ling say, "Yes, my love, you will leave me in the morning," or "don't ever forget me."

She fell asleep and dreamed of ships gliding through the night.

CHAPTER 7

Turtle Dreams

Orientation.

Knowing one's place in time and space.

There's a name for it. They say that turtles are somatic navigators—that they feel their way from island to island—but this is not a small answer to the question of how turtles find their way. It's a big answer, like God or the uncertainty principle. Sea turtles may be both particle and wave, knowing intimately what no outside observer might.

If you wake me from my sea turtle dream to ask me my position, I will surely lose my course. And if you draw me up in great nets to ask me of my course, do not be surprised if, for a moment, I do not know where I am.

Marina did indeed leave the next morning. She woke early and saw a ship far off on the horizon. It was not the ship for her, but she knew it was a sign. The world of the living was calling her.

Mai-Ling was quiet as they ate breakfast and had their morning tea. She said nothing about Marina's leaving, though they both knew it was inevitable.

Mai-Ling was sad but also light. There was an unusual sense of peace about her. She tied back her hair with a scrap of red silk, exposing her whole face in a way she'd never done before. Marina said nothing about this, but did notice that she didn't touch her scar all morning.

After breakfast, when they might have gone off to work together on one of Mai-Ling's circles, they were both suddenly awkward around each other. Mai-Ling spoke first.

"I would say let me help you pack, but you have so little to take with you that it seems silly." Marina was surprised but grateful that Mai-Ling was able to joke about it. "Do you have anything to pack things into?"

Even Marina laughed at that. "I have my shoulder bag," she said in mock defiance. She looked down and realized she was wearing Mai-Ling's clothes. She had worn different pieces of Mai-Ling's clothing during her stay, but today, without really thinking about it, she'd wrapped the yellow silk skirt around her hips and pulled on the red and orange patterned top, the clothes Mai-Ling had first given her.

"Keep them," Mai-Ling said, anticipating Marina's dilemma. "They suit you."

Marina only had one other piece of clothing: the colorful woven jacket that Rafael had given her. Mai-Ling had washed it, and it had come close to clean. Mai-Ling had taken to wearing it in the evenings when it got cooler. She said she could smell both Marina and Rafael on it. It was hanging on a peg near where Marina slept. She took it down and gave it to Mai-Ling. "I have so little to give. I wish I could give you more."

"You've given me plenty," Mai-Ling said, as she took the jacket and hugged it to her chest. "I think perhaps I will follow you soon."

"Come with me now!" Marina said excitedly. She had wanted to say this before but was unsure how Mai-Ling might respond. "You don't need these circles anymore. Come with me, build new ones." She was not sure what she was asking or offering, but Mai-Ling interrupted her.

"You know I can't. I'm almost there but just not yet. I'll come soon enough."

"I could wait for you."

"No, you can't . . . any more than I can hold you here."

"Perhaps we could find each other, you know . . . after."

Mai-Ling knelt near Marina's altar and took the string of coral and black pearls from the little branch it decorated. She took Marina's foot in her lap and began tying it around her ankle. "If we are meant to find each other again, I think we will . . . but I don't think we should seek each other out." Marina did not answer. She knew that, hard as it was for her to say this, Mai-Ling was speaking from her heart. "It will be enough to see your photographs and read your name. And perhaps you will come across one of my circles in your travels."

Marina sensed the wisdom in this as almost a palpable thing. There was really nothing else to be said. She packed her stones and her pendulum in the little box Mai-Ling had carved. She wrapped the inlaid bowl and the bottles of essential oils in little scraps of silk. She chose some of the feathers and leaves and one of the pebbles she'd found. She put all of this carefully into her shoulder bag and slung it over shoulder. Mai-Ling helped her tie the little branch onto the bag so that it didn't poke her or stick out awkwardly as she walked.

She drank some water before leaving but took no food with her. She kissed Mai-Ling and they held each other fondly for a long moment, but the fever that had come over her seemed to have passed now, and she parted from Mai-Ling as she might a sister or dear friend.

Marina walked slowly down the trail beside the cliffs to the lower island. She was in no hurry now and made a morning of her slow descent. She stopped to listen to the calls of birds. She stopped to smell the moist, fragrant air. She stopped to practice seeing the little shimmer of silver and blue around the trees and plants and found that it came to her easily.

In the afternoon she came upon a stream and took the opportunity to rinse her feet. She'd walked over rough terrain in the past days. She'd cut and scraped and banged and bruised her feet, but they seemed now unscathed. She pulled up her skirt to examine her legs. They were smooth and unmarked, save for the faint old scars. All signs of her rough crossing had healed. She'd fallen, and marked her legs on her journey. She could remember the falls and the wounds, but she couldn't recall where any specific injury had been.

She continued her inspection, unwrapping her skirt and pulling off her shirt with the pretext of rinsing in the stream. She could find no evidence of the journey on her body. She recalled that her skin had, at one point, seemed different, somehow new again, but this was the skin she remembered from before Turtle Island. It made her happy, this feeling of being back in her own skin, the skin she'd earned.

She splashed herself with water, dried in a patch of warm sun, and dressed again, deftly tying the skirt on so that she knew it wouldn't slip off.

As she continued on, the path grew level and sandy. She could see more palm trees around her and became aware of the steady rhythm of waves. Not far, she thought, and then, not far to where?

When I'm dreaming, she began a conversation in her own mind, I don't think about how real I am. And when I'm awake, I don't think about it, either. So I wonder why I am so aware of it now. Marina did feel more real, more solid, full of more energy than she had before. Was this coming back to life? she wondered.

She'd been alive, then dead, then dreaming, somewhere between dead and alive, now she was alive, or very close to it. She felt excitement and a certain amount of apprehension. She wondered if she was really ready. The pouch at her side with the makings of her altar was reassuring. I can do this, she thought. I wonder what happens next?

It occurred to her that there must be some mechanics, some logistics involved with this return to life. She hadn't really thought about it before. Each step in her journey had, in its own way, seemed to have been supported by such a fragile reality. At first she had not been able to accept that she might come this far back to life. She had not wanted to believe it. Then it seemed as if she had dreamed her way across the island, always afraid that practical questions, anything that challenged the reality of the dream, might wake her. And where would she wake? she wondered. Drowning again? In a real heaven or hell?

Now the practical questions began to creep back into her mind. How long had she been dead? How long had she been on Turtle Island? Were they the same thing? There were people who, by now, surely thought her dead. Erin would know. Her family would know. She would have caused them terrible grief. Would she simply make her way back to civilization and call them? Hi, Mom, Dad, guess who? It was a morbid thought. What would she say? She'd left a note clearly announcing her intention to die. She could not now claim to have fallen accidentally. Would she say that she tried to die but it didn't take? Would she say that she had died and come back to life?

She wondered if there would be some prohibition on her speaking of her experience. Perhaps it happened to people all the time, and perhaps they did talk about it. Maybe before Turtle Island she would have seen these people as crazy or disturbed individuals. Or, more likely, perhaps she simply looked right past these people, not even seeing them or registering their stories. Maybe she would not want to speak of her time on Turtle Island. Or perhaps she would forget about it.

This thought bothered her most. If I forget about this, I will forget the lessons of this place. No . . . I can't forget about this. I won't allow it. She patted the bag at her side. It somehow made her feel better to have these tangible reminders with her. Their weight was reassuring, but still she worried.

You are not thinking in the present. This came in a voice that was not Marina's, but it came from inside her. At first she did not realize this and looked around for the person who had spoken. She was, by now, well used to being surprised by people. But she saw no one. It slowly came to her that she had thought this and not heard it, but it was a strange kind of thought, as if she now carried the spirit of the Turtle Woman, or Rafael, or Atana, or Téves, or even Mai-Ling inside her. It was the kind of wisdom she would not have been surprised to have heard from any of them, but, it had come from inside of her.

Yes, she answered herself, I am thinking too far out. I've taken each moment as it's come to me here. It's a good way to go. I don't think my journey is completely over yet.

Suddenly Marina realized she was facing a choice. She'd come to a stop when she thought she heard a voice speaking to her. She'd listened and looked, but all she heard was the sound of waves off to her left. Now she was aware that there were two directions she could take. The wide trail continued on ahead and disappeared around a turn, but to her left was a narrow, less-traveled trail. It was this path that beckoned her.

The trail ended at the beach, a beach not much different than the one on which she'd begun. The sand was creamy white with few shells, decorated with the occasional piece of sun-bleached driftwood or fallen palm husk. The sand was hot and felt good beneath her toes. Despite having gone barefoot for days, she stood and squirmed her toes in the sand just to feel it.

She walked to the water's edge. Waves lapped ashore gently, but she could see them breaking more violently far out where the coral reef created sandbars and breaks. She lifted the edge of her yellow silk skirt and waded into the water up to her knees. It was warm and flecks of foam splashed about her legs.

She looked up and down the beach and contemplated swimming. She could see no sign of other people. There were no footprints on the beach. There were no sounds other than the natural music of ocean and jungle and sky. She laughed at herself when she realized that she was concerned about taking off her clothes. She'd had only barely perceptible traces of modesty since waking up on Turtle Island. It had been liberating and awakening to live with her skin, her body, so open to experience and physical sensation. She did not now want to lose that feeling, but realized that there must be some balance.

Perhaps that's why I'm here, why I turned off the main path, she thought. Maybe I need to learn how I'll integrate Turtle Island into my new life.

For the moment Marina decided against swimming. Instead she turned and walked back up the beach to the place where the trail had been. Set back from the edge of the tree line she noticed a primitive hut like the ones Rafael and Mai-Ling had lived in. It had a simple plank floor and thatched roof, but this hut had walls of woven mat on three sides and split bamboo shades that could be rolled up or down on the fourth side, facing the sea. They were rolled up now, which revealed the inside of the hut.

It was bigger than the other huts had been and furnished simply. There was a low platform for sleeping, several low tables and chests, and a tall cabinet with double doors. There was also a low counter with a stone top near a big opening on the back side of the hut. There were pillows and carpets and grass mats on the floor and the stuffed mattress on the platform was covered in ivory sheets.

Marina walked completely around the hut. It was clearly lived in, but she found no one around and no footprints other than her own on the ground. At the back of the hut was a small stone-lined fire pit. The ashes in it were cold. There was a pile of firewood beside it and a round stone cistern filled with fresh water. A coconut-shell cup sat on the edge of the water basin and Marina dipped water for herself. She looked in through the back entrance to the hut and saw that the stone counter was a place for preparing food. Neatly arranged on the counter were several small wooden bowls, cups and plates, and a long chef's knife.

She continued around the hut until she was standing in front of it again. Still seeing no one, she climbed the two steps up into the hut and looked around. There was a mirror in one corner. There was some stationery, block-printed with a crude sea turtle, sitting on one of the low tables. There were clean towels in one of the chests on the floor and a bowl of sweet-smelling soap. The tall cabinet contained a pair of sandals and several cotton sundresses and gauzy Indian print skirts that looked as if they might fit her. Another chest contained more odds and ends of clothing, neatly folded, but other than that, the place had no personal items.

Marina tried her foot in one of the sandals and it fit her perfectly. She lifted one of the dresses in her hand and brought it to her nose. She could smell no perfume or fragrance on it. She let it fall back into the cabinet and shut the door.

★ ★ ★

She waited for the owner of the dresses to return, even though she suspected no one would come. She waited three days, gradually settling in. The first two nights she slept on one of the carpets on the floor.

She slept in her clothes and rolled three of the four split bamboo screens down each night before retiring. She did this out of more than just abstract concern. Each morning when she woke, she found a tray of fresh fruit and sliced bread neatly covered with a red cloth on the edge of the stone cistern outside of the hut. She neither heard nor saw the person who delivered it. She could not even distinguish tracks in the sand that might have belonged to this person.

The tray would vanish just as mysteriously late in the morning when Marina walked down to the beach, and other meals would replace it whenever Marina was away from the hut or napping. The trays of food sometimes contained soups and each evening there was a simple dish of cooked fish with vegetables in different sauces flavored with ginger, mangoes, and peppers.

It took her some time, but gradually she overcame the sense that she was constantly being observed and relaxed into her new home. Late on the afternoon of the third day she washed and rinsed her yellow silk skirt and red top and hung them to dry outside the hut like the flags explorers once put down to claim a place for king and country. She swam naked in the warm sea and scrubbed her skin with sand. Back at the hut she rinsed herself with fresh water and washed her hair with some of the sweet soap. She dried herself with one of the thick, clean towels she'd found and, after feasting on a delicious fish soup and balls of rice wrapped around a core of sweet potato, she slipped luxuriantly between the clean sheets of the raised platform bed and slept.

When she woke the little hut had become hers. She tried on one of the sundresses, a pattern of leaves and flowers in warm earthtones, and it fit her well enough to wear. It fell to just below her knees, but left her shoulders and arms bare except for the thin straps that held it up.

She still had no use for the sandals. She put her anklet on every morning, but otherwise wanted nothing about her feet or ankles. She found but did not put on a straw sun hat, though she appreciated a scarf she found in the back of the cabinet. She used this to tie back her hair.

She also unpacked her little bag and spread the contents of her altar out on one of the tables. She placed her little tree in its box stand and dangled her crystal pendulum from its branches. She carefully arranged Rafael's stone pendant and the shiny black pebble from the mirror pool. She placed Mai-Ling's bowl in the center and laid the feather and some of the other things she'd found around it. She filled Mai-Ling's bowl with water and floated upon it the blossom that always accompanied her food tray.

Each day thereafter she would explore a little ways around her hut, often bringing back items for her altar. Though she never saw anyone, Marina would sometimes hear voices in the jungle around her. They were not speaking to her but seemed to be carrying on conversations of their own. She always retreated from these voices. She needed time, she told herself. But time for what? Her days were filled with simple meditation before her altar, walking along the beach, swimming, napping, eating, watching the sun rise, watching the tide come in, retreat, and come in again.

For the first time in her life she spent little time thinking about her past. She did find herself looking for objects for her altar that might, in some way, honor the little girl in her who had once lain buried to her face in mud in the middle of a steamy summer storm. She might like this crab's shell, or this feather, or this fish bone, Marina thought, fully aware that the "she" to whom she was referring was a part of herself. She would like signs of the nature she stalked with her camera.

In the same way, she brought back flowers and the leaves of plants to honor the part of herself most like her mother. She recalled her mother's studio as always being filled with flowers and plants. If I can, she thought, I will sit again in my mother's studio and watch her paint, and listen to her talk, half to me, half to her canvases, as I once did. Perhaps I can learn again to make art that satisfies the deep places in me. My mother knows this secret, Marina thought, she always has.

Marina also brought back odd little pieces that struck her in some way as being playfully erotic: a peach-colored conch shell with undulating vulva-like folds of pink on the underside, a smooth, brown seedpod that spiraled and twisted in a phallic dance, a twining branch of coral that reminded her of the tangled legs of sleeping lovers. These pieces also honored some part of her long ignored, but she did not think of this as dwelling in the past. She had no regrets now, had, in fact, no place for regrets.

She also tried to avoid anticipating the future. Sometimes she would catch herself thinking of things she might do, but, like a meditation, she let these thoughts come and go without dwelling upon them.

Sometime after she'd lost count of the days she'd spent in her little home on the beach, she came to realize she was waiting for something.

Marina had fallen asleep in the afternoon and woke to the awareness that someone was watching her. She was sleeping on her side on the raised platform bed and opened her eyes slowly. A child squatted on the floor about five feet away studying her. There was within her a certain quality of sadness.

The little girl looked to be about eight or nine years old, though Marina was never a good judge of the ages of children. She was slender, with lightly tanned skin and pale blonde hair that fell straight, if a little wildly, over her shoulders. She wore the bottom piece of a green bathing suit but nothing over her torso. She had a little necklace of shells and had put a small flower behind one of her ears.

"Are you a ghost?" she asked matter-of-factly.

"A ghost?" Marina responded.

"You know. Are you real?" She pinched her own arm to emphasize her point. "Or are you a ghost?"

Marina did not know quite how to answer this. It was in fact the question she'd tended to want to ask of everyone she'd encountered lately.

By way of answer she extended her own arm to the girl. She realized as she did this that she too was naked from the waist up. She was wearing one of the gauzy skirts she'd found, but had taken off the shirt she'd been wearing with it. Somehow, though, this did not seem a problem but instead put them on an equal footing.

For a moment the child did not move. Then she dropped to her knees and crawled close enough to pinch Marina's arm gently.

"Ghost?" Marina asked with a smile.

"I guess not . . . but I've seen 'em, you know."

"Ghosts?"

"Yeah, they're all around, especially up the trail, toward the volcano.

You see 'em and they look just like a person. Only when you get close they aren't there anymore. It's weird."

"So you're pretty sure I'm not a ghost?"

"Yeah, I guess. Why?"

"Nothing. I've just been feeling like a ghost lately. It's good to know that I'm a real person." Actually, it really was a relief to know that someone considered her alive, though why she trusted this child's opinion, she couldn't say. The child thought about what Marina had said for a few moments before answering.

Marina wanted to put her arms around this little girl and hold her, but instead she sat up and stretched. "My name's Marina," she said, extending her hand.

"I'm Grace Carolyn DeVries," she answered, shaking Marina's hand enthusiastically. "But you can call me Gracie."

"Well, Gracie, where are your parents now?"

"Oh, they have one of the inland huts by the waterslide."

"The waterslide?"

"Well, it's not really a waterslide, not like an amusement park or anything, but you can slide down on this real slippery rock into a pool. It's kind of like a waterfall."

"Is it far?"

"Not too far." Gracie seemed to think about this a moment. "Probably farther than I'm supposed to go though. You won't tell them will you?"

"No, I don't think so. As long as they won't be worried about you."

"They won't." She seemed sure of this but the certainty was nothing she took pleasure in. "I don't think they'd notice if I didn't come back at all."

"Of course they would," Marina answered quickly, though it hadn't been too long ago that she'd believed the same thing about herself.

"I don't know. I mean we eat dinner together, and sometimes one of them makes the other do something with me, but never together. Mostly they say to go play, but there's no one to play with. There are no kids on this island. There are the ghosts, and some other grown-ups, and the big house, and you. That's it."

"What's the big house?" Marina asked.

"You know, the big house. It's like a hotel or something. It's near the pier. It's where the ship brings you. You had to see it."

"No, not yet. I came from the other side of the island."

Gracie looked at her suspiciously. She rolled back up into a squatting position as if to be ready to bolt suddenly. "You know what I think?" She waited for Marina to answer.

"No, what do you think?"

"I think only ghosts come from the other side of the island." She said this with a deep seriousness, checking Marina carefully for any suspicious moves.

"And why do you think that?"

"'Cause that's where all the ghosts are, stupid." She realized she'd said something she shouldn't have and apologized immediately. "Sorry. I didn't mean that you were stupid."

"But that's where I came from, and you already decided that I'm not a ghost."

"Yeah, I guess," Gracie conceded. "But ghosts can fool you."

Marina laughed at this and soon Gracie was laughing with her.

They talked some more about little things, what Gracie liked and didn't like about the island. At one point Marina flinched when Gracie referred to it as Turtle Island. She somehow felt as if she had named the place herself and that others only used the name out of deference to her journey. But Gracie called it Turtle Island and referred to big turtle shells that hung on the patio of the big house.

She also realized at some point that Gracie was making her fantasy island, her dreaming place, a reality. Like a goddess or Devic spirit, Gracie's naming of things, her confirmation, was making Marina's dream a thing of substance.

Eventually, however, Gracie cocked her head to one side, listening to a sound Marina could not hear. "I better go now, I think they're looking for me."

Marina didn't want her to go. Gracie got up and danced down the back steps, then turned back. "Hey, can I come back tomorrow?"

"That would be nice," Marina said, and, in an instant, Gracie was gone.

I wonder what this means, Marina thought to herself later as she ate alone. Her food had arrived as usual, though whether it had come while she slept or while she talked to Gracie, she could not say. Everyone I've met has had some message, some lesson for me. I wonder what Gracie's message is?

As soon as she'd thought this though, another observation came to her. I've assumed all along that my experiences have been arranged to meet my needs. What if I'm here for Gracie?

★ ★ ★

The next morning Gracie was back before Marina woke. She was polite and stayed outside, but Marina could hear her rearranging the shells Marina had placed on the edge of the cistern. She was glad Gracie was back. She stretched and wrapped the sheet around her.

"Good morning," she said from what would have been a doorway, if there had been a door.

"Hi. I hope it's okay that I came back, I mean so early." There seemed to be something else she wanted to tell Marina, some other explanation she wanted to make, but didn't.

"It's fine. Have you eaten breakfast?"

"Yeah, but I'll sit with you while you eat, if you want."

"That would be nice." Marina went back inside and selected a full skirt of several sheer layers of blue and green and a vest with a pattern of green leaves on it. "Would you bring the tray inside?"

"Sure." Gracie seemed excited to be useful to someone. She was dressed in torn blue jean shorts and a little T-shirt with a big question mark printed on the front. Her toenails were painted an electric shade of blue and she wore a necklace of shells. She bounded up the steps with the tray in hand, almost tripping in her enthusiasm.

Marina took the tray and set it on one of the low tables, gesturing for Gracie to sit. When Marina uncovered the tray she discovered two sweet rolls instead of the usual one and two ceramic mugs of tea, still steaming.

"I suppose you were meant to join me after all." Gracie nodded and picked up first one, then the other mug of tea, sniffing each and selecting one.

"This is mine," she announced.

"How can you tell?"

"Honey. I like honey in my tea." Marina tasted the tea Gracie had pushed to her side of the table. Sure enough, it was unsweetened.

"Did you sweeten it before?"

"No, it comes like that. My tea always comes sweet."

"Do you know who brings this?" Marina said, gesturing at the food tray.

"The people from the big house. They bring it. You never see 'em though. But they're not ghosts, they just move real quietly."

"And they know about me?"

"Sure. You're living in one of their cabins, just like my mom and dad. They have to know about you."

This was a puzzle to Marina. This is some part of the process of return, she thought. It makes sense in a way. It's gradual, gentle. But still she wondered how.

"Hey, wanna go exploring with me?" Gracie said after devouring her sweet roll and tea.

"Sure," Marina answered. "Where shall we go?"

"I'll show you."

Gracie waited impatiently as Marina rinsed the dishes and cups with water from the cistern and placed the tray back outside. There was never food left on the tray, but Marina never felt full after eating. They, whoever they were, seemed to know just how much was enough.

"You don't have to do that, you know," Gracie said as Marina rinsed the plates. "They don't expect you to. My mom and dad don't do it. It's like room service or something."

"Ahh," Marina acknowledged, continuing to clean up. "Still, it feels good to do it. Do you mind?"

"No. Suit yourself." This seemed an unlikely phrase to have sprung from Gracie. Marina imagined Gracie picking it up from her mother or father.

After splashing some water on her face and tying her hair back, Marina let Gracie lead her back up the trail that forked off the main trail. At the main trail Gracie turned right, the direction that led back up the way Marina had come. This made Marina vaguely uncomfortable. She'd vested so much energy in going forward on her journey that going backward just felt wrong. Gracie seemed to sense Marina's unease because she stopped and took Marina's hand in hers.

"It's okay. You're with me. I won't let anything happen to you." Marina had no idea what Gracie meant by this, but she found it oddly reassuring.

She let herself be led up the trail until they came to another fork, one that Marina did not recall passing on her way down. Gracie took this path and they climbed for a while. They crossed two small streams and one they had to wade through, but Gracie seemed to know where she was going so Marina let herself be led.

After about an hour they reached a level plateau and Gracie left the trail. Marina followed her to the edge of a clearing. Gracie put a finger up to her lips, indicating quiet and sat in the shade of a tree with low-hanging branches. Marina sat beside her.

"Just kind of squint your eyes," Gracie whispered, "and you'll see 'em."

"See who?" Marina whispered back.

"Ghosts."

Marina could see nothing, but she closed her eyes and then opened them again, squinting as Gracie had advised. Gracie looked at her to see if she was squinting properly. Marina still saw nothing. It was clear that Gracie saw something. Her head moved back and forth, eyes tracking some movement invisible to Marina. After several minutes, out of boredom more than anything else, Marina tried seeing auras. She looked with the kind of softening of vision that helped her see the shimmering energy patterns. She saw the glow around the leaves nearest to her, around the trees on the other side of the clearing, and a bright glow around Gracie.

Then she saw the others.

At first she saw only their outlines, faint auras, barely visible, more of a disturbance or fluctuation of light than real auras. Then they popped for her, the way optical illusions sometimes did—one minute she couldn't see the pattern, the next she could.

It was an old woman and a younger woman sitting and talking in the clearing. The old woman wore a long purple robe, the young woman, a short gray tunic belted with a wide black belt. Marina did not recognize them, and she could not hear what they were saying, but seeing them appear so suddenly made her gasp.

Gracie squeezed her hand to comfort her. "It's okay. They aren't real."

Marina wondered what she was looking at. Were these wandering spirits? Had she been a ghost like this? Mai-Ling had said that people from the lower island couldn't really see her when they got close. Was that because on the upper plateau they'd both still been insubstantial? She remembered her own journey and wondered if she'd been observed like this. It made her feel uncomfortable, and after a few minutes she stood and walked back to the trail.

Gracie followed her and began leading the way back down the trail. "Pretty cool, huh." It was not really a question, but something Marina was supposed to agree with.

"Yes, pretty cool," Marina repeated, though without much enthusiasm. "Do you know what happens to them?" She wasn't sure why she was asking this of Gracie, wasn't sure what she thought Gracie could tell her.

"They're ghosts. What do you think happens to them?"

"I don't know. I mean do you ever see them again?"

"The real ghosts I don't. Sometimes I think it's a ghost but later I find out it was a real person . . . like you," Gracie added.

Marina swallowed hard. "Did you see me before you saw me down at the beach?"

"I thought maybe I did," Gracie explained. "But then I found out that you're real, so you can't be a ghost."

Marina let this pass. She didn't know why it bothered her, but it did.

The two of them shared lunch back at Marina's cabin. Once again, food for two was waiting for them. After lunch they swam in the ocean, but then Gracie said she needed to check in with her parents and left.

Marina went shell collecting along the beach and found several more large conch shells and some big round bowl-like shells. She added these to the collection she had started around the cistern and sat looking at them for a while.

She remembered Mai-Ling's circles and suddenly felt the urge to create her own. She had not known why she'd been collecting the shells; now it seemed obvious. She could not pretend to create anything as elaborate as Mai-Ling's circles, but something simple would serve her needs.

She took a handful of shells, as many as she could easily carry, and began to walk in big circles around her cabin. She walked slowly, purposefully, shifting her weight deliberately, as the Turtle Woman had taught her. She paid attention to the physical sensations as she walked—sand, leaves, twigs underfoot, the light of late afternoon, the breeze off the ocean, salt smell, green tree smell. She tried to empty her mind and see as Téves had taught her. Energy patterns glistened and glowed around things as she made her slow spiral outward. Finally, she found the spot she was looking for. She felt it tingling beneath her bare feet, looked down and saw the subtle pattern of it.

She kicked away the loose debris to uncover a layer of sand. She dropped the shells in this spot and set about clearing a circle of sand about twelve feet in diameter.

Next, she carefully arranged her shells at even intervals around the circumference of the circle and raked the sand clean and even with a palm frond.

Satisfied with her work she stepped back from her circle. She had to admit that she had no idea why she had built it. It's a calling, she heard a voice in her head say. It sounded like Mai-Ling, she thought, or maybe it's just something Mai-Ling had told her. Was it a calling to build it? she wondered. Or was it built to call something?

★ ★ ★

Gracie was back again the next morning, once again waiting out by the cistern when Marina awoke. This time she seemed more troubled than she had the previous morning. Marina noticed that her eyes were puffy and red as if she had been crying.

"Do you want to talk about it?" Marina asked as they shared her breakfast.

"No," she said, and sounded as if she meant it, then added, "Well, maybe."

"Is it your parents?"

"They're not going to stay together." Gracie was silent after announcing this. She seemed to be gathering her strength before speaking, fighting the urge to cry again. "I mean, I didn't really think they would. They fight all the time, but now I'm supposed to say who I want to live with." A little gulping sob escaped from Gracie despite her best efforts to control it. "It's like they want me to say who I love best." And now she was crying, punching her own thigh with anger and frustration. "How can I choose? How? How?"

Marina had no answer for this. She held out her arms in invitation. Gracie resisted for a moment, then came to her, allowing herself to be cradled.

"It's not fair. I wish I was dead, just dead, that's all."

Marina did not scold her for this expression, but stroked her hair and rocked her in her arms. She let Gracie tire herself with tears before speaking.

"You know that this isn't your fault, don't you? You know that this isn't about you?"

"That's what they say," Gracie sniffled, "but it still hurts."

"I know, but the question is, what will you do with that hurt?"

"What?" This question caught Gracie off guard. "What do you mean?"

"I mean what will you do with your hurt? How will you live with it?"

"I don't want to live with it."

"But it's a guest now. It may be an unwelcome guest, but it's still a guest. It lives with you now. How will you live with it?"

"You mean like a game?"

"A game if you like."

"Then if this was my guest, I'd make it stay in the basement, and I wouldn't ever let it out."

"And would you feed it?"

"Nope."

"Then what would happen to it?"

"It would die."

"And what would happen to your basement?" Gracie thought about this a second, then responded.

"It would stink."

"And everyone would say that your basement smelled bad."

"Oooh, gross." Gracie thought a bit more. "I'd run away."

"Your house is in your head. How can you run away from that?"

"Okay, I would feed it, but it would have to stay in the basement."

"And then wouldn't it get bigger?"

"I don't like this game." Gracie pulled away from Marina, still pouting but not crying anymore.

"I know. But think about it, okay? How could you live with something that hurts inside you?"

They were both quiet for a while. Marina couldn't tell whether Gracie was thinking about the dilemma she had posed or not, but after a long silence Gracie asked, "How would *you* live with something that hurts?"

"Well, I haven't done a very good job of it in my life, I'm afraid." Actually, she realized that she did not know what she was going to say, but she knew that she owed Gracie some kind of answer. "I guess I would try compassion. Do you know what that means?"

"That's when you're supposed to be nice to somebody even if you don't like them, right?"

"Well, not exactly, but that's a good start. Compassion means to really love someone who is suffering."

"Yeah, but I'm suffering. How will that help me?"

"Do you think you could love the part of you that hurts or the thing that's causing you pain?"

"No!" Gracie was direct and emphatic.

"How about this, then. Can you imagine how you might forgive a person or thing that's hurting you?"

Gracie was silent. Marina too was silent for a moment and a new thought occurred to her. "What does your hurt look like?"

"I don't know."

"Imagine it. Give the thing that's hurting you a face."

Again Gracie was silent, then she brightened. "It's a bear, a mean bear with big teeth and claws."

"So what's hurting your bear?"

Gracie looked confused. "My bear?"

"Yes, it's your bear. Close your eyes." Gracie shut her eyes obediently. "Now see the bear. Look at all of him. Do you see what it is that makes him so mean?"

After a few moments Gracie spoke without opening her eyes.

"He has a trap stuck on his leg. One of those metal traps with sharp points."

"Can you take the trap off?"

"He might bite me." Gracie was now fully playing this imaginary game.

"Try it anyway."

Marina watched Gracie, eyes still closed, tentatively mime removing the trap.

"Okay, I took it off."

"Now what does his face look like?"

"He isn't so unhappy now."

"Do you feel like you know him better."

Gracie nodded.

"That's what it's like to forgive. It doesn't mean you have to approve of the bear's behavior. It doesn't make everything better right away, but it's a start. What do you think?"

Gracie was quiet for a while, obviously thinking about the question.

"I don't know, maybe."

"Well, start there. Just try to understand the bear and forgive a little bit each day. And, if you can forgive, maybe you can imagine how you might come to do the same thing if you were in a similar situation. Maybe you can get to compassion that way, maybe not. But in the end, if you can't forgive, I think it will only hurt worse."

"So you're saying that I shouldn't be mean to the bear, even if he's being mean to me?"

"If he's hurting you, it may be that he's hurt. Maybe you can help him not hurt anymore."

"I don't know," Gracie repeated, and Marina let the conversation trail off.

★ ★ ★

They did not speak of it again that morning or that afternoon.

They swam together and Marina helped Gracie repaint her toenails. Gracie chose a hot pink polish from the little collection of colors she'd brought. She tried to talk Marina into painting her own toenails. Maybe later, Marina had said, smiling at the thought of her own toes accented with one of Gracie's eccentric selection of colors.

After lunch they gathered more shells, and Marina showed Gracie the circle she was making. She expected Gracie to ask her why she was making it, but Gracie didn't seem to need an explanation and, unexpectedly, offered one of her own.

"You're calling ghosts, aren't you?"

The question surprised Marina and made her think. She did not know why she built the circle. She could not say if she was calling ghosts or not. But Gracie didn't really seem to need a confirmation.

Marina was about to answer, but some signal that she, once again, could not hear, caught Gracie's attention.

"Sorry. Gotta go." She skipped off into the jungle, but turned and called back. "You know, they only come at night."

"What?" Marina called after her.

"Ghosts," Gracie shouted. "They only come at night."

★ ★ ★

Later, Marina carried several armloads of firewood to her circle. She hadn't thought to make a fire in it, but Gracie's comment about ghosts coming at night gave her the idea.

She found some matches in one of the chests in her cabin and carried one of the little carpets with her back to her circle as the sun began to set.

She lit a fire of dry kindling and fed it pieces of driftwood and some of the cut wood she'd found around the fire pit in back of her cabin. Soon she had a nice crackling fire and she settled herself onto her carpet, cross-legged, to watch it burn.

Mesmerized by the dancing flame, she lost track of time. She had no purpose, no clear idea of what she was doing, only the strong urge to sit in her circle and wait.

When she heard rustling in the leaves, just beyond the range of the fire's light, she would not have been surprised if it had been a ghost, but when she called out softly, Gracie appeared. She was wearing a long T-shirt that reached to her knees, probably what she slept in, Marina thought.

"I'm sorry," she said meekly. Even in the firelight Marina could tell Gracie had been crying again.

"Come," she patted the carpet beside her. But after Gracie had joined her, Marina asked, "What about your parents? Do they know where you are?"

"They had another fight. Mom said she was going to sleep up at the big house, and Dad left after he thought I was asleep. They don't care about me."

Marina wanted to swear. She had no children of her own. She knew she had no right to be angry, but she wondered how people could waste something so precious as a child. They don't deserve you, she wanted to say, but knew it was not her place.

"Have you ever heard the story of Saba the turtle?" she asked instead.

"No." Gracie answered.

"Well, if you'll lay your head right here, I'll tell you of Saba and the story of turtle dreams." Gracie laid her head in Marina's lap, and Marina began stroking her hair.

Marina's mother had told her the tale of Saba when she was a little girl. Her mother used to tell Marina and her sister folk tales that, later in life, Marina came to suspect were not folk tales at all but were inventions of her mother's. This made them no less magical, and in a way even more special. She hadn't thought about this particular story in years, but now it came flooding back to her.

"Well, you see Saba was the first turtle. She was one of the Great Mother Spirit's four magical children, so she was a kind of princess—like you."

Gracie looked up. "I'm a princess?"

"Of course."

Gracie seemed pleased with this. "Was the Great Mother Spirit a turtle, too?" Gracie asked.

"No, the Great Mother Spirit had four children and they each took the shape of an animal. Kazah, the eldest took the form of a raven. He was jet black and a beautiful flyer. Shana, the next oldest, took the form of a dolphin. She was smooth and sleek, a fast swimmer, and a great jumper. Nebu became a bear. He was strong and tall and a fierce warrior."

"Was he like my bear?" It took Marina a moment to remember what Gracie was referring to—the imaginary bear that she had earlier envisioned as her pain.

"Yes, perhaps," she answered, then continued. "Saba became a turtle, but no one had ever seen a turtle before, and to her brothers and sister she just seemed slow and ungainly, with a hard, dull shell, liable to tip onto her back and be unable to right herself. In addition to their physical forms, for this was before there were ravens and dolphins and bears and turtles, each of the Great Mother Spirit's children had special talents that made them unique."

"Like superpowers?"

"Sort of. But the Great Mother Spirit never told her children what those talents were. She wanted them to discover their talents on their own.

"As a child, Saba played with her brothers and sister and she watched as they began to discover their secret gifts. Her brother, Kazah, seemed to know so many things and seemed always hungry for more knowledge. He was very smart, and knew the names of everything and anything. Nebu was strong and brave. There was no tree he could not climb, no creature he was afraid to fight. He was, however, at times overbearing, and Saba would turn to her sister Shana, for comfort. Shana was the caring one, always concerned with the feelings of other and the fairness of their actions.

"The gifts of her sister and her brothers seemed obvious to Saba, but her own secret talent remained a mystery to her. Though she was pretty to look at, her brothers thought her dull-witted and singularly unremarkable. She moved slowly and always seemed to be daydreaming.

"And so her childhood passed and Saba prepared to become a woman, still unsure of her gift. She almost resigned herself to not having any special talent. Perhaps, she thought, her mother had no gifts left for her. Perhaps she had been a mistake, unwanted and unnecessary.

"One day Shana came to her and told her that Sha Feru, the wolf, wished to see them.

"Now Sha Feru was no ordinary wolf. He was a kind of wizard or magician in the form of a wolf. He was also consort and lover to the Great Mother Spirit. They had loved each other once and he was in reality the father of her children, but the two had quarreled ferociously and found it best to live apart." Gracie looked up at Marina but said nothing. Marina had been reciting the story as it was told to her and hadn't thought about the parallel with Gracie's parents when she began to tell it. She wondered if it would upset the child, but Gracie let it pass. "The Great Mother Spirit lived in the sky, and Sha Feru walked the earth. Sometimes he would sing to the Great Mother Spirit. . . ."

"Was the Great Mother Spirit the moon?" Gracie interrupted. She sounded sleepy but still interested.

"Very good, Gracie. Yes. My mother used to tell me that the moon was the Great Mother Spirit and that's why wolves still howl to the moon." Gracie giggled.

"Well, anyway, all the Great Mother Spirit's children gathered at the cave of Sha Feru to hear him speak. Kazah was certain that he could answer any question. Nebu was sure that his strength and courage would see him through any quest, no matter how dangerous. Shana knew that her heart would serve her well. But Saba was unsure of how she could compete in such gifted company.

"When Sha Feru appeared on the singing rock beside his cave he spoke solemnly. 'You are the children of the Great Mother Spirit. Each of you has a gift, but these gifts are untested. It is time for you to make a great quest. You must go into the world and try your gifts. Come back to this place in one year's time and we shall see whose gift served them best.'

"Saba wanted to interrupt, to remind Sha Feru that she had no gift she knew of, but he was gone in the blink of an eye.

"Each of them picked a direction and set off. They traveled in the world in their own fashion—by land, by water, and by air. Saba traveled more slowly, but this also gave her more time to see and talk with the creatures she encountered. She crawled through lands of death and strife, saw pain and heard suffering. But she also discovered great joy and beauty. She changed little things as she went. She left marks on stones. She painted deserts, arranged the branches of trees, and placed ponds just to catch the sunlight. Her changes were not large and grand, but she brought magic into the lives of those she met.

"When they all gathered back at the singing rock the following year, Saba thought her brothers and sister much changed. When they spoke of their trials and ordeals she understood why.

"Kazah said, 'I have shared my great wisdom and knowledge. I have been a master and a teacher. My words have become legends, my legends stories, my stories books. All the creatures of the world come to me for answers and guidance, but the more answers I give, the more questions they ask. It is unending and I am tired.' Saba noticed that Kazah looked tired. His once-shiny black feathers were dusty and dull and his head hung down. 'I longed all the time to return home.'

"Shana spoke next and agreed with her brother. 'I have traveled the world as a healer. I've comforted the sick and the dying. I've nursed injured and the wounded spirits. I've given so much of myself that I fear I am all used up.' Saba saw that Shana did look haggard, pale, and thin—a mere shadow of what she had once been. She swam with no vigor and never splashed the surface of the water. 'I too could think of nothing but returning home to rest and renew my strength.'

"'I am also weary,' Nebu admitted. 'I've fought the good fight, stood for justice and everything fair. I've won a hundred battles, but I've endured a hundred wounds. I've been fearless in the face of the mightiest enemy, but now I face a fear I cannot defeat. I'm afraid of my own dark nature. I think one cannot be a warrior all the time.' Saba noticed that Nebu's fur had lost its luster. It was matted in some places, and great hunks of it were missing. He seemed barely able to lift his mighty club. 'I want nothing now but to sleep in my own bed.'

"When Saba did not speak they turned to her and gasped as one. They had each been consumed in their own tribulations and had not noticed their youngest sister. Now they gathered around her with great shows of pity. For, though she could not see it herself, Saba looked the worst of them all. Her shell was scarred and gouged, stained with dirt and blood, and even chipped in places. They begged her to tell of her journey.

"'Surely you have seen the worst of the world.' Kazah said.

"'I've seen the worst and the best,' she answered honestly.

"'But your shell is so badly marked,' Shana said.

"'Only on the outside,' Saba answered.

"'But did you not long for your home—for a place of rest and safety?' Nebu asked.

"'I took my home with me. I carried my place of rest and renewal on my back.' With that Saba drew her head, legs, and tail into her shell and sealed herself within. But still her brothers and sister did not understand. When she peeked her head out again she saw Sha Feru standing on his rock with great blanket over his shoulder. 'Help me show them what it is like inside my shell,' she asked the great wizard.

"Sha Feru smiled and cast his blanket over them all. For Kazah, Shana, and Nebu, it was like being drawn into Saba's shell. All was peaceful and serene and beautiful. Saba had painted maps and murals of her travels on the cavelike walls within her shell. She had collected signs, symbols, and artifacts of her journey. The beauty and joy she had seen was represented, but so was the pain and suffering. Each step of her quest was rendered with truth and passion. It made Kazah bow, Shana weep, and Nebu kneel.

"'Your sister Saba has traveled in the world as each of you has,' Sha Feru said as he drew back the blanket. The world outside Saba's shell seemed colder, but, in some way, each felt renewed. 'Each of you served the world with your gifts. Kazah was a great teacher, Shana a gifted healer, Nebu a brave warrior, and Saba an artist. But Saba has a second gift, and this gift served her as well as it served the world. She has the capacity to walk in balance—to find renewal—to carry her sanctuary with her. You would all do well to learn her secret. For your fiery gifts, as great as they are, will be as nothing if they consume you.'

"Saba's brothers and sister honored her then. They begged the blanket from Sha Feru and laid it over their sister's shell. The blanket molded to her shape and became hard like her shell, but now her shell was alive with subtle shimmering color, and almost as beautiful on the outside as it had been on the inside. And Saba was happy, for at last she understood her gifts. As evening fell over the world, Sha Feru sang to the Great Mother Spirit of their daughter's gift and of her coming of age.

"My mother used to tell me that the spirit of Saba was embodied in turtles. Turtles move more slowly, as if time was not something to be used up, and they have hard shells like Saba's to protect them. And when she would catch me or my sister staring for long moments at nothing in particular, she said we were having turtle dreams.

"Turtle dreams." Gracie repeated this so softly that Marina could tell she was barely awake.

"Yes, turtle dreams. That means that you're traveling an interior landscape of dreams and sanctuary—that you're recharging and reimagining your world," she leaned close to whisper in Gracie's ear, "and listening to the words of turtles."

Gracie said nothing else, and Marina could tell by her breathing that she'd fallen asleep. She tossed a few more logs on the fire and eased herself down on the carpet, pulling Gracie to her and snuggling close. As she drifted off to sleep, she wondered if, together, they had called any ghosts.

★ ★ ★

Gracie was gone when she woke in the morning. She wondered if she had dreamed her coming. But Gracie was back by lunch asking her about Saba.

"I know it's just a story, but is it a true story?" Gracie asked. They both sat on the floor of Marina's cabin.

"It's as true a story as my mother knew how to tell," Marina offered.

"Did your mother love you?"

"Yes. She still loves me. I haven't seen her for a while, but I'm sure she still loves me." Marina thought she should reassure Gracie and say something about Gracie's mother still loving her, but Marina had never really known how to relate to children in a way that was different from how she would relate to an adult.

"Hey!" Gracie had picked up the little black pebble from the mirror pool and was turning it in her fingers. "It looks like a turtle."

It did sort of look like a turtle's shell, but Marina hadn't noticed it before now. It was oblong and smoothly rounded.

Gracie held it close to her eye. "I think Saba must be inside here. What do you think?"

"She might be." Marina smiled.

Gracie set the stone back down on the table that had become Marina's altar. "What's all this stuff?" she asked.

"That's my altar . . . my special things."

"What's it for?"

"It's a special place I can go to. See these things?" She picked up and set down several of her treasures. "They each remind me of something important that I know or want to remember."

"Like what?"

"Well," Marina picked up the pendulum, "This reminds me that if I look carefully and softly, and if my heart is open, I can see more things. It also reminds me of the person who gave it to me. And this little branch reminds me that I can be strong if I need to be."

"What about the bowl?" Gracie said, fingering the bowl Mai-Ling had given her.

"That full or empty is my choice, no one else's." She hadn't voiced this thought before. The awareness came over her suddenly, but it felt correct.

Gracie needed to know what each piece meant, and Marina explained them all patiently. Speaking her thoughts out loud was almost a form of prayer. When she finished, Gracie was quiet for a long while. When she finally spoke again it was with great seriousness.

"Do you think I could have an altar?"

"Anyone can have an altar, Gracie. You just have to make one."

"Will you help me?"

"Of course. But you might want to start with just a few things and collect more as you go. It's more important to have the right things than to have a lot of things."

"Okay. How do I start?"

"Let's start with what's most important to you. What would you want in your secret sanctuary?"

"A sanctuary is like a hiding place," Gracie announced proudly.

"Yes, it is."

"Then I guess I would start with my mom and my dad."

"And what might represent them on your altar?"

Gracie thought of several things and discarded them just as quickly. Marina suggested that they take a walk and see what they could find.

They spent the afternoon finding, inspecting, discussing, and usually discarding shells, stones, branches, and feathers. In the end they returned with four things for Gracie's fledgling altar: a cowry shell to represent her mother, a little green feather to represent herself, a white stone to represent her father, and a small, gray branch of driftwood, just big enough to support her miniature family.

Marina encouraged her to play with the arrangement until it felt right to her. She made space on her own altar table for Gracie's items. When Gracie finished arranging her pieces, the green feather was stuck in the center of the piece of driftwood and the stone and cowry shell were as far out on the ends of the branch as they could be without falling. She did not offer to explain her arrangement to Marina. They sat together in silence, each contemplating their altars. Marina was surprised at how long Gracie could sit still.

A little while before sunset, Gracie was called away again by the signal only she could hear. Marina carried more firewood to her circle and lit a small fire. She was more tired than she had been the night before and quickly fell into a trance before the flames.

One moment it was light, the next moment it was dark. It was dark and she was studying the patterns of the fire. She could see shapes in

the fire. She could see shapes through the fire. She could see eyes looking back at her, the eyes of a shadow. Slowly she realized that the
shadow had a face. It had a mouth with white teeth. It was smiling at
her. Then it spoke.

"Everybody comin' and goin'."

Marina was surprised at how real the shadow sounded. She shook
her head as if to shake the fire trance off. She looked away, blinked
hard, and looked back. The shadow was still in front of her. She could
see it even more clearly now, sitting opposite her, the fire between
them.

"I'm still here," it said, he said, it was a man's voice. "Not for long
though." He laughed then, and the laugh became a long cough.

"Who . . . are you?" Marina asked softly, her voice barely a whisper,
not sure she wanted an answer.

"Jus' a ghost. Come for the dyin'. Who are you?" The question surprised Marina. Since coming to Turtle Island, no one had asked her so
directly and immediately who she was. Usually they either seemed to
know who she was or were content for her to tell them when she
chose to. It was silly, she knew, but she wasn't sure how to answer this
ghost.

Who was she? Was she still Marina Hardt? Certainly she was not the
same person she had been. She'd only recently come hesitantly to
accept that perhaps she was still living, or living again. Could she still
lay claim to the same name? Wasn't there a different person dwelling
in her body now?

"I'm . . . Marina . . . Marina Hardt."

"The photographer?" Again the question surprised Marina. While
she'd experienced some small degree of celebrity as a photographer,
that was usually within the more limited community of artists, photographers, journalists, and editors. However, most of the people
Marina met, while they might have remembered and, in fact, been
deeply touched by her work, seldom attached a name to the photographer.

"Yes," she answered, hearing the uncertainty even in her own voice.
"I guess I am."

"Hah! You're good. Been aware of you since, oh . . . the late seven-
ties, Beirut I think."

"Yes." Marina laughed in spite of herself. I have a reputation among
the dead, she thought.

"Name's Clarence, Clarence Mudder." The name was familiar to her, but only in a distant and abstract sort of way. It was a name she'd heard somewhere. "Stinkwater Jack's, the Burning Boys . . ." He was helping her, giving her clues. They sounded like titles. "Ginsburg, Burroughs, LeRoi Jones . . ." She made the connection.

"The poet?" There had been a Clarence Mudder that she'd read in college. She recalled him as being a minor black poet of the beat generation, famous more for his political writing in the early civil rights movement than for his poetry.

"That's me."

Marina was aware that what had seemed to be a shadow before was in fact just the dark skin of an old man. She could see him more clearly now. He was thin, but he looked as if he'd once been strong and barrel-chested. His skin hung about him like a damp sheet. He wore no shirt and his baggy black trousers were cinched up by a belt that he'd added holes to. A silver-gray fuzz dusted his dark chest and the top of his head.

"I didn't know . . ." Marina stopped herself. She was going to say she didn't know he was dead, but it seemed an awkward statement. She still did not understand the protocols of Turtle Island. They seemed to be constantly shifting, constantly appropriate for a different place.

"Yeah, Kiyoko loved this place. We used to come here once every year just to . . ." His thought trailed off. It seemed to Marina that he had begun to respond to a different question, something about Turtle Island, not about death.

"Kiyoko?" Marina decided to pursue this course. It took Clarence a moment to respond.

"My wife. She died last year. Nothin's been the same since. I shoulda' been with her by now, but she made me promise to write a poem for her. I couldn't ever refuse that woman." Marina was confused, but Clarence seemed to have begun a story. She seemed to have accidentally triggered some need in him to tell it.

"I was stationed in Japan at the end of the war. I met Kiyoko there. She was a beauty, all of seventeen and so full of life. Her family had died in Hiroshima while she'd been away visiting relatives and she was pretty much on her own. I don't know why she agreed to marry an American, much less a black man, but she did and I brought her back to New York with me, proud and on top of the world.

"I worked my way through City College and started writing poetry.

Hung out with Ginsburg and Kerouac, all them cats. You know that line in 'Howl,' the one about Negro streets?" Marina nodded her head, aware only that she should know it. "That was my line. I gave it to him. It was late and we were at some party. Ginsburg looked out the window and said something about walking home on black streets. I said to him, 'Those ain't just black streets, they're my streets, Negro streets.' He laughed, but he also made a note of it. I could see his mind working. He never forgot a good line." Clarence laughed to himself. "I don't mind though. It was a great poem, much better than I ever wrote.

"Well, times were good for a while, then, I don't know, I guess I began to see America more and more through Kiyoko's eyes. When you grow up black in America, least when I grew up, and people treat you like you ain't there. Well, you sort of get used to it. But Kiyoko wasn't used to it. She couldn't understand it. Drove her crazy. Then it started to drive me crazy. We stuck it out for a while, but in the end we left, went back to Japan." Marina remembered a little now. Clarence Mudder had been an expatriate poet and writer. Some of his books were published, a few collections of poems, but then he just dropped out of sight.

"I taught English and literature. We had a good life. We used to come here for a couple of weeks every year, just to remember who we were. Then last year she died. Cancer." Marina wanted to say something like I'm sorry, but Clarence continued too quickly. "No, she was everything to me. There's just not much point without her. We never could have children and I know that made her sad, but we loved each other about as much as two people can, I guess—maybe more.

"I've just been hangin' around. But I'm tired now. I came here to write the poem I said I'd write and to be with Kiyoko again."

They were both silent. There seemed to be nothing for Marina to say.

"Well, I wouldn't have troubled you with all this if I hadn't needed a favor."

"What can I do?" She wanted to help and meant it when she said, "Anything."

"Well, I wrote that poem for Kiyoko. I don't know that it's any good, but it took all the fire that's left in me to write it. She made me promise I'd read it out loud for her on Turtle Island, that I'd come here one more time for the both of us. The problem is that I can't read it. I can't say it out loud. It's like sayin' good-bye and I can't do it." Marina could see moisture glinting in Clarence's eyes through the fire.

"Then I was out walkin' last night and I heard this beautiful voice telling this story and I listened. It was the story of a turtle. I heard you tell it to that little girl and I thought, well, maybe you could read it for me, for me and Kiyoko."

"I'd be honored to read one of your poems, but how . . . ?"

"I'm an old man. I don't have much time left. If you make a fire, I'll come back tomorrow night, maybe the next night, just lie here, wait for death. I'll know when the time is right for you to read the poem. Is that okay?"

"Yes. I'll be here."

★ ★ ★

When daylight woke her, Marina was again alone by the warm coals of the fire.

She now had a secret to share with Gracie and felt like a schoolgirl herself. She wanted to tell the child that she'd been right, that the circle really had called up a ghost, but when she finally saw Gracie, it was clear she had something else on her mind.

Around lunchtime Gracie showed up. This was late for her, but she offered no explanation. She went immediately to her little altar, rearranged some of her treasures and sat before it quietly.

At last she spoke. "We're leaving the day after tomorrow. Mom says this isn't working—only making things worse—and she wants to leave. We move into the big house tomorrow afternoon and take the early boat the next morning."

"Will I see you tomorrow?" Marina asked, running her hand absentmindedly though Gracie's hair.

"Sure. I have to pack in the morning, but they won't care what I do in the afternoon. They could probably leave without me and not even notice."

"You know that's not true."

"Almost."

"I'll miss you, you know."

Gracie was tearing up. She was about to cry but clearly didn't want to, so Marina changed the subject.

"I saw a ghost last night," she announced conspiratorially.

"A real ghost?" Gracie was clearly excited. She wanted to be distracted, but she was also genuinely interested in the phenomenon of ghosts.

"He seemed pretty real. He said his name was Clarence Mudder."

"You mean old Mr. Mudder, the black man?"

"Yes, I guess. How do you know him?" Marina was surprised.

"I've seen him a couple of times. He lives in the next cabin up the beach. My dad says he's pretty sick, and that I shouldn't bother him. Did he die?"

"I don't know." Now Marina was confused. "He said he was a ghost."

"Did you touch him?"

Marina felt like a child who had overlooked something obvious. She was embarrassed to admit that she hadn't, that she'd simply believed what he'd said.

"No," she said sheepishly.

Gracie rolled her eyes and smacked her own forehead with the palm of her hand. It was another gesture, Marina noticed, that seemed adopted from someone older.

"You have to touch them to see if they're a ghost. They're very tricky." The logic of this was somehow flawed. Marina wondered who Gracie was referring to—ghosts, or people pretending to be ghosts. And why would someone pretend to be a ghost?

"Oh." Marina sighed. "I thought the circle had called a ghost." She hung her head and Gracie comforted her.

"Don't feel too bad. Just because Mr. Mudder isn't a ghost doesn't mean that the circle didn't work."

★ ★ ★

Later in the day, after Gracie had gone, Marina thought about her. She wished she could make sure that Gracie would be happy, that her parents would stay together, and that everything would work out, but she knew that the opposite was most likely. Things wouldn't work out well, the parents wouldn't stay together, and Gracie would be hurt.

She looked at Gracie's little altar next to hers and a thought struck her. She realized that she wanted to give Gracie something for her altar. All along she had been gifted with things for her own altar. Now she wanted to give something to Gracie, but she wasn't quite sure how to find something. She could give her something from her own altar, but that didn't seem quite right. She needed something that represented their time together and their shared experience. So she went for a walk.

As she walked along the beach she looked hard for something, but she felt as if she was forcing the process. It didn't feel right. When she had found things for her own altar, they had just sort of called to her, but now she wanted to call to them. She tried closing her eyes and walking slowly.

She walked as if she was stalking something. She walked deliberately, feeling the shift in balance that the Turtle Woman had taught her when she learned to walk again. She moved like a blind hunter. She found that she could tell where she was walking by the dampness of the sand. If it became too dry she corrected her course to the left. If too wet, she moved to the right. She had no idea how far she had walked in this blind, trusting meditation, but just when it seemed most absurd to her, she stepped on something hard.

She opened her eyes to find a round knot of driftwood half buried in the sand. It was about the size of her fist, and when she picked it up and rinsed the sand off the bottom, she knew she had found what she was looking for. Within the knot of wood, Marina could see a face, but not a human face, the face of a bear. It's Gracie's bear, she thought, and carried it back to her cabin.

She cleaned it again with fresh water and let it dry in the sun. When it was dry she took some of Gracie's electric blue nail polish and accented the eyes of the bear. She considered painting in more of the face, but with the eyes highlighted, the face came alive on its own. It had a split beneath the snout that made the bear appear to be smiling and this pleased Marina. She touched the bear with a drop of the essential oil she always wore so that the bear would smell of both saltwater and herself. She wrapped the bear in a silk scarf and tied it with a piece of ribbon.

★ ★ ★

As the sun began to go down, Marina found herself carrying more wood to her circle and lighting another fire. She stayed awake for a long time, but Clarence did not appear. Finally she lay down on the carpet and closed her eyes.

When she awoke, sometime deep in the night, Clarence was there. He was lying on his back with his head near Marina's. Still barefoot and shirtless in baggy black trousers, he now wore a yellow brocade vest, woven with tiny threads of gold that seemed to glint in the glow of the fire's hot coals.

The fire had burned down, but there was a good bed of ruby red coals. Marina carefully placed several pieces of wood on the fire and turned on her stomach to watch Clarence.

His eyes were closed and he was very still. She looked for evidence of breathing. She held her own breath, waiting to see if his chest would rise and fall. If he was breathing, he made no sound and gave no sign.

Is he dead? Gracie had been convinced that he wasn't a ghost when Marina had seen him the previous night. But is he a ghost now? she wondered. What was it Gracie had said, that she had to touch him to know for sure? While she accepted this bit of wisdom from Gracie on the surface, it did not seem to correspond to her experiences as a ghost. Touch had been as real as anything she could remember. Sometimes it had been more real. The only thing like the kind of ghost Gracie talked about that Marina had encountered had been Rafael's wraiths. They had been insubstantial to Marina's touch. Her hand had passed right through them. But had this been because Marina herself was a ghost? It all seemed too confusing.

And still she felt the urge to reach out and touch Clarence.

She reached a finger out to touch him gently. She did it slowly, ready to pull her hand quickly back if she did not meet solid flesh. But her finger did touch something solid. It was thin skin, easy to push around, eerily disconnected from underlying tissue like the skin of a cat or dog. But it was skin. She recalled her grandmother's skin being like this, pale, translucent, and loose over her muscles and bones. She knew that her own skin might one day grow loose like this; that she might come to old age, ready to throw off her skin for the return to Turtle Island or someplace like it.

"I'm not dead yet." Clarence whispered, his eyes still closed. This startled Marina, and she jerked back her hand.

"But last night you said you were a ghost."

"Oh, I'm a ghost. Been a ghost for nearly a year now. I'm just not full dead yet." His voice was weak and breathy with a bit of a rattle to it. He started to speak again but coughed instead—a long, deliberate wheezing.

Both Marina and Clarence were silent for a while, then he opened his eyes. They were the eyes of a blind man, dull and unfocused. He didn't seem to be taking in any more information by having them open than by having them closed, but opening them meant something to him. He gestured for her to come close to him by twitching his head. He wanted to say something and had not much strength with which to say it.

"Tell me," he gasped. "What's it like?"

Marina could have pretended she didn't know what he meant. She did not understand how or what he knew about her. Was it a scent? Was it the way she looked? Did her voice have the peculiar ring of the recently dead? But it seemed like an honest question, a question from the heart.

"It isn't what I thought it would be like." It was all she could think to say. There was no simple answer to this question. She wasn't even sure that her experience had not been totally unique and totally constructed out of her own life experiences and expectations. "I'm sorry. It's hard for me to describe."

"Is there pain?"

Marina thought about this. "I think there's pain if you bring it with you. I think there's pleasure, too, though, at least the possibility of pleasure."

"What about answers? What about the big questions?"

"I found some answers, but I still have a lot of questions. Maybe I wasn't there long enough. Maybe I wasn't paying attention. Maybe it's because I chose to come back so soon. I don't know."

"So no real answers, then, no big reason for it all." He seemed disappointed.

"Listen, I'm not an expert. I still don't really know what happened to me. But I seemed to have a choice at one point, and I chose to come back here. I think if I had made the other choice, well, this is just my intuition, but I think it would have been such a new game that none of my big questions would have mattered any more. If I'd chosen to really enter death, I think I would have remembered that I already knew the answer to those questions. I knew them before I was born, I had a chance to remember and act upon some or even all of them while I was alive, and I would remember them all after death. Only then it wouldn't matter. They would be like quiz-question answers after the quiz is over—so important one moment, trivial in the next."

Clarence lay still for a long time mulling this over. "One more question . . ." He hesitated. "Will I see her again?" There was such love, such heart in this question that Marina didn't know how to tell him that she didn't know. She too hesitated before speaking, but in that hesitation, Clarence interrupted her. "No, don't tell me. I promised her that we would see each other again, and we will. I don't need anyone to tell me if it's so or not. I believe it. I have to believe it."

Marina put her hand on Clarence's head. "I think believing is about the most powerful thing there is. So, if you believe it, it will happen."

Clarence closed his eyes again and seemed content.

"What about that poem?" Marina asked. "Are you ready for me to read it."

"Don't rush me, girl. That poem goin' be the last thing I hear."

"Anytime," Marina offered, a little embarrassed.

"Not anytime. Soon—real soon."

Clarence was silent after that, and eventually Marina lay back down and closed her eyes. On the edge of sleep she heard, or thought she heard, Clarence speak again.

"You know now they goin' to come to you. You can try to hide it, but they'll know. They'll know you been there and come back and they'll want to know what it was like." Marina wasn't sure who "they" were, but she had an idea and it scared her. She didn't want to become a guru for near-death experience groupies. "You can't fight it, so you better figure out how you goin' tell this story in a way that helps people like you're helpin' me."

Marina wanted to answer, she wanted to speak, to reject this calling, but sleep and dreams washed over her first.

CHAPTER 8

Theatre of the Bardo

The shamans of Tibet have a Book of the Dead—chart and guide for the land-scape of dreams. Before I sleep I ask a question: How shall I know if I'm dreaming or dying?

In my dream a great sea turtle swims before me. He opens his shell like the cover of an ancient book of water. I see tiny letters carved on the inside of the shell. The sea turtles' Book of the Dead says this:

> *Dreaming and dying,*
> *they are one in the same.*
> *But when you wake from death,*
> *you must find a new shell.*

Marina woke from a dream in which she was living in the late 1800s and was trying to gather a huge extended family together in one house. It was a dream of some frustration. She was aware of trying to bring various things together, but for every three people she gathered in a room, she would lose one.

Clarence was still there. He lay where he had the night before, tak-ing shallow and infrequent breaths, barely clinging to life.

When Gracie found them together, her first question was, "Is he alive?" She was wearing a little sundress and sandals and her normally tangled hair had been brushed and pulled back in a ponytail.

"Yes," Marina explained. "He's resting."

"He's dying," Gracie corrected with the firmness of a child who will not tolerate being talked down to. Marina agreed, checked Clarence, and asked Gracie to come with her.

Back at the cabin she helped Gracie roll her altar treasures up in a cloth and slip them into a little canvas bag. "You can set this up anywhere you are, and it will be your secret place. Add more things when you feel like it, and give things away when that feels right. Don't become too attached to any one thing, but remember they are powerful objects. After they have lived in your sacred space for a while they will be even more special."

Next she gave Gracie the bear wrapped in silk.

"It's my bear!" she exclaimed. She recognized the face immediately. She laughed and studied the bear.

"When you put this on your altar, you'll remember me and what we've shared. It'll make me feel good to know that in some way we're connected. It'll be like I'm sitting on your altar somewhere." Gracie was quiet and Marina noticed tears in her eyes. Marina's own eyes began to get moist.

"I don't have a present for you," Gracie sniffled through the tears.

"Just knowing you has been a present for me." Marina swiped at the tears running down her cheeks. "I won't forget you."

"I gotta go now." Gracie stood up and started for the door with her bear and her altar in its canvas bag. "My mom wants me at the big house today. We have to look like a family." She made a face with a grimace of a smile. "Maybe I can come back before I leave, but I don't know if they'll let me."

She started to leave, then turned back quickly to hug Marina tightly. Marina hugged her back and smelled soap and the sweet smell of a little girl.

"I wish you could be my mom," she whispered in Marina's ear. Then she broke her hug and was gone.

The cabin felt empty after that. She had no appetite for breakfast or lunch and did not even uncover the dinner tray. She checked on Clarence regularly but observed no change. She brought water in Mai-Ling's bowl, should he want some, but he never asked, and she did not want to disturb him. She brought the two blue bottles of essential oils that Mai-Ling had given her and she brought the ivory sheet from her bed.

By late in the day she'd carried more firewood from the magically replenishing supply outside the cabin to her circle. She had not let the fire go out completely during the day, so when she added new dry wood, it sprang to life quickly. As darkness came she settled in before the fire and waited.

"S'time now," Clarence whispered. Marina had not dozed off, but her mind was elsewhere and she thought at first that she might be dreaming when she heard him. "S'time now."

Marina leaned close to Clarence. "Are you ready for me to read the poem?"

"Vest pocket." Clarence spoke economically, as if he had little breath left in him, each exhalation more precious than the last. Marina found a folded piece of paper in his vest pocket and held it up to him. He nodded. "You sing it out, now. Don't be shy 'bout it."

Marina unfolded the piece of paper delicately.

"Sing it out. That's how you have to say one of my poems. Sing it out till I don't need it no more." He paused. "And don't cry for me when I'm gone. I'm a happy man." He closed his eyes.

Marina began to read.

"'Circus Requiem'

> I had a three-ring circus,
> she and me and we,
> the greatest show on earth.
> I jumped through hoops of fire
> with the big cats,
> and I had tigers in my cage
> a rage within 'em,
> a Cajun rhythm.
>
> I had three rings.
> Bright gold round your finger,
> buried now.
> Binding steel tight across my chest,
> rusting now.
> Tarnished brass round my finger,
> slipping now,

as my fingers curl and shrink
round ticket stubs for this tawdry show.

I have no wild animals now.
Second-hand, sideshow unicorn,
all the magic I can muster.
A goat bleating,
a heart bleeding,
afraid of the sacrificial knife
that comes for my throat.

I have one tumbling, free-falling flyer.
Swinging out, night after night,
letting go my hold,
adjusting my trajectory,
hoping you'll be there
to catch me.

I have one sad clown
left in the spotlight,
and I chase myself
round and round,
and beat myself with a rubber bat
for no one's amusement.

I have one bag of stale peanuts
left to feed the pachyderm
that no longer stands
gently on the head
of the woman with the uneasy smile
and the sequined breasts.

I have one long last blast
of calliope circus music in me,
playing slow like a funeral dirge.
Then I'll fold up this big top
this grave plot,
this soft spot,
and carry my poor circus

on my back
like a peddler into the flames.

My hissing, popping flesh
will sing out to you.
My crackling bones
will tap out a dancing rhythm.
My sparks and cinders
will light the night sky
searching for you.
My ashes will be carried
on the wind that whispers
in your ear
a love song from the high wire."

Tears filled Marina's eyes. She looked down at Clarence. His eyes were still closed, his breath almost still, but he smiled.

She said the poem again, louder this time, with more feeling. She heard it differently this time, but still she cried. She said the poem aloud a third, then a fourth and fifth time, growing more comfortable with it each time. She got inside the poem, put it on like an old shirt, said it again.

She was crying now, not for Clarence and his love, but for the love she hadn't had. She had loved. She had been in love. But she had not known this kind of love. This was a love that had had time to grow. It'd grown into something Marina had no experience of, and she felt a great emptiness.

She said the poem again with rage and anger. She said it with frustration and disappointment. She said it with sadness and longing. In the end, however, she said it with hope. That someone could love this much gave her a kind of hope she hadn't felt before.

She never knew at what precise moment Clarence died or which reading of the poem had been the last he heard. But even when she knew he was dead she still said the poem. Spirits sometimes linger around bodies, she thought. They need time to move on. So she continued reciting the poem until her throat was sore and her voice cracked.

When she was certain that she had given him enough time, she put the piece of paper into the fire and held it while it burned. She held

onto it as long as she could, then dropped it in the sand while the
flame consumed the last of Clarence's words. Before it had completely
cooled, she took the charred bits back in her hand and crumbled them.
She rubbed her blackened hands on her face, mixing tears and ashes to
mark her skin with snakelike streaks of mourning.

Then she straightened Clarence's body and arranged his clothes. She
cleaned his face and hands and feet with a cloth dipped in water and
touched him with drops of scented oil: forehead, eyelids, lips, heart,
palms, and the soles of his feet. After anointing him, she covered him
with the sheet. She thought of saying a prayer for him, but he'd written his own prayer and she'd read it, and there was nothing better she
could say.

She put all the remaining wood on the fire and stood for a moment
as the flames leapt to life. She hoped that his Kiyoko would see it. She
left the circle then and walked back to the cabin in the darkness before
dawn. She did not wash or drink, but pulled her clothes off and fell
onto her bed.

★ ★ ★

When she woke next it was late in the day. She did not know what
day. She was suddenly tired of having no way of telling the passing of
time. Her mouth was dry and she was feverish. She was thirsty but too
tired to go out to the cistern. She reached for the little bowl on her
altar. She always kept water in it to float blossoms, and she was tired
and thirsty enough to drink from it now. It was not there. She'd
brought it for Clarence and left it in the circle.

What she did notice, however, were the flowers. There were little
coral and pink orchid blossoms all over her altar. They were the kind
of orchids the Turtle Mother had covered her in before burying her.
She'd found one while exploring with Gracie and commented on how
beautiful it was.

Gracie was here, she thought, she came back to say good-bye, and I
was asleep. This made Marina feel heavy and sad. She'd missed seeing
Gracie one last time. There was nothing she could do then but sink
back into sleep.

She slept a hot, alchemical sleep, drifting in and out of dreams.

She woke but did not dress. She walked naked to the circle.
Clarence's body was gone. The fire she had burned for four nights was
covered and buried with sand. Many of the shells had been scattered.
Only a skeleton of the original circle remained. How long have I slept?

she wondered. She walked back to the cabin but lost her way. She headed out onto the beach to get her bearings. She walked up and down the beach but could not find the cabin. Everything seemed strange and out of place.

From a long way off she saw a figure walking toward her on the beach. As it approached she saw it was a man, a black man. It was Clarence, still barefoot, still dressed in his baggy black trousers and his yellow vest. He came up to her and stopped.

"What you still doin' here?"

"What?"

"You heard me. What you still doin' here?" He sounded gruff.

"I'm . . . I'm . . ." She stammered, stuttered, could think of nothing to say. "I don't know."

"Haven't you learned anything? Is it so easy for you to get lost all over again?"

"I don't know. I don't know what I should do next."

Clarence grabbed her firmly by the shoulders and shook her. "You get up now and go. Don't you hear that?"

Marina couldn't hear anything.

"Listen, they're calling you."

Marina listened again. She heard something. It was faint and far off, but she heard something.

"You've done all you need to do. Do you hear me?"

Marina nodded. She found herself more and more distracted by the noise. It was almost something she could recognize.

"You think they can't come for you here, just because you crossed over that mountain? Well, you're wrong. You stay here too long, and you'll find yourself going back up that trail looking for something you lost, something you're sure you left behind. Are you listening to me?"

Marina nodded abstractly. She was naked, standing on a beach, a dead man was shaking her, a horn sounded in the distance. A horn, yes, she thought, a ship's horn. My ship.

She woke then. It was morning again, but what day? The sun was shining across the water. The sheet she slept on was stained with sweat and streaked with black ash. She felt weak, but she got up and walked to the cistern. She drank six ladles of water before her thirst was slaked. Then she poured water over herself, washing her hair and the black marks from her face with the sweet little soaps. One pitcher at a time she rinsed her body and dried with one of the towels. Without much thought she tied on her yellow silk skirt and pulled on the red and orange top.

She looked around the cabin. Her altar was still covered with the little orchid blossoms. They still looked fresh, as if they had just been picked. Mai-Ling's bowl was there, as were the little bottles of oil. She did not remember bringing either of them back from the circle.

She drank some more water, then walked with some thought of visiting her circle. She could not find it. It had not been far from her cabin, but she had now lost it completely. There was no body, no charred remains of a fire, no circle of shells. She found herself walking out onto the beach, so like in her dream.

She headed east on the beach. She knew by her observations from the upper plateau that around the point was a little bay and a pier, but she'd never walked far in this direction. Now, with no real purpose she would admit to, she set out for the point.

It took her longer than she thought it should have. She found herself looking back to see if she was leaving footprints. She was. They only disappeared when she walked into the water to cool her feet. The sand was hot as well and she found this reassuring.

By noon she saw the outline of the pier ahead. It was not large or particularly long, but it still took an unusual length of time to reach it. Then she saw the big house. It was clearly the place Gracie had described.

She approached it from the side first as it faced, not east, but south, onto the little bay. It was set up on rocks that overlooked the bay, and there were long wooden and stone steps to reach the front entrance. The porch was wide and covered with a thatched roof. It featured fan-back rattan chairs, low-slung bamboo recliners, little tables, and benches.

The shells of sea turtles hung as decorations. Marina hoped they hadn't been hunted or killed. A sign with artistically primitive green letters hung over the big open double doors. It read TURTLE ISLAND RESORT. This struck Marina as funny, or at the very least, surreal.

She saw no activity, so she climbed the steps to the porch. She peeked through the doors, but it was dark and her eyes did not adjust quickly. She heard low voices, but saw no one.

The view from the porch was beautiful. It overlooked the aquamarine bay. Marina could see several small groups of people lying full in the sun or partially shaded by beach umbrellas painted to resemble turtle shells.

She had no intention of staying long. She had, she thought, a long walk back to her cabin. But she was tired from her walk and, she thought, not fully recovered from her recent fever, so she sat in one of the rattan chairs and put her feet up on one of the little benches. There were little cushions on the chair, and it was more comfortable than it looked.

She closed her eyes, but only for a moment.

★ ★ ★

When Marina woke she was not alone. She knew this without opening her eyes, but it was not some supernormal sensitivity. She smelled perfume, heard ice clinking in a glass, was aware of even the gentle breathing of the person across from her.

She opened her eyes. A woman sat opposite her. She had in fact moved her chair to face Marina. Her bare feet were propped on the same bench Marina's feet were resting on. She had a tall glass of what looked like iced tea in her left hand, which she held from the top and twirled to make the ice spin.

She looked to be about fifty, with fair skin and long straight hair more silver than brown. A blue blossom was tucked behind one ear. She wore a simple white dress embroidered with wave patterns in different shades of blue thread. There were sandals on the floor by her chair.

Marina took this all in within seconds of opening her eyes. The woman smiled at her.

"Hi. I'm Ingrid, Ingrid Goeller. I'm sorry I wasn't here to greet you when you arrived. I was away doing some buying for the island. You met my husband, Max, though. I'm sure he took good care of you."

Marina looked around, trying to identify the person to whom this woman was speaking. "I'm sorry. I've been a little ill for the past several days, I'm not thinking too clearly." She didn't want to be rude, but she had no idea who this woman was.

"Yes, Akoni told me. He's been looking in on you, but he didn't think you were in any danger."

"Akoni?"

"Akoni is the caretaker for cabins one through five. He brings food, cleans up, stocks the cabins, whatever needs doing."

"I don't believe I've met Akoni."

"Oh no, you wouldn't have. We are very discreet here. We try to anticipate the needs and desires of our guests and cater to them. Akoni prides himself on serving without being seen." While this woman, Ingrid, sounded rational, nothing of what she said made sense to Marina.

"And what about Gracie?" Marina decided to try a little test. "Is she here?"

"Gracie? You mean the little DeVries girl? No, she and her parents left over a week ago." Marina was stunned. Had she been sleeping that long? What had happened to her? Marina decided to try another test.

"And Clarence, Clarence Mudder, when did he leave?"

Ingrid looked solemn. "Mr. Mudder passed away almost a week ago. He was very ill. He came to us to die. He's buried in a little graveyard on the other side of the bay next to his wife, Kiyoko. They were regular guests at Turtle Island. We will miss them. Did you get to meet Clarence before he died?"

"Yes," Marina answered dumbly.

"He was a truly gentle man. I remember one year—"

"Excuse me," Marina interrupted. "Do you know me? I mean, where are we? Where do you think we are?" She realized she sounded desperate, but Ingrid looked at her like a compassionate nurse. When she spoke, she spoke slowly and clearly as if Marina were dull-witted, foreign, or a child.

"You're Marina Hardt. You . . . we are on Turtle Island. This is a resort island. My husband, Max, and I own the island, though we let more than half of it go wild to preserve the natural balance." She gestured west in the direction of the volcano. "You made a reservation, well actually your assistant Erin made the reservation. . . ."

"She's my agent, my friend, really." Marina corrected her.

"Well, she reserved three weeks for you in cabin one. It's our most remote cabin, while still offering full services of course."

"And how did I get here?" Marina realized her questions sounded irrational and almost hysterical, but Ingrid answered her patiently.

"Your cruise ship, the *Blue Pearl*, makes regular port calls here to pick up and drop off our guests. Don't you remember?"

"No, no, I don't remember. I mean, I do remember. It's just that what I remember is very different from what you're telling me."

"Why don't you tell me what you remember, then, and we'll work from there."

"I came from the other side of the island. I washed ashore there and walked here. I was dead . . . I think I was dead . . . but I had a chance to come back to life and I took it. I've been here for weeks, no, longer than that, several months at least. It took me a long time to get here. I . . . I . . ."

Ingrid was looking at her gently. "You know Turtle Island isn't very big. You could walk completely around it in a day and a half. Even crossing over it wouldn't take more than two and a half days." Ingrid said this gently, not as confrontation, but in an effort to nudge Marina back to rationality.

Marina was silent. How could she prove anything that had happened to her? Had she gone mad? Had she dreamed the whole thing? Was she dreaming now?

"No!" She said this out loud with more force than she'd intended. "It did happen. I remember it all very clearly. I was dead, really dead. I drowned." She said this louder than she'd intended as well. She was aware that there were other people around her, but her eyes were filling with tears and she chose to ignore everyone else and focus her attention on Ingrid. The woman had shifted her chair closer and put her hand over Marina's.

"It's okay, dear, no one is saying that what you experienced wasn't real. People come here for all sorts of reasons. They often have very emotional experiences here. For some reason, a number of people have come here to die over the years. Turtle Island is a very peaceful place to spend one's last days. There's a strong spirit here. Perhaps you felt that spirit."

"Yes, I did feel it, but it was more than just a feeling or a dream. It really happened to me. My soul came here after death."

Ingrid nodded her head sympathetically, but Marina could tell she didn't believe her.

"You think I'm hysterical," she said, as calmly as she could. "You probably think I'm mad."

"Not at all." Ingrid looked to either side of Marina. People had moved chairs to form a loose circle around her. She didn't know how many. She refused to look at them, refused to allow them into her world. Not yet, she thought. I'm not ready for this.

"I really should be heading back to my cabin now," Marina said. "It's a long walk and I've rested long enough." She wanted nothing more than to escape back to her little cabin, to sleep some more, to find her altar.

"You stay here too long and you'll find yourself going back up that trail looking for something you lost, something you're sure you left behind." It was Clarence's voice. She heard it as clearly as she had in her dream, but one look at Ingrid, and she knew that only she had heard it. Ingrid looked puzzled.

"But your room is here now. You came back here yesterday. Max will take you out to the *Blue Pearl* in the morning. Remember?"

Marina did not remember. She did recall that Gracie had said that she and her parents were to spend their last night at the big house, but . . .

"All guests spend the last couple of nights in the big house. It seems to help people reaccustom themselves to civilization."

"But my things . . ."

Marina put her head in her hands. She didn't want to continue crying in front of this woman. She didn't know what to think. She felt like Dorothy, trying to explain Oz to her family.

"Your things are all here." Ingrid patted her hand. "Look, maybe it would help if you told us what happened to you." The use of the word "us" forced Marina to look around her. No one was as close to her as Ingrid, but a group of people had arranged their chairs around her.

To her left was an elegant old man with a long, drooping, silver mustache and carefully combed hair of a matching shade. He was dressed in a wrinkled white linen suit with a blue striped bow tie. A silver-handled walking stick leaned against his chair.

To her right was a younger man in khaki shorts and an olive green T-shirt. He was deeply tanned and wore round rimmed glasses joined at the back by a strap that allowed him to take them off without setting them down.

Beside him sat a large soft woman in a loose purple dress. She had silver and turquoise bracelets on her arms and rings on her fingers that flashed with different color stones as she moved the cigarette from her mouth to the ashtray and back. She turned her head away each time she exhaled even though the breeze tended to carry the smoke right back onto the porch.

They all seemed attentive to what she might say, but she suspected they had very different reasons for being interested.

Ingrid made no move to introduce these people. Marina wondered if she'd already been introduced to them. Was she supposed to know who they were?

"Just start from the beginning and tell us what you recall," Ingrid was saying.

Start from the beginning. Start from the beginning.

Where was that? she wondered. The beach, the cruise ship, Chechnya, Baghdad, Afghanistan, Beirut, her childhood?

"I took my own life," she began. "I know it makes me sound incredibly self-centered, ungrateful, spoiled, but I truly could find no reason left to live. I couldn't feel anything. I jumped from the *Blue Pearl*. I drowned. I had a vision of an angel . . . or a sea turtle. I'm not really sure now, but everything went black for me. Then I found myself here. Well, not here, on the other side of the island. I couldn't move or speak. My body was burned, I think bones were broken. I couldn't feel anything below my neck."

She told them then, in great detail, about the Turtle Woman, the Turtle Mother, about learning to sit, to stand, and to walk. She told them what she'd learned about balance. She wished she could show them the turtle tattoo, but it seemed too fantastic even for her story, so she did not mention it. Marina noticed for the first time that she was not wearing the coral and black pearl anklet. I could have shown it to Ingrid as proof, she thought, then added, to herself, but proof of what? What would it prove? I could have had it when I came here. Mostly, she missed the feeling of it about her ankle.

She told them about Rafael, though she kept some of the more intimate details to herself. She described what it was like as her senses returned and she learned to attend to each moment.

Then there was Atana and her experience at the mirror pool. This was harder to explain because she lacked terminology for it. She talked about Téves and Adytum Wood. She tried explaining about auras but, again, couldn't find the right words.

She saw Ingrid's aura. It was a silver sheen with bursts of blue and green. The old man's aura was irregular, but vital, with hints of gold in it. The young man to her right had a fine silver iridescent aura with a lot of green in it, and the woman next to him had an irregular pale aura of white and blue. She was not sure what this meant exactly. She felt as if it was telling her things about these people but it was speaking in a language she only half understood.

Marina tried to convey the sense of urgency she felt about crossing to the eastern side of the mountain before her time ran out. She backtracked to tell them about the tattoo at this point. She knew it sounded far-fetched, but by this point it seemed no stranger than the rest of her story.

She detailed her night crossing of the volcano, but this required her to digress and recount her experience in Chechnya. She also found herself talking openly with these strangers about the death wish she had been pursuing for the past several years. After her crossing and her escape from the death shadow, she spoke of Mai-Ling and her circles. Again, she kept some of the more intimate details to herself, but she tried to convey the sense of power she'd discovered through the use of the altar.

From Mai-Ling to the cabin, to Gracie and Clarence, to her fevered dream sleep, to the porch she found herself on, the remainder of her story poured out of her and she felt drained.

The sun was setting. She had talked for several hours straight. No one had moved. No one had interrupted her. Occasionally she'd been aware of one guest nodding or murmuring something. She'd caught side glances between them. But if they thought her mad, they were, at least, very polite. A glass of tea had appeared for her on the little table next to her chair, and she drank this now in one long gulp. Some of the cool liquid ran down her chin and dribbled onto her chest. No one spoke.

At last Ingrid stood up. "Well, Marina, if it didn't happen just as you said it did, it should have. That was beautiful."

"But you still don't believe me."

"Let me think about it awhile, okay? Right now I have some other things to attend to, but I'd like to continue our conversation later if you don't mind."

Marina nodded.

"Since you are new here, you won't have met your fellow guests." Ingrid gestured to the company that had assembled around her. Marina wondered if she was hearing condescension in the woman's voice, but decided she wasn't. "This is Dr. Arenbough." She indicated the tall, thin, old man in the white linen suit and he bowed slightly. "Nigel is an anthropologist."

"Cambridge University, retired," he added.

"And this is Corrine Carr. Corrine is from New York. It's her third visit with us." The large woman in purple smiled and nodded her head.

"I'm Jack Davis." The tan young man extended his hand.

"Jack is a scientist," Ingrid went on. "He studies the protected turtle habitat that we have set up on the west side of the island." Marina shook his hand.

"Now, I'll be back shortly. Stay and talk if you'd like. I have a feeling these people have some questions for you." There was something mildly conspiratorial about her tone, but Marina let it pass. "We have a late dinner tonight, so you have time to talk and still shower and change before dinner, if you'd like. If you'd rather, I can show you to your room now." Marina sensed the disappointment in her fellow guests at this suggestion.

"No, I'll stay awhile," she said.

Ingrid walked off through the double doors, and Marina heard her speak to someone inside the door. "Michael, please bring Ms. Hardt some more tea, and see if anyone else wants anything."

Marina looked at the guests who had remained behind. They looked at her. She wasn't sure if it was politeness or discomfort that kept everyone from speaking. Finally she decided to break the ice. "So, do you all think I'm crazy, too?"

They all started to speak at once, laughed, started to speak again and stopped.

"Please," Jack deferred to Corrine.

"No, first the professor." Corrine nodded in his direction.

"Thank you." The old man paused a moment, making a tent out of his fingers and pressing the point into his chin. "Ms. Hardt . . ."

"Please, call me Marina."

"Very well, Marina, Each of us has a rather different interest in your story, but I, for one, can say that, while I don't understand it completely, I don't think you're crazy. I think something profound has happened to you.

"This island, Turtle Island, has been in the Goeller family for generations, but its history goes back much further. As near as we can tell, this island was never regularly inhabited by natives of this area. But they did have a myth about it. They believed their dead came here to pass on to the next life. There is some evidence that their old people sometimes journeyed alone to this island across hundreds of miles of open sea. They called it Turtle Island because their navigators would follow sea turtles to the island. It's still a rookery for a rare form of sea turtle. . . ."

"Yeah, Chelonia Somnio," Jack interrupted.

"Dreamer's Turtle," Marina said with an assurance she did not recognize.

"Yeah, right. Do you speak Latin? I mean, how did you know that?"

"I don't know."

"It's just that they're very rare. Only maybe a hundred left in the whole world, and this island, at least on the west side, is the only place we know for certain that they lay their eggs. They call them Dreamer's Turtles because of their markings."

"Green and blue with highlights of reddish brown and yellow. The markings look like little islands or continents," Marina said softly. Jack looked at her suspiciously.

"You've seen one. You were on the other side of the island, weren't you?" Marina said nothing. "You had to have been. Unless you're an expert in turtles, it'd be very unusual for you to know about their markings. They call them Dreamer's Turtles because sailors on watch who caught a glimpse of them were accused of dreaming them."

"And you're here to study them?"

"Yeah. There's a research station the Goellers have on the west side of the island. They allow sea turtle specialists access on a controlled and rotating basis. They discourage their guests from using that side of the island so the turtles are pretty safe."

"So they come here to lay their eggs?"

"Well, that's the odd part. Chelonia Somnio do lay their eggs here, but both male and female turtles of other species also seem to come here . . . well . . . to die."

Marina remembered Tarzan movies she watched when she was young. Films whose plots revolved around white ivory hunters and the existence of secret elephant burial grounds, places elephants went to die.

"It's really most unturtlelike behavior. Turtles can live a long time if they're not caught in nets or killed by predators, but old turtles seem to return here to die." He gestured to the shells hanging on the walls of the big house. "We find the shells every once in a while. Never Dreamers, though—don't you think that's interesting?"

"Perhaps that's the origin of the myth the islanders have about Turtle Island," Corrine offered.

"Perhaps it's not just a myth," Dr. Arenbough said. Everyone was quiet for a moment. "I'm just speculating, mind you, but I find some aspects of Ms. Hardt's . . . Marina's story fascinating. My dear, are you familiar with the culture of the islanders in this area?"

"No," Marina answered honestly. "This cruise was my agent's idea. I've traveled a lot, but never much in the South Pacific."

"Then you didn't read up on the area or research it?"

"No," Marina conceded again.

"Then is this familiar to you?" He pulled back his jacket sleeve and unbuttoned the cuff of his shirt. He extended his arm to her and turned his wrist face up.

Marina gasped! It was the turtle tattoo, tiny and intricate, almost a match to the one that had crawled from her ankle to the top of her head before disappearing.

"Where . . . I mean how . . . how did you get this?" Marina looked into Dr. Arenbough's eyes, searching for some hint of what she had seen in the eyes of the Turtle Woman or the Turtle Mother.

"Years ago," Dr. Arenbough rebuttoned his sleeve and straightened his jacket, "I was given this tattoo in a ceremony for elders. The turtle tattoo, you see, was a mark of having found Turtle Island and returned. Some of the old ones, it seemed, made the journey to Turtle Island and returned to live for years longer. They claimed that the spirits were not ready for them and had sent them back to their communities. They often became powerful healers or spiritual guides. I suppose I earned the tattoo because I'd visited Turtle Island and returned. I don't know whether it was visiting this place and returning or just the acceptance I earned by undergoing the tattooing ceremony, but it did mark quite a breakthrough in my work. My little turtle friend here," he held up his arm, "gained me an insider's access. It was extraordinary. I've written three books on the customs and culture of the islanders around here."

"So you think maybe Marina earned her turtle tattoo as well," Jack said smiling.

"It's possible," Dr. Arenbough said, leaning back into his chair. "I'm an old man, Jack. I've seen too many things I don't have an easy answer for. I can tell you one thing, though. If you looked for an answer that reflected popular opinion, you'd find far more people in the surrounding hundreds of miles of ocean and island that would take Marina's story as a fact."

"It's also possible she dreamed the whole thing." Corrine had not said much during their conversation and now she seemed annoyed. "Let's get real here," she said in the manner Marina associated with abrupt and to-the-point New Yorkers. "The Goellers say she came on the *Blue Pearl* several weeks ago. They say she's been staying in one of their cabins for the past three weeks. She says she drowned and washed ashore on the other side of the island. She can't have done both. I mean what about her suitcases, her things. Do you think the ship would have just dropped them off if she'd really jumped overboard."

Corrine had been speaking to the others as if Marina didn't exist, but she turned to her afterward and said, "I'm sorry. It's not personal, you know. Believe me, I'd give anything to think your story really happened, but . . ." She didn't finish. Even in the fading light Marina could see tears in the woman's eyes, sense some unspoken pain.

She put her hand out and touched Corrine's arm. "It's okay. Now that I've told it, I'm not sure I even believe it." She laughed, but something about her hand on Corrine's arm bothered her. She felt as if she knew more than she should about the woman, like she was eavesdropping on a private conversation. She pulled her hand back, trying not to make the gesture seem abrupt.

"You have to admit it is pretty far-fetched," Corrine said to the others. Jack nodded, but Dr. Arenbough matched her gaze and said nothing. She looked back at Marina. "Well, I just had to say that. I'm sorry if I've hurt your feelings. You seem like a nice person." Corrine seemed to be assuming or forcing a consensus on the group.

"Well, I could sure use a beer," Jack said. Marina was almost grateful for his changing the subject.

"Corrine," Dr. Arenbough asked, "how would you know if you were dreaming right now?"

"Come on, Nigel, not that again. I'm not dreaming right now. I'm wide awake."

"But when you dream you don't know you're dreaming. You wake up screaming. Sometimes you walk in your sleep. When you dream it seems as real as this." Dr. Arenbough seemed to be talking about something other than idle speculation. He'd heard Corrine wake screaming from some nightmare. He'd seen her walk in her sleep. Marina was certain of this. She also noticed that Corrine was suddenly uncomfortable with the conversation.

"That's different. I may not know when I'm dreaming, but afterward I know that I was dreaming. Just like I know I'm awake now." She lit another cigarette nervously.

"Have you ever heard of the Tibetan Book of the Dead?" Corrine didn't answer. Dr. Arenbough looked at Marina.

"I've heard of it, but I can't say I know much about it."

"Well," Dr. Arenbough continued, "it's not really about death at all, at least not in the way that we think of it in the West. I mean on some level it is connected with their rites and rituals of death, but on a deeper level it's a kind of training manual for passing over from one reality to another. It describes the stages one goes through after death. They are a series of dreamlike illusions, some terrifying, some serene and peaceful, but all, in some sense, both lessons and traps. The reason for the manual is to prepare the dying person for the nature of these illusions."

Marina noticed that Corrine was fidgeting uncomfortably in her seat. "And how is this connected with dreams?" Marina asked.

Dr. Arenbough smiled. "The realm of dreams and the place you go after death are both the same place. Even the waking world is just a kind of dream realm with specific attributes. I mention it as a possibility for you to think about."

"What do you mean?" Marina asked.

"It might explain the discrepancies Corrine pointed out. Perhaps what happened to you really happened and yet was also merely a dream."

"Give me a break, Nigel. . . ." Corrine was near to exploding. Marina could feel pent-up tension in her voice.

"I'm not sure I understand," Marina interrupted, hoping to defuse the tension, but realizing too late that she was only adding to it.

"Maybe you did dream all of your story. You said that you'd been feverish and sick for the past several days. Perhaps it was the dream of a sick woman. But what if it was no less real for having been a dream? What if you lived it on some level of what the Tibetans call the Bardo? It could have been as real as any of this. If you had not done the things you did, made the choices you made, perhaps you would have succumbed to that fever. If you had died in your sleep, in the middle of your dream, who's to say what that would have been like. You may indeed have gone back to your Turtle Woman. None of us can say for certain how true your experience was."

"Speak for yourself, Nigel." Corrine pushed her chair back abruptly and stood up. "And you can keep your Book of the Dead. I'm not dreaming now. I'm wide awake. And I'm not dying, either."

Marina knew this was not true. She couldn't say how she knew or that she had known before that very moment, but she knew that Corrine was dying. There was some shadow in her chest, a little wisp of what had chased Marina off the summit of the volcano. She'd felt it when she touched Corrine's arm, though she had not identified it until that moment.

"When you die, you die. There's nothing after that. It's . . . it's . . ." She couldn't finish her sentence. Marina could almost read her mind, though. She knew the fears Corrine could not voice.

Corrine turned then and walked briskly away. Marina stood quickly and started to follow her, but Ingrid intercepted her at the door.

"It's best to let her go, dear," she said softly. "Corrine is just beginning her stay with us. Nothing you could say now would change what she is feeling or what she has to discover within herself. You were the same when you first came here. Give her time. She'll either heal or she won't, but it's out of our hands."

Then, as an afterthought, she added, "When people first come here they seem to bring all their problems with them, but when they leave, well, they're different somehow, though I can't say Turtle Island did much for the DeVries." She seemed a little frustrated by this, as if she had somehow failed.

"Perhaps it was the child, Gracie, that Turtle Island was supposed to help," Marina offered.

"I'd like to believe that we helped some member of that family. It's just that Turtle Island usually has a rather profound effect on people."

"Well, I must confess that I don't feel like the same person anymore," Marina admitted.

Then, as if remembering her role as hostess, Ingrid added, "Dinner will be served in about an hour. You have time to shower and change. Do you need for me to show you to your room?" Marina sensed that Ingrid was still being cautious with her.

"I'm afraid you will."

Ingrid led her through a large, comfortable room with couches and chairs. There were a few people about, but none that Marina recognized. They went down two hallways before Ingrid stopped at one of the doors. The little brass plaque on the door read GARDEN ROOM II. Marina waited, realizing she had no key. After an awkward moment, Ingrid turned the handle for her and opened the unlocked door.

The room was simple but beautiful. The furniture was hardwood and looked as if it had been made by a true craftsman. There was a table with two chairs, a comfortable-looking chaise longue, a dresser, and a wardrobe cabinet. The floor was smooth, polished wood partially covered with a tatami rice mat. There was a ceiling fan spinning slowly and a lacy mosquito net hanging over a large bed. There were no windows on three sides, but the forth wall had French doors that opened onto what looked to be a garden courtyard.

Ingrid had stepped into the room with Marina and watched as she wandered around it. She stuck her head through one door and found a bathroom. Cosmetics she recognized were arranged on the counter. She never traveled with much, but this was exactly what she usually had with her: shampoo, toothpaste, toothbrush, deodorant, perfume, hair brush, moisturizer, sunscreen.

She opened the wardrobe cabinet. There were clothes in the cabinet that she recognized. She'd bought these dresses for her cruise, but had never unpacked them. They'd also been the clothes she'd found waiting for her in the cabin on the beach, though she had not recognized them at the time. She saw her shoes neatly arranged on the floor of the wardrobe: several pairs of comfortable sandals, a dressier pair of heels, and a pair of low-top hiking shoes.

Her two small but well-worn suitcases were stored between the dressers. She opened one of the drawers and found more things she recognized. With a sigh she closed the drawer. Her adventure was rapidly collapsing into a dream, and it saddened her. She looked around the room, wanting to find something she now doubted the very existence of.

"Did you say everything of mine had been moved up from the cabin?"

"Yes. Why? Are you missing something?" Marina thought about her altar: the anklet, the pendulum, the little branch in its wooden base, the essential oils, Mai-Ling's bowl, Gracie's flowers. All of it a dream? she thought.

"No. No, I guess not. I'm still adjusting, I suppose."

She found her camera bag next to the chaise longue. She hefted it and, by its weight, knew everything would still be inside it. She noticed a letter sticking out of one of the back pockets and drew it out. It was addressed to Erin. It was her suicide note.

She sat heavily on the chaise longue and sighed.

"It never really happened, did it? I dreamed it all, didn't I?"

Ingrid sat on the edge of the bed. "I don't know, dear. It's a wonderful story, though, maybe more important than the truth. But let me tell you a different story. A woman takes a cruise to a resort island. She's deeply tired inside, disappointed with life, unhappy. She can't feel. She has a fog about her and can't see more than a little way at a time. She comes to Turtle Island almost in a walking coma. She spends several days drifting in and out of conversations, never engaging anyone, never fully present. She overhears the theories of an eccentric anthropologist. Perhaps she catches a glimpse of his tattoo. She hears about sea turtles from a research scientist. She absorbs who knows what from the conversations of visitors passing through, all without really processing any of it.

"Then she goes into isolation. She lives alone for several weeks with no distractions, nothing to occupy her time but her own state of mind. She's overwhelmed, lethargic, she sleeps a lot and dreams. Her dreams run together. She develops a fever of some kind that intensifies the reality of her dreams. She wakes, confused, still half in the dream, and returns to the place she started. Only now she doesn't recognize it. She doesn't remember it because she never really saw it when she was there before.

"Slowly she comes out of the dream. She is changed by the dream, changed for the better, perhaps. Still the dream seems more real for her than the waking.

"So, what will she do?"

Marina had no answer.

"Dinner in about forty-five minutes," Ingrid said, standing and slipping out the door, pulling it closed behind her.

★ ★ ★

Later, after her shower and dinner with Dr. Arenbough, Jack, and several other guests, Marina found herself back in her room. She'd worn a little black dress that she liked because it packed well and was still flattering. She'd even put on the dressier black heels, but had slipped them off during dinner and carried them back to her room. She took the dress off and found her silk robe laying across the bed. *I was wearing this robe when . . .*

She let this thought trail off. She put the robe on and walked to the French doors. She found that they were designed so that she could open up almost the whole wall. Gauzy white curtains hung in front of the doors. They now blew around her legs in the lightest of breezes.

She lay down on the bed, pulling the mosquito netting around the mattress. From inside she felt like she was seeing the world through a mist. She closed her eyes and drifted.

"So, what did you think it would be like?" A high-pitched, musical voice woke her.

"What?" Marina sat up in bed. She heard laughter, familiar laughter.

"Did you think you would just go back?"

Marina strained to see in the dark. There was moonlight coming in through the French doors, creating a silhouette of the person seated on the chaise longue. "What?" Marina asked again.

"Stop saying what, you silly child." Marina thought she recognized the outline of a small old woman, wild hair cascading around her shoulders.

Turtle Mother? Marina thought.

"Well, did you think there would be no way back? Just because you did not see the path that led you here, doesn't mean there wasn't one. And just because you did not imagine this path, doesn't mean you aren't walking on it." Marina's head spun.

"Turtle Mother!" she called out, batting the mosquito netting out of the way and standing up.

There was no one there. No one was sitting on her chaise longue. No one was in her room.

Marina ran to the French doors, pushed through the filmy curtains, and stepped out into a little garden. It, too, was empty. There was a little fountain and the moonlight sparkled on the water. The garden was surrounded by a low bamboo wall, but she could see palm trees above the wall that made the garden feel much bigger.

She stood for a while looking into the jungle. She imagined she could see through it to the high plateau, over the volcano, down to Adytum Wood, past the mirror pool, around Rafael's hut, to the beach where she had first found herself. Or where I dreamed I found myself, she corrected.

She turned, suddenly sleepy, to go back inside. To the side of the garden was a low stone slab. Something familiar attracted her to it.

She caught her breath!

My altar.

She crossed and knelt in front of it. She smelled Gracie's coral and pink blossoms. They seemed as fresh as she remembered them. She handled and lifted her shells, stones, feathers, and bones. She caressed Mai-Ling's bowl, turning it in her hand like the cup from a Japanese tea ceremony. She opened the two blue bottles and smelled the essential oils. She lifted the branch from its box and replaced it carefully. She dangled the pendulum between her fingers and felt it dance lightly.

She caressed Rafael's circular stone pendant and Atana's stone from the mirror pool.

The coral and black pearl anklet was suspended from the branches of the little tree. She lifted it and fingered each bead like a rosary. She tied it loosely around her wrist.

There was a candle on the altar, a tall ivory one with matches in a little dish beside it. She lit the candle. She felt something stiff in the pocket of her silk robe.

It was a letter, the note she'd left for Erin. It seemed like such a long time ago.

She held the letter to her lips for a moment, then passed it into the candle's flame. It caught and burned. She held it as long as she could, watching little cinders take to the night like fireflies, before dropping it into the bowl Mai-Ling had carved for her.

Epilogue

A woman walks out onto the deck of a ship. It is a cruise ship famous for its level of luxury. It is filled with happy couples, people escaping, people paying for an illusion of the exotic, but it is early morning and still, and she passes no one as she pads softly on bare feet from her stateroom to the lowest of the outer decks—the one that offers no obstructions between the railing and the sea.

She is calm, perhaps more tranquil than she has been in a very long time. Her stateroom is in order. There is a little space she has cleared on her dresser. It contains an odd assortment of treasures, things found in her travels, things she travels with. They are carefully, purposefully arranged, telling some story through their positions and relationships.

She finds a point along the railing more in shadow than the rest. She looks out across the moon-sparkled night sea. It is warm, and the only breeze seems to come from the ship's forward motion. It is barely enough to lift her dark curly hair from her shoulders. Except for the humming vibration of the ship's engines, all is quiet. She breathes in the salt scent. She is still, her mind totally clear.

She unties the belt of her silk robe and lets it fall open. She stands as if bathing her body in moonlight reflected from the sea. From the pocket of the robe she pulls a handcarved wooden bowl inlaid with mother-of-pearl. She has wrapped a silk scarf around it to keep the contents from spilling. She unties it. There is in the bowl a strange pot-pourri of dried orchid petals and ashes. She extends the bowl out over the sea with her left hand and pours the mixture into her right. She slowly crushes the petals and the ash into a fine powder that slips between her fingers into the sea.

She checks the compass she carries inside her heart. With subtle adjustments in position she finds the point on the horizon where an island should be. If it is there, if it was ever there, it is beyond sight now, but that doesn't matter. She carries it with her. It is her past and also her future.

★ ★ ★

A sea turtle's head breaks the surface of the water among a powder of sweet flowers and ash. It pauses for a moment, tasting the water. It is a beautiful creature, rare and magical, with markings of a whole world upon its back in green and blue, deep red and yellow. It does not stay long on the surface, but dives once again with eyes closed, dreaming a woman, dreaming an island, dreaming a story.

About the Author

Tom Crockett is a writer, an artist, an educator, and a shamanic practitioner. After spending four years as an award-winning photojournalist in the United States Navy, Tom pursued undergraduate and graduate degrees in fine art. He is a summa cum laude graduate of Old Dominion University in Norfolk, Virginia, with a Bachelor of Fine Arts degree. His Master of Fine Arts, with an emphasis in photography, is from the School of the Art Institute of Chicago, Chicago, Illinois.

Tom is the author of *The Artist Inside: A Spiritual Guide to Cultivating Your Creative Self.* This book is a guide and manifesto for a spiritually awakened approach to artistic expression and creativity. It draws on the work Tom has done both as an art teacher and a shamanic practitioner. Helping people find "The Artist Inside" has become a passion for Tom— a kind of shamanic retrieval for the creative soul.

Working the intersection of dreams and visionary artwork drew Tom to shamanism. He has studied shamanism and energetic healing for ten years. He also currently directs ArtQuest, a multicultural arts-based mentoring program at the Hermitage Foundation in Norfolk, Virginia. This program for area high school students uses art and ceremony as a kind of urban tribal initiation program. With adult groups, Tom teaches a form of urban contemporary shamanic practice synthesized from the traditions he has studied. He conducts Dream Artist Path apprenticeships, and weekend workshops in addition to seeing clients as a shamanic counselor. He is the editor of *Dream Artist Tribe: A Newsletter of Urban Contemporary Shamanic Practice.*

Tom is a member of the Foundation for Shamanic Studies and the Association for the Study of Dreams. He is forty-three years old and lives in Norfolk, Virginia.